Praise for

"... Wyatt effectively mixes political intrigue with action. This high-stakes adventure, full of violence, magic and suspense, should entertain gamers and epic fantasy fans.
—*Publisher's Weekly*

"Innovative twists, like the cyborg-like warforged and the tattoos that determined the character's house and how powerful they were with magic, gave the book an upbeat edge. *Storm Dragon* ... is recommended for lovers of fantasy fiction."
—Bret Jordan, *Monster Librarian*

"James Wyatt's writing is good and quick with a lot of action throughout the story. I will wait with baited breath to find out what happens next."
—Conan Tigard, *Reading Review*

"... an action-packed adventure ... Wyatt churns out an exciting tale of power and self-destiny.
—Mania.com

The books carry a contemporary, yet distinctly fantasy, feel to them and are packed with adventure and mysticism that is the hallmark of entertaining and fast-paced writing.
—Galaxy Books, *Faves & Raves*

There's plenty going on here and, once again, it's not just 'another D&D quest shoehorned into novel form'. There are magic items that have to be found, but there are also political machinations and ... a world that is slowly beginning to embrace some forms of technology ...Wyatt doesn't hang around or take you off down blind alleys, he starts you off at point A and you just know that things will end where they're meant to."
—Graeme's Fantasy Book Review

EBERRON

JAMES WYATT
EBERRON

DRAGON WAR

DRACONIC PROPHECIES

BOOK THREE

The Draconic Prophecies, Book 3
Dragon War

©2010 Wizards of the Coast LLC

Published by Wizards of the Coast LLC

EBERRON, WIZARDS OF THE COAST, and their respective logos are trademarks of Wizards of the Coast LLC in the U.S.A. and other countries.

Printed in the U.S.A.

Cover art by Raymond Swanland
Map by Robert Lazzaretti

Original Hardcover First Printing: August 2009
First Paperback Printing: March 2010

9 8 7 6 5 4 3 2 1

ISBN: 978-0-7869-5482-7
620-25356000-001-EN

The Library of Congress has catalogued the hardcover edition as follows

Library of Congress Cataloging-in-Publication Data
Wyatt, James, 1968-
  Dragon war / by James Wyatt.
    p. cm. -- (Draconic prophecies ; bk. 3)
  ISBN 978-0-7869-5122-2
1. Dragons--Fiction. 2. Prophecies--Fiction. I. Title.
PS3623.Y33D76 2009
813'.6--dc22

                                                                    2009016150

U.S., CANADA,   EUROPEAN HEADQUARTERS
ASIA, PACIFIC, & LATIN AMERICA   Hasbro UK Ltd
Wizards of the Coast LLC   Caswell Way
P.O. Box 707   Newport, Gwent NP9 0YH
Renton, WA 98057-0707   GREAT BRITAIN
+1-800-324-6496   Save this address for your records.

Visit our web site at www.wizards.com

This one's for Mom.
Thanks for reading my crazy books
and displaying them on your shelf.

FAIRHAVEN

A: Royal Court of Fairhold
B: University of Wyrnarn
C: Chalice Center
D: Distant Exchange
E: House Jorasco Citadel

Aundair river

PART

I

↓

Thunder is his harbinger and lightning his spear.
Wind is his steed and rain his cloak.
The words of creation are in his ears and
on his tongue.
The secrets of the first of sixteen are his.

In the darkest night of the Dragon Below,
storm and dragon are reunited,
and they break together upon the legions
of the Blasphemer.
The maelstrom swirls around him.
He is the storm and the eye of the storm.

His is the new dawn.
In him the storm cannot die.
His are the words the Blasphemer unspeaks,
his the song the Blasphemer unsings.

CHAPTER
1

It began as an itch, a minor annoyance that grew until it woke him in the night. Gaven sat by the door of his cell, scratching at his neck, his shoulder, his arm, until his skin was raw. By morning it was a raging fire on his flesh, and he began to feel the lines.

He hadn't understood them then, the twisting lines of his dragonmark. Or had he? His mind was so lost in the Prophecy while he was in Dreadhold. Had he unknowingly mumbled the verses that wrote themselves on his skin?

They first appeared as white marks against his red skin, raised like welts. A guard noticed them while Gaven was out in the yard. He yanked Gaven's hair to pull him down for a closer look, ready to summon a healer. His eyes grew wide when he realized what he was seeing, patterns similar to the one on the warden's hand. He ran to tell his superiors, and Gaven stood in the yard, looking up at the clouds that churned the sky.

When the first fork of lightning struck the prison tower, Gaven laughed. He spread his arms and tasted the rain on his lips. The guards began to clear the yard, herding the prisoners back indoors. They sent four guards for Gaven. When they laid hands on him, the rain turned to searing acid, and cries of pain and surprise filled the yard. Another blast of lightning hit the high tower, and for a moment it seemed that the prisoners might revolt, as though the storm raged in their own hearts. Ducking their heads against the rain, the guards dragged Gaven to the nearest door. Gaven laughed at the acidic shower that seared his skin, laughed at the fist-sized hailstones that pummeled the last stragglers, laughed as lightning speared a guard on the outer wall.

He didn't resist as they dragged him through the corridors, carried him up the stairs, and threw him in his cell. He could hear the hailstones clattering on the stone roof above him, and he marveled at the elegant blue loops and swirls that stood out clearly on his skin, still burning, but also cool, refreshing.

He was marked after all. Wouldn't his father be proud?

* * * * *

"Gaven?"

The thunder of the storm had been so loud that Aunn could no longer hear his own voice. He stepped closer and saw the dragonshard clutched to Gaven's chest. Gaven rocked the shard like a baby, gently, back and forth, his glassy eyes fixed on the stone in his hands, the brilliant red lines of his dragon-mark coiled within it. The wrecked husk of the Dragon Forge loomed around them, the roof wrenched open by Gaven's storm, steam rising in great billowing clouds from the infernal furnaces.

"Gaven, look at me." Aunn still couldn't hear himself speak. Perhaps Gaven had been deafened, too. He reached out a hand but stopped just short of Gaven's shoulder. Last time—

They had been in the jungle of Aerenal, the cool of the evening beginning to clear the humid air. Gaven clutched the Eye of Siberys to his chest, rocking it forward and back. Aunn shook Gaven's shoulder, trying to jolt him out of his trance or stupor. When it didn't work, he threw a punch at Gaven's chin. But he never connected. A clap of thunder sent Aunn sprawling on his back.

Aunn wished they were back in Aerenal, holding the Eye of Siberys as Haldren puffed toward them. Aunn would do everything differently. He'd show Gaven his true face, and they'd work together to find Rienne, put a stop to Haldren's scheme before it cost hundred of lives at Starcrag Plain, stop Kelas too. There would be no clash of dragons, no Dragon Forge. And they wouldn't end up in the wreckage of the Dragon Forge, with Gaven lost in the depths of his dragonshard.

We wouldn't be here now, he thought.

"Come on, Gaven," he said, shaking Gaven's shoulder. His ears had begun to ring as they rebounded from the thunder's assault. Gaven gave no sign that he could hear any better than Aunn could.

There was so much he wanted to say, so much he had to explain, so many questions he needed answered. He shook Gaven's whole body, pushed him from side to side, but he couldn't break Gaven's glassy stare.

"Please come back," he said, taking Gaven's head in his hands and staring into his eyes, trying to will Gaven to meet his gaze.

He felt Cart's hand on his shoulder, glanced back, and saw Ashara there, her hands folded around Cart's arm, fear etched on her face. In Aerenal, Cart had knelt beside him after Gaven's thunder knocked him back, making sure he wasn't badly hurt, while Senya stood beside them both.

He dropped to his knees beside Gaven and rested his head on Gaven's unmoving shoulder. At last he heard his own voice, howling his grief.

* * * * *

Arnoth stood over Gaven, holding out his hand and smiling. Gaven looked up, weak from his ordeal. Why was his father smiling? He had failed the Test of Siberys.

"A Siberys mark," Arnoth said. "Gaven, I'm so proud."

Gaven looked down at his skin. No, he wasn't the young man on the brink of death, scorched by the sun and parched by the ocean wind. He was strong, and the Mark of Storm flowed over the rippling muscles of his chest and arm.

"Thank you, father." Gaven took his father's hand and stood, then stepped into Arnoth's embrace.

"I love you, son."

"I—"

Searing pain choked the words from his throat. Something wrenched Arnoth out of his arms. His dragonmark burned, scorching his skin.

His father was pulling away, eyes wide with terror. "Help me, Gaven!"

Smoke rose from his shoulder and arm—his mark was burning away to nothing. He stretched a feeble hand toward his father, but then Arnoth was gone.

Gaven slumped to the ground, his dragonmark stripped from his skin.

* * * * *

Without Starcrag Plain, there would have been no clash of dragons, no Soul Reaver, no Crystal Spire. Gaven would not have been the Storm Dragon. The Prophecy would unfold in a different way, a different time and place, far beyond Aunn's own tiny life.

He could have stopped Kelas before it all got out of hand, before Aunn outlived his usefulness. He would never have gone to the Demon Wastes, never have led Sevren and Zandar to their deaths or witnessed Vor's sacrifice. He would never have fought alongside the Maruk Dar, and the proud orcs of that city might still be alive, safe from the advancing hordes of Kathrik Mel.

And yet . . . Aunn wiped his eyes. Without Vor and the Maruk Ghaash'kala, without the utter desolation of the Labyrinth, who would he be? Would the Traveler's question still haunt him? Where would he have found the will and the conscience to stand against Haldren and Kelas, if not for all the events they set in motion?

"What's wrong with him?" Ashara's voice jolted him back to the present.

"I don't know," Aunn said. "He seems . . . gone."

Ashara walked around Aunn, kicked aside a shard of twisted iron from the forge's destruction, and knelt in front of Gaven. "Interesting," she said. Her voice held no trace of emotion, as if she thought Gaven were an unusual magical artifact. Indeed, her attention was focused on the shard, not on Gaven. "I might expect that of a Khyber shard, holding his mind or spirit inside it. But not an Eberron shard."

"It has his dragonmark," Aunn said.

"And it has for some time." Ashara put a hand out to the shard. "Why should it take his mind now?"

Aunn almost stopped her, afraid of Gaven's reaction. He was too slow. Ashara's fingertips touched the pink surface of the bloodstone and she closed her eyes in concentration.

Cart shifted, and Aunn looked back over his shoulder. The warforged looked distinctly uncomfortable, flexing his hands into fists and stretching them wide in turn.

Seeing Aunn's glance, Cart said, "What if it captivates her as well?"

Aunn looked back at Ashara. She smiled without opening her eyes. "She's fine," he said. "She knows what she's doing."

* * * * *

Gaven was a storm, looking down upon the water churning in his wake. He was a hurricane, riding a blasting wind as long rolls of thunder announced his coming. He was a god, as blindly destructive as the Devourer.

> *Thunder is his harbinger and lightning his spear.*
> *Wind is his steed and rain his cloak.*

He shot toward his prey, a city perched on the water's edge. His winds tore at its banners and stripped the leaves from trees within and outside its walls. Waves broke upon the wharves, washed over the decks of ships and dragged them under, crashed against the city walls. He hurled lightning like spears at towers and parapets, and his rain sizzled on streets and roofs. People screamed and ran for cover, but there was no shelter from his storm. He blew away shingles and thatch, knocked over walls, stripped away every shred of protection. He stopped his advance and hovered over the city, pouring out destruction.

> *His storm flies wild, unbound and pure in devastation,*
> *going before the traitor's army*
> *to break upon the city by the lake of kings.*

His rage was unrelenting, fueled by dragon fire and the blood of fiends. His storm did not stop until the city's streets became canals, its outer wall lay in ruins, and half its people lay dead. Only then did his thunder fall silent, his rain and hail cease, his churning clouds disperse back into the clear blue sky. He retreated and coiled once more into fire and blood at the heart of the Dragon Forge.

* * * * *

Ashara opened her eyes, shaking her head, her brow furrowed.

"What did you find?" Aunn asked.

She shrugged. "What our plans anticipated, nothing more. The dragonshard's magic is structured to hold his mark, and that's exactly what it's doing. I didn't see any flaw or addition that might have caused his stupor."

Her words made no sense at first. "Your plans . . ." Slowly it dawned on Aunn, and he looked around the ruin of the Dragon Forge. "You were part of it? You helped build all this?"

"Of course," she said. "What did you think I was doing here?"

Hot anger rose in his chest. "You did this to him!" He rose to his feet, looming over Ashara, his hand fumbling for his mace. "You—"

Cart seized his arm and yanked him back from Ashara. "We have all played our parts in this scheme," he said. "I served Haldren. Ashara served her House. You were part of it as well, from the day you helped us get Gaven out of Dreadhold. None of us are innocent."

Aunn slumped, and Cart let him fall back to his knees. Grief drowned his anger, and he mumbled an apology to Ashara.

Ashara turned her attention back to the dragonshard. "Rather than casting blame, perhaps we should focus on how to get out of the mess we're in."

* * * * *

He was a dragon in the form of two-legged meat. Shakravar didn't remember how he got into that form, but it was proving useful in bringing the Prophecy to its fulfillment. The opportunity had at last presented itself: the twelve dragon-marked Houses would soon become the thirteen dragons of the Prophecy.

He sat in a dirty, noisy tavern in eastern Khorvaire, and an elf sat across the table, leaning forward over his untouched mug of ale. Shadows pooled beneath the elf's hood and clung to his black clothing like cobwebs. The Prophecy had written itself on the elf's pale skin, starting on his cheek and disappearing beneath his armor.

"Listen, Gaven," the elf said.

Shakravar knew his own name, but somehow Gaven was also his name. It didn't matter. Like the meat, the name was useful. He looked up from the ring and met the elf's dark eyes.

"I have an associate in Karrnath," the elf continued. "Very well-connected. He says that one branch of my family is work-ing with Breland in a plot against the regent and the young king of Karrnath. I think it's even worse than that." The elf paused, his eyes fixed on the table.

"Go on," Shakravar said.

"You have to understand, Gaven. My House has been troubled for a long time. We claim three different lines of descent, and the head of each one believes that his own family should control the House. Few people outside our House know this, but we spend nearly as much time spying on each other as we do in our more lucrative endeavors."

"So you think that the plot extends beyond Karrnath?"

"Exactly. I believe that the Paelion family plans to destroy the other two—the Phiarlans and my own Thuranni line."

"Why are you telling me this?" Shakravar knew the answer, but he played his part, feigning ignorance.

"I have no proof. I need evidence I can show the baron, something to prove the Paelions' guilt."

"What does that have to do with me? Your family is full of master spies."

"If I infiltrated a Paelion enclave and was discovered, the Paelions would have an excuse to strike against us. They could justify it to the Phiarlans and the rest of the world, if they had to. We need someone who's not connected to our House to do it."

It was perfectly clear. Shakravar could help the Thurannis and help the Prophecy. If he found the evidence he needed, proof of what the Thuranni suspected, the Thurannis would attack the Paelions before the plan could be set in motion. The Phiarlans would condemn the Thurannis, and the stalemate would be broken—House Phiarlan would split. Twelve dragons would become thirteen, and the Prophecy could be fulfilled.

"What's in it for me?" Shakravar asked. He didn't care, but his Thuranni friend would be suspicious if he didn't ask.

"There's the Gaven I know." The elf allowed himself the hint of a smile. "My House will pay you well. Name your price."

The price didn't matter. His goal was within his grasp. Shakravar would find the evidence the Thuranni sought, even if he had to create it.

* * * * *

"Perhaps if we take the shard away, he'll snap out of it," Cart said.

"Perhaps you should try," Aunn said. "I don't want another taste of Gaven's thunder."

Cart shrugged and leaned over Gaven. He hesitated only a moment before grasping the dragonshard and yanking it out of Gaven's grasp.

Gaven didn't move. He didn't even cling to the shard—his hands just fell away.

"Gaven?" Aunn said. He shook Gaven's shoulder again.

Ashara slapped Gaven's face. The force of it knocked him off balance, and he fell over on his side. His body slowly curled inward.

Aunn scowled at Ashara. "Was that necessary?" he said.

"Evidently it wasn't enough. Maybe we need to hit him harder. Cart?"

Aunn jumped to his feet and put himself between Cart and Gaven. "I don't think that's the answer. He needs more help than we can give."

Cart looked down at him. "Don't you have a wand for this sort of thing, Darraun?"

Aunn's hand shot to his face as panic seized his chest—the fear that he was supposed to be someone else, that he'd let his identity slip without realizing it. No, he realized, he hadn't been Darraun since Starcrag Plain. Darraun was dead. "Aunn," he said.

"Sorry. Aunn."

"And he's beyond the help of wands, I think. A ritual scroll might . . ."

Gaven's body curled on the ground suddenly became Vor, bleeding out his life into the scorched earth of the Labyrinth. Aunn saw the scroll he'd tried to use to bring Vor back, felt an echo of its magic flowing through him, and then felt again the void that followed, the desolate silence of his failure.

"No," Aunn said. "We need to take him somewhere. A Jorasco healing house perhaps."

"Shall I carry him?" Cart said, stooping down beside Gaven.

It seemed they were back in Dreadhold, standing over Gaven in the wreck of his cell. Aunn's eyes stung.

"Not yet," Ashara said. "We need a plan."

CHAPTER
2

Aunn's mind couldn't handle making plans yet. Cart cleared away enough of the forge's debris that he and Ashara could sit on the ground near Gaven, and he started tracing a rough map in the sand. Aunn heard them talking, but his mind couldn't process their words. His eyes kept wandering to Gaven, to the wreckage of the Dragon Forge all around them, and finally he left them to their planning and wandered away.

The iron dome of the forge was open to the sky, torn asunder and strewn in masses of twisted metal around the canyon. The towering apparatus at the forge's heart had collapsed into a pile of rubble, half filling the trenches beneath it, scattered plumes of smoke and steam still billowing into the air around it. The camp that had grown around the forge was deserted, and its tents and structures were a shambles, torn up in the fury of Gaven's storm. The sky was clear and blue, the air perfectly still and warm. The shaft of clear crystal that towered over the end of the canyon, though, had clouded over into blue-gray stone, smooth and hard, only slightly out of place among the other rock formations of the canyon. The sense of malevolence that had spread from it was gone.

What of the Messenger? Aunn had felt its presence, too, like velvet whispers in his mind, reassuring him and guiding him. That feeling was gone as well, and Aunn's heart felt empty without it. He slid his hand absently into a coat pocket and felt the cool metal of Dania's torc against his fingers.

He drew out the torc and examined it closely for the first time. When he first brought it to Kelas, he had barely given it a second glance—professionalism, he'd told himself at the time, but the truth was that it hurt to see it. It reminded him of Dania's death, and pricked at his conscience. When it fell from the surface of the blue crystal prison, he stuffed it into his pocket and moved on to deal with more pressing matters, like finding Gaven. Now he held it up to the sunlight and took in every detail.

It was pure silver coiled into the shape of a serpent, about as thick as his thumb. It was hinged at the back, but the hinge was so well concealed that it seemed like a single piece of metal. Each one of the serpent's feather-like scales was carefully engraved, and two feathered wings were barely noticeable near the head, held close to the body. The glittering eyes were pools of quicksilver, somehow liquid but firmly rooted in the solid metal head.

Tiny black pockmarks dotted the edge of the torc, where the silver tracery had joined it and siphoned power through it to the Dragon Forge. He ran his thumb along their rough edges. His skin scraping against the metal sounded like the harsh whisper of the Secret Keeper.

The torc had been a gift to Dania—a gift of the spirit that imprisoned a different fiend beneath the earth in a distant place. It had appeared around her neck in a blaze of silver fire. As Aunn held it, it seemed that it had become a gift to him, the Messenger's acknowledgement of the good he had done. But still marked by evil, much like his own heart. He took a deep breath, pulled open the torc's hinge, and placed the metal around his neck.

Aunn couldn't say what he had expected, but what he felt was . . . nothing. The metal was cool against his skin, but quickly warmed at his touch. It fit him, which was a bit surprising since it had coiled close around Dania's slender neck. But there was nothing more, no sudden surge of power or great revelation. He ran his hand across the front and considered taking it off, but decided against it. There was a reason for the Messenger's gift, if that's what it was, and he would honor the gift and the giver by wearing it.

He turned and looked at Ashara and Cart, still sitting close and talking quietly. They no longer looked at the map on the ground, but at each other, and Aunn looked away, not wanting to intrude on what seemed like an intimate moment. Or would have, if Cart had been a man of flesh and blood. He looked back at them, but the moment—if that's what it was—had ended, and their faces were turned back to the ground.

Then his eyes fell on Gaven again, still curled into a ball, lost in his own mind. It was time to do something. He walked back to Cart and Ashara and sat down, facing them across the map.

"What is this all about?" he said.

"What?" Ashara's face was flushed, and her brown eyes glistened.

"All this." Aunn gestured vaguely around at the wreckage. "The Dragon Forge, House Cannith, the Arcane Congress, the queen. It's not just about the war, reconquering the Reaches, and it's more than just seizing power in Aundair, isn't it?"

"There's a great deal I don't understand," Ashara said, not meeting his eyes.

"It seems we all have fragments of information," Cart said. "We were all tangled in different parts of the web. Perhaps combining those fragments will give us a better picture of the whole."

"Exactly," Aunn said. "So—" He stopped. Cart and Ashara knew nothing about him or his role in Kelas's plans from the start. His first inclination was to extract information from them, stitch it together with what he knew, and keep them in the dark. To do otherwise could be a deadly breach of security.

But he didn't care anymore. He drew a slow breath. "So I'll start," he said. "I'm a Royal Eye. I've worked for Kelas my whole life." He saw Ashara's eyes widen, and he had Cart's full attention. "Kelas sent me to join your expedition to free Haldren and Gaven, and after Starcrag Plain I took Haldren back to Kelas. My main purpose was to bring Haldren around to where he'd help Kelas, instead of trying to seize the throne for himself. That done, Kelas sent me to the west, to the Demon Wastes—I think primarily to get me out of the way while he did whatever he was doing here. To kill me, most likely. But if I also managed to achieve my stated purpose, so much the better."

"And that purpose . . . ?" Ashara asked.

"To provoke a barbarian warlord into attacking the Eldeen Reaches. Which I did." He saw in his mind the plume of smoke rising above Maruk Dar, and his voice faltered. "The goal was to give Aundair an excuse to invade the Reaches from the east, ostensibly to protect its own borders from the threat of the barbarians."

"Which Aundair has now done," Ashara said. "The war has begun."

"But they're not taking the threat seriously," Aunn said. "Kelas wanted a pretext, but he roused a dragon." Farren's words rang in his mind: *I want you to make sure that a big enough army meets him soon, before his evil can spread far.* Because of Aunn, the Maruk Ghaash'kala had failed in their sacred mission, to confine the evil of the Demon Wastes, to keep it from spreading beyond the Shadowcrags.

"You think the barbarians actually threaten Aundair?" Cart asked.

"I fear that they do."

Why did he say that? Farren's foreboding, Marelle's warnings, the verses of the Prophecy that Gaven had mentioned—*Dragons fly before the Blasphemer's legions.* They combined into a sense of impending doom, as though the approach of the barbarian horde spelled the end of the world.

Ashara shook her head. "They'll never reach the Wynarn, much less cross it and enter Aundair."

"Kelas was counting on the Dragon Forge to stop them," Aunn said. "We've destroyed that hope."

"We had to," Ashara said. "We never should have tapped into the fiend's power."

Aunn looked around at the wreckage of the Dragon Forge. "Weapons more terrible than their foe . . ." he said, and Marelle's pearl-green eyes shone in his mind. He could almost feel her cool hand on his cheek. "You built it?" he asked Ashara.

Ashara cleared her throat. "My House, the Arcane Congress, and Kelas worked together to construct the Dragon Forge. At first, we—House Cannith—believed that it was simply a new source of magical power, something that would increase our production, create new weapons. Kelas offered it to us in exchange for our support in his attempt on the throne. We were not initially aware of the role that Gaven's dragonmark would play in the use of the Forge, and we—well, I overlooked the risk of the fiend's evil corrupting the power."

"But the Forge was actually a weapon," Cart said. "It created that storm we saw and sent it toward the Reaches. So Kelas planned to use it against the barbarians?"

"And the Eldeen Reaches would shower praise on their Aundairian liberators," Aunn said.

"So that's what the queen was here to see," Ashara added. "A demonstration of this new weapon Kelas offered her. But why . . ."

"Why should Kelas offer the Forge to the queen if his goal was to overthrow her?" Aunn said.

Ashara nodded. "Exactly."

"To win her confidence, her trust. To make Thuel look bad, shown up by one of his underlings."

"Thuel?" Cart asked.

"Thuel Racannoch," Aunn said, "the head of the Royal Eyes. Sea of Fire, I've just committed treason by telling you that." He pressed his hands to his temples, trying to sort out the jumble of thoughts. "Why is Jorlanna involved in all this?" He looked at Ashara, who frowned. "Why chase after power in Aundair, rather than trying to unify House Cannith? She already has holdings in the Reaches and Thrane as well as Aundair. Why limit herself?"

"Well," Cart said, "if Aundair retakes the Reaches, she hasn't lost much, has she?"

"She's playing a dangerous game," Ashara said. "She's making such a break with tradition that she could lose some of her own enclaves, leave them open for Merrix or Zorlan to step in."

House Cannith was fragmented, Aunn knew. It hadn't split like House Phiarlan had, with the Thuranni family forming its own house, but many people believed it was just a matter of time. Jorlanna controlled the house enclaves in the northwest, but Merrix d'Cannith held sway in the south from his head-quarters in Sharn, and Zorlan oversaw the house operations in the east. Anything that tipped the balance of power among the three factions could lead to a true schism, or to one baron finally claiming victory over the others. Ashara was right—it was a dangerous game.

"But I don't think that's all," Ashara said. "I think it has to do with the Dragon Forge."

"How so?" Aunn asked.

"Well, what if Jorlanna could rule a nation that didn't need the other dragonmarked houses? What if Aundair had its own lightning rail and airships, its own banks and security, its own message stations, all operated by the Cannith family?"

"Using dragonmarks stolen from the other houses," Aunn said. "With the Dragon Forge."

"Exactly."

"So it's not a question of choosing national power over the economic power of a dragonmarked house. She wants both."

"Who wouldn't?"

Aunn drew a deep breath and let it out slowly. "So what about the dragons? What was the dragon king doing here?"

"Malathar was interested in the Prophecy," Cart said, "and in Gaven's mark. Kelas spoke of the Forge as a refinery, separating the gold of the dragonmark from the dross of Gaven's flesh."

"Kelas certainly had an interest in the esoteric side of it all. This torc, the Ramethene Sword, the Prophecy—they were all part of it."

At Aunn's mention of the Prophecy, Cart turned his head to look at Gaven, and Aunn's eyes followed. Gaven hadn't moved.

"I think there's only one person left alive who can help us sort out that part of Kelas's plans," Aunn said.

"But in the meantime," Cart said, "Aundair is at war."

"And we're still stranded in the middle of the wilderness," Ashara added, "four days from Arcanix or Vanguard Keep and not likely to be welcomed in either place."

"I'm sure we can find supplies in the camp," Aunn said. "Certainly enough for a short journey."

Ashara frowned. "But all the soldiers who fled the camp when we fought Malathar are sure to make their way back eventually, with their eyes on the same supplies."

"We'll need to be careful," Cart said.

"What were you two talking about?" Aunn said. "Before I came back?"

Ashara's face turned red again and she looked away.

Cart answered, "Xandrar."

"Xandrar? That's at least ten days from here. And the wrong direction."

"What do you mean?" Ashara said. "Where were you thinking of going?"

Aunn blinked. "I . . . I suppose I assumed we were going back to Fairhaven, sooner or later."

"Why?"

Why? Aunn realized that he didn't know. He always had returned to Fairhaven—was it simple habit? His mission accomplished, he'd return to the Royal Eyes and await his next orders? What would happen now that Kelas was dead? Would he go to Thuel and tell him of Kelas's treason? Warn him that the queen's life might still be in danger? Wouldn't Thuel just throw him in prison or have him killed?

When he had killed Kelas, Aunn had dealt the final blow to his old life. And he didn't know yet what his new life would be.

"Wherever we're going," Ashara said, "how do we take him with us?" She nodded toward Gaven.

"I can carry him," Cart said.

"Even you'd get tired with that much weight on your shoulder for ten days."

"No, I wouldn't."

"So we get him to Xandrar," Aunn said, "or Fairhaven, or wherever we're going—then what?"

"I hoped you had an answer in mind," Cart said.

"I don't. I don't have any answers." He stood up. "I need to think."

"Think quickly," Ashara said. "People will start trickling back to the camp any time, now that the storm has died."

Aunn stalked away from the pair and found himself beside the blue-gray monolith again. He leaned his head against the cool, smooth stone and tried to think. Only a short time ago, he'd been filled with a sense of purpose—a driving force that spurred him into action, the goal of destroying the Dragon Forge and ensuring that the evil of the Secret Keeper didn't escape into the world. Not only had he been driven into action, he felt he'd been helped along in that action, supported and guided by the Messenger. He'd been helped in the Labyrinth, given purpose by the Traveler or Kalok Shash or the ghost of Dania or some other presence. He needed to find that same sense of purpose. And that same source of help.

Help me, he thought. Please.

Be not afraid. I will be with you.

Had he heard the Messenger's voice again in his thoughts, or just remembered it speaking before? He couldn't tell. He put his hand to the torc at his neck, and felt a tingling chill course through his body.

It was still there, he realized—the magic that had fueled the Dragon Forge. It sprang into his mind, not a knot or weave of magic, but a raging fire, alive and unbound. It still burned in the heart of the monolith, and in the silver torc around his neck, and in himself. It was magic as he'd never seen it before, power he could taste but didn't dare touch, a force and a presence that left him awed and humbled.

Slowly a purpose took shape in his mind again.

* * * * *

"I'm returning to Fairhaven," Aunn announced. "I'll take Gaven with me—there has to be a mule or horse around here that can carry him there for me. You two don't have to come—maybe it'd be best if you don't. I can hide myself, but I'm not sure I can hide you."

Ashara's eyes widened. "And what are you going to do in Fairhaven?" she said.

"Aundair's in danger, thanks to me. I need to warn them, to make sure the queen and her generals take the threat of the barbarians seriously. I also need to find help for Gaven. And I want to find out more about Kelas's plans. There were others involved in his plot, and someone else might be ready to pick up where he left off."

"That's hard for me to imagine," Ashara said. "The plan belonged to Kelas—no one else there had the initiative or the intelligence to pull it together."

"You're probably right. Even so, knowing Kelas, there were probably other pieces of the plan, pieces we don't know about, that might have enough momentum to keep moving without him."

Cart got to his feet. "I suppose I was being foolish to think I could just walk away from all that."

"You can," Ashara said, standing beside him and taking his arm. "You're a free man."

"I'm not asking you to come with me," Aunn said. "I really don't know what I'd do with you."

"I'll take care of myself." Cart turned to Ashara. "And freedom doesn't mean running away from responsibility. I played a part in Kelas's plans because I thought I had a duty to help and obey Haldren. Now I have a duty to help make it right."

Aunn smiled at the memory of walking with Gaven and Cart in Whitecliff, what seemed like years ago and worlds away. He had just started to see the mind behind Gaven's distracted appearance, and Gaven observed that Aunn, too, had been concealing his true face. No one had ever seen through him so easily. Cart had shattered the tension, though, by taking pains to point out that he, too, was "really quite complex. Many-layered." It had seemed like a joke at the time.

"I'll be glad to have you along, Cart," he said.

"Will you come as well?" the warforged asked Ashara.

"How can I?" Tears welled in Ashara's eyes. "I've betrayed my family. I'll be excoriated!"

"You'll be in excellent company," Aunn said, nodding toward Gaven.

"True," she said, smiling up at Cart.

"We'd better gather supplies," Cart said. "We have a long journey ahead of us."

Ashara's eyes widened, and her mouth spread slowly into a grin. "Not necessarily." Her gaze drifted to the upper rim of the canyon, the area where Aunn had fought Kelas.

"The circle!" Aunn said. The queen's party had used a ritual circle to transport themselves back to Fairhaven.

"Exactly," Ashara said. "Working together, I'm sure we can activate it again."

"Where will we appear?" Cart asked. "And how do we stay hidden?"

"Ah, that's where my plan gets devious." Aunn's face melted away, passing quickly through the blank gray of his natural face before it became the smiling visage of Kelas ir'Darren.

CHAPTER
3

R ienne stood looking down over the airship's railing as the sun descended toward the green and gold expanse of the Towering Wood. The Aundairian army kept growing as more squads and companies trickled in from the ruins of Varna and the surrounding forest. They stood at attention, waiting for the command to march, but in their stillness she sensed an energy, a drive that would carry them forward to overwhelm the Eldeen Reaches.

The Reaches had been part of Aundair once, and the loss of their fertile farmlands and vast forests during the war was a hard blow. But with Thrane to the east and Breland to the south, Aundair couldn't mount a concentrated effort to take them back while the Last War still raged. Haldren ir'Brassek, the former general who had helped Gaven escape from Dreadhold, had earned his place in that prison by refusing to let the war end, continuing his campaign in the Reaches in violation of the Treaty of Thronehold—that, and his brutal treatment of prisoners and civilians, in defiance of every convention of war.

With the war over and after a few years passed to rebuild its military strength, Aundair could manage a more concentrated effort to retake the Reaches—at least until the other nations became involved and threatened its other borders again. Then Khorvaire would be back in the full heat of war, and what would Aundair have gained? Already, in their travels across Aundair, Rienne and Jordhan had heard rumors that Brelish troops were massing in the south, prepared to help defend the Reaches from Aundair's aggression.

The difference, Rienne supposed, was the barbarian horde sweeping into the Reaches from the west. It was Aundair's pretense for the invasion—Aundair couldn't rely on Reacher forces to fight back the barbarians, so it had to protect its borders with its own army, before the barbarians started pillaging Aundairian lands. It was a thin excuse to begin with, and the ruins of Varna proved that Aundair took the business of retaking the Reaches far more seriously than it did the barbarian threat.

And that, Rienne feared, was Aundair's deadly mistake.

Heavy footfalls on the deck stirred her from her thoughts. For a moment she dreamed that it was Gaven stepping up behind her, ready to enfold her in his arms. But it was Jordhan's voice that asked, "What's our course from here, Lady Alastra?"

She turned around and tried to smile at him. "I'm not sure," she said.

"Something tells me Gaven is somewhere south of here, if those storms were any indication." Jordhan's smile seemed forced as well. "Shall we head that way and look for him?"

Rienne sighed and turned back to the railing, gazing across Lake Galifar to the hazy silhouettes of the distant Blackcap Mountains. Jordhan's question had said a great deal, and his face had told her more. They had sighted two great storms in the last days of their journey west, both forming somewhere on the Aundairian side of the lake, near those mountains. The storms appeared in clear skies and flashed with lightning. The second one, though, had swept across the lake and crashed into the city, leaving it in ruins. Rienne didn't want to believe that Gaven was responsible for demolishing the city, for Aundair or any other cause. Perhaps the storm was some new weapon of Aundair, nothing to do with Gaven at all.

More than three weeks had passed since she last saw Gaven, and not an hour had gone by without some thought of him surfacing in her mind and pricking at her heart. But she had chosen to pursue her own destiny, whether that course brought her back with Gaven or not. She wouldn't veer from that path now.

"No," she said. "We'll continue west. Gaven will have to find us."

* * * * *

Evening found Rienne back at the railing, looking down at the farmland drifting along beneath them. She heard Jordhan's footsteps on the deck behind her and her grip tightened on the rail.

"We need to talk," Jordhan said, coming to stand behind her. Rienne took a breath and tried to brace herself for what was coming next.

Things with Jordhan were different than they had been before, when Gaven was in Dreadhold. Gaven had said, when they met Jordhan again in Sharavacion, that he always expected Jordhan to start courting Rienne as soon as Gaven was out of the way. He might have, if the circumstances of Gaven's arrest had been different. As it was, spending time together was a painful reminder of what had happened, and Gaven was always there, a haunting presence that squelched any feelings that might otherwise have blossomed between them.

On their journey to Argonnessen together, Gaven was a physical presence with them, and Jordhan kept his distance. But Gaven was gone again—dead, for all they knew. Rienne had chosen not to look for him, and that seemed to give Jordhan permission to show his feelings a little more openly. He held her gaze just a moment too long, stood half a step too close, touched her elbow or her shoulder as they spoke.

Jordhan was the best of friends, the only person—other than Gaven—she had ever been able to share her deepest thoughts and dreams with. She loved him. She would have been devastated to lose his friendship, but there was no passion in her feelings for him. But she didn't want to have to tell him that, to see the hurt in his eyes and watch him slowly drift away. She turned slowly to face him, to hear what he wanted to say.

Jordhan's face was serious, and he put both hands on her shoulders. "Rienne," he said, "you know how much I care about you."

"Of course." She couldn't meet his intense gaze.

"I'm worried about you," he said.

She looked into his eyes then, surprised. "Worried? Why?"

"You spend half of every day staring over this railing. You're wearing a rut in the deck from your pacing. I'm not sure this ship can support the weight on your shoulders much longer." A hint of his warm smile danced at the corner of his mouth, but his eyes remained serious.

Jordhan's hands fell from her shoulders as he turned away. "You're mocking me."

"No, I'm not. I know you have a lot on your mind. I'd like to help you, if I can. If you'll let me."

"Help me how?"

"What do you need? What can I do for you? There's no one else who can help you, not until we find Gaven, or he finds us. Please let me help."

Rienne stared down at the Eldeen fields passing beneath them like a patchwork of greens. What did she need? She wasn't sure she knew. And she wasn't sure she wanted help. "My whole life, I've depended on everyone—on my family and my noble name, on Gaven, on Maelstrom, on you. I need to figure out who I am."

Jordhan touched her elbow. "I've never known anyone more sure of herself."

"No, that's not it. My training is all about emptying myself, seeing myself and everyone around me as a part of a network, a web of being and motion. Without that web, at rest, I don't know . . ." She shook her head. "I don't know what I mean, I can't expect you to."

"It'll be all right, Ree." Jordhan's arms encircled her and his warmth surrounded her.

She closed her eyes and for a moment imagined it was Gaven calling her Ree, and his strong arms around her. But Jordhan was far leaner, and he smelled wrong—like the sea, like the citrus fruit he'd just eaten, like her friend. She pulled away from his embrace. "Jordhan—"

"I know," he said. "I'll leave you alone."

Rienne watched him slouch back to the helm, and she felt the weight on her shoulders grow heavier.

* * * * *

A day's journey past Varna, the airship approached the edge of the Towering Wood. The ordered lines of tended fields came to an abrupt end, and the forest rose like a wall dividing the agricultural east from the lands of the druids and rangers. But it was a wall that would give the eastern farms no shelter from the barbarians, whose approach was heralded by a smear of gray smoke on the western horizon.

Jordhan pointed the airship's prow at the smoke, and they floated over miles of forest green, autumn red and gold scattered among the branches. The smoke grew into a cloud like a raging storm, the fires beneath it painting splashes of scarlet across the darkened sky. As the sun's light drained away, the conflagration came into view. Flames leaped into the sky, pouring smoke into the air. Trees burned like torches as the fire consumed them and moved on, leaving them broken, blackened skeletons. The fires formed a long, curving line like a ripple spreading out from the Shadowcrags beyond. And thousands of campfires burned among the smoldering bones of the trees, glittering on the dark ground below like distant stars.

"Sovereigns help us," Rienne breathed. Images from her dream in Rav Magar stormed into her mind again—the tumult of the field of battle, barbarian soldiers falling before the fury of Maelstrom, the bone-white banners of the Blasphemer. And the words of the Prophecy: *Dragons fly before the Blasphemer's legions* . . .

"Jordhan, get us out of here!" she cried. They were high out of bowshot, but if there were dragons—if the dragons spotted them they'd be vulnerable to attack, all too easy to bring to ground.

The airship jerked as Jordhan urged the elemental bound within her to greater speed.

Rienne leaned over the bulwarks to peer down at the shadowed ground. The campfires illuminated clumps of people, but she didn't see any of the dragons mentioned in the Prophecy.

"What is it?" Jordhan called. "What do you see?"

Rienne turned back from the bulwarks to see Jordhan, eyes wide and knuckles white as he clenched the tiller. "We're flying over the horde now," she said. "And there are supposed to be dragons with them."

"More dragons." The constant threat of dragon attack had driven Jordhan and his crew half mad on their journey to Argonnessen.

"I don't see any, though . . ." As she spoke, Rienne turned back to look over the bulwarks—just in time to see a winged shadow pass before the fires that raged in the forest. "Oh no."

"How many?" Jordhan asked.

"I think I saw one. Hard to be sure—it's dark down there."

"Well, I've always wondered whether a little airship like this could outpace a dragon. Shall we find out?"

Rienne saw it clearly for just a moment, leathery wings spread wide as it rode the updraft over the flames. "Fly like the wind!" she cried. "It's coming!"

CHAPTER
4

Aunn stood outside Kelas's tent and drew a slow breath. For a moment he imagined that he was about to have another meeting with the man who had been his mentor, his superior officer, and the closest thing to a father that he had ever known. But that man lay dead at the edge of the canyon, dead by Aunn's own hand, and Aunn was wearing his face. Aunn would never again have a face-to-face meeting with Kelas ir'Darren.

Letting the breath out, Aunn pulled back the flap of the tent. There could be no doubt that the ordered, austere tent belonged to Kelas—it was almost a replica of his study in the Royal Eyes' offices in Fairhaven, with the addition of a simple bedroll in the back corner. A plain table had been erected to serve as a desk, and it was as bare as Kelas's desk always was, a single sheaf of papers neatly stacked on one side. The chair behind the desk was plain wood. A low bookcase held a few favorite books, two other stacks of paper, and a small glass orb on a plain tripod. A small chest near the bedroll was the only other furnishing.

Still half-expecting Kelas's voice to accost him, Aunn swept around the room, stuffing papers into his backpack. The chest's lock only slowed him for the seconds it took him to slide a pick from the pouch at his belt and find the right catches inside. A few clean clothes followed the paper into his pack, and a handful of gold and silver coins went into his belt pouch. Less than a minute after he entered, he stood at the flaps of the tent and cast his eyes around the inside of the tent again. He scanned the books on the shelves—he was familiar with them all, from the classic treatise on tactics in war and politics, *The Chimera of War,* to the worn collection of the plays of Thardakhan, an ancient hobgoblin playwright Kelas revered. Nothing essential. He turned to leave, but dashed back and snatched the glass globe from the shelf, sliding it into the pouch with his wands. He wouldn't know until he took more time examining it whether it was anything more than decoration, but if nothing else it was a pretty trophy.

He hurried out of the tent and into the deserted camp. The battle with the dragon king, and Gaven's fierce storm, had strewn debris over the whole end of the canyon—a twisted metal beam ripped from the Dragon Forge impaled the tent nearest Kelas's, and wooden flinders littered the sandy ground. Aunn made his way up the ridge to the circle they would use to teleport back to Fairhaven. Cart and Ashara, still gathering supplies somewhere in the camp, weren't there yet, so Aunn was alone with Kelas's corpse. He froze with a sudden rage.

"You bastard!" Aunn shouted.

The surge of fury in his chest surprised him. He had expected, he realized, that killing Kelas would calm the storm of emotion he'd been caught in since he set out for the Demon Wastes.

He couldn't look at the dead man's face, though he was wearing it as his own. Falling to his knees beside the body, he undressed it, careful not to let his eyes meet the dead man's glassy stare. He made a quick scan of the corpse to make sure he hadn't missed any details in copying Kelas's appearance, but his memory had served him well. He took off his own clothes and armor, which Farren had secured for him before he left Maruk Dar, and replaced them with Kelas's garb. The contents of his belt pouches, including Kelas's glass orb, he transferred into the pouches Kelas had worn, and he took a quick inventory of Kelas's gear. Finally he lifted the sword from the ground beside Kelas's dead hand and slid it into its sheath at his belt, praying he'd never have to draw it.

"Oh, Kelas," he said, forcing his eyes to the face. "I'm . . . I'm not sorry!" He slapped his own face. "I do not care!" He dropped to his knees. "You failed," he croaked, "so you died. Damn you!" He curled around the knot of anguish in his gut. "Damn you damn you damn you . . ."

He thought at first that the heavy hand on his arm belonged to Kelas, come to shake him out of sleep and inspect his body. He threw a child's frantic punch and scraped his knuckles against the metal plate of Cart's shoulder.

"Aunn?" Cart's voice was heavy with concern.

Aunn pressed his fists to his temples and tried to steady himself with a long breath. "Sorry," he said. "I . . . lost control. It won't happen again."

Cart lifted him to his feet and put a hand on his shoulder. "I understand."

Aunn looked at the warforged, and his confusion must have been plain on his face.

"I killed Haldren," Cart explained.

Aunn's eyes met Cart's, two green circles cut into the metal plate of his face, faintly glowing with inner light. The warforged normally seemed utterly inhuman, made of wood, metal, and stone assembled into an automaton designed for war. It was all the more surprising to see such empathy from him.

"Thank you," Aunn said.

Cart clapped Aunn's shoulder. "It's a good resemblance. You look just like Kelas."

Ashara stood by Gaven, a few yards away where Cart had left him. Gaven stared blankly at the ground. Cart had discovered that Gaven would stand with help, and he'd walk if he was led, but he remained otherwise unresponsive, his eyes wide but unseeing. Walking around the camp with Cart hadn't improved his condition, evidently. Ashara let go of his arm and came to stand before Aunn, and Gaven slowly sank into a crouch.

"Let me see," Ashara said. She examined Kelas's face carefully, lingering at his eyes, then repeated the examination of

Aunn's assumed face. Aunn stared into her rich, brown eyes as she checked his.

"The eyes will give me away," he said, shaking his head.

"Kelas could never hold anyone's gaze," Ashara said. "He knew his secrets were there. You'll do fine."

Aunn looked away. Could that be true? He had always believed that Kelas overlooked the importance of the eyes in a disguise—he had never checked them carefully enough. But perhaps he had been afraid of revealing too much of himself.

"We can't leave the body here," Ashara said. "Is there any fire left in the forge?"

"I'll take care of it," Cart said. "You two start working on the circle." The warforged lifted Kelas's body over his shoulder and started down the ridge without looking back.

"Have you worked with a teleportation circle before, Aunn?" Ashara asked, crouching to examine the circle traced in the ground.

"No," Aunn said. A permanent portal was a dangerous way for a spy to travel, since the destination circle was usually a fixed location that was carefully watched. It was a bit like blustering one's way through a city's main gate, drawing as much attention to oneself as possible. Not his preferred way of doing things—and as he considered it, he questioned again whether their plan made any sense.

Ashara kneeled at the edge of the circle, retracing its outline with a slender silver rod. The dirt glowed faintly silver-blue where the rod passed. "You're a Royal Eye," she said. "Tell me about the teleportation circles in Fairhaven."

"House Orien has one." The same house that ran lightning rail lines across Khorvaire also maintained permanent circles in major cities, facilitating the instant transportation of couriers, and even goods, if the price was right.

"And its sigils are so closely guarded that even the queen probably can't use that one."

Aunn nodded. Each teleportation circle had a series of magical sigils engraved into it, identifying it as a unique destination for any portals that linked to it. Ashara must have been trying to reconstruct or verify the sigils traced into this circle, to make sure their destination was the same as the queen's.

"There's one by the university," Aunn said.

"Very public. I don't think the queen would use that one." Ashara stopped tracing lines in the ground, and most of the circle stood out clearly in the dirt, glowing softly. Aunn closed his eyes, and the lines of magic that formed the real circle appeared in sharper focus in his mind. But they were incomplete—a few of the sigils were clear, but the rest must have been wiped away in his fight with Kelas.

"Does House Cannith have a circle?" he asked.

"Yes, these could be the sigils for the Cannith circle. But that would mean . . ."

"That we'll arrive right on the doorstep of your House, where you're not exactly welcome."

"Right. With a warforged, an excoriate from House Lyrandar, and a dragonshard that's worth about three kingdoms to the right people."

Aunn wheeled to look at Gaven, but his hands were empty. "Where is the shard?" he said. Panic set his heart drumming.

"I have it." Ashara patted a pocket in her coat. "Believe me, I haven't forgotten about it, or the need to keep it safe. Can you imagine what people would do to get their hands on it?"

"First they have to know it exists." Aunn felt like an idiot for having forgotten it—his mind had been on Gaven, not on the shard that Cart took from his hands. It was a terrible oversight.

"Well then," Ashara said, "let's start with the people who know it exists—like Baron Jorlanna and Arcanist Wheldren. And Phaine d'Thuranni. Perhaps one of the dragons that flew out of here when Gaven wrecked the Dragon Forge. That's enough, but it won't stop there. Word will spread."

"Is that thing ready?" Cart called from somewhere behind Aunn.

Aunn saw Ashara brighten, and he smiled to himself. Strange as it was, her affection for Cart seemed genuine, and it was touching.

"The circle's ready," she said. "Now we just need—Oh! You're hurt!"

Aunn turned and saw Cart running toward them. A gash on Cart's arm, just above the top of his shield, streamed with brownish fluid. His axe was in his hand, blood staining the blade, and he shot a glance over his shoulder as Ashara hurried out of the circle to meet him.

"It's nothing," Cart said, pulling his arm away from Ashara's reach. "But we should get out of here now, if the circle's ready."

The tramp of running feet followed Cart up the hill, and Aunn reached for his mace. His hand grabbed empty air, and he glanced down to his belt, where Kelas's sword hung at his left side. He sighed and fumbled in his pouch for a wand.

"Get in the circle!" Ashara said. "I'll finish the sigils."

"But your House—" Aunn began.

"We'll cross that threshold when we get there." She knelt near the center of the circle, and Cart joined her, turning back to shield her from the soldiers who were cresting the ridge. Aunn took Gaven's arm, stood him up again, and led him into the ring of twisting lines and symbols. A soldier shouted and a spear stabbed into the ground just outside the circle. Aunn stretched his mind to feel the lines of magic coursing around the completed circle.

"Just one thing," Ashara said. "When we get there, nobody move."

* * * * *

Activating the circle took only a moment. Once again, Aunn and Ashara were joined together by the weave of magic formed by the circle, and their hands and minds darted over the loom in perfect unison. Aunn saw another spear clang against Cart's shield, and the world went black.

At first he thought they had failed, and somehow hurled themselves into the Outer Darkness beyond the world. Then his senses caught up with him: he felt the hard stone beneath his feet and hands, heard Ashara and Gaven breathing beside him, and noticed the magic weave of the Cannith teleportation circle. They had arrived in Fairhaven. He almost stood up, then remembered Ashara's warning.

"What now?" he whispered.

He heard Ashara let out a long, slow breath. "We're in a large room warded by traps, with a guard outside the door."

Aunn sighed. "Quite a threshold to cross." His mind started tracing a possible course, anticipating the traps that were likely in place and how to disable them. The last thing he wanted was to raise an alarm, to be forced to explain what Kelas ir'Darren was doing sneaking around the Cannith forgehold. "Wait a moment," he said aloud.

He had to start thinking like Kelas, Aunn realized. He drew a deep breath, stood up, and listened. He didn't hear anything to indicate that he'd sprung a trap, so he called out in a perfect imitation of Kelas's most authoritative voice, "House Cannith! Open this door, in the name of the queen!"

"What are you doing?" Ashara cried. Before Aunn could answer, magical lights around the room blazed to life and a door swung open.

They were in a large, square chamber, perhaps thirty feet on a side. At a glance, Aunn saw nozzles in the ceiling, probably designed to release a gas that would knock intruders unconscious—or possibly jets to bathe invaders in fire. Holes in the walls were almost certainly designed to release darts or arrows. Every flagstone on the floor, beyond the etched lines of the teleportation circle, could have been a moving plate concealing a trigger for one of the room's traps.

The two warforged soldiers in the doorway commanded his attention, however. They gripped halberds, and one had a hand on a copper panel on the wall beside the door. Aunn didn't wait for them to speak.

"I am Kelas ir'Darren and I am here on the queen's business," he said. "Please escort me and my companions to the nearest exit."

The two warforged exchanged a glance, one nodded, and the other moved something on the copper panel. "Please approach," the one at the panel said, "and I'll need to see your identification papers."

Aunn strode forward without glancing at the others, hoping that Cart and Ashara were playing their parts. As he walked, he produced the papers he'd found in Kelas's pouch, and he handed them to one of the warforged. "The half-elf is a prisoner," he said, nodding toward Gaven, who was shuffling along under Cart's guidance. He tried to force his heart into a slow, steady rhythm, but it was like pulling the reins of a wild stallion.

The warforged studied the front page of Kelas's papers carefully, then turned the page to read the part that identified him as an agent of the crown. He looked at the first page again, examined the portrait and compared it to Aunn's face, then handed it back and turned his attention to Ashara.

Her Mark of Making was hidden beneath a sleeve of leather armor, so he didn't recognize her as an heir of the House until he read her name from the papers she offered. "Lady Cannith!" he exclaimed, and both of the warforged bowed deeply.

The other warforged, rising from his bow, held a hand out to Cart.

"I have no identification papers," Cart said.

"He's mine," Ashara said. That seemed to satisfy the guard, though Aunn saw Cart stiffen.

The first warforged still held Ashara's papers. "Lady *Ashara* d'Cannith?" He exchanged another glance with his comrade, and Aunn saw Ashara's eyes widen with sudden fear.

"I'm sorry, master ir'Darren," the warforged said to Aunn, "but we are going to have to take Ashara into custody. House Cannith has declared her excoriate."

CHAPTER
5

ouse Cannith?" Aunn said.

"Whose enclave you have just barged into, yes," said the warforged, Ashara's papers clutched in his fist.

"House Cannith no longer exists in Aundair," Aunn said. "The Cannith family no longer has legal authority over its members—you're all Aundairians now. And Ashara *ir*'Cannith is an agent of the queen's Ministry of Artifice, to which this building belongs. She's coming with me. Give her back her papers."

If the warforged said anything, Aunn couldn't hear it over the pounding in his ears. From what Ashara had told him, Jorlanna should have sworn her fealty to the queen already, if everything had gone according to plan. But nothing was going according to plan, and if Jorlanna remained the head of a House Cannith still protected by the Korth Edicts, he had just talked himself into a very bad position. He could barely breathe as he waited for the warforged to respond.

Then Ashara had her papers again and the warforged were leading them out of the room and up a narrow stone passageway. Aunn glanced back at Gaven, grateful that the dispute over Ashara had distracted the guards from the "prisoner" who shuffled along beside Cart. Satisfied that Gaven was not attracting attention, Aunn concentrated on his stride—purposeful, proud—and tried to become Kelas. For thirty years, he thought, Kelas tried to make me the perfect spy, shaping me into a replica of himself. Now I need to *be* him.

There's too much I don't know, he thought as he strode behind the warforged, too many ways I can give myself away. I know more than anyone, probably, about Kelas's past, but not enough about the plots he was embroiled in when he died. What in the Traveler's ten thousand names am I getting myself into?

The passage opened into a hall that Aunn recognized as the primary audience chamber in the Cannith enclave, close to the main entrance from the street. He could just hear the sounds of the busy street outside as evening settled over the city—a donkey braying, voices raised in an argument. A moment more, he thought, and we'll be out of here. Free.

The warforged stopped in front of a man who bore the Mark of Making, smaller but no less elaborate than Ashara's, on his left temple. A streak of stark white hair, contrasting with the rich black that covered the rest of his head, started right beside his mark. The warforged bowed slightly and leaned in to explain the situation.

The man stepped around the warforged to confront Aunn. "I'm Harkin d'Cann—" He stopped, grimaced, and corrected himself. "Harkin ir'Cannith, steward of this house."

Clearly, as a dragonmarked heir, he needed some adjustment to the idea of being an Aundairian noble, changing the honorific in his name from the dragonmarked d' to the mark of a noble family of Galifar, the ir'- prefix.

"Kelas ir'Darren," Aunn said. When he needed to be, Kelas could be charming, all smiles and ingratiating warmth. But in situations like this, Aunn knew, Kelas was cold fire.

"Look, ir'Darren," Harkin said, "I don't know what Ashara did, but the baron wants her head."

"I'll discuss the matter with Jorlanna, then. It's no concern of yours."

"It'll be my head next if the baron finds out that I let her go."

Aunn folded his arms. "And I'll have you in a court of law if you try to detain this woman. You have no legal authority to arrest her."

"Why don't I just see if the baron's here now, and we can get this sorted out before Ashara goes anywhere?" His eyes ranged over Cart and Gaven, then settled on Ashara for a moment. Aunn thought he saw the hint of a smile.

"Harkin—" Ashara began, but Aunn cut her off.

"Ashara is helping me on the queen's business, and it can't wait. You may tell Jorlanna that I'll speak with her about this in the morning. But we are leaving now. Good evening."

Aunn turned his back on the man and swept toward the door. His heart was still pounding, but it was not an altogether unpleasant sensation. Exhilarating, almost. A taste of the power that Kelas wielded. Nobody moved to intercept him before he reached the door, and a glance over his shoulder showed him that Cart and Ashara were right on his heels, leading Gaven along between them. Gaven's face registered no thought or feeling.

Sorry, friend, Aunn thought. You're missing quite an adventure.

Harkin watched them leave with his arms crossed and his brow furrowed, his eyes fixed on Gaven. So Jorlanna would know that both Gaven and Ashara were in his custody, as well as a war-forged who was most likely the one who killed Haldren.

How am I going to talk myself out of that? he wondered.

We'll cross that threshold when we get there, he thought as he turned his back to the Cannith enclave and stepped back onto the Fairhaven streets.

*　*　*　*　*

"You did it!" Ashara said, once several blocks lay between them and the Cannith enclave. "You got us out!"

"Lower your voice," Aunn said. "I haven't spotted anyone yet, but it's a safe bet we're being followed. Keep up appearances."

Ashara glanced over her shoulder, and Aunn rolled his eyes. It didn't matter—if the Cannith following them knew what he was doing, he would assume that his quarry knew he was there. And following their strange procession would hardly be a challenge. Gaven walked with Cart, but slowly, and they drew entirely too much attention. The streets were crowded with workers heading home and the well-to-do beginning their nightly revels—far too many people who might remember the strange sight of a warforged leading a catatonic half-elf through the streets.

"I might have gotten us out of there," Aunn said, "but I'm afraid I talked us into more trouble. Now Jorlanna knows you're with me—and we have Gaven. That rules out a lot of good lies."

"Well, at any rate we're walking through the city, not in a cell somewhere." Ashara looked around. "Where are we going?"

"House Jorasco. I want to get Gaven back as soon as possible."

"Do you think that's wise?" Cart said, speaking for the first time since they left the Cannith enclave.

"Bringing Gaven back to his senses?" Aunn said, stopping and turning to face the warforged.

"No, taking him to House Jorasco. We just had one adventure in a dragonmarked enclave. Are you in such a hurry to rush into another?"

"But House Jorasco—"

"Loves to be underestimated," Cart said. "They took Senya in when she was injured, nursed her back to health, and then summoned the Sentinel Marshals as soon as she was well enough to travel. And that was in Vathirond. I think it's wise to assume that House Jorasco in Fairhaven will be at least as well-informed."

"Damn, you're right," Aunn said. "What do we do, then? If not House Jorasco, who can heal him?"

"I have an idea," Cart said. "A sergeant I knew once had some unusual interests, and a friend of hers here in the city took her once to meet someone she said . . . hrm. It's a bit hard to explain." Cart shrugged. "What if I just find him and bring him to the cathedral?"

"Can I come with you?" Ashara asked.

"If you like."

"The cathedral?" Aunn said.

"Kelas was using the old cathedral as a meeting place," Ashara explained.

The old cathedral of the Silver Flame. It struck Aunn as an odd choice of a meeting place for Kelas's conspiracy. Kelas had never shown anything but contempt for the Church of the Silver Flame, and of all Aundair's neighbors he hated Thrane the most, with its theocratic government, the Keeper of the Flame at its head. Perhaps, in Kelas's mind, meeting at the cathedral symbolized Aundair's victory over Thrane. The idea made Aunn's stomach turn.

"No," he said, "meet me at Kelas's real office, in the Tower of Eyes. It faces the west side of Crown Hall."

Crown Hall was the queen's palace. It made Aunn nervous to get so close to the heart of the whole affair, but he needed a secure place to take Gaven, and few places were safer than the stronghold of Aundair's Royal Eyes.

"I know where it is," Cart said. "I went there with Haldren once. But how will we get in?"

Aunn pulled some paper and a small writing set from one of Kelas's pouches. Using Cart's back as a desk, he scrawled a hasty note and signed it in a perfect imitation of Kelas's hand. He touched a ring he'd pulled from Kelas's dead fingers to the paper, felt with his mind for the tiny knot of magic contained in the ring, and tripped it. A pattern of faintly glowing lines appeared on the paper beneath the signature, and Aunn smiled in satisfaction.

"Show this to the guards at the door and tell them you have an appointment to see me. Tell them to summon me if they give you any trouble. I'll take Gaven there now and wait for you."

Cart took the paper, scanned the words and nodded.

"Be careful," Aunn added.

"Always." Cart held Gaven's arm out for Aunn to take, then Ashara took his arm and they strolled off together toward the eastern side of town.

Aunn looked at Gaven and smiled. "All right, Gaven, we're going this way. Can you walk with me?"

Slowly Gaven shuffled along beside him as Aunn made his way to the Tower of Eyes.

* * * * *

Walking beside Ashara was the opposite of marching in a unit of soldiers, Cart thought. His stride was long and even, like the steady cadence of a drum keeping soldiers in step. Her shorter legs made her steps quicker, and she had trouble keeping up with him, so she'd occasionally take a flurry of little, half-running steps, her boots pattering like hail on the cobblestones. There was a pleasing music to it, somehow—her melody playing against his constant drone.

Aunn and Gaven were long out of sight, and the busier streets of Fairhaven's downtown soon fell away behind them, replaced by quiet rows of homes and apartments. Cart was lost in the rhythm of their steps.

"What's wrong, Cart?" Ashara asked, breaking the silence.

Cart took a few more steps before he answered. "You don't really think I'm yours, do you?"

"What?"

"Back there. I said I didn't have papers and you said, 'He's mine.' Like it was nothing."

"Oh, Cart, no. I just wanted to make sure they didn't give you any trouble, that's all. Sometimes House Cannith can still be very possessive about warforged."

"But those were warforged we were talking to."

"Warforged who might as well still be slaves owned by the House," Ashara said. "They're not legally slaves, but they don't get paid what human guards do."

It came to Cart like a dawning realization, full of wonder. "Nobody owns me," he said.

Ashara clutched his arm. "Of course not."

Cart walked in silence again. They approached a group of young men, who stopped their boisterous conversation and stared as they walked past, arm in arm. Ashara shifted her grip and Cart thought for a moment that she might release his arm in embarrassment, but she held on. Her hands were warm where they touched the cords and sinews between his armored plates.

"I think," Cart said, "that I would like to get identification papers. Would you help me?"

"You've never had papers?"

"I had military identification, but that was before the Treaty of Thronehold. Those papers showed me to be the property of Aundair. I belonged to Haldren. Right up until I killed him."

"So now you're free."

"I suppose I am," Cart said. "I'm not sure what to do now."

"What did you do while Haldren was in Dreadhold?"

"I waited."

"That's all? Just waited?"

"I did odd things here and there to pass the time. I worked in Passage for a while, carrying crates. Senya dragged me into an old Dhakaani ruin once with some half-elf wizard who promised her a fortune. Mostly I waited."

"So what do you want to do with your freedom?"

Cart looked down at her, into her warm, brown eyes. He eased his arm free of her hands and wrapped it around her shoulders, pulling her close to his side. She put one arm around his waist and laid the other hand on his chest, and her head rested beside her hand. It was confusing to him—he hated the thought of being owned: her dismissive words to the Cannith warforged had cut him like daggers. But the urge to hold her close, keep her beside him, protect her—it was a fiercely possessive urge.

"Freedom is a strange thing," he said. With her body so close to his, he slowed his step and she matched it, so they found a slower rhythm together. "Nobody owns me, but Gaven and Aunn and you seem to have a hold on me anyway. What I want to do is to be with you."

"Freedom is the ability to choose your commitments," Ashara said, "to choose what owns your loyalty."

"Then perhaps I am yours after all."

Her smile spread all across her face, touching every one of the tiny muscles beneath the skin—such an intricate construction, he thought, like the work of a divine artisan.

"And I'm yours," she said.

* * * * *

Aunn stood at the door to Kelas's study. Out of habit, he cast his mind over his body, from the crown of his head to the soles of his feet, making sure every detail was in place for Kelas's inevitable scrutiny. Only this time the details were those of Kelas's own appearance, and no one would be in the study to inspect him. He glanced at Gaven, motionless at his side, then pulled a ring of keys from one of Kelas's pouches and found the right one. Taking a deep breath, he turned the key in the hole and pushed open the door.

Nothing had changed. He knew the room at least as well as his own suite, which he hadn't seen in months. The large oak desk gave the room its color and character, dark and solid. For an absurd moment, Aunn wasn't sure where to sit. A wooden chair between the desk and the door was Aunn's accustomed place; the one behind the desk, upholstered in leather, was where Kelas would sit. He shook his head to clear it, then led Gaven to the wooden chair and walked around the desk to Kelas's chair.

"Well, Gaven," he said, "perhaps you're wondering why I've brought you here."

He ran his hands over the chair's leather, worn but well cared for. He sat gingerly, then settled back against the cushions. It was a comfortable seat—it fit Kelas's body perfectly.

"Frankly, I'm wondering the same thing. This seems a bit like madness."

He spread his palms over the oak of the desk, which he had never touched before. It was smooth, immaculately clean, warm. Only a single sheaf of papers on his left side marred the dark, polished surface.

"But here we sit, until Cart and Ashara come back with whoever they think can bring you back to your right mind." He looked at Gaven, whose eyes were fixed on some point behind the wall, then pulled the sheaf of papers closer. "Let's see what Kelas was reading, shall we?"

The writing on the paper was written in thick, angular letters that made Aunn think at first they were in Dwarven, but the letters were Common:

> *The servant seeks to free the master,*
>   *seizing flesh to unbind spirit,*
>   *to break the serpent's hold.*
> *Touched by flame, the champion*
>   *recapitulates the serpents' sacrifice,*
>   *binding the servant anew*
>   *so the master cannot break free.*

"What in the Traveler's ten thousand names . . . ?" Aunn breathed. He thrust a hand into a pouch at his belt and rummaged until he found a piece of stone, a fragment of the masonry wall that he had picked up at random while he stood in Gaven's cell. On it, scratched with the metal stylus the Dreadhold guards had allowed him, Gaven had written the same words, or at least the last two lines. Part of the Prophecy.

Aunn pushed that page aside and read the next. The hand was the same, presumably one of Gaven's jailers, a dwarf of House Kundarak. Another verse of the Prophecy: *Showers of light fall upon the City of the Dead, and the Storm Dragon emerges after twice thirteen years.*

"How did Kelas get these?" Aunn said, looking up at Gaven as if he expected an answer. But Gaven's eyes had closed and his chin dropped to his chest.

"You're right, my friend. It has been a very long day."

CHAPTER
6

Jordhan wasn't the Storm Dragon, but he was a dragonmarked heir of House Lyrandar, with the Mark of Storm etched across the side of his head. When he needed to, he could bend the wind to his will and urge it to fill his galleon's sails. And with a dragon rising up from the Blasphemer's horde to pursue them, there was great need; he coaxed the wind to speed his little airship along.

Rienne clutched the bulwark rail at the aft of the ship, squinting into the darkness behind them for any sign of the dragon. A ring of elemental fire surrounded the airship, arching high above Rienne's head and bathing the deck in warm firelight, which hurt her ability to see far beyond the lit circle. She strained her ears for the beat of the dragon's wings. Just as she started daring to hope they might have outdistanced it, she saw the glitter of its eyes reflecting the light of the fiery ring.

"Here it comes!" she cried.

A gust of wind shot the airship like an arrow away from the onrushing dragon, and its eyes disappeared into the darkness again. Rienne heard it roar, and a liquid sound like the eruption of a geyser, then the wind brought a spray of fine mist that stung where it touched her skin.

"We'll never get away from it," she called to Jordhan. "It can see us from miles away."

"But if it can't catch us, it might give up," Jordhan said.

"Who do you think can keep this up longer? You or the dragon?"

"What's your plan?"

Rienne looked over the railing to the darkened ground below. They had flown over the barbarian horde, and its fires were a glimmer in the distance. The dragon was still shrouded in the darkness behind the ship.

"Take us down," she said. "Let's fight this thing on the ground."

"You want to *fight* it?"

"I don't think we have a choice. We're outrunning it now, but you're going to get tired eventually, and I'm guessing it can outlast you. But we *can* choose whether to fight it in the air or on the ground. In the air, it can wreck our ship and send us plummeting to the ground without ever coming within our reach. On the ground, we have a chance."

"Even without Gaven?"

Rienne's heart was a jumble of emotion—regret over the harsh words she'd said to Gaven on their last journey together, grief that he wasn't there to fight by her side, an irrational anger that he'd left her to take care of herself. She found a scrap of joy and clung to it: she imagined telling Gaven the story, when it was all over and they were together again, of the dragon she killed.

"Even without Gaven," she said. "Trust me."

Jordhan clutched the helm and the ship veered downward. "How high are we?" he asked.

Rienne leaned over the bulwarks. The airship's fiery ring lit only empty air below, as far as she could see. "I can't tell."

"Pretty high, then. You have to be my eyes, Ree. I'll try to watch for the dragon, but I need you to shout as soon as you see ground—or anything else we might hit on our way down."

Rienne nodded her understanding and took a slow breath to focus her mind. She heard the faint roar of the elemental fire, the creaking of the wooden hull, and the rush of air past the ship as she descended. The air smelled of burning wood, with a lingering hint of the acrid scent of the dragon's caustic breath. Finally the ground came into view, painted in pale orange light.

"Sovereigns help us," she breathed, before she called to Jordhan, "We're still a bowshot above the ground, but it's going to be a rough landing." The charred skeletons of the forest thrust jagged stumps and branches up toward them, as if reaching up to pull them down.

"It always is," Jordhan said. "Airships aren't meant to be landed."

"To starboard, just a bit," she called. "Fewer trees. Gently!"

The airship drifted downward at Jordhan's command, floating a few yards to starboard, then a few more when Rienne shouted a warning. Rienne marveled at the precision of its movement—unlike a seagoing galleon, which had to obey the ocean currents and winds as well as the pilot's commands, the airship went exactly where Jordhan willed it to go.

"Dragon!" Jordhan shouted.

Rienne whirled, then darkness swallowed her. The airship's burning ring, the distant glow of fire in the forest, even the dim scattering of stars that had shone through the cloud-burdened sky—all light disappeared. For an instant, Rienne thought she was floating alone in a void, then she heard Jordhan's sputtering curse, the continuing roar of the flaming ring, and the flap of the dragon's heavy wings, very close above her. The dragon must have conjured the darkness to blind its prey.

"Just take her straight down," Rienne said, "as fast as you can without crashing." She slid Maelstrom from its sheath and stepped to the center of the deck, bracing herself to meet the dragon. She heard the beat of its wings, and its slow intake of breath, and she realized her mistake.

As the roaring sound of the dragon's breath erupted overhead, she dove for the wheelhouse but hit the deck harder than she intended, sending Maelstrom skittering from her hand. She rolled several times before the acidic spray splattered over her, searing her back and left side. Gritting her teeth against the pain, she lifted herself to her hands and knees before the airship tilted sharply to port with a splintering crash of wood, sending her rolling across the deck again.

The airship slowed, then stopped, listing to port. Rienne heard the clatter of Maelstrom sliding down the deck and crawled after it. The dragon's wings beat once, twice, closer . . . a third time, and then it slammed into the ship. The airship tore free from the trees that had held it in place and fell through splintering branches until it settled again, this time slanted to front and starboard. As the hull settled into its new position, though, the darkness fell away—Rienne saw the dragon in all its terrible majesty, filling the deck, ready to spring. Beyond it, she could see the charred branches that held the airship in place, just above the ground, outlined against the fires on the horizon. The airship's own fiery ring was extinguished, probably at Jordhan's command, to avoid reigniting the trees around them.

Terror coursed through Rienne's body as she looked up at the dragon. It dwarfed the ones she had faced before—if it had stretched its legs and arched its back, she could have walked under its belly without stooping. Its scales were gleaming black, resembling polished jet, though its wings were like great cloaks of utter darkness draped across its flanks. Two ridged horns curved forward around a face that seemed almost skeletal, with leathery black skin stretched over its skull. Its tail lashed behind it, tipped with a serrated blade that scratched long cuts into the airship's deck. Its mouth opened and emitted a long, low hiss that only slowly registered on Rienne's mind as a series of changing sounds, presumably Draconic words she couldn't understand.

This story would be better, she thought, if I could report on the witty banter I exchanged with the dragon. Sorry, Gaven.

The thought of Gaven seemed to soothe her fear, and she spotted Maelstrom beneath the dragon's hind foot. The dragon's yellow eyes were on hers, and its mouth opened and closed quickly in what seemed almost like a laugh. It believed Rienne was at its mercy, she realized—helpless without her sword.

Well, let it think so, she thought.

Slowly, keeping her eyes fixed on the dragon's, she got to her feet. It watched her intently, its eyes gleaming, as if eager to see how she would try to extract herself from this situation. She heard Jordhan's stifled breathing, trying not to be noticed. Had the dragon noticed him at the helm? That might affect how it would respond to her movements. She decided to test it.

Crouching low, ready to dive away from any attack, she shifted a few steps to her left, toward the prow. It countered with a few shuffling steps to its left, toward Jordhan, dragging Maelstrom along beneath its clawed foot. The airship creaked and rocked, and Rienne heard branches snap. The dragon's movement suggested it didn't know Jordhan was there, or it didn't care about being trapped between two foes it considered insignificant. Mostly, it was trying to keep the bulk of its body between Rienne and Maelstrom.

Its mouth flapped open and closed again, and it spat a jet of acid at her—just to keep her moving, it seemed. She sidestepped the spurt of black slime, circling back to her right, toward the wheelhouse. The dragon countered her move again, and for just an instant one foot scrabbled on the slanting deck. The dragon's wings spread slightly as it fought for its balance, and Rienne used that moment to strike.

She threw herself directly between the dragon's front legs, at the space below its plated belly. It reared in surprise, throwing its wings wide and flailing at her with its claws. One claw raked across her back, but the blow had no strength behind it. Rienne rolled beneath the dragon, braced herself with her arms, and kicked with all her strength at the leg that pinned Maelstrom to the deck.

With a roar of fury, the dragon slid toward the prow. It kicked off from the airship and flapped wildly to get itself aloft, spraying acid across the deck. Rienne snatched Maelstrom up and leaped into the nearest tree, dodging the worst of the spray, then hopped through its branches to the ground.

Solid earth beneath her feet and Maelstrom in her hand again, Rienne fell easily into a ready stance and waited for the dragon to follow her, trusting that its rage would make it come to her without lingering to destroy Jordhan's airship—or Jordhan himself.

She wasn't disappointed. Shrieking its frustration, the dragon hurtled down at her, fangs and claws bared. It snaked between the trees more easily than she had thought possible, folding its wings close and falling more than flying. Terror seized her again, and she rolled beneath its onslaught. She shouted as its claws raked her, but answered their bite with an upward thrust that drove Maelstrom deep between two of the heavy plates that protected the dragon's belly. Black blood spurted out over her hand, stinging like the acid of its breath, and the dragon crashed into the ground behind her.

She rolled to her feet and leaped to where the dragon had landed, swinging Maelstrom in whirling arcs around her. The dragon kept its feet despite its wound, and its head darted forward to bite at her as she came within reach. Its teeth closed around her arm, and pain seared through her as acidic spittle ate into the wound. Her other arm brought Maelstrom to slash into the dragon's neck, just behind its jaw. The jaws opened and Rienne tumbled to the ground, then darkness swallowed her again.

She could still hear the dragon beside her and feel the heat of its body. Biting back the pain, she swung Maelstrom in a relentless dance of arcs and jabs, driving the dragon away from her assault. She followed its retreat, and after a few steps found herself outside the dragon's magical orb of darkness. The dragon looked nearly beaten, its wings pulled close to protect it, its head drooping and bloody, its belly still oozing thick blood that sizzled in puddles on the ground.

She advanced a few more steps, and the dragon backed away. Its head swung to one side, and Rienne saw what had attracted its attention: Jordhan, holding an axe with both hands in front of him, stepping toward Rienne and the dragon. She seized the moment of distraction and leaped at the dragon.

"Get down!" she screamed, as a gout of black acid sprayed from the dragon's mouth. Maelstrom bit deep into the dragon's throat, cutting off the spray of its breath and nearly taking the head off its long neck. The dragon fell to the ground, and Rienne ran to where Jordhan lay.

"Sovereign Host," she said, "let him be—"

"I'm alive," Jordhan said. His voice was strained, though, and he drew a shuddering breath.

Rienne dropped to the ground beside him. He lay on his side, his axe forgotten a few feet away. Rienne pulled off the silk cloth that was wrapped around her waist and dabbed at a few splashes of viscous acid still burning into his chest and neck. The spray had hit him full on, and his body was covered with welts and open wounds.

"What were you thinking?" she said, taking his hand.

"I couldn't let you face it alone." He smiled, but it changed to a grimace as he tried to sit up. He gave up and fell back to the ground.

"That was noble of you. And foolish. You're a dear friend, and the best pilot in House Lyrandar, but you're not a warrior."

"A few more steps and that dragon would've had my axe buried in its shoulder."

Rienne smiled, squeezed his hand, and decided not to point out that, the way he was holding the axe, he would have been lucky to get enough power in his swing to nick the dragon's scales.

CHAPTER
7

A knock at the door jolted Aunn out of a doze.

Make it solid, he thought. I'm Kelas ir'Darren, and this is my office.

He ran a hand over his face to make sure he was who he thought he was. He cast his eyes around the office. Gaven's eyes were open again—perhaps awakened by the knock—but still vacant, staring at something other than the blank wall aross from him.

"Come in," he said. Kelas was warm and polite, most of the time.

The door swung open and Cart's massive body filled the frame. The warforged hesitated for a moment, swinging his head to look at Aunn and Gaven as if making sure he'd found the right room.

"Come in, Cart," Aunn said, standing up behind the desk.

Cart stepped into the room, which suddenly seemed much smaller, and gestured to a tall, handsome man behind him. "This is Havrakhad," Cart said. "And this is—"

"Kelas ir'Darren," Aunn said, stepping around the desk and extending his hand to the newcomer, who clasped it and bowed slightly.

Havrakhad was human, though he carried himself with a graceful elegance that reminded Aunn of the eladrin he'd met in the Towering Wood. His black hair was very long, cascading over his broad shoulders with a small topknot held in place by a silver ring. He wore a heavy, midnight blue cloak that hung almost to the floor, and beneath it a sky-blue shirt of gleaming silk, open in front to reveal a muscular, hairless chest. Breeches the color of his cloak were tucked into the tops of his boots. No weapon hung at his belt.

"I am honored to meet you," he said to Aunn. His words had an accent Aunn couldn't place.

"Likewise," Aunn said, uncertain how to respond. But Kelas was confident, assertive. "Cart explained the nature of our problem?"

"Somewhat," Havrakhad said, turning to face Gaven. "I take it this is our patient?"

"Yes. And what techniques will you use to heal him?"

Havrakhad didn't look like a healer—more like a noble in exile, from some indeterminate foreign land.

"I will enter his mind and attempt to lead him out."

"Havrakhad is a kalashtar," Ashara said, squeezing into the little room behind him and closing the door. Havrakhad shifted away from her, though there wasn't much space for him.

A kalashtar. That explained a great deal, though Aunn's knowledge of the kalashtar was limited. They were a distinct race, not quite human, native to the distant continent of Sarlona. Their reputation painted them as beautiful mystics who had mastered the powers of their minds, able to communicate telepathically, move objects from afar, and perform other feats of what might as well be magic. It was a magic, though, that Aunn's artifice couldn't mimic or even fully comprehend.

"I see," Aunn said. "Well, are you ready to get started? Would you like my chair?"

A knock at the door cut off Havrakhad's answer. Aunn froze. It was late in the evening. Who would be looking for Kelas in his office at this hour?

"Excuse me," he said.

Havrakhad, Ashara, and Cart shifted around to let him through to the door. He pulled it open.

"You're here late, Kelas." It was a man Aunn didn't recognize.

"Yes." Kelas hated to be interrupted when he had people in his office. He jerked his head back toward the crowded office. "Important meeting. Can it wait?"

The man's face changed. The dark hair became sandy, tanned skin turned pasty white, eyes lightened to hazel. It was a face Aunn knew quite well, though the eyes were wrong. It was one of his own faces. It was Haunderk's face, the one Aunn used most often when talking to Kelas.

Aunn fought to keep his pulse and breathing under control, but rage and fear fought against him. What other changeling was using his face? Did he expect Kelas to be fooled? Was he trying to discredit Haunderk somehow? Or was he sending a subtle message that he saw through Aunn's disguise?

"It's not urgent," the changeling said, smirking. His eyes were everywhere but on Aunn, trying to see past him into the study. "I'll come back tomorrow."

Tomorrow, Aunn thought, I already have an appointment with Jorlanna. I think I'll be out.

The changeling strode off down the hall without another word, and Aunn retreated back into Kelas's study, closing the door. Ashara shot him a quizzical glance, but he shook his head and followed Cart's gaze. Havrakhad was kneeling in front of Gaven, looking into his eyes.

Hearing the door close, Havrakhad stood and looked at Aunn. "It would be best if there were no more interruptions."

"There shouldn't be any more. Please begin when you're ready."

The kalashtar kneeled again, put one hand on Gaven's shoulder, and gazed into his eyes.

* * * * *

Two ogres held Shakravar's arms, the meat that was his body now, and a dwarf stood behind him with a bludgeon. But the dragon would not be restrained. If only he could emerge from this body, revert to his true form, fill the room with lightning and spatter it with the blood of his enemies . . .

The judges of the tribunal stared down at him from their high seats. They called a witness to give testimony—an elf, the head of the Thuranni family.

"Lord Elar Thuranni d'Phiarlan," one of the judges

intoned, prompting shouts of protest from both the witness and another elf in the great hall.

"He's no Phiarlan!" came a woman's voice. "He is excoriate!"

"I am Baron Elar d'Thuranni," the witness said.

"The status of the Thuranni family is yet to be settled in the eyes of this tribunal," another judge said. "For now, we shall address you as Lord Elar and move on with the proceedings."

"Very well." Lord Elar bowed his head in deference to the judges.

"Lord Elar, please state your claim against the defendant, Gaven Lyrandar."

Hearing his name, Gaven woke from what felt like sleep, and found himself in the firm grasp of two ogres, rage and violence churning in his heart. What was going on?

A dark-eyed elf was speaking, pointing an accusing finger at Gaven. Rienne was there, tears streaming down her face, avoiding his eyes. Judges glared down at him.

They had to understand, had to know, had to be prepared. "When the Eternal Day draws near," he cried, "when its moon shines full in the night, and the day is at its brightest, the Time of the Dragon Above begins."

"Silence!" one of the judges shouted.

He couldn't be silent. He had to warn them. "Showers of light fall upon the City of the Dead, and the Storm Dragon emerges after twice thirteen years."

"Silence him," another judge commanded.

"Tumult and tribulation swirl in his wake!" Gaven shouted. "The Blasphemer rises, the Pretender falls, and armies march once more across the land!"

"That's enough," the dwarf behind him said, and the club came down on his head. Darkness swallowed him.

"Arnoth d'Lyrandar," a judge's voice intoned in the darkness, "please state your claim against the defendant."

"My son," Gaven's father said, "he is my firstborn, my heir. But he has failed me. He failed the Test of Siberys. He refused to assist me in my business and chose instead the life of a dragonshard prospector." Light slowly grew in the darkness, outlining Arnoth's body. "I waited twenty-six years for him to return to me, until I couldn't wait any longer. Finally he came to me, but too late. I died that morning." The light shone full now on Arnoth's face, showing Gaven the flesh rotting away from his skull.

"Guilty!" came a voice from the tribunal.

A chorus answered, "Guilty as charged!"

Darkness again.

"Rienne ir'Alastra, please state your claim against the defendant."

"When we delved into Khyber together," Rienne's voice said from the darkness, "when we sailed with Jordhan, when we worked for your House together, we were partners. Equals. We fought as a team. You covered my back, and I covered yours. We don't fight like that any more. You used to give a damn about me—you used to love me, and I don't think you do anymore."

"Of course I do," Gaven called. "Rienne!"

"You left me here to die, Gaven. Here in the land of dragons. You abandoned me."

"I couldn't—! They captured me—!"

"Gaven?" Her voice was fading. "Gaven, help me!"

"Rienne!"

She was gone.

* * * * *

The kalashtar stood, staggered away from Gaven, and slumped against Cart, exhaustion etched onto his face.

"What happened?" Aunn asked. "What did you see?"

"I'd accept that chair now, if the offer is still open," Havrakhad said.

"Of course," Aunn said.

Cart helped the kalashtar around the desk to Kelas's chair as Aunn waited, breathless.

Havrakhad slumped into the chair and covered his face with his hands. "He carries many burdens," he said, "along a twisting path."

Aunn's thoughts jumped to the Labyrinth, and the demon he fought there after leaving Maruk Dar. He looked at Gaven. Was a similar battle raging inside his mind?

"I don't understand," Cart said.

Havrakhad wiped his face and dropped his hands to his lap. "Something has trapped him, imprisoned him in a maze of his own thoughts. There his guilt, his shame, and his fear can prey on him, devouring his spirit. I tried to break through the maze, to find him and lead him out, but there were too many obstacles. Too much darkness."

"You have to try again," Aunn said, a sudden urgency seizing him. "If the darkness takes him—"

"I will try again," the kalashtar said. "In a few hours. I must rest."

"We all could use some rest," Ashara said.

Cart shrugged. "I'm fine," he said.

* * * * *

A distant light appeared in the darkness, dim and flickering, like a beacon calling him home. Gaven tried to lift himself from the ground and move toward it, but he was mired in mud and filth. It took all his strength just to lift his head, to see the light a little better.

At the sight of it, though, he felt strength surge in his limbs, and he fought harder to pull himself up. The sludge slithered and hissed around him, resentful of the disturbance. He kept his eyes on the light, and he thought he heard a voice calling his name.

"Stay with us," someone whispered in the darkness. "You belong with us." Bony hands gripped him, and faces surrounded him. They were dark-eyed and gaunt elves, the phantoms of the Paelions—the third branch of the Phiarlan family, slaughtered because of him. "Your destiny lies with us."

"No," Gaven murmured, "I'm sorry. No."

The distant light sent a tingle of warmth into his icy skin, and he longed to let it fill him, penetrate to his bones.

Mustering his strength, he lifted one foot from the mire and set it down in front of the other.

"You can't leave," the voices around him said. "You deserve this fate, though we did not. Stay."

"I'm sorry," Gaven said. His voice sounded stronger. He raised the other leg. Sticky tendrils of shadow snapped off him, leaving behind round sores on his skin. His strength surged, and soon he was walking in slow, stumbling strides toward the amber glow.

Faces crowded around him, smears of shadow trying to hide the light from his eyes, Paelion ghosts seeking to keep him in their clutches. He pushed them aside.

Rienne's voice wailed behind him, "Bring me with you! Don't leave me here!"

He turned around to find her, and the darkness enfolded him again. He tried to turn back to the light, but it was gone, and shadows coiled around him again.

* * * * *

"Another will is opposing me," Havrakhad said. His face was pale, and shadows pooled beneath his eyes. "Someone is trying very hard to keep him imprisoned."

"Who?" Aunn asked.

"I don't know. It might be helpful if you could tell me what happened to him."

Cart and Ashara turned to Aunn, and Havrakhad followed their eyes.

"Very well," Aunn said. "Ashara, you still have the shard?"

"Of course," she said. She drew the dragonshard out of a pouch at her belt. The lines of Gaven's mark burned red as hellfire in the pinkish crystal, throwing stark shadows on the walls. Havrakhad recoiled.

"Already I think I understand a great deal more," the kalashtar said. He looked at Ashara. "That's the evil I sensed around you. I apologize for misjudging you."

Ashara set the shard down on the desk in front of Havrakhad, who leaned forward for a closer look without touching it.

"What is this?" Havrakhad said. "The pattern inside—it resembles a dragonmark."

"That's what it is," Aunn said. "It's Gaven's dragonmark, the Mark of Storm."

Havrakhad's eyes shot to Gaven and scanned his skin. "You say it's his mark. Do you mean . . . ?"

"Yes. His mark was removed and transferred into the dragonshard."

"Leaving him in this state."

"Actually, no," Ashara said. "He endured the loss of his mark well enough. He seemed normal for some time. He didn't fall into this stupor until after the shard was back in his hands."

"I take it that his dragonmark was removed from him against his will," Havrakhad said.

"Correct," Aunn said. He wasn't pleased with this line of questioning, but he was loath to withhold any information that might help the kalashtar save Gaven. After two failed attempts, Aunn was beginning to feel an urgency, as though Gaven could be utterly lost if Havrakhad couldn't restore his mind soon. Never mind the additional challenges morning would likely bring, starting with Jorlanna ir'Cannith.

Gaven's hand fell onto the dragonshard, making Aunn jump in surprise. Gaven held his arm as though it had lost all circulation, but he had fixed his eyes on the shard and was moving his whole upper body in an effort to pull the shard from the desk into his lap.

Aunn started to reach for the shard, but a rumble of thunder outside stopped him short. "Cart, would you . . . ?"

Cart's armor-plated hand closed over the dragonshard and pulled it away, and in one smooth motion he deposited it back into Ashara's belt pouch. Gaven slumped back into his chair, like a discarded puppet.

"That was strange," Ashara whispered.

"And very enlightening," Havrakhad said. "I think that now I have what I need." He stood. "Ashara, will you please stand and face me?"

Ashara hopped down from her seat on the desk and faced the kalashtar, turning her back to Gaven.

"Now can you slowly withdraw the dragonshard from your pouch again? Let your body block Gaven's view of it, please."

Ashara did as he instructed, holding the shard gingerly in the fingertips of both hands. Havrakhad reached toward it, but he didn't touch it.

"Let it go," he murmured, and the shard floated up from Ashara's fingers. "Thank you."

He stepped around Ashara, the dragonshard suspended in the air between his hands. Gaven stirred slightly, and Havrakhad shifted the dragonshard so that it hovered over one hand. He extended the other hand to touch Gaven's shoulder, and Gaven slumped down again, though his eyes remained fixed on the shard.

"Excellent," the kalashtar said. "The third trial is the favored one."

CHAPTER
8

The light reappeared, brighter than before, but this time Gaven turned away from it, buried his face in his arms to shield his eyes. The darkness stirred in response to his movement, then settled in around him again, rustling softly, cold but comfortable.

"This is where I belong," he murmured. "What I deserve."

A chorus of whispers voiced its assent. "What you deserve."

"No, Gaven." An unfamiliar voice cut through the whispers—a voice made of light, clear and strong. Gaven tried to lift his head, but the darkness held it down. "You are a prisoner here," the clear voice said.

"I was sentenced," Gaven said, "sent to Dreadhold . . ."

"But now the Keeper of Secrets holds you bound."

"It lies," Gaven said, a reflex. "Truth would burn its tongue."

"It speaks nothing but lies," the voice said. "Cast it off. Stand up, Gaven."

Gaven lifted his head, pulling against the tendrils of darkness that held him down. The light was close beside him, and a man stood at the center of the light. Tall and slender, the man was a vision of beauty, like the light made flesh.

"Are you the Messenger?" Gaven asked. The darkness stirred in angry whispers around him.

"I'm Havrakhad, and I'm here to lead you to freedom," the man said. "Take my hand, get up, and follow me." He bent over Gaven, extending a hand.

Gaven wrenched a hand free of the darkness and seized Havrakhad's hand. The whispers turned to shrieks of pain and fear as the darkness fled. Gaven stood on a floor of pale pink crystal. Red fire burned just beneath his feet, leading off in both directions, forming a maze of whirling lines stretching as far as he could see.

"I know this path," he said. His eyes traced the pathways, seeing more than the glowing lines. They were the words of creation, and they spoke to him of what had been and what might yet come to pass.

"We can lead each other," Havrakhad said.

"Wait—Rienne . . ." Gaven turned. A cloud of darkness formed before him, and Rienne's crying face appeared in the midst of it. She stretched her arms out to him.

"Don't leave me here, Gaven!" she wailed.

"Rienne isn't here," Havrakhad said. "Follow me to freedom, then you can find her."

"He's lying, Gaven!" Rienne cried.

"It lies," Gaven murmured. "Truth would burn its tongue." But that was the darkness—the Keeper of Secrets. He turned back to Havrakhad and the light. He surveyed the pathways again, and he made his choice. "This way," he said, and together they started walking.

"What is this path?" Havrakhad asked.

"It's my dragonmark," Gaven said. But it was more than that. "It's my life, spoken in the words of creation, part of the Prophecy."

"But there are many paths here."

"Many paths and many destinations."

"Why are we going this way, then?" Havrakhad asked. He stopped and gazed into Gaven's eyes.

"This is the path I choose."

They were in a room, and the light was only a single lamp on a table beside him. The dragonshard floated just above Havrakhad's fingertips. Other faces crowded behind Havrakhad—Cart, Ashara, and . . . Kelas ir'Darren?

"No!" Gaven cried. He leaped up from his chair and pulled the sword from its sheath on his back, then swayed as dizziness washed through his head. Havrakhad jumped back, and the dragonshard clattered onto the floor. "What have you done to me?"

"Gaven, calm down," Havrakhad said.

Cart stepped closer, wary of Gaven's sword. "You're safe," he said.

"Whose side are you on today, Cart? I can't keep track any more."

"Yours, Gaven."

"Then what's he doing here?" He turned his gaze to Kelas. "You were dead. I saw Aunn kill you. Am I still dreaming?"

Kelas met his eyes, and then—just for an instant—he wasn't Kelas anymore. Darraun's face appeared where Kelas's had been, and just as quickly vanished. Then his eyes flicked over to Havrakhad and back. Gaven stared, uncomprehending, for a moment, all the more convinced he was still dreaming, but then he understood.

"I'm sorry, Kelas," Gaven said. He sheathed his sword, trying to think of something to say that would allay any suspicion his behavior had stirred up in Havrakhad, but he decided to keep quiet until he had a better understanding of what was going on.

"I understand," Kelas—or rather, Aunn said. "You've been through quite an ordeal."

"Where are we?" Gaven said, looking around the unfamiliar room.

"My office in Fairhaven."

"Fairhaven?" Gaven wasn't sure exactly where the Dragon Forge had stood, but he knew it was near the Blackcaps, and it would have taken three or four weeks to get from there to Fairhaven on foot. "How long was I . . . ?" He realized he didn't know what state he'd been in. Had he been unconscious?

"Not long. Twelve or fourteen hours, perhaps." Aunn looked as though he were about to say more, but he glanced at Havrakhad and closed his mouth.

Havrakhad must have noticed that he was crowding the small room. "My work here is done," he said. "But you should contact me again if Gaven's sleep is particularly troubled—or if you can't wake him up, of course."

"Wait—the dragonshard," Ashara said. "What should we do with it?"

Gaven's gaze followed hers to the dragonshard on the floor. The lines of his dragonmark beckoned him to walk their pathways.

"I should think that House Cannith would be best qualified to find an answer to that question."

"But should we . . . keep it away from him?" Cart asked.

"What do you think, Gaven?" Havrakhad said.

Gaven stooped to pick up the dragonshard, hesitating just a moment before curling his fingers around the smooth crystal. A tingle of soft lightning ran down his neck and chest, the tender skin where his dragonmark had been, and he thought he heard a distant rumble of thunder. He stared at the twisting lines for a moment, the path he'd chosen shining clear in his mind.

He smiled at Cart. "You want to try to take it?" he said, laughing. "I'll wrestle you for it."

"It's yours," Cart said. "I want no part of it. Oh, uh, Kelas—I told Havrakhad that he should work out the details of payment with you."

"Of course," Aunn said, moving to sit in the chair behind the desk. "Did you agree on terms?"

"Cart generously assured me that I could name my price," Havrakhad said. "But I live simply. I don't need much."

"But you were here all night, and it was very taxing work." Aunn produced paper and a quill from the desk and began writing out a letter of credit. "I want to ensure that you feel properly compensated for what you've done. And I trust that we can also rely on your complete silence." He pressed a seal onto the finished letter and handed it to Havrakhad. "Will that be sufficient?"

Gaven saw Havrakhad's eyes go wide, and he looked at Kelas with a mixture of wonder and fear.

"That is more than enough, I assure you," Havrakhad said. He bowed to Kelas, then turned to Gaven. "Remember, Gaven:

Whatever you deserve, freedom is what you have been given. Use your freedom as if you deserved it."

Gaven nodded. "Thank you."

Havrakhad clasped Cart's hand. "I hate to cause any further trouble, but I wonder if you would be willing to see me safely to my house?"

"Of course," Cart said. "The city at this time of night can be daunting."

"I suppose there is that, yes," Havrakhad said, as if the threat of street thugs hadn't occurred to him. Gaven wondered what danger he did fear.

"I'll come as well," Ashara said.

After a last round of bows and farewells, Havrakhad left.

Cart closed the door behind him, and Aunn let out a long breath.

Gaven wheeled on him. "Now will you tell me what in thunder is going on?" he said.

"I'll try." Aunn rubbed his temples. "But I'm not entirely sure myself."

"Why don't you start by explaining why you're pretending to be Kelas?"

"I was hoping to learn more about Kelas's plans," Aunn said. "It also gives me a position where I can warn the army."

"Warn them about what?"

"Kathrik Mel. The barbarians."

Gaven remembered fragments of dream—a corpse-strewn battlefield, a sky darkened by vultures' wings, the earth torn open. He sat down across the desk from Aunn.

"Kelas thought he was creating a pretext," Aunn continued, "giving Aundair an excuse to invade the Eldeen Reaches. He assumed that the army would have no trouble defeating the barbarians, especially with the Dragon Forge at its disposal."

"With my Mark of Storm," Gaven said. "The storm breaks upon the forces of the Blasphemer . . ."

"What's that?" Aunn asked, looking up at Gaven. "Oh, the Prophecy. Which reminds me." He collected a sheaf of paper from the side of the desk and straightened the pile. "Here's another thing I want to figure out about Kelas. While you were in Dreadhold, the dwarves recorded everything you said or wrote down about the Prophecy. They sent a copy to House Lyrandar, at your family's request. But how did Kelas get a copy?" He pushed the papers across the desk to Gaven.

Tumult and tribulation swirl in his wake: The Blasphemer rises, the Pretender falls, and armies march once more across the land.

Gaven didn't remember that verse, but according to the paper in front of him, he had written it on the wall of his cell sometime during the night of Zarantyr 29, 973 YK. One of his first nights in Dreadhold. He flipped through the pages, ignoring the Prophecy in its neat dwarf-printing, looking only at the dates. One entry every week or so, two or three entries to a page, covering all twenty-six years of his imprisonment—he held more than five hundred pages.

"Maybe the Sentinel Marshals or Bordan d'Velderan came to Kelas after I escaped," Gaven said, "looking for help from the Royal Eyes."

"That would be strange," Aunn said, "the dragonmarked houses asking for help from a national government. And why the Royal Eyes? You haven't spent much time in Aundair."

"But Kelas had his own interest in me. He wanted me for the Dragon Forge. Or he wanted my mark."

"And he was interested in the Prophecy as it pertained to you and the Dragon Forge, certainly. But that doesn't explain how he got these documents."

"He could have . . ." Gaven had reached the last pages of the stack. These were written in a different hand, a flowing script nothing at all like the block letters of the dwarves. His father's hand.

My dear friend Kelas.

"What is it?" Aunn asked.

I hope this letter finds you well. I've enclosed the latest reports from House Kundarak—more of the same. I certainly hope they mean more to you than they do to me.

Gaven's own father, writing to Kelas as if to an old friend?

"Gaven?"

"My father sent them."

Gaven flipped through the last pages, scanning dates again. The last letter was dated the fourth of Eyre, 999 YK—less than a week before Gaven escaped from Dreadhold, just over a month before his father's death.

Dear Kelas,

My younger son and all Stormhome are sleeping soundly as I write this, but sleep eludes me. Perhaps I have let my mind be influenced too much by Gaven's ravings, if that's what they are. I feel the weight of the future pressing on me. My health, I must accept, is failing. But how can I accept that if it means I am never to see Gaven's face again?

You have long assured me that I would live to see Gaven walk free of his prison, his innocence proven at last, and that hope has sustained me through these years of our correspondence. But unless you know some way to prolong my life—or Gaven's release is somehow imminent—I fear you have been mistaken.

So now I am preparing myself for death. Thordren will carry on my business, as he has ably done for many years now. If you wish, I will send a letter to House Kundarak, asking them to continue sending their reports to Thordren, and instruct him to send them on to you as I have done. And I will go to the Land of the Dead and strive to retain my memories there in the endless gray, so that when Gaven joins me there—many years from now, if it please the Host—I might still know him and be able to tell him what I couldn't tell him while I lived.

Thank you again—a thousand times—for all that you have done for me and my son. I hope you will continue your efforts on his behalf after I am gone, for the sake of our friendship.

Your friend,
Arnoth d'Lyrandar

Gaven read the letter three times—the first time, blinking back tears as he thought of his father, gripped with the pain of having missed the chance to see him by a few hours. The second time, he hunted through every sentence for a hint of what Arnoth had wanted to tell him. The third time, his tears dried, he looked for a better idea of what Kelas had supposedly been doing on Gaven's behalf.

"You worked for Kelas," he said at last.

Aunn was holding a glass orb and peering intently into its depths. "I did," he said, setting the orb aside on the desk.

"He sent you to join Cart and Senya, to get me out of Dreadhold."

"I'm afraid so."

"Why?" Gaven asked.

"Why did he send me? Isn't it obvious? He wanted your mark for the Dragon Forge."

"Did you know that at the time?"

"No," Aunn said. "I knew he wanted your knowledge of the Prophecy. Please believe me, Gaven, if I'd had any idea—"

Gaven shook his head. Cart had said the same thing. It didn't matter. "Did you know he was corresponding with my father?"

"I had no idea."

"He thought I was innocent," Gaven said. "He called me his son, even though I was excoriate, and he always believed he'd live to see me walk free."

"And he did, right?

"No. He knew I'd escaped, but that's not the same thing. I'm still not free. I'm still guilty, they'd still throw me back in Dreadhold if they could."

Aunn leaned forward over the desk. "But are you really guilty?"

"What do you mean? I did the things they accused me of."

"But the dragon—"

"I wasn't possessed. Its memories confused me, to be sure, but it was still me, doing what I did. As much as I'd like to avoid responsibility, I can't. The Thurannis killed all the Paelions because of me."

Aunn sat back in his chair, his gaze fixed on the desk.

"Bordan d'Velderan kept saying that I was no different from any other common criminal," Gaven said. "I have to prove him wrong."

"And how—" The glass globe on the desk began to glow, cutting him off. He looked at it for a moment, as the light grew from a faint shimmer to a brilliant glare, then reached for it. As soon as his fingers touched the smooth surface, the light faded, but Gaven could see the hint of an image inside the sphere.

"Kelas?" A woman's voice came from the globe, as clear as if she were in the room. "What's going on? I've been waiting all night!"

CHAPTER
9

T he forest to the east burned with the false promise
of dawn as Rienne kept watch over Jordhan. The
airship's fiery ring held the vessel aloft just above
the tops of the charred trees, but its harsh light was a small
flicker in a much larger darkness, leaving Rienne to peer
nervously at every hint of movement at the edge of the
encroaching shadows.

No attack came, and at last the eastern sky came alive with
fiery red and yellow heralding the sun's true arrival. No bird
calls greeted the dawn light, though, and as the light spilled
across the ground beneath her Rienne saw the extent of the
devastation left in the barbarians' wake.

The earth was a wide field of black rock and gray ash,
the charred trunks of once-mighty trees jutting up like the
crumbling stone pillars of an ancient ruin, many of them half
toppled, inclined almost to the ground in their grief. Bones
littered the ground as far as she could see—the snarling skull
of an Eldeen bear nearby, shattered ribs jutting from the blackened tatters of a chainmail coat just beyond it. Among the
bones vultures hopped, flapped, and swarmed over the fresh
corpse of the dragon.

*Vultures wheel where dragons flew, picking the bones of the
numberless dead.*

The words from Rienne's dream sprang to her mind, and
brought with them images of battle—dragons flying overhead,
a bone-white banner marked in blood, wave after wave of
the enemy crashing down over her and Maelstrom. A demon
standing before her, his sword burning with hellfire.

Rienne shook herself—had she fallen asleep?—and walked the perimeter of the deck. She and Gaven had visited the Towering Wood once, chasing a rumor of a dragonshard deposit, and she had loved the feeling of shelter she found beneath the arching branches of the ancient trees. The ground seemed like a magical twilight world where the sun never quite reached, yet it was warm and alive. Now the ruin of the forest was laid bare to the dawn, extending as far as she could see in every direction.

She turned Maelstrom over in her hands, searching the blade for the hundredth time for any pit seared into the steel by the dragon's acidic breath or blood, any nick left behind as the blade pierced its armored plates. Maelstrom was perfect, as sharp and whole as the day she'd received it.

"Lady Alastra," the messenger said, bowing low, "your presence is requested at the home of Master Kevyen."

She knew instantly what had happened. Her master was dead. It was not a shock—he had been ailing for months. Still she was too numb to feel the grief, and she would later be ashamed to realize that the first thing she felt was a tiny surge of joy. Maelstrom would be hers.

The tears came as she followed the messenger through Stormhome to the master's home, hurrying to keep up with his fast pace, wondering if it would be the last time she walked this particular path through the city's winding streets.

The modest house had been a blur of confusion in the wake of the master's death, and she stood in the midst of it, trying to find a still center of calm and patience. At last the steward had found her and carelessly thrust the case into her suddenly awkward hands.

She fell to her knees and the commotion around her faded. She ran her hands over the velvet that covered the case, the color of wine, and breathed in the musty smell of it. The smell awakened such memories in her! She remembered kneeling before the master at the beginning of her studies, at the age of three, and seeing the blade for the first time. Every day for nearly seventeen years she had admired it.

And now it was hers. She lifted the lid of the case at last and stretched out her fingers to touch the blade. Then she curled her fingers around the hilt and lifted it from the blade, swearing a rash oath in her heart that she would never let Maelstrom hang on display as the master had. She would wear it, carry it into battle, and let it do what it was made to do.

According to Kevyen, Maelstrom had been the sword of the great explorer Lhazaar, who carried it on her legendary expedition from Sarlona to Khorvaire, three thousand years ago. In her hand, the blade had helped to tame the wilderness of the eastern islands and fight back the remnants of the fallen Dhakaani Empire that threatened the first human settlers. There it had earned its name, for in Lhazaar's hand it had been a whirlwind of steel that caught all her foes in its inexorable grasp and drew them in to annihilation. That was as much as her master had known or chosen to reveal, but after Maelstrom came into her possession, Rienne learned as much as she could about its history.

Two thousand years ago, a hero named Darven, native to the city-state of Fairhaven long before it became the nation of Aundair, wielded Maelstrom in battle against the armies of Karrn the Conqueror. Cathra d'Lyrandar carried the sword in the War of the Mark, five hundred years later, and used it to cut off the head of Maggroth the Warlock Prince before she herself was killed by the aberrant lord Halas Tarkanan. Less than two hundred years ago, a paladin used the blade to kill the werewolf queen Ragatha and each of her twelve sons, the leaders of twelve vicious werewolf packs across the Five Nations. The paladin, strangely, used Maelstrom's name as his own, supposedly to convey the idea that he was merely a sword in the hand of the Church of the Silver Flame. She never learned how Maelstrom came into Master Kevyen's possession, but she had always suspected a connection of blood or training between her master and that nameless paladin.

"The day you first touched that sword," Gaven said, *"you set a course for a much greater destiny. It's a sword of legend, Ree. Great things have been done with it, and more greatness will yet be accomplished."*

Rienne had called Maelstrom hers for forty-two years, carrying it into the depths of Khyber, across the Five Nations, and all the way to Argonnessen in her adventures at Gaven's side. Before Gaven's madness, she used it to kill the monstrous prophet of a cult of the Dragon Below, a hideous, tentacled foulspawn with burning eyes. In the months since Gaven escaped from Dreadhold, Maelstrom had nearly killed the red dragon that attacked their airship on the way to Starcrag Plain, then she had cut a swath through the Soul Reaver's hordes and killed a beholder. And she had killed the black dragon that was feeding the vultures beneath the airship. To her mind, though, all her adventures did not seem like the stuff of legends. She was no Lhazaar, and the monsters Maelstrom had slain in her hand were not villains on the scale of Ragatha or the Warlock Prince. Great things had indeed been done with the weapon, but her own greatness was yet to come. The sword of Lhazaar, Darven, Cathra d'Lyrandar, and the paladin known as Maelstrom was in her hand, the sword of champions, and her destiny was linked to that sword.

Something had impelled her westward, from the time Jordhan extricated her from the jail in Thaliost, as if a silent voice had been calling her to this place. Her destiny, she felt increasingly sure, was bound to the barbarians that had ravaged this land, that were continuing their advance eastward, toward the edge of the forest, toward the farms and villages of the Eldeen Reaches and Aundair beyond. Her dream in Rav Magar, at least, had seemed to suggest that a confrontation with the demonic chieftain of the barbarians was her fate— or perhaps Maelstrom's, no matter what hand was wielding the blade.

She squeezed down the stairs to the little cabin where Jordhan slept and kneeled beside him. He stirred and moaned when she lifted his bandages, but he didn't wake up. Bathed and bandaged, his wounds looked much better than they had the night before. With Olladra's blessing, he'd be well enough to pilot the airship again by the next morning.

Rienne returned to the deck and gazed to the east, dread clutching at her heart. The sun hid behind a curtain of smoke, staining the sky red. More dragons flew in the midst of the smoke, igniting the sky with flashes of fire and lightning, clearing a path through the forest for the Blasphemer and his legions.

* * * * *

Two guards brought in the leader of the beast-men, clutching his arms and forcing his head down before pushing him to the ground, prostrate before the throne. Four more guards escorted two more beast-men, forced to their knees in the same way. Kathrik Mel clutched the skulls that capped the arms of his throne and smiled down at the three humiliated figures.

"You are in the presence of Kathrik Mel, chieftain of the Carrion Tribes," one of the guards said.

"You may speak," Kathrik Mel said.

The leader of the beast-men started to raise his head as if to set his eyes upon Kathrik Mel. A guard smashed it down to the ground.

"You may not lift your head, animal! Speak, if you can." Kathrik Mel saw blood on the dirt from the beast-man's head, and he ran his tongue over his lips.

"Great chieftain," the beast-man said, his voice muffled— partly because he was speaking into the dirt and partly, Kathrik Mel suspected, because he had blood in his mouth. "I am Varish Blackmane, chief of the Blackmane tribe."

"You are nothing and your tribe is nothing."

"As you say, great chieftain. If you grant it, I will be your servant, and the Blackmane shifters will join your horde. We wish to fight the Aundairians under your banner."

"I grant part of your request. Tell all the beast-men formerly known as Blackmanes that they have no tribe. They serve only Kathrik Mel. They will add their pitiful strength to the might of the Carrion Tribes."

"Part of my request, great chieftain?" The beast-man started to lift his head again.

This time, the guard did not need to intervene. A word from Kathrik Mel's mouth seized the Blackmane, wrenching a gasp from his throat. The guards fell to their knees and covered their ears, and Haccra beside his throne covered her head and wailed a wordless scream. Kathrik Mel spoke, and Varish Blackmane tried to scream. Blood gurgled in his throat as he sprawled in the dirt, clawing at the ground.

"On his lips are words of blasphemy, the words of creation unspoken." The dragon snaked around the throne and whispered, its words a hissing undercurrent to the booming cacophony of Kathrik Mel's speech. "In his ears are the screams of his foes, bringing delight to his heart."

Varish Blackmane ceased to exist. To Kathrik Mel's regret, not even a drop of blood remained. But the screams—they seemed to echo in the black pavilion, to his delight.

* * * * *

When Gaven appeared before her on the deck, draped in a black traveling cloak, Rienne knew she was dreaming. He cocked his head to look at her, and she laughed.

"What are you doing here, love?" she said.

"I wanted to see what you're like without me."

"I'm lost without you, Gaven. Just lost."

"You don't seem lost," Gaven said. "It seems like you found your purpose."

"I found a purpose. I don't know if it's mine."

"Whose purpose is it, then?"

Rienne buried her face in her hands. "Maelstrom's, maybe. Maybe yours. It's your fault I'm all tangled in the Prophecy."

"None of us is tangled in it, Ree. It's a path we walk. A labyrinth perhaps. But you're above it, not caught in it."

Gaven stepped, almost hopped closer to her, cocking his head strangely again, and she laughed at him again.

"You look like a bird when you do that," she said.

He turned his head in surprise, then spread his cloak into big black wings and flapped into the air. She heard more wings behind her, and footsteps on the deck.

"Jordhan," she murmured, then she realized she was awake.

"I'm no help against a dragon," Jordhan said, "but at least I can chase off the vultures." He tried to smile, but either his wounds or his pride turned it into a grimace of pain.

Rienne jumped to her feet and rushed to Jordhan's side. "You shouldn't be up," she said. "Come back to your cabin and rest some more."

"I'm fine," he said. "You're the one that needs rest. You've been worrying over me all day. Point me the way you want me to fly and we'll get a few hours on our way while you sleep. With no vultures this time."

"No, no. Your wounds—"

"Aren't serious enough to keep me from flying. It's really not strenuous work, as long as the elemental knows who's in charge. So where are we going?" He grasped the helm, and Rienne could feel a surge of power through the ship. Jordhan was right—the elemental did the work of flying the vessel, and it was clearly ready to answer to his command.

"East," she said. "We have some idea of the size of the invading force and what they're capable of. So this time we circle around them, keeping clear of the dragons, and look for a place where the Reachers are mustering their defenses. That's where we'll take our stand."

"East it is," Jordhan said, and the airship began to rise.

Rienne put a hand on his shoulder. "Jordhan?"

He lifted an eyebrow, but didn't look at her. His attention seemed wholly focused on the ship.

"Thank you," she said.

He half smiled, met her eyes for an instant, and looked away. She went to the cabin and curled up in Jordhan's bunk, hoping to dream more of Gaven.

CHAPTER
10

Aunn wiped the surprise from his face and peered into the crystal. A woman's face looked back at him, her sharp features and dark eyes conjuring the image of a raven in his mind. He knew her at once—Nara ir'Galanatyr, former head of the Royal Eyes. Why was she expecting contact from Kelas?

"I'm sorry," Aunn said. How did Kelas address Nara?

"What's going on? Where are you?"

Two questions meant the opportunity to answer only one. "I'm in Fairhaven," he said.

"I saw the storm, Kelas. It was breathtaking. And I'm told that Varna lies in ruins. Was the queen pleased?"

So she knew about the Dragon Forge. That meant she was involved in the conspiracy—had Kelas been reporting to her all along? She'd been removed from her position at the end of the Last War, which could mean that Kelas had been plotting against the queen for three years or more.

"She was impressed," Aunn said. "The device worked exactly as planned."

"His storm flies wild," Nara said, "unbound and pure in devastation." She sounded reverent, almost breathless.

Was that the Prophecy? Aunn glanced at Gaven, who had leaned forward at Nara's words. Gaven's eyes were fixed on the globe, but his lips were forming words—finishing the verse Nara had begun, no doubt. Could he see her image in the glass? Could she see Gaven?

"What's wrong?" Nara said. "Is someone else there?"

"No." Aunn brought his eyes back to the glass. "I was just thinking."

"Thinking what?"

"About what comes next."

"Indeed. The Time of the Dragon Below is upon us at last. All our planning is coming to its fruition." She looked for a moment as though she were gazing into the glorious future she imagined, then her eyes hardened. "Why are you in Fairhaven? It isn't safe."

If he hoped to learn anything more from Nara, he had to tell her as much of the truth as he dared. "There's a problem," he said.

"Go on." Her voice was steel.

How much did she know already? When had Kelas spoken to her last? "The Dragon Forge is destroyed."

"What?" she shrieked.

"As soon as the queen departed, we came under attack."

"The dragon king? Or the excoriate?"

Aunn almost blamed the dragon king, because Malathar was already dead. But too many people knew the truth—if Nara got a report from anyone else who was there, she would know he'd deceived her. "The excoriate," he said, keeping his eyes fixed on her.

"Damn it, Kelas! I told you to kill him quickly! I warned you not to let the Thuranni toy with him like that! Is he still alive? Is he free?"

He had paraded Gaven through the Cannith enclave that evening—Jorlanna would certainly know by morning that Gaven was in his custody. "I have him here with me. He's in a stupor. As he destroyed the forge, he shattered the dragon-shard that held his mark, and it seems to have shattered his mind."

"He destroyed the dragonshard?" Her voice was a gasp, as if the news had been a physical blow to her gut.

"Yes." Aunn felt confident in that lie—no one but Cart, Ashara, and the kalashtar could tell her otherwise. And he didn't want her to come looking for the shard, or order him to bring it to her.

"His mark—it hasn't returned to his skin, has it?"

Aunn glanced at Gaven, who was staring into the dragon-shard again. The lines of the Mark of Storm still coiled within the rosy stone. Gaven's skin was still red where his mark had been. It looked tender.

"No, there's no sign of it."

"Twelve moons," she said. "So we have no Storm Dragon. But he has a few verses yet to fulfill." Nara tapped a finger to her lips. "Damn it, Kelas. I've been planning this for a very long time. You know I don't like surprises like this. We'll survive the loss of the Dragon Forge—it has played its part in the Prophecy—but without the Storm Dragon, what happens to the Blasphemer?"

"The barbarians," Aunn blurted. Kelas had been counting on the Dragon Forge to stop their advance through the Eldeen Reaches—or so he'd said. "Without the forge—we have to find a way to stop them."

"Stop them?" Nara chuckled. "And undo all of your dear changeling's hard work? 'The Blasphemer's end lies in the void, in the maelstrom that pulls him down to darkness.' You're teasing me . . . Kelas." Her eyes grew hard as she said his name.

Aunn swallowed. He had to convince her he'd been joking, allay whatever suspicion had just formed in her mind. "Of course I am. I neglected to tell you that my changeling also returned to the Dragon Forge with Gaven, panicked about the onrushing barbarians." He saw Nara's eyebrow rise and a smile play at one corner of her mouth—good signs. "He did not survive the attack."

"Excellent," Nara said, chuckling. "Still, it says a great deal that he survived as long as he did. He could have been a tremendous asset."

"Where did I go wrong with him?"

"You were always too quick to punish him, Kelas. You made him hate you. He was always loyal, but to the crown, to his work, not to you. Did he try to kill you in the end?"

"He did." Aunn was amazed—Nara's words echoed many of his own thoughts of the last months.

"So you were forced to kill him. That must have been difficult for you."

"No." That was a slip—he'd answered from his own perspective, not Kelas's. Was that the right answer?

Nara laughed. "Well, some of my lessons stuck at least. I must say, Kelas, I was growing worried that you were too attached to him, just as he clearly cared too much about you."

What had Kelas thought about him? "He was extremely useful."

"He was, and his last mission was his greatest. The Blasphemer rises." Something shone in her eyes for an instant, then they turned back to steel. "So why did you flee to Fairhaven? Who's in command at the forge, or what's left of it? I assume the excoriate didn't manage to kill every last soldier there."

"I had to get the excoriate away from there before he did any more harm."

"You said he's in a stupor, and the forge is destroyed. What more harm did you fear?"

"I don't know how long he'll stay like this, and I want him locked up someplace where he can't escape."

"Why Fairhaven? It's too dangerous. He could be seen and recognized, and without his mark . . ."

"Speed. Arcanist Wheldren used the circle portal at the forge to bring the queen back to the palace, so I could get here quickly."

"How did you activate the portal?"

"With the assistance of a Cannith artificer."

"So House Cannith knows you're there."

"Yes." He had, after all, marched defiantly through House Cannith's Fairhaven headquarters.

"With the excoriate?"

"Yes." Aunn thought of the way that Harkin ir'Cannith's eyes had lingered on Gaven.

"That's less than ideal." She scowled. "Still, I can see why you did what you did. Who's in command at the forge?"

"No one. It was in chaos when I left. I know I should have—"

"Yes, you should have. But you didn't, so that's the situation we have to address now. We need those soldiers, however many are left, and we need them marching back to Fairhaven as soon as possible. Send Tolden—is she still alive?"

"I believe so." Aunn hadn't seen Janna Tolden at the forge.

"Send her and Wheldren to clean up the mess down there. You get Gaven locked away—he must not escape again. We need him in place when the time is right for the reunion. And then move ahead with the next stage of the plan. Is there anything else you need to tell me?"

What plan? "I think that's everything," he said.

"Good. You know better than to lie to me, Kelas. Nothing can hide from these eyes."

He felt a surge of panic—was there something in her voice when she said his name? He was sure she'd seen through his disguise. But why not call him on it? He leashed his fear and nodded. "Of course. I won't fail you."

"I know. I'll contact you tomorrow night. I have to get out of here before too long. I don't want barbarians at my doorstep just yet."

Where was she? He had a vague memory that she'd retired to the west after the war, perhaps to Wyr, north of Varna on the Wynarn River. "How long until they reach the river, do you think?"

"Two or three weeks, I expect. But they'll be driving the Reachers out of their villages soon, and we'll see a flood of refugees across Aundair's borders. With Varna destroyed and all." Something about her smile sickened him—that was part of her plan. She'd arranged for the destruction of Varna so that the Reachers couldn't take shelter in its walls when the barbarians approached. Why?

"Until tomorrow, then, Kelas."

He still didn't know how to address her. "Tomorrow, then."

The light in the globe faded, and the distorted reflection of the room replaced Nara's image in the glass. Aunn dropped his head to the desk, taking comfort in the cool stability of the oak against the pounding in his temples.

"What was that all about?" Gaven said.

Aunn looked up. He'd all but forgotten Gaven was there. "I have only the vaguest idea," he said. "But one thing is clear—this plot doesn't begin and end with Kelas. I need to learn more."

"You could just disappear. We could all get far away from Fairhaven, out of Aundair entirely—"

"No." His eyes met Gaven's, and he smiled. "We have to prove Bordan wrong."

"What?"

"I was trying to tell you before that it's not your fault— that you're not responsible for the crime they sent you to Dreadhold for."

"But I am," Gaven said.

"You are. Just as I'm responsible for all the things Kelas made me do. We've both done some evil, Gaven. But together we're going to make it right."

Gaven returned his smile. "Does that mean you're not going to lock me up, then?"

"I wouldn't dare try. I saw what you did to Malathar."

* * * * *

Cart had never feared a city street at night. He understood that fear—he'd known other soldiers who never made it back to camp after revels that went too late in the wrong parts of town. A drunk soldier was unable to defend himself and made a tempting target.

But a warforged was never drunk. A warforged soldier during the war was the army's property and didn't go into town for rest and recreation. And even a lone warforged was a daunting opponent, sure to be a tough fight for a group of thugs, and rarely in possession of enough coin to make the risk worthwhile. The worst he'd had to face in the past had been taunts, the derision of people who thought of warforged as inferior beings. Sometimes they threw garbage at him with their insults, but he just walked on in silence.

Havrakhad, it turned out, wasn't concerned about thugs, either. He carried himself through the dark streets like a proud warrior, though he held no weapon. Still, there was fear in his voice, fear that took root in Cart's mind as well.

"The turning of the age draws near," Havrakhad said. His eyes scanned the sides of the street. "The dreams of your people grow dark indeed."

Cart shrugged. "I don't sleep," he said. Ashara's tight grasp on his arm, though, suggested that the kalashtar's words resonated with her.

"But you have felt the tumult of fear when those around you dream in darkness," Havrakhad said.

Cart remembered long nights during the construction of the Dragon Forge, and he nodded.

"Are you saying there's some kind of epidemic of nightmares?" Ashara asked.

"You do well to compare it to a disease," Havrakhad said. "It's a symptom—a sign, a harbinger of the evil that is coming."

"What do you see in your dreams?" Cart asked him.

"My people, like yours, do not dream, though we sleep. We are exiles from the Region of Dreams, for the masters of that place are our enemies."

"Who are they?"

"The quori. Ensconced in human vessels, they rule Riedra. But in their true form, as creatures of nightmare, they are the lords of Dal Quor. My people are kin to them, but we have chosen to fight against their tyranny and guide the world into the next age of light."

"Are they responsible for what happened to Gaven?" Cart asked. "These nightmare lords?"

"No—at least not directly. There was a fragment of an evil presence in the dragonshard that bound him. But without question the quori were aware of it and drew sustenance from it. Just as they are feeding now on all the nightmares in this place."

Something in the way the kalashtar's eyes ranged over the city around them, just above the streets, set Cart on edge. The fear that had gnawed at his mind seized him in a surge of panic, and he felt suddenly beset by enemies on all sides—foes he couldn't see. He drew the axe from his belt, just to feel the comforting weight of it in his hand. Havrakhad chuckled.

"You sense it, though you can't possibly understand it," he said, resting a hand on Cart's shoulder.

Then Cart saw what Havrakhad's eyes had seen. The buildings that lined the streets rose from solid foundations but faded into smoke and mist as they approached a nightmare sky. The stars were gone, along with the Ring of Siberys that stretched between them, and in their place was a roiling storm of angry red and violet clouds. Blue and green lightning streaked in silence across the sky, shedding lurid flashes of light on scenes of nightmare.

Mobs of people screamed and ran through the haze, falling beneath the swinging clubs and cleaving swords of onrushing barbarians. Shadowy buildings erupted in flames, adding pale firelight to the underbellies of the clouds. Close by, an unspeakable horror crouched over a trembling human form, clutching one arm in an enormous claw as glittering insect eyes examined the body.

"That is a quori," Havrakhad whispered in Cart's ear. "It must not see me. Come!"

The kalashtar removed his hand, and the city returned to normal. At Cart's side, Ashara looked at him with wide eyes as the kalashtar started along the street again.

"Did you see it too?" he asked.

"You have seen it, I believe," Havrakhad said over his shoulder. "You visit the Region of Dreams nightly."

Ashara nodded. "I have seen it. I don't need to see it again."

Cart took a few quick steps to catch up with Havrakhad, shaking his head in a vain effort to dispel the memory of his vision. "Why?" he said. He wasn't sure what he meant.

"The turning of the age draws near," Havrakhad said again. "The light must die before it can be reborn."

Ashara fell into stride beside him and clutched his arm, and Cart decided not to ask any more questions.

CHAPTER
11

With Havrakhad safely returned to his little apartment, Cart and Ashara walked in silence back to the Tower of Eyes. Ashara's hand on his arm was a comfort, but her furrowed brow told him that her thoughts were as troubled as his.

"Ashara!"

Cart felt Ashara jump and her grip on his arm tighten, and he yanked his axe from his belt. They had almost reached the tower, but the shout had come from behind them, near the palace. Cart whirled, planting himself between Ashara and whoever had called out to her.

A man hurried toward them. The hood of a cloak hid his face from the glowing dragonshard lamps that bathed the broad street in pools of golden light. His hands were empty, but Cart saw a scabbard slapping against the man's legs as he ran.

"Do you know him, Ashara?" Cart asked. He glanced over his shoulder and saw her shrug. "Stop where you are and announce yourself," he called out.

"Tell your warforged to stand down," the man said, but he stopped and lowered his hood. Cart recognized him from the Cannith enclave—one broad streak of white hair identified him as the man who had tried to persuade Aunn to hand Ashara into his custody. The man held up his open palms. "It's Harkin. I just want to talk."

"He's not my warforged," Ashara said. "He's my friend. And we'll relax when you've shown you're not a threat. Last night you tried to hand me over to Jorlanna."

Harkin took a few slow steps toward them, keeping his hands up. "I'm sorry about that, Ashara. I had to keep up appearances."

"Hand Cart your sword and your wands," Ashara said, "and we'll talk."

Harkin chuckled, but started unbuckling his sword belt as he walked closer. "Cart, is it? I suppose you used to carry your squad's whole camp on your back?"

Cart expected some condescension from members of House Cannith, and as recently as a few months ago he would have accepted it without a second thought. Meeting Ashara had changed that. He decided he didn't like Harkin at all.

"They called me Cart because I always brought the wounded back," he said. "Alive."

"Fancy yourself a war hero, then?" Harkin said. He tossed his sword at Cart's feet and started on a second belt, the one that held a quiver full of wands.

Cart didn't answer. He had never thought of himself as a hero, but as a dutiful soldier. Ashara had changed that, too.

"Listen, Ashara." Harkin was close enough now to hand Cart his wands, treating them much more carefully than he had his sword. Cart took them but left the sword where it lay. "I never wanted to hand you over to Jorlanna. I want your help."

Ashara stood with her arms folded across her chest, no hint of a smile in her eyes. "My help with what?"

"Stopping Jorlanna."

Ashara stared at him for a long moment.

"Look, this isn't the time or place to talk details. But I'll tell you that I've been talking to Merrix, and he's promised his support as well." Cart recognized the name of Merrix d'Cannith, one of three barons who vied for control over House Cannith. Merrix oversaw the House's operations in the south, from his headquarters in the Brelish city of Sharn.

"Of course he has," Ashara said. "With Jorlanna out of the way, he'll have two-thirds of the House under his thumb, and Zorlan won't be able to oppose him." Zorlan was the eastern baron, who lived in the Karrnathi capital.

"Would that be so bad? Better that than to be a ministry of the Crown, or divided like the Phiarlans." Harkin took another step closer to Ashara, ignoring Cart entirely, and put a hand on her shoulder. "Listen, Ashara. We were friends once, and more than that. Can I count on your help, for the sake of that old . . . friendship?"

Ashara looked at Cart, her face a little flushed. "We've already set ourselves against Jorlanna's schemes," she said.

"I knew I could count on you," Harkin said. He had assumed Ashara was still talking to him, Cart realized, liking Harkin even less. "I'll be in touch again soon."

Harkin snatched his wands from Cart's hands and held out his hand for his sword, still smiling at Ashara. Cart turned his back on the Cannith and walked toward the Tower of Eyes. A moment later, Ashara's hands were on his arm again, and he felt his anger ebb.

* * * * *

Aunn sat in Kelas's chair with his feet on the desk and his chin on his chest, but Gaven didn't want to sleep. He paced the small room, feeling trapped, his mind circling around thoughts of his father and Kelas, his disturbed dreams, and Havrakhad's parting words: Use your freedom as if you deserved it.

Aunn had spoken of making restitution for the wrongs they had done, but how could he do that? He couldn't bring the Paelions back, not any more than he could bring his father back.

A gauntleted fist knocked at the door, and Gaven pulled it open. Cart shuffled inside with Ashara leaning on his shoulder, looking too tired to support her own weight. Gaven glanced at Aunn and saw him fighting to open his eyes, still surfacing from his dreams.

"You all need sleep," Cart said.

"I don't," Gaven said. "There's enough room in here to put two bedrolls on the floor. You and I can keep watch, Cart, while these two sleep."

"Don't try that on me," Cart said. "Sleep is no weakness,

and you're not some kind of great hero if you can fight it off for a few hours or days."

"What are you talking about?"

"I used to see it all the time in the army—soldiers would decide that they were as tough as a warforged, try to go without sleep, and nearly every time they ended up dead."

"I don't need to sleep now—I've been dreaming for the better part of a day."

"And you're afraid of dreaming again, is that it?"

"I'm not—" Gaven broke off. Actually, he realized, Cart was exactly right. He didn't want to dream again of Paelion ghosts, or of Rienne. And after being trapped in his dreams, he was afraid he might not wake up again.

"We can go to Kelas's home," Aunn said. "In fact, we should. It's what Kelas would do."

"Does he have any family?" Ashara asked.

"No. There'll be a servant or two, but I can handle them. And we can all get a good rest in a warm, soft bed."

A bed. Gaven hadn't slept in a bed since he and Rienne boarded the Sea Tiger in Sharavacion. Without Rienne, though, he feared a bed would seem painfully empty.

"How far is it?" Ashara asked. She looked as though her only concern was whether she could make it all the way to a bed before she fell over.

"Not far," Aunn said. "A few blocks."

"I'll help you," Cart said, and Ashara smiled up at him.

Aunn stood. "Let's go, then, before the sun rises."

Gaven lifted the sheaf of papers from Kelas's desk, his fingers scrabbling to get the bottom page off the smooth wood. He glanced around the room to make sure he wasn't forgetting anything, but his only possessions were on his person—the armor and sword that Cart and Ashara had secured for him while Phaine held him captive. He clutched the papers to his chest.

Aunn led the way out of the quiet white tower and onto the street. Crown's Hall rose in stately majesty just off to the left, and Gaven saw a pair of royal guards watching as Aunn led his friends away from the palace. Gaven imagined that the guards stared particularly keenly at him, though he knew it was unlikely they'd recognize him. Following Aunn's lead, he ignored them and walked with the others down the wide street, kicking at the dry leaves on the cobblestones.

Kelas's house was everything his study in the Tower of Eyes was not—large and well lit, with tall, glass-paned windows offering a pleasant view of the tree-lined neighborhood. Aunn produced a key, but the door swung open before he could turn it in the lock, and a pretty young woman smiled at him.

"Welcome home, Master Kelas," she said. "We weren't expecting you back so soon." To Gaven's eyes, her smile seemed forced.

"Plans change," Aunn said. He was gruff, aloof. The woman gave way as he stepped through the door and into a long entry hall. "We haven't slept, and we mean to. Are the guest rooms ready?"

"Of course, master."

"And send some wine to the rooms as well."

"The vintage?" She didn't look at Aunn when she asked that, but at Cart.

Aunn hesitated. The servant's eyes fluttered back to him. "Bluevine '92," he said, and she seemed to relax.

"A fine choice," she said. "Will you be needing anything else?"

"Just sleep."

"As you wish." She bowed deeply and withdrew.

"This was a terrible idea," Aunn whispered. "We should just leave."

Gaven looked at the shadows beneath Aunn's eyes. Ashara was leaning heavily on Cart, and despite Gaven's earlier protest, he felt the weight of exhaustion. "We need to rest," he said.

"We'd have been safer at an inn," Aunn said, glancing around the hall.

"Why?"

"Kelas was a spy master. He had so many precautions in place—" The sound of footsteps cut him off. "The guest rooms are this way," he said, louder, and he led the way through a door into another hall.

"Like the business with the wine?" Gaven whispered as they climbed a flight of stairs.

"Exactly. I think I said the right thing, but I'm not positive. It's probably best not to drink the wine."

They reached another hall, and Aunn pushed a door open. "Here's one room," he said, "and the next two doors. I, unfortunately, will be at the other end of the house."

Gaven looked into the open doorway. It was large for a guest room, with space enough for a low table and two upholstered chairs in addition to the soft-looking bed. The first morning sunlight streamed in through a tall window on the far side of the room.

"Avoid conversation," Aunn added in a whisper. "The servants will hear everything you say."

Cart led Ashara down the hall to the next door and opened it for her. Gaven didn't wait to see them say good night. "Get some rest," he said to no one in particular. He tossed the papers onto the bed in the first guest room, closed the door with a last nod to Aunn, pulled off his boots, and squirmed out of the chainmail shirt Ashara had given him in the cave temple behind the Dragon Forge.

Pain flared from a dozen scrapes and wounds on his chest and arms. His shirt was in tatters, thanks to Phaine's ministrations, and some of his cuts oozed fresh blood when he pulled the mail away. He wished Aunn had ordered the servants to draw a bath, and briefly toyed with the idea of summoning them himself. He remembered Aunn's warning, though, and decided to avoid the servants. He fell into bed, and immediately sleep reached to enfold him.

"No," he said, and he heaved himself to a sitting position, propped against the elegant headboard. When he closed his eyes, the darkness was like the blackness of his dreams, pulling him down and holding him captive. Best not to close his eyes, then. He grabbed the papers from Dreadhold, straightened the pages on his lap, and started to read.

Tumult and tribulation swirl in his wake: The Blasphemer rises, the Pretender falls, and armies march once more across the land.

The Storm Dragon, Gaven thought. He couldn't remember the rest of the verse, but it was something to do with the Storm Dragon.

He ran a hand over the tender skin where his dragonmark had been. Am I still the Storm Dragon? he wondered. He reached into the pouch at his belt and pulled out the dragonshard that held his Mark of Storm.

Or is this the Storm Dragon now?

Turning the shard in his hand, he thought for a moment that he saw in his mark the same words he'd just read on the page. Something about the Blasphemer, anyway.

He placed the bloodstone on the skin of his chest and balanced it there as he turned to the next page in Kelas's papers.

The cauldron of the thirteen dragons boils until one of the five beasts fighting over a single bone becomes a thing of desolation.

The twentieth day of Olarune, 973 YK. Gaven had scrawled those words on the wall of his cell twenty-one years to the day before the Mourning, when Cyre became "a thing of desolation." They were transcribed without comment—surely no dwarf at Dreadhold could have guessed in 973 how those words might be fulfilled. Gaven remembered that verse and its conclusion:

Desolation spreads over that land like wildfire, like plague, and Eberron bears the scar of it for thirteen cycles of the Battleground. Life ceases within its bounds, and ash covers the earth.

Apparently the Mourning had been foretold in the Prophecy. Did that mean it had to happen? Were the deaths of millions of Cyrans somehow necessary, because the Prophecy predicted it?

Or had someone brought the Mourning about in order to fulfill the Prophecy? No one knew for certain what had really happened on the Day of Mourning. Perhaps some dragon or sorcerer, obsessed with the Prophecy, had decided that killing all those people was the best way to fulfill those words, words found written in the the depths of the Dragon Below or encoded in a dragonmark, or signified by the movement of the moons and stars. Where had Gaven learned them? In a nightmare?

What nuance of meaning was obscured by the bald translation he'd scribbled in his cell? All the verbs he'd chosen seemed clear, painfully direct, making it hard to imagine any other possible interpretation. Could the Prophecy have been fulfilled in a less devastating way? Could Cyre have been spared?

He closed his eyes as he thought, then jolted awake as sleep tried once more to claim him. He scowled, shook his head to clear it, and turned the page.

Thunder is his harbinger and lightning his spear. Wind is his steed and rain his cloak. The words of creation are in his ears and on his tongue. The secrets of the first of sixteen are his.

Malathar had echoed those words back to him during their final battle—why? Was the dragon-king seeing his own doom in the Prophecy? And then Malathar said another verse. Gaven looked at his dragonmark again, and saw it:

The Storm Dragon flies before the traitor's army to deliver vengeance. The storm breaks upon the forces of the Blasphemer. The maelstrom swirls around him. He is the storm and the eye of the storm.

Gaven stood for a moment upon the burning line of his dragonmark, red fire in the rosy crystal floor. The maze of twisting lines threatened to overwhelm him. How had he chosen a path with such clarity before, with Havrakhad beside him? Consequences and destinations eluded him, paths trailed off into darkness before he could discern their significance. Shadow closed in on him again, and he thought he heard Rienne's voice.

"No sleep," Gaven said aloud, forcing his eyes open and then away from the dragonshard. He turned another page.

A clash of dragons signals the sundering of the Soul Reaver's gates. The hordes of the Soul Reaver spill from the earth, and a ray of Khyber's sun erupts to form a bridge to the sky.

There was a note on this page, written in the same angular Dwarven hand: "The prisoner's sleep was very troubled."

Of course it was, Gaven thought. He remembered his dreams of the Soul Reaver and its hordes, though now the dreams were jumbled with the memory of the actual event. It didn't matter—the dreams had been true to reality in every detail. He had lived through a nightmare.

He looked at the date, 21 Eyre 973 YK. Twenty-six years later, he'd been in New Cyre with Senya—he remembered the date from the forged identification papers she'd secured for him there.

"Destiny is . . . it's like the highest hopes the universe has for you." Gaven couldn't see Senya's face, but he heard her voice as though she were in the same room. "Like—like my mother wanted the best for me. And you can either fulfill your destiny, or you—"

What had Senya's mother dreamed for her daughter? Gaven hadn't really known his own mother. She died shortly after Thordren was born, leaving just a vague impression of a comforting presence in his toddler mind, an encompassing love he associated later in his life with Rienne's embrace. What had been her highest hopes for her son? Gaven thought of his father, whose hopes for Gaven had always felt like very high expectations—the hope, disappointed at every turn, that Gaven would grow into a replica of himself. Rienne, though, had always accepted who he was, and somehow at the same time inspired him to become someone better.

He threw himself out of bed, scattering papers to one side, the dragonshard clattering to the floor on the other. A weight gripped his chest, squeezing the breath from his lungs, and he couldn't sit still. He strode to the door, thought about opening it, then turned and paced to the window at the other end of the room.

"Where are you, Ree?" His eyes scanned the streets and buildings outside as if he expected Rienne to show herself to his view, but for all he knew she was still half the world away, rotting in some dragonborn prison. "I need you so much."

He pressed his forehead against the cool glass and closed his eyes, drawing a slow breath to calm his racing heart. Rienne's face appeared in the darkness, streaked with tears.

"You left me," she sobbed.

"I'm coming to find you, love," he mumbled, his lips thick with sleep.

He stood on a battlefield. Bodies blanketed the ground, slick with gore. Howls of fury and sobs of pain assaulted his ears. Exhaustion pulled at his limbs and dragged his shoulders toward the blood-soaked ground. Thunder crashed in the air, then all human sounds ceased, leaving only a string of syllables. They held the absence of meaning, and their sound was the unmaking of all things.

All around him, soldiers in Aundairian blue and savages clad in hide and fur fell as one to the ground, clutching their ears, their mouths forming silent howls of agony. He saw Rienne still standing, her face wrenched in pain, both hands on the hilt of her sword. Before her was a demon in the shape of a man, bound in bloodstained plate armor. He lifted a curved sword as the sounds of destruction kept spilling from his mouth.

"No!" Gaven screamed, and lightning arced from the red dragonshard to his body and exploded toward the Blasphemer.

Glass shattered and fell in a hail around him on the hardwood floor.

CHAPTER
12

"R ienne!" Jordhan's voice was a distant siren, drawing her
out of sleep.

She awoke in his cabin, her cheeks wet with tears,
wisps of dream clouding her thoughts, Gaven's name on her
lips. Jordhan was calling down from the deck, and as the haze
of sleep lifted she could hear the urgency in his voice.

She sprang out of the bunk, snatched up Maelstrom in its
sheath, and bounded through the hatch to the deck. Sunlight
cast long shadows across the polished wood beneath her feet,
but she couldn't tell whether the sun was about to dip below the
horizon or just emerging above it. Jordhan stood at the helm,
alert, watching something off the starboard bow.

"What is it?" she asked, hurrying to the bulwarks. She saw
before he could answer—three pairs of wings, fierce eagle beaks
and talons in front, powerful body and horse-like hooves in back.
Hippogriffs—each one carrying a rider. The sun gleamed on the
riders' metal armor and shone on the tips of the long lances they
carried. The majestic beasts soared on wide-spread wings, on a
course that would intercept the airship's in just a few moments.

"Have they hailed you?" Rienne called back to Jordhan.

"Not yet."

"Where are we?"

Jordhan scoffed. "The middle of nowhere. We're almost
back to the edge of the forest, ahead of the barbarians again."

"These riders aren't from the horde, though."

"No. There seem to be Eldeen forces coming together
somewhere near here—I've seen quite a few contingents moving
beneath us."

"So the hippogriffs are part of the Eldeen defenses."

"I'd assume so."

Rienne slid Maelstrom into the sash at her waist and tried to relax as the hippogriffs closed the distance. She should have nothing to fear from the Reachers—she was here, after all, to help them defend their land from the barbarians. Ostensibly, though, that was the same reason that Aundair had sent troops into the Reaches. House Lyrandar had close ties to Aundair, so she wasn't sure of the reaction she should expect from these riders.

The hippogriffs approached in a tight wedge, the wingtips of the two in the rear almost touching each other near the front one's tail. Rienne backed toward the helm to make room on the deck for one of the beasts to land, and a moment later the two rear hippogriffs split off to either side as the front one fluttered into a graceful landing, its rear hooves clattering against the deck. The rider was a human in thick hide armor, covered with a sage green tabard bearing the oak-tree emblem of the Eldeen Reaches. His skin was a shade darker than Rienne's, almost black. He set his lance into a sling attached to the saddle and dismounted.

"Captain Lyrandar," the man said with a small bow toward Jordhan, "and lady, I apologize for this intrusion. I am Sky Warden Kyaphar."

Rienne glanced over her shoulder at Jordhan, who smiled at the Sky Warden. "I am Jordhan d'Lyrandar—you'll forgive me not leaving the helm to greet you properly. This is Rienne ir'Alastra, of Stormhome."

"What can we do for you, Sky Warden?" Rienne said.

"Can I inquire as to your business in this part of the Reaches? Are you carrying cargo?"

Rienne drew a deep breath. "We are here to offer our support to your leadership, to help defend the Reaches from its attackers."

Kyaphar's face twisted in anger. "Which attackers do you mean? The Carrion Tribes or the armies of Aundair?"

"I believe the Carrion Tribes to be the greater threat," Rienne said, "with dragons as their vanguard."

"And vultures at their rear. But Aundair is no less an invading army. The defense of the Reaches is a Reacher concern, not Aundair's, and not yours. What is your stake in our fate?"

Kyaphar's words echoed the words of her dream, and she shuddered. *Vultures wheel where dragons flew, picking the bones of the numberless dead.* "I had a dream," she said, to herself as much as to him.

"And your dream led you to the defense of the Eldeen Reaches?"

Rienne threw a sharp glance at Kyaphar, but his face held no mockery—rather, he seemed intrigued.

"Yes," she said. "I believe my destiny is intertwined with that of the barbarian leader." *The Blasphemer,* she thought.

"And you believe that the two of you, and your airship, can make a difference in this war."

"We already have," Jordhan said from the helm. "One fewer dragon flies before the horde already, thanks to Rienne and this airship."

Rienne felt embarrassed at Jordhan's boast and looked away. Kyaphar's hippogriff shifted nervously on the deck, while the other two riders circled their mounts around the airship. The sun was sinking behind the distant mountains, streaking the smoke-filled sky with red.

"All our fates are intertwined," she said. She stepped to the bulwarks and looked eastward. The forest dwindled away into the farms of the eastern Reaches, and beyond them the writhing line of the Wyr River glowed red in the evening sun. The land across the river was Aundair—more fields, vineyards, and bustling Fairhaven at their heart. She struggled to find words to make sense of something that hovered at the edge of her understanding. "The Blasphemer is coming," she said. "This isn't a war of conquest. He doesn't want your land, or Aundair's. The barbarians aren't going to settle down and start farming these lands when this is over. It's about annihilation. He will sweep through behind his dragons, and leave nothing in his wake. I don't know if I can stop him, but I have to try."

Kyaphar stared at her for a long moment, then he nodded slowly. "I would welcome your help against the Blasphemer," he said. He turned to Jordhan. "If you would be kind enough to bring your vessel to the ground, I would like to introduce you both to the Mosswood Warden."

Jordhan looked to Rienne, and she nodded. The airship started to descend, startling the hippogriff. It squawked and flapped its wings, spreading its legs to keep its balance. Kyaphar turned to the beast and laid a hand on its neck, soothing it.

The Mosswood Warden, Rienne thought. The Eldeen Reaches were governed by druids, nature priests of various sects who led by wise guidance and example, striving to keep their people in harmony with nature as much on the farms of the agricultural east as in the wilds of the Towering Wood. What would the druids have to say about the Blasphemer?

Kyaphar returned to his saddle and raised a hand in salute to Rienne and Jordhan. "I will guide you to a safe moorage," he said, "then escort you to the Warden." He gently pulled on his mount's reins, and the hippogriff's wings spread out wide. Catching the wind, it lifted off the deck as the airship continued her descent, and Rienne watched Kyaphar and his mount soar over them, then swoop down past them to a towering oak in the forest below.

As the airship followed Kyaphar down, the ground came alive to Rienne's eyes. Soldiers massed in ragged lines, spear tips glinting in the sun—militia called from their farms to defend against the invaders. Clumps of warriors in thick hide armor formed around enormous Eldeen bears, clad in their own plates of metal-studded leather. Men and women in flowing robes of green, brown, or gray huddled around menhirs and obelisks of rough-hewn stone, raising their voices in droning chants. Rienne couldn't see a settlement of any sort, let alone a wall that could help hold the barbarians back. What were the Reachers hoping to defend here?

The spreading branches of an ancient oak made a perfect mooring tower for the airship. Kyaphar left his hippogriff on the ground and climbed a rope ladder into the branches. He walked nimbly among them, tying ropes to hold the ship in place, then helped Jordhan and Rienne off the deck and led them down the ladder to solid ground. At the bottom of the ladder, he extended an arm toward where a small clump of people waited for them.

Rienne had formed a picture in her mind of the Mosswood Warden, based in part on Sky Warden Kyaphar—an old man, as dark as Kyaphar but with gray hair and a long beard, so hunched he was almost lost in his moss-green robe. Her image could hardly have been more wrong. As Rienne approached, one woman stepped forward to greet her, and Kyaphar introduced her as Mosswood Warden Elestrissa.

She did wear some moss green in her cloak, but that was where the resemblance to Rienne's mental picture ended. She was a gray-skinned half-orc, taller by a head than Kyaphar and powerfully muscled. Her long black hair was strung with beads that clattered as the wind stirred them, and her powerful chest was wrapped in armor made of thick bark sewn to tough leather. In one hand, she held an ornate shield carved of darkwood, and the other clutched a short spear tipped with a gleaming crystal point.

The Mosswood Warden's face was grim as Kyaphar repeated what Rienne and Jordhan had told him on the airship—about their desire to help defend against the barbarians, and Rienne's conviction that her destiny was linked to the Blasphemer's.

"Tell me your dream," she said to Rienne.

Rienne felt the half-orc woman's eyes bore into her. They were steel gray, intense, perhaps haunted. "I was in darkness," Rienne said. Her dream suddenly was as vivid in her mind as when she'd had it in Argonnessen, four weeks earlier. "All I could see was my sword, suspended in the air, so I took it by the hilt and it lifted me into the air. I heard words—no, I didn't hear them, I just knew them. The words of the Draconic Prophecy." She closed her eyes and recited them.

" 'Dragons fly before the Blasphemer's legions, scouring the earth of his righteous foes. Carnage rises in the wake of his passing, purging all life from those who oppose him. Vultures wheel where dragons flew, picking the bones of the numberless dead. But the Blasphemer's end lies in the void, in the maelstrom that pulls him down to darkness.'"

She opened her eyes, feeling the weight of the Mosswood Warden's stare, and found Kyaphar and a circle of retainers all staring at her intently. "Then I was on a battlefield. I saw dragons in the air, and the barbarians' white banner in the wind. I was fighting, and I killed many soldiers before I finally stood before the Blasphemer."

Elestrissa didn't move, but kept staring, as if waiting for more.

"That's all," Rienne said. "That's when I woke."

The half-orc's shoulders slumped. "So you did not foresee the Blasphemer's death," she said, clearly disappointed.

Rienne thought back over the dream. It seemed strange, but Elestrissa was correct—she had seen herself standing before the demonic figure of the barbarian leader, but there her dream had ended. She had associated the dream with the Blasphemer's death because of the words of the Prophecy. In her mind, the maelstrom was *her* Maelstrom, the blade that had led her into the dream in the first place. She shook her head as she repeated the words: "'But the Blasphemer's end lies in the void, in the maelstrom that pulls him down to darkness.'"

"Look around you, lady," Elestrissa said. "Does this place look familiar to you? Might this be the place where the battle took place in your dream?"

Rienne looked at the forest behind the Warden, and turned to see the trees thinning off to the east into farms and fields. "No," she said. She closed her eyes again. She had not been in the forest in her dream. She saw open sky, and heard the shouts of soldiers and the screams of the dying . . . and the rush of the river. "No—in my dream I was at the river."

"Then it appears your destiny is bound to the defense of Aundair after all, and not the Reaches."

"I have to help stop the Blasphemer, if I can."

"And perhaps you will, when he crosses the Wynarn. But by then, it will be too late for us. We take our stand here, even if it is our last."

"I will fight here," Rienne said, "if you will let me."

"We will not refuse another sword pledged against the barbarians," Elestrissa said, shaking her head and turning away. "But I fear it will do precious little to help us. Kyaphar will put you and your airship where he thinks you can do the most good."

"Wait—"

"Good fortune, Lady Alastra, Captain d'Lyrandar." The Mosswood Warden and her retainers walked away, leaving Rienne and Jordhan alone with Kyaphar.

"Well, that was strange," Jordhan said.

"Ten Seas! There's so much more I wanted to ask."

"Ask me," Kyaphar said. "You seem to have been placed under my command." He smiled, and Rienne couldn't help but return the warmth of it. "Let's go back to your airship, and you can ask me anything you need to know."

"The most important thing is, what are we defending? Why make our stand here?"

"I suspected that might be your first question. And it's a question best answered from the air."

CHAPTER
13

Gaven stared up at a storm-wracked sky where dragons wheeled like vultures. Darkness slowly poured into the sky until it was a whirling cloud of shadow, and Gaven saw the souls of the fallen drifting into that new storm. *He is the storm, and the eye of the storm,* he thought. *In him the storm cannot die.*

The harsh chant of the Blasphemer was gone, but no sound dared to take its place. He felt but did not hear heavy footsteps drumming the floor beside him, and then Cart crouched over him. Cart's mouth opened, but no words emerged. Gaven tried to focus on Cart's face, but his eyes kept drifting past the warforged to the storm of souls. Cart turned away for a moment, then leaned close, putting a steadying hand on Gaven's shoulder.

Ashara came then and leaned over him, and Cart shifted away to give her room. A slender wand was in her hand, and she moved it slowly over his body, as if it were a tool knitting his wounds closed. Her touch was cold on his skin, but it woke his nerves, first to a cacophony of pain, then as the wand worked its magic, to the hard floor and sharp glass beneath him.

"What happened?" Kelas's voice, somewhere behind him, was the first clear sound he heard. "Damn! Is she hurt?"

"The servant?" Ashara said, glancing up. "She'll be fine. Don't move her! I have more work to do yet. But we almost lost this one."

"Gaven?" Kelas's face appeared in his vision. Gaven felt a surge of rage and fear before he noticed the lines of worry and the genuine concern in the man's eyes and remembered it was Aunn looming over him, not Kelas. Aunn looked him over, then surveyed the room. Something caught his attention, and his eyes shot wide. "Fire!"

Cart sprang to his feet, following Aunn's eyes. Gaven managed to turn his head enough to see the warforged snatch a blanket from the bed and beat it against the floor, sending smoke in eddies toward the open door. After a moment the warforged stopped and stood back.

Aunn barked orders. "Ashara, see to the servant. Cart, as soon as Ashara says you can move her, carry the girl into a bed and find out what she saw." He turned to address someone Gaven couldn't see. "You, put that wine on the table, then go and bring me a fresh bottle." He crouched beside Gaven and sighed. "I think I'm going to need it."

Ashara stood and strode toward the door, leaving Gaven in Aunn's care.

"Can you hear me, Gaven?" he said.

Gaven opened his mouth and found that he had no voice. He managed a slight nod.

"Can you tell me what happened?"

Gaven turned his head to the side. Even if he could speak, he wasn't sure he knew what had happened.

"Well," Aunn said, "it looks to me like we had a lightning storm in here. If I had to guess, I'd say that a bolt of lightning connected that dragonshard to the sky, with you and the window caught in between. Which resulted in a burning rug, a shattered window, a wounded servant, and you . . ." His brow furrowed. "On the brink of death. Which seems odd."

Gaven closed his eyes, trying to remember the lightning.

"I've seen lightning go through you quite a number of times," Aunn continued. "But I've never seen you burned like this." With a glance at the door, Aunn slid a wand out of a pouch, hiding it halfway in his sleeve. Warmth flowed into Gaven's body where the wand and Aunn's hands touched him, and he felt a surge of renewed strength.

"The Blasphemer," Gaven said. He could manage a rasping croak, no more.

"You were dreaming," Aunn said. "By the window?"

"A vision. Rienne."

"I see." Aunn looked around, lifted a sheet of paper from the floor beside him, and read it aloud. "'In the darkest night of the Dragon Below, storm and dragon are reunited, and they break together upon the legions of the Blasphemer.' That's pleasant bedtime reading. No wonder he was haunting your dreams." He turned and started collecting the other pages strewn across the floor.

"Wait," Gaven said. "Read that again."

Aunn did, and Gaven felt his pulse quicken. Storm and dragon reunited . . .

That could just mean Gaven holding the dragonshard that contained his mark. Or it could point to his mark being somehow restored to his skin—or, he supposed, to the involvement of some dragon. "Is there anything else on that page?" he asked.

"Just the date, 22 Dravago 988. Why?"

"I've forgotten so much."

When he had first left Dreadhold, the Prophecy swam in Gaven's mind. He remembered every dream that had haunted his sleep, every scrap of writing he'd collected and deciphered in his expeditions through the depths of Khyber, and even verses he'd never read—fragments held in the dragon's memories trapped in his mind. Haldren and Vaskar had questioned him about the Time of the Dragon Above, the Eye of Siberys, the Soul Reaver—and those memories had flooded over him and spilled out of his mouth. Flashes of memory still surprised him occasionally, but the Prophecy no longer felt like a part of him.

"Just set it down and leave us alone," Aunn said, looking toward the door again.

With an effort, Gaven sat up and looked around the room. A young man stood in the door, eyes wide, clutching a bottle of wine. The floor around him was covered with shards of glass, and only a few jagged pieces remained in the frame. A faint smell of smoke lingered in the air, but Gaven couldn't see the damage his dragonmark had caused. Cart and Ashara had vanished.

The servant placed the bottle on the small table beside the bed, knocking it into a glass that was already there, sending a splash of red wine over the lip. Flustered, he looked around in vain for something to clean up with, but Aunn barked at him and he scurried away.

"Let's get you into bed," Aunn said, extending a hand to Gaven.

"I'm fine." Gaven managed to stand, glass crunching against the wood under his feet. Now he could see the rosy dragonshard on the other side of the bed, resting in a blackened crater in the woven Talentan rug. Between the window and the rug, Gaven's outburst had probably caused a thousand gold galifars of damage. He stepped carefully out of the glass and bent to retrieve the shard.

Its heat surprised him, and a sharp surge of anger shot through him. For an instant, the man before him was really Kelas, who had stripped his mark from his skin. A prickle ran over his chest and shoulder, where his mark had been, and he heard thunder crack outside. He dropped the shard back on the bed.

Aunn's hand shot to the hilt of his sword, as if the thunder heralded an imminent attack. "What was that?" he said.

"His storm flies wild," Gaven muttered, "unbound and pure in devastation."

"Nara said that," Aunn said. "Is that the Prophecy?"

Gaven nodded.

"What's the rest of it? You were saying it with her."

"Pure in devastation, going before the traitor's army to break upon the city by the lake of kings."

"The city of Varna, on Lake Galifar."

"Going before the traitor's army," Gaven said. "Kelas? Did he send the army marching to Varna?"

"Or Nara. Is there anything else about the traitor's army, or the traitor herself?"

"I don't know." Gaven slumped onto the bed. "I don't remember. Why don't you look in there?" He gestured vaguely toward the papers still strewn on the floor.

"You didn't sleep at all, did you?" Aunn asked.

"No. You?"

"A little. I'm sorry. I'll stop interrogating you."

"What do you know about Nara?"

Aunn laughed. "It's only fair, I suppose. But let me find Cart and Ashara first. They should hear this as well."

Gaven gathered the papers from the floor while Aunn ventured down the hall in search of the others. He didn't give the pages any more than a glance until he saw his father's writing. The sight of the flowing script made something in him break. He fell on his knees, felt glass bite through his skin, and dissolved into grief.

"She was bringing the wine." Ashara's voice came from the doorway. "She said she had just knocked on the door when it flew open and threw her back."

"Where's Gaven?" Aunn said.

Gaven tried to compose himself and got to his feet, fumbling with the papers in his hand. Aunn stood in the doorway, relief plain on his face as Gaven returned to his view. Cart and Ashara crowded the hallway behind him.

"Is the servant badly hurt?" Gaven said.

"She'll be fine," Ashara said. "You're bleeding again."

Gaven looked down and saw blood soaking into the knees of his pants, where glass had cut through the cloth and sliced his skin. "It's nothing," he said. The cuts burned, but they weren't serious. He looked at Aunn. "So tell us about Nara."

Aunn took a deep breath and let it out. "Very well. Nara ir'Galanatyr led the Royal Eyes from 975, I think, to 996. She was supposed to be close to Queen Barvette, but I've heard nasty rumors that she had something to do with the old queen's death. When Aurala took the throne, though, Nara became one of her closest advisors, and she stayed that way right up until the end of the war."

"When she was dismissed," Cart said. "She didn't want Aurala to sign the treaty, so Aurala appointed a new spy master who would work for peace."

"Something like that," Aunn said, "but there was more to it." He paused, biting his lip.

"What?" Gaven asked.

Aundair's internal politics were a mystery to him, for all that he'd been caught up in them since leaving Dreadhold in Haldren's company. But opposition to the Treaty of Thronehold was something that Nara and Haldren evidently had in common.

"Well, first of all it's not entirely clear that Aurala has ever been interested in peace, except a peace that results from her sitting on the throne of a reunited Galifar. So it's possible that she replaced Nara purely for show, to convince the other nations that she was serious about the treaty—serious enough to remove her most trusted advisor."

"What has Nara been doing since the end of the war, then?" Ashara asked.

"To all appearances, she's been in seclusion—I think in Wyr, by the Eldeen Border."

"But you think she's been working for the queen in secret all this time?" Ashara said.

Aunn scowled. "Actually, the thought hadn't occurred to me. But it's possible. Perhaps they've spent three years plotting the next stage of the war. But that would mean . . ."

"That all of this goes back to the queen," Gaven said. "The barbarians invading the Reaches, the Dragon Forge, my dragonmark. What about Haldren? Were Kelas and Nara behind all that as well?"

"Indirectly," Aunn said. "But that would also mean that Aurala is planning her own assassination, or planning to stage an attempt on her life at least. Because that's what Kelas thought he was doing."

"Ending a thousand years of Wynarn rule over Aundair," Cart said. "At least, that's what he told Haldren."

"Kelas might have lied," Ashara said. "Or Nara might have lied to Kelas. Think about it. Poor Aurala—she has rogue generals starting hostilities in Thaliost, barbarians threatening her western border, and insurgents plotting against her. Naturally, she has to take drastic measures to secure her throne—destroying Varna, invading the Reaches, taking control of House Cannith and Arcanix. What's next? Some kind of assault on her own people under the guise of putting down a rebellion?"

Aunn shook his head. "I got the sense that Kelas knew everything Nara does, or just about."

"Which puts you in a difficult spot," Gaven said, "as long as you're wearing his face."

"I've survived worse."

Gaven looked at Aunn and scratched his chin. What did he actually know about the changeling? He was a Royal Eye—deception and intrigue were his life's work. He had been sandy-haired Darraun, a whispering dwarf opening Gaven's manacles, tall and proud Aunn, and now Kelas, the master-mind behind the Dragon Forge. Gaven had never seen his real face, and he wondered if he would ever know the real man. Aunn lived in a world Gaven could barely imagine, and he seemed perfectly at home in all this discussion of conspiracies and betrayal.

"What did she say?" Ashara asked.

"First she asked about the storm—the demonstration for the queen." He snapped his fingers. "She said she saw it, so she can't be in Wyr, that's two hundred miles from Varna."

"Unless she was using magic to watch it," Ashara said.

"Anyway, she asked about the queen's reaction to the demonstration."

"And she cited the Prophecy," Gaven added. "She saw the storm as a fulfillment of the Prophecy."

Aunn frowned. "So did she plan the Forge in order to fulfill the Prophecy, or is the Prophecy just an extra?"

"I don't think it's just an extra," Gaven said. "If Nara is trying to shape history so the Prophecy is fulfilled, it's because she wants whatever she thinks the Prophecy promises. Like Vaskar—he brought about the clash of dragons at Starcrag

Plain because he wanted to be the Storm Dragon. He wanted to cross the bridge to the sky and become a god."

"So what does Nara want from the Prophecy?" Aunn asked.

"The destruction of Aundair?" Ashara said. "Barbarians plundering the land as some kind of revenge against Aurala?"

"Perhaps," Aunn said, "but then why all the intrigue? It would be enough to stir up the barbarians, perhaps weaken the armed forces from within. She wouldn't need House Cannith and Arcanix for that."

Gaven ran his fingers through his hair. "But she needed them to build the Dragon Forge, to take my dragonmark. To make that storm that she thought fulfilled the Prophecy."

"And she thinks she needs you for the Prophecy as well. 'We need him in place when the time is right for the reunion,' she said."

Reunion—the word sparked a memory, and he shuffled through the papers in his hands. "Storm and dragon are reunited," Gaven said. Then he found the page Aunn had read. " 'In the darkest night of the Dragon Below.' The Time of the Dragon Below is beginning now."

"What else is supposed to happen in the Time of the Dragon Below?" Cart asked.

Gaven closed his eyes and tried to remember. "The rise of the Blasphemer," he said, and an echo of a vision flashed through his mind, an impression of bone-white banners. Beyond that, his mind was a blank. "I can't remember what else."

"The Prophecy makes my head spin," Aunn said.

Gaven sighed. "All this political scheming does the same to my head."

"I need some of that wine now." Aunn moved to the table by the bed and stopped, staring down at the wine bottle and the glass beside it.

"Are you sure it's not poisoned?" Gaven said, trying to laugh.

Aunn turned and pointed at Ashara. "The servant who was hurt—she told you she was bringing wine to Gaven."

Ashara nodded. "She said she was just about to knock on the door when it flew open."

"And the glass broke on the floor in the hall. So why is there a full glass of wine here?"

"There was a young man," Ashara said. "He came just after you did, holding a glass of wine. You told him to set it down and bring the bottle."

Aunn shook his head. "How long has there been a spy in Kelas's house?"

CHAPTER
14

Aunn bolted to the room at the end of the hall, where Cart and Ashara had placed the injured servant. The bed was empty. He forced himself to walk back to Gaven's room, though he wanted to run.

"We're leaving," he said from the doorway. "Gather your things."

"Where are we going?" Gaven asked.

"No more discussion." The servant had probably heard everything they'd said. "Let's move."

Ashara edged past him to retrieve her pack from her room as Gaven pulled his mail shirt back on. Aunn reviewed the morning's events, trying to fix the two servants in his mind. The young woman's disappearance suggested that she had been the spy, not the boy, but he couldn't be certain. She'd had a round face, dark hair hanging over her eyes, thin lips, the pale skin of a household servant who lived her life indoors. Her eyes had been closed in pain or veiled behind her hair—perhaps hidden on purpose.

Ashara emerged from her room and Gaven stood ready. Without another word, Aunn led the way back to the front door. Halfway down the stairs, he remembered—his pack was still in Kelas's chamber. When he'd heard the thunder in Gaven's room, he'd bolted out, stopping only long enough to pull on his boots. He had to go back.

"Listen," he whispered. "You three go to the Ruby Chalice, near Chalice Center. You know it?"

He glanced behind him and saw Ashara nod, at least. Good—she could lead the others. The plaza called Chalice

Center held an airship docking tower and a lightning rail station, making it a good place to blend in among travelers.

"I'll be right behind you. I just have to get some things from my room."

"We can wait," Gaven said. "No need to split up."

"No. In fact, it would be better if you split up, and be careful you're not followed." They had reached the front hall, and the same servant who had met them at the door stood smiling, ready to hold it open for their departure. "Go," Aunn whispered.

"I hope you had a pleasant rest," the woman said. Her smile almost looked genuine, for a moment while she looked at Gaven. Aunn watched her eyes as his companions filed past her out the door, and he saw only venom and steel.

I've spent my whole life crawling through a nest of vipers, Aunn thought. So far I've managed to bite before getting bitten, but how much longer can I do that?

He left the hall by a different door and strode down a wide hallway floored in marble. He turned and started up another flight of stairs, but a voice at the top brought him to a halt.

"You're not Kelas."

Aunn looked up and saw the young woman Gaven had injured, though no sign of the injury remained. She held a long knife to the throat of another young woman . . . no, the same woman, staring at him with pleading eyes. One was a changeling—presumably, the one with the knife—and the one who had been spying on Gaven in his room. Her pale blue eyes bore into him, as if she thought she could see through his disguise if she stared hard enough.

"Of course I am," Aunn said. "One changeling in this house is enough."

"Kelas wouldn't care if I slit this girl's throat."

Aunn had to will his heart into a steady rhythm. She was right—Kelas wouldn't care. And a year ago, he wouldn't have risked his disguise to save a servant's life. He was a servant of the crown.

"What is his death," Kelas demanded, *"if Aundair is served by*

it? What does it matter if I die, if you die, if hundreds of soldiers march to their death, so long as Aundair remains?"

Laurann's knuckles were white on the hilt of her dagger. The man—a Brelish spy, Kelas had said—stared up at her, pleading in his eyes.

"You serve the crown!" Kelas shouted in her ear. "You are a Royal Eye of Aundair! You are not a person, you're an eye, an appendage, a part of Aundair. The queen relies on you to do her work. Do it!"

The dagger cut quickly across the captured spy's neck. For Aundair.

"Neither would any spy worth a damn," he said. "You prove nothing by doing it." Please don't, he thought. Not another life's blood on my hands.

The spy hesitated, confused, and he saw the hand holding the knife relax ever so slightly. Aunn climbed another step, then the captive woman exploded in a blur of motion. Aunn heard bones crack as the knife changed hands, then blood sprayed him as the knife plunged into the first woman's chest. Aunn watched her sink to the floor, waiting for her face to change in death, but it was the other woman who changed, smiling wickedly.

"Thank you, *Kelas*," the changeling said. Then it was Haunderk's face sneering at him, ridiculously perched atop a serving-girl's smock.

Aunn's heart pounded, refusing to be quieted. Who was this changeling who had stolen his face? Did he expect Kelas to believe he was Haunderk? Or was he taunting him somehow, trying to show that he saw through the Kelas disguise? Whatever he intended, he had demonstrated how dangerous he could be.

Until he knew more, he had to stick to his own disguise, at least hope to sow enough confusion to find an opening. "Not that face," he snapped. "You know I hate talking to dead people." Words straight from Kelas's mouth.

It worked—the changeling was visibly surprised. "Dead?"

"Yes. I killed him myself. Do you mean to be next, pointing

that knife at me?" He was Kelas at his most imperious, and the changeling took a step back from the top of the stairs. Aunn climbed two more stairs.

Haunderk's face melted off the changeling, leaving only a gray blankness and white eyes. Long white hair fell in unruly shocks down to the shoulders. The mouth was a lipless slit in a featureless face. "But you're Haunderk," the changeling said.

"Don't be a fool." Aunn took two more steps up. He had to browbeat the changeling into believing his lie before he was asked for proof he couldn't give. He jerked his chin toward the servant's body lying at the changeling's feet. "You've made enough of a mess as it is."

The changeling took another step back, giving Aunn room to stand beside the dead woman. "I'm sorry, master."

Aunn twisted his face into a fury and howled. "You are not sorry!" He stepped forward again until his face was a hand's breadth from the changeling's. "Her death is nothing!" Ignoring the knife in the changeling's hand, he slapped the featureless face. "You don't feel regret, you don't know shame, you don't care!" He punctuated his words with slaps and punches until the knife clattered to the floor and the changeling cowered before his rage. With one final kick, he strode past the changeling and away down the hall.

Before turning the corner, though, he shot a glance back. The changeling was glaring after him with a searing hatred that mirrored Aunn's own feelings toward Kelas. As their eyes met, though, Aunn realized his mistake—Kelas would never have looked back. And the changeling knew it.

Aunn reached the sanctuary of Kelas's chamber and sank against the door. Nausea gripped his stomach and chilled his brow, and his pulse still pounded in his ears. In the space of moments, he had let an innocent woman die and—perhaps worse—he had become everything that he had despised in Kelas. What happened? he wondered. Didn't anything change in the Labyrinth?

"Make it solid," he muttered. But nothing was solid—he couldn't find a firm place in the quagmire. He dragged himself to his feet, but nausea brought him back to his knees, vomit splattering on the floor.

* * * * *

"Where is he?" Gaven said for the third time. He searched the faces in the crowded tavern for Kelas or anyone else who could be Aunn—anyone, really, who might be heading for the table where he sat with Cart and Ashara.

"Stop it, Gaven," Cart said. "You're drawing attention. Look at us, look at your drink, or look at the pretty women. But don't stare at everyone, and don't make eye contact."

Gaven laughed. "The warforged is giving me lessons in behavior." He saw Cart stiffen, and he put a hand on the plated arm of his warforged friend. "I didn't mean it like that. Clearly, I need the help."

"When's the last time you cut loose in a tavern?" Ashara asked.

The smile fell from Gaven's face as he thought about the question.

"There was our wrestling match in Darguun," Cart offered. "That wasn't so long ago."

"True. But we were just waiting for Haldren, the way we're waiting now for . . . whatever his name is." He started to look around the tavern again, but forced his gaze back to Ashara's face. "It's been a very long time."

"Well, we'll have to remedy that," Ashara said, smiling at Cart. "Though I have to say, I wish I'd been there for the wrestling match. Who won?"

"He did," Cart said.

"Cart was holding back," Gaven added. "He'd been wrestling hobgoblins and bugbears, so he wasn't prepared for a real challenge."

"No, I stopped holding back when I realized what I was up against. You won it fairly."

"It must have been an epic struggle," Ashara said. Gaven noticed for the first time how her smile crinkled the corners of her eyes—and how her eyes shone when she looked at Cart.

Rienne's absence hit him suddenly like a mace in his gut. He stared down into his wine glass and saw the red of her silk wrap.

"Sorry I took so long."

Gaven looked up with a start and saw Aunn, still wearing Kelas's face, standing by the table. "There you are!" he said. "Is everything all right?"

"I ran into a little trouble."

He was wearing different clothes than he'd had on an hour before, and his movements were strangely stiff. "Are you injured?" Gaven asked.

Aunn shook his head and sat in the empty chair. He looked down at his clothes and absently brushed at a dark spot on his coat that might have been dried blood.

"So are you going to tell us what in the Ten Seas is going on?"

Aunn blinked at him, then his face came alive. He leaned forward on the table and words spilled out in a fierce whisper. "There was a spy in Kelas's house. Another changeling. I think he followed us from the Tower of Eyes. She was the servant you injured and Ashara took care of, and I suspect she heard everything we said in your room after Cart and Ashara left her. He accosted me in the hall when I went back to my room."

"And you killed her . . . him?" Gaven said.

"No. I convinced him I really am Kelas."

There was more to the story than Aunn was telling, Gaven knew—starting but not ending with the spray of blood on his coat. He decided not to press for more details, though . . . at least, not until he saw Aunn smile again.

"So the spy was a Royal Eye?" Cart asked. "Not spying on the Royal Eyes?"

"As far as I know, yes," Aunn said.

An awkward silence fell on the table. Gaven could see in Ashara's face that she wanted to know more, and was holding back as he was.

"We need a plan," Cart said at last. "And a safer place to talk it over."

"Right," Aunn said, sitting back and planting his hands on the table. "That's why I suggested this place—they have private rooms that are really private, if you know who to talk to. I'll be right back." He stood up and weaved his way through the crowded tables to the back of the room.

"Is anyone else getting tired of looking at Kelas's face?" Gaven said.

"It is unnerving," Cart said.

"I keep forgetting which side I'm on," Ashara said. "I worked with Kelas many times . . . before."

"Which side?" Gaven dug his fingers into his hair. "I don't even know how many sides there are, let alone who's on which one."

"How long can he keep it up, do you think?" Cart asked.

"He's good at what he does," Ashara said.

Gaven thought again of the blood on Aunn's coat. "I think I want to stay on his side."

Ashara gave him a grim smile. "Let's hope he stays on ours."

* * * * *

"I'd like to speak to the master cook," Aunn told the gangly young man at the kitchen door. *What if they've changed the password?* he thought. But the boy nodded and disappeared into the kitchen.

I've been out of this for too long, he thought. *The mad trip to Xen'drik with Janik and Dania, crossing Khorvaire with Senya and Cart to free Gaven and Haldren, the brief time as Caura and Vauren and General Yeven, then the long trek to the Demon Wastes—I've been so many other people, I haven't had time to be a spy.*

He recognized the man who emerged from the kitchen, a broad dwarf in silk and lace, a thick beard hiding most of his face. Lukas looked him up and down, but gave no indication that he knew Kelas's face. "What can I do for you?" he growled.

"I need a quail in silver," Aunn said.

Lukas's expression didn't change. "Certainly, master," he said. "Will there be anything else?"

Aunn thought for a moment. *If he asked, Lukas would send agents throughout the tavern and the rest of Chalice Center,* listening for anyone who might be asking after Aunn or his party. But he doubted the other changeling would be so careless. "No, thank you."

"Very well. Is the rest of your party here?"

"Yes. I'll gather them. Thank you." He nodded a slight bow to Lukas and returned to the table where he'd left the others.

"Ready?" Gaven asked as he approached.

"Ready. Lukas will show us the room."

The dwarf led them outside and into a wide alley beside the tavern. A well-kept staircase took them above the dining room where they had sat before, and Lukas opened a door into a luxurious private dining room. It was little more than a table with benches on either side, but the benches were padded with upholstered cushions—and so were the walls, to keep sound from escaping the room.

Lukas bowed as they filed past him into the room. "I hope you find the quail satisfactory," he said.

"I'm certain we will. Thank you."

Lukas pushed the door closed, and the din of the tavern and the street faded away. Aunn collapsed onto one of the upholstered benches, overwhelmed with exhaustion and anxiety. The relief was so great that he felt his face begin to change under his hands, fading to its natural blank.

Make it solid, he told himself. He fixed Kelas's face in his mind and molded his face to match, hoping the others hadn't noticed the slip.

"Are you all right?" Gaven said.

Aunn took a deep breath and lowered his hands, Kelas's visage fixed firmly on his face once again. "I'm fine," he said. "And now we can talk."

CHAPTER
15

R ight," Gaven said. "Let's talk. But can we talk to a different face?"

He saw Aunn stiffen. "What?"

"I'm sick of staring at his face. Could you be Darraun again, or Aunn, if you prefer?"

"I'm sorry," Aunn said, and Kelas's face was gone.

Gaven had never seen the changeling alter his appearance before, and he watched in fascination. First the features that most defined Kelas's face softened—the black hair lightened to gray, thick brows thinned and faded, and the dark, deep-set eyes lightened as their surrounding wrinkles smoothed. Gaven caught just a glimpse of a face that wasn't a face at all, just a blank gray surface waiting for shape and color, then it molded into the proud, commanding face the changeling called Aunn. That was his real name, he'd said, but it clearly wasn't his real face. Was this face somehow supposed to represent his true self? he wondered. Or was it just another disguise?

"Nice to see you again, Aunn," Gaven said.

Aunn didn't return his smile. He seemed lost in concentration, as if perhaps he were still shaping some part of his face or body. Gaven noticed that his clothes didn't fit this new form well—Aunn was taller and more muscular than Kelas. He wondered why Aunn didn't alter just his face, especially when he knew he'd be changing back into Kelas before long.

"So now what?" Ashara asked.

Gaven stared at the table. For a brief moment, his path had seemed clear to him, shining in the darkness, and he had accepted it with all its consequences. That clarity was gone, crowded out in all the scheming and intrigue going on around them, which Aunn seemed to understand so much better than he did. One thing burned like a beacon in his mind, though—he had to find Rienne.

No one had answered Ashara's question. Aunn still seemed lost in some aspect of his transformation, so Gaven cleared his throat. "I need to go to Stormhome," he said. "I have to find Rienne, and I want to find out why my father was corresponding with Kelas."

"Stormhome?" Aunn said. "Last time you were there, I had to break you out of manacles." His voice was deeper and clearer than it had been as Kelas.

"You were also part of the team of dwarves it took to get the manacles on me in the first place. They'll never capture me without your help."

"Rienne threw me into the kitchen. Believe me, I wasn't much help."

Gaven laughed, but it was strange to think of the man sitting across from him as the dwarf who had barged in through Thordren's back door, as well as Darraun, and also Kelas. The changeling could take any face, could be anyone. How could Gaven trust him?

"Nevertheless," Gaven said, "that's where I have to go."

"But there's so much we have to do here," Aunn said. "I have to make sure that the army takes Kathrik Mel seriously and prepares to meet him, instead of just fighting the Reachers. Kelas can do that. I need to figure out what Nara is going. And assuming Jorlanna doesn't give up on her plans just because the Dragon Forge is destroyed, we need to stop her from seizing the throne and stealing any more dragonmarks."

"So it seems our destinies lie along different paths," Gaven said.

Aunn frowned. "Nara said I should keep you here until the reunion, whatever that means. If you leave now, and she finds out about it, it's going to be very hard for me to explain."

"Are you thinking about locking me up after all?"

"Of course not. I'm just saying maybe you should wait, see what Nara has in mind—"

"And continue to be her pawn? No, I've done enough of that. Even when I thought I was doing what I wanted, I was playing into her hands."

Aunn leaned forward and opened his mouth, ready to argue, then slumped back on the bench. "What can I say to that?" he said. "Except that I'm sorry for the part I played in it all."

Gaven frowned. He had always liked Darraun, but he'd never quite understood his role in events so far. He had used his intelligence contacts to get himself invited along with Cart and Senya to free Gaven and Haldren—which meant that Kelas had arranged it, most likely. At Nara's command? When Gaven escaped Haldren's custody, it was Darraun that brought him back to Starcrag Plain, but not to help Haldren. Was Nara behind that as well? Then Darraun had faked his own death and disappeared. When Gaven saw him next, he'd just killed Kelas at the Dragon Forge. Presumably Nara had not ordered that, since she had addressed Aunn as Kelas without a hint of irony. He couldn't help it—he still liked Aunn, this new incarnation of Darraun, even if he couldn't think of a reason to trust him.

Aunn interrupted his musing. "Cart? Ashara?" The changeling's gaze flicked between the two of them, who had been listening in silence. "Where do your destinies lie?"

Ashara looked at Cart, and Gaven thought he saw her hold her breath.

"I was made to be a soldier," Cart said, looking at the table, "and trained to fight for Aundair."

Gaven smiled. "I'd be proud to fight the Blasphemer beside you, Cart."

"I hadn't finished," the warforged said. "Like you, Gaven, I think it's time to make my own decisions. And also like you, I need to follow my . . . heart."

"What?"

Cart turned his head so his gaze met Ashara's, and a smile spread across her face until it reached her eyes. "I don't know what the future holds for me," the warforged said, "but I know my destiny lies with you."

Gaven and Darraun had laughed at Cart's insistence that he was many-layered, and Gaven suddenly felt ashamed of his laughter. It was all too easy to think of the warforged as an automaton, with his expressionless face and his body formed of wood, stone, and metal. Whatever process House Cannith had used to imbue Cart with life, though, had clearly given him more than animation, more even than the capacity for reasoning thought. Gaven had been impressed before with Cart's loyalty, even when it seemed misplaced. At the Dragon Forge, the warforged had proven he had a moral compass after all, when he tried to rescue Gaven from Kelas's clutches. Why should Gaven be surprised, then, to learn that Cart was in love?

Ashara cleared her throat. "We'll help you stop Jorlanna, Aunn. I know the workings of House Cannith."

"Excellent," Aunn said. "I appreciate the help."

"So it seems I'll be traveling alone," Gaven said. It would be the first time in many years, he realized. But only until he found Rienne.

"I'll get you papers," Aunn said. "We'll get you on the lightning rail to Thaliost, get you there about midday tomorrow, then a ship to Stormhome—"

"I want to fly there," Gaven said. "An airship."

"I can't get you another airship," Aunn said. "At least, not quickly."

"So I'll buy a fare. There must be airships going to Stormhome daily."

"You want to travel right under the nose of House Lyrandar? Do you think that's wise?"

"It's faster. I'll cut my hair, and without my mark no one will know me."

"Few Lyrandars ever saw your mark," Aunn said.

"But anyone who's looking for me now will be looking for the mark. It was rather distinctive." Gaven put his hand on the pouch that held the dragonshard, fighting a sudden urge to look at the lines of his mark tracing through the crystal.

"Very well," Aunn said. "I'll get you traveling papers. Do you have identification?"

"Not any more." The papers Senya had secured for him were still in Rav Magar, or destroyed.

"Then I'll get you identification papers as well. Who do you want to be?"

The question caught Gaven off-guard. Aunn might be accustomed to changing faces and identities at a moment's notice, but Gaven found it harder to think of being anyone else. He wanted to be himself. More than that, he wanted to be the Gaven he'd been thirty years earlier—before Dreadhold, before he gained his dragonmark, before he attained the power of the Storm Dragon. He wanted Rienne back, and his father, and his family name. He wanted a clear conscience, without the weight of the dead Paelions on his shoulders. But Aunn couldn't give him any of that.

"I don't know," Gaven said. "I suppose I just want to be able to travel without being harassed."

"Is that all? I can give you a noble title, a military rank, a government post. You name it."

"I . . . I don't know. I guess I don't care."

"Very well, I'll take care of it. How about a name?"

Senya had made a good case to use a given name that was similar to his own. "Keven," he said. It was close enough that if someone shouted that name, he'd turn to look, and if he accidentally blurted his real name, listeners would hear what they expected to hear.

"Good choice." Aunn scratched some notes on a piece of paper he'd produced from a belt pouch, and sat back in the bench. "I'll need a few hours at the Tower of Eyes. It's probably best if I go alone, now that it's daylight." He opened another pouch and pulled out a handful of coins. "You don't have any money, do you?"

Gaven shook his head, and Aunn slid a small pile of coins, mostly gold galifars with a few silver and copper coins in the mix, across the table to him. "Thank you," Gaven said.

"Thank Kelas," Aunn said with a grin. "He's become

uncharacteristically generous since his death." He turned to Cart. "Do you need any?"

"We're fine," Ashara said.

Aunn put his palms on the table. "Very well," he said. "Let's meet back here for dinner. In the meantime, everybody lie low, don't attract attention, don't get in trouble. Or start trouble. And Gaven—it's a nice day, and I don't think Fairhaven has too many more of those in store before winter. Don't ruin it."

Gaven laughed. "I'll try. No promises, though."

* * * * *

Jordhan lifted the airship gently up from its treetop mooring as Rienne and Kyaphar stood at the bulwarks, looking down on the gathered Eldeen defenders.

"The barbarians have moved quickly through the Towering Wood," Kyaphar said. "The people of those lands are so scattered that they couldn't mount an effective defense. Some fled, others made a valiant stand and perished. A few, I'm told, have joined the barbarians in order to fight against Aundair."

"Joined them?" Rienne said.

"Mostly shifter tribes, and a few of the Children of Winter. It appears that the Blasphemer accepted them under his banner just as he accepted all the warring Carrion Tribes."

"So this is the first time he's met concerted resistance."

"I believe so."

"So again, why here? What are you defending?"

"Look there." Kyaphar pointed over the bulwark and down.

Darkness draped the forest floor, but scattered bonfires spread rings of light here and there among the trees. Rienne couldn't see what Kyaphar was trying to show her.

"You see the cluster of three fires there?" he asked. "Imagine they're an arrowhead, pointing to your left. Now look for the shaft of the arrow."

Rienne squinted, and she saw it—a line of faerie fire, dim greenish-white light that stretched across the land. Trees blocked her view of it in places, but it continued for at least a hundred yards. "Now I see," she breathed.

"You begin to see," Kyaphar said. His pointing finger traced the line from the fiery arrowhead to a point just to their right. "Another line crosses it there, where those fires are. Do you see?"

The light of the bonfires hid the fey glow, so Rienne searched the area just above the fires, and quickly found the crossing line. This one was pale purple, and it crossed the first at a sharp angle then curved away from it before disappearing into the forest.

"What are they?" Rienne asked.

"Do you know the daelkyr?"

Rienne nodded as a chill ran down her spine. The gibbering hordes that had bubbled up from the ground at Starcrag Plain were the spawn of the daelkyr, kin to the hordes that ravaged the ancient goblin empire of Dhakaan thousands of years before.

"The armies of the daelkyr came through portals that led from the Realm of Madness to our world," Kyaphar said. "One of those portals was here."

"But it's sealed now. The druids—"

"The Gatekeepers were the first druids of the Eldeen Reaches, and they saved the world by sealing the daelkyr portals."

"And you fear that the Blasphemer will break the seal?"

"We know he will. Since leaving the Demon Wastes, he has led his horde from one seal to the next. So far he hasn't done irreparable harm, but the Depravation is spreading behind him. The influence of the daelkyr and their brood corrupts nature, twists it into unnatural forms."

"This seal is enormous," Rienne said. She could see the conclusion of Kyaphar's explanation. "If he breaks it, it will be much harder to repair."

"Exactly. The Reaches might take thousands of years to recover."

Rienne fell silent, memories of Starcrag Plain crowding her mind. What greater horrors might spill out of this portal if the Blasphemer managed to wrench it open?

Jordhan let the airship drift higher, clear of the tallest trees. The faerie fire of the Gatekeeper's seal was too faint to see at that height, but the bonfires gave Rienne some sense of its size—the glow and smoke of the fires suggested a circle large enough to encompass Fairhaven.

"Can he break the seal, do you think?" Rienne said.

"'When he speaks all doors are opened and all chains are broken, all law is repealed and chaos is unbound.'"

"What is that? The Prophecy?"

Kyaphar shrugged. "It is a prophecy, I suppose. It is what the spirits say about the Blasphemer."

"What else do they say? What do you know about him?"

"I know what I have seen." Kyaphar swept his arm out across the bulwark, drawing Rienne's eyes out to the west.

The farthest bonfires' smoke rose into a sky already choked with billowing gray clouds. The Blasphemer's horde was close, no more than a day away. Rienne saw fire and lightning flash in the midst of the smoke, like a storm out of nightmare, a harbinger of annihilation. The past few months, she suddenly felt, had been just one storm after another.

She imagined Gaven at the eye of that storm and tears sprang to her eyes. What had he become? His power at times seemed so wild, too strong to control. She thought again of the storm she'd seen over Lake Galifar, hurtling to bring Varna to ruin—had that been his power, broken free of his reins?

She clutched the airship's railing and tried to quiet her mind. The words of the Prophecy danced through her thoughts, the words she'd heard in her dream. She saw herself again on the battlefield by the river, saw the demonic face of the Blasphemer leering at her, and realized suddenly what she feared most about her dream.

Gaven wasn't there. She was going to face the Blasphemer alone. And she might never see Gaven again.

Part

II

Dragons fly before the Blasphemer's legions,
scouring the earth of his righteous foes.
Carnage rises in the wake of his passing,
purging all life from those who oppose him.
Vultures wheel where dragons flew,
picking the bones of the numberless dead.
But the Blasphemer's end lies in the void,
in the maelstrom that pulls him down to darkness.
On his lips are words of blasphemy,
the words of creation unspoken.
In his ears are the screams of his foes,
bringing delight to his heart.
When he speaks all doors are opened and
all chains are broken,
all law is repealed and chaos is unbound.

CHAPTER
16

Nara jabbed her knife at the meat on her plate, just to see the blood well up and drip onto the plate. Her conversation with Kelas had ruined her appetite.

"Does the meal not please you?" the steward asked, a perfect mask of solicitude.

"It's terrible." She pushed the plate away and stood. "I'm going downstairs."

"Yes, madam." He bowed, then scurried to open doors ahead of her as she stormed down to her sanctum.

Nara reached the last door and glared at the steward until he left. No one else could open this door, and no one but her was permitted beyond it.

The steward departed, careful not to let the antechamber door slam behind him, and Nara turned her will to the wards protecting her sanctum. She touched her fingers to the whorls and lines engraved in the burnished bronze door and whispered Draconic words. The doors groaned and swung open to admit her.

The chamber beyond had been carefully chiseled out of the bedrock beneath her Aundairian estate and every surface plated in bronze. At a word, a brazier at the far side of the room burst into flames, filling the room with warm golden light. Her eyes ranged over the Draconic characters etched into the bronze. The words covered every surface, from floor to ceiling, recording key verses of the Prophecy.

She allowed herself a smile, remembering Kelas's report that Gaven had scribed the Prophecy in the walls, floor, and ceiling of his cell in Dreadhold. He had remembered.

The thought of Kelas made her scowl again. Nara swept across the room and touched one of the bronze panels in the wall, and it sprang open. Reaching behind it, she withdrew a gleaming Siberys dragonshard, pale yellow with a coil of liquid gold in its heart. She brought the shard to the center of the room, where a circle of gold stood out from the bronze, untouched by the words of Prophecy, but surrounded by them. At a hissed command, the dragonshard floated in the air above the circle.

"Kelas," she whispered, closing her eyes and slowly inhaling the brazier's heady smoke. She began a low chant, and the coil in the heart of the dragonshard sprang to life.

Her eyes half-closed and unfocused, she watched the dragonshard's core twist and writhe. She allowed her mind to be drawn into snaking tunnels lined with the words of Prophecy, to meander through familiar passages that spoke of the Storm Dragon and the Time of the Dragon Above, the Time Between, and the rise of the Blasphemer. Soothing as they were in their familiarity, she forced herself back to the task at hand, speaking Kelas's name again.

She walked his path through the world's destiny, from his wretched birth, naked and mewling, to his rise through the ranks of the Royal Eyes under her tutelage. His was a feeble creek tumbling along beside the great rivers of her own path and that of the Storm Dragon. And then . . . then it tumbled into the void.

She gasped. "Why did I not see this before?"

So who had she spoken to that morning?

In a surge of fury, she dashed the dragonshard out of the air, sending it clattering into a corner of the room. The brazier's smoke billowed from her nose and mouth as rage seethed in her chest. She ran over every word of her conversation with the imposter, combing her memory for information.

A harsh laugh burst from her throat. She clenched her fist in the air and the brazier's flames were extinguished, and in the darkness she turned to the door and rested her burning cheek against the cool bronze. Kelas's death meant nothing—the Prophecy would continue to unfold just as she had planned.

* * * * *

He was Kelas again—at least, his face was Kelas's. In the Ruby Chalice, taking Kelas's face off had been like removing a bandage over an infected wound. It showed him just how much he'd become the man he despised, how much his newfound conscience had rotted in the short time since he'd come back to Fairhaven. Becoming Aunn—the proud, noble hero who strode out of the Demon Wastes just a few days before—had been inexplicably hard.

Before leaving the private room, he changed back into Kelas, and the ease of it bothered him. It was like changing into comfortable clothes after wearing stiff formal garb, and not just because the clothes he was wearing belonged to Kelas and fit his body better than they fit the taller Aunn. He was Kelas, and he was walking back to the Tower of Eyes. That meant immersing himself in the world of the Royal Eyes and getting his hands dirty. Kelas had no time for conscience or qualm—Kelas was the one who had beaten such things out of Aunn when he was a child.

Nausea churned his stomach as he walked, Kelas's short, quick strides cutting a path through the busy streets of the city. He hadn't slept enough at Kelas's house, just a fitful hour or two before Gaven's lightning blast had jolted him awake and into action. Just like the Dragon Forge—it was another mess in Gaven's wake that he would have to deal with, one way or another, if he wanted to keep up the appearance of being Kelas.

The Tower of Eyes was never crowded, but it was very different in midday than it had been in the dead of night. He strode past the soldiers at the door, flashing Kelas's identification papers, and found himself in a crowd of mostly familiar faces. He fought a surge of panic—how many of these people did Kelas know? What was his relationship with each of them?

He decided it didn't matter. When he was under pressure—which was most of the time, in Aunn's experience—Kelas was brusque with everyone. He fixed his eyes on the floor and strode up the stairs to Kelas's office, ignoring the few people who made an attempt to catch his eye or nod a greeting.

"Kelas!"

He couldn't ignore the voice of Thuel Racannoch, as much as he wanted to. He looked up and saw the Spy Master standing in the open door to his office at the end of the hall. Thuel jerked his head toward the inside of his office, waited an instant to make sure Aunn had seen, and disappeared back into the room.

The other people in the hall looked away as he passed them, and Aunn wondered what they were thinking. He knew that Kelas could be charming when he needed to be, but his sense was that Kelas was not particularly well liked by his colleagues. Were they embarrassed for him, or hoping that Thuel would humiliate him?

A fire crackled in a small fireplace, making the room a little too warm for Aunn's taste. Thuel stood, arms folded across his chest, beside an upholstered chair that faced the fire. Another chair stood at the third point of a perfect triangle, but Thuel did not invite him to sit.

"What in the Ten Seas are you up to, Kelas?" he said. "Close the damned door."

Aunn carefully pushed the door closed, making sure it latched, buying time to formulate an answer.

"Well?" Thuel demanded. "Why was Jorlanna d'Cannith looking for you at the crack of dawn?"

"Lady ir'Cannith," Aunn said.

"Don't correct me!" Thuel's face was red with rage. Aunn had never seen him like this. Thuel was a calm, cultured man with an appreciation for fine music and excellent wines.

"My sincere apologies."

"And answer the damned question. Why was she in a fury this morning? What have you done?"

No harm in telling the truth, Aunn decided. "I refused to turn over a House Cannith excoriate who is working with me."

"Working on what?"

Except that the truth led naturally to more questions he didn't know how to answer. More truth? "Keeping an eye on Jorlanna."

"You're spying on our queen's newly-appointed minister of artifice?"

"I am not convinced of her loyalty to the queen."

"Perhaps you should have considered that before you arranged for the queen to reward her loyalty in this way." Thuel was no longer blustering—his anger calmed into quietly seething rage. "Are you surprised that I know about that? You shouldn't be."

"I suppose not," Aunn said. He had said enough. It was time to hold his tongue and ride out the storm of Thuel's wrath.

"So does Jorlanna's visit mean that your operation has been compromised?"

"It appears that I no longer have eyes inside the Cannith enclave."

"Why did Jorlanna excoriate your agent?"

"I'm not certain," Aunn said. How much did Jorlanna know about what Ashara had done?

"You don't think Jorlanna knows that your agent was spying on her and reporting to you?"

"It's a little more complicated than that."

"If you say so." Thuel turned toward the fire and rested his hands on the back of a chair. "Does this Cannith agent of yours have any ties to the other Cannith barons?"

Aunn frowned. Jorlanna had used Ashara in all her negotiations with Kelas, suggesting that she had absolute confidence in Ashara's loyalty. But that confidence had clearly been misplaced. "I don't believe so," he said.

"Well, find out. You and Jorlanna and the queen might think you can ignore the Korth Edicts, but let me tell you, the last thing I want is to get Aundair caught in the middle of Cannith politics."

"Of course." Aunn tried to hit just the right mix of deference and arrogance—Thuel was right, of course, but he wasn't saying anything Kelas wouldn't know.

"I don't like this, Kelas." Thuel stared into the fire for a moment, then wheeled to face Aunn, his face red with rage again. "I don't like it a bit. First you cozy up to the baron and Arcanix, playing games behind my back to curry favor with the queen. Now you tell me you don't trust Jorlanna. Either you're making a mess of things, or you don't know how deep you're getting. Either way there's trouble."

"I know what I'm doing," Aunn said—his first outright lie.

Thuel stared at him, frowning, his eyes narrowed. Without shifting his gaze, he reached inside his jacket and pulled a small wooden case from a breast pocket. He glanced down at it as he opened it, and Aunn realized his danger—the case held a crystal lens, presumably enchanted with magic of seeing, a spell that would show Thuel Aunn's true face.

"Listen, Thuel—"

He was too late. Thuel raised the lens to one eye and closed the other, then stepped back in surprise.

"Start talking," Thuel said. He tossed the lens and its felt-lined case down on a chair and slid a rapier out of its sheath at his belt, pointing the tip at Aunn's chest. "Are you one of Kelas's changelings?"

Aunn sighed, cursing himself. He had never been so careless before. No one had ever seen his true face unless he chose to show it. He was slipping, and if he wasn't careful, he knew, that first mistake might prove fatal.

No more lies, he reminded himself, thinking of the man he'd been when he strode out of the Labyrinth.

He held his hands out from his body, away from his own sword. "I'm Aunn," he said. "Haunderk." He changed his face to match the name, which was how Thuel knew him. "Everything I just told you is true. You're right that Kelas was plotting behind your back with Baron Jorlanna and Arcanist Wheldren." He decided not to bring Nara's name into the discussion—not yet. "Kelas was plotting against the queen, and I believe Jorlanna still has her eyes on the throne."

"Kelas is dead, then?"

"Yes." He felt a surge of anger, remembering the dead body on the lip of the canyon.

"At your hand." It wasn't an accusation, but a statement of the obvious.

"Yes."

"And the world's well rid of him. The question is: What do I do with you?"

"Let me continue what I'm doing. Please."

"So far, you haven't convinced me that you have the situation in hand. After I had the baron screaming in my halls this morning, demanding Kelas's head, I have to wonder how useful it is to pretend Kelas is still alive."

"She'll talk to me. Kelas was part of her plot. No one else has her confidence."

"Then I should find another changeling to become Kelas— one who won't get caught."

"No one knows Kelas as well as I do." He wondered if that were true, remembering the other changeling he'd found in Kelas's house. An acrid taste like blood soured his mouth.

The point of Thuel's sword dipped slightly. "Show me," he said.

Aunn drew a steadying breath and changed again, hiding himself behind Kelas's arrogant smile. Thuel stepped closer, lowering his sword point to the floor. He peered at Aunn's face, scrutinizing the details, staring into his eyes. Aunn didn't meet his gaze, just as Kelas wouldn't. Thuel made a slow circle around him, examining every detail.

"Kelas always said you were the best," Thuel said from behind him.

He heard the rustle of Thuel's coat and a soft intake of breath, then Aunn twisted around and away as Thuel thrust his blade forward. The rapier's point cut through Aunn's coat and shirt to scrape across his back as he whirled to face Thuel. His hand fumbled at his belt where he usually kept a mace.

"Don't," he said. He reached for the hilt of his sword, at the other side of his belt, and yanked it from its sheath.

Thuel took a dueling stance—sword arm forward, body turned to the side, and his off hand thrust behind him. "I'm sorry, Haunderk, but I can't let you run free any longer." He stepped forward, and Aunn scurried back away from his blade. "Kelas should have kept you on a tighter leash."

Aunn gripped the short sword's hilt and held the blade clumsily in front of him. "I'm not his dog," he said.

"No, you're his changeling, which is worse. You know too much, and your assessment of your own importance is greatly inflated." Thuel punctuated his words with a quick lunge that Aunn beat aside.

Aunn felt rage wash through him like poison in his veins. He was trapped, he knew. Even if he managed to defeat Thuel—an expert swordsman—while he fumbled with an unfamiliar weapon, he would never get out of the Tower of Eyes alive. His only hope lay in convincing Thuel that his knowledge was valuable.

"I know more than you think," he said.

Thuel apparently wasn't convinced, as he launched a fierce barrage of jabs and cuts with his rapier. Aunn fended off as many as he could, but the blade nicked an arm and both legs. Stepping back with a smirk, Thuel said, "You talk too much."

"I can give you details of the conspiracy," Aunn said. "Help you save the queen."

"You don't know anything I don't already know, or have agents finding out." Thuel lunged again, and Aunn's awkward parry only managed to deflect the blade to scrape across his stomach instead of piercing it.

Aunn had no choice but to play his best card and hope it was enough. "So you know that Kelas was reporting to Nara?"

"Nara?"

It worked—Thuel went wide-eyed and lowered his guard. Swinging the short sword with both hands, Aunn knocked Thuel's rapier from his grip and sidestepped to plant a foot on the blade where it lay.

"I spoke to her yesterday, and I expect to hear from her again today. Do you have another agent in her confidence?"

Thuel's look of bewilderment and anger melted into laughter. "Well played, changeling. You're probably lying, but you've bought yourself a few more hours, at least. Why don't you put that sword away and have a seat? Then we'll talk this over."

Warily, Aunn crouched to pick up Thuel's sword. Gripping its hilt, he slid Kelas's sword back into the sheath at his belt. He kept the rapier pointed at Thuel as the Spy Master walked around one of the chairs by the fire and took a seat, then he settled himself in the other chair. He kept the rapier in his hand, resting its point on the floor.

"So how is my dear predecessor?" Thuel said. His tone was light, completely out of line with both the circumstances and the subject of the conversation. "You say you spoke to her yesterday?"

"Yes. She contacted me—well, she tried to contact Kelas." Aunn's heart was racing. As he ran through his conversation with Nara ir'Galanatyr the night before in his mind, he realized how little he actually knew, and how little he wanted to share with Thuel, particularly after their duel.

"How?"

"Kelas had a crystal orb, which I took after his death. She spoke through that."

"And you saw her? Her face appeared in the orb?"

"Yes."

"You're sure it was her?"

"She looked more or less as I remembered her. It hasn't been that long." It was a subtle jab, reminding Thuel that up until just a few years ago, the office they were sitting in had belonged to Nara. Aunn saw it register on Thuel's face, his brow crinkling in distaste.

"And why was she trying to contact Kelas?"

"She had been expecting word from him and she was concerned."

"And he didn't contact her because—"

Aunn finished his sentence. "Because he was dead, yes."

"So Kelas was acting on her command?"

"Definitely."

"Did she give you any new orders?"

Aunn thought for a moment—Nara had told him to lock Gaven away, to send Janna Tolden and Arcanist Wheldren back to clean up the Dragon Forge, and . . . "Just to move ahead with the next stage of the plan."

"What's that?"

"I don't know," Aunn admitted.

Thuel tapped his fingertips together and sighed. "Very well, Haunderk," he said. "Either you're not telling me everything you know, or you're even more useless to me than I first thought. So here's what's going to happen. You're going to back up, start at the beginning of the story, and tell me every scrap of information you can dredge up from your memory, whether you think it's useful or not, and we're going to put a stop to whatever Nara and Jorlanna are planning. If you fail to cooperate, you will die. Is that clear?"

Aunn fingered the hilt of Kelas's rapier, hesitating.

"You hold my rapier," Thuel said, noting the motion. "And you hold information that might prove important to the queen. That is all you hold. You are not in a position to negotiate, or to fight. You are in the seat of my power, and you do not want to learn the full extent of that power."

Aunn closed his eyes and changed. He felt Kelas's suspicious and scheming thoughts clutching at his mind even as Kelas's clothes pulled at his body, but he shed them and put on his new face, the proud visage he dared to call by his own name. He was a Royal Eye of Aundair, a servant of the queen—and so was Thuel. There was no reason to mistrust him.

He nodded, shifted his grip to the blade of Thuel's sword, and handed the weapon back to the Spy Master. "My life is in the service of the queen," he said. "Let's get started."

CHAPTER
17

O n a cedar bench near the Ruby Chalice, at the edge of the red brick plaza of Chalice Center, Gaven sat gazing into a clear blue sky. The plaza was thick with people—travelers spilling out from the lightning rail station or filing in to board the next coach bound for Passage or Thaliost, as well as visitors and residents enjoying all the trinkets and treats the busy marketplace had to offer. Few people went in or out of the mooring tower at the far end of the square, built to accommodate House Lyrandar's airships. Gaven hoped to see an airship arrive before it was time to reconvene for dinner, but in the meantime he was enjoying a rare taste of sunshine.

The sun gleamed on metalwork in the distant spires of the palace, baked the tile roofs of government buildings and upscale homes, cast his dark shadow onto the ground in front of him, and warmed the back of his neck and shoulders. He couldn't remember ever enjoying its touch so thoroughly. It filled him with an eager expectation and made him restless to start his journey.

He scratched at his neck and shoulder, the tender skin where his dragonmark had been. It was healing, he supposed— though his dragonmark had started as an itch. Would it return, blossoming back on his skin like a weed growing back from the remnant of its roots?

If it did, would there then be two Storm Dragons? He rested a hand on the pouch at his belt, felt the smooth hardness of the dragonshard inside, and a tingle of power responded to his touch. The itch on his shoulder flared into pain, and the light of the sun seemed to diminish a shade. He yanked his hand away and rubbed his thumb against his stinging fingertips, scowling.

His dragonmark hadn't made him the Storm Dragon of the Prophecy. It hadn't given him the power to defeat Vaskar in the Sky Caves and destroy the Soul Reaver beneath Starcrag Plain. But somehow that power seemed bound up in the lines of his mark, the lines that spelled out the myriad possibilities of his destiny and wrote him into the Prophecy. His mark said that he was the one who drove the Eye of Siberys through the Soul Reaver's black heart. He was the one who closed the bridge that linked starry Siberys to Khyber's depths. But his mark was scribed in a dragonshard, and it seemed as though someone else had done those things. And whatever the Prophecy said about deeds the Storm Dragon had not yet done—well, anyone might do those things. Anyone who held the dragonshard or managed to extract the mark from it and wear it on his own flesh.

Had that been part of Kelas's plan, or Nara's? Kelas had fulfilled part of the Prophecy by using his mark in the Dragon Forge, the verse Nara had cited: "His storm flies wild, unbound and pure in devastation."

For her part, Nara had seemed quite distressed at Aunn's lie, that Gaven had destroyed the shard. She clearly believed that the Storm Dragon had yet to fulfill some verses of the Prophecy, something related to the Blasphemer. Gaven rummaged in a different pouch and brought out the papers he'd brought from Kelas's office. At the top of the sheaf was the page Aunn had read from: "In the darkest night of the Dragon Below, storm and dragon are reunited, and they break together upon the legions of the Blasphemer."

Storm and dragon reunited—it sounded like a reference to the Storm Dragon, especially given the separation of Gaven's dragonmark from his skin. What did the Prophecy say about that separation? Did this verse mean that his mark would be restored to his skin before he confronted the Blasphemer? Which was the storm, and which the dragon? Or did the verse refer to something else entirely?

Gaven pulled his pouch open and peered at the dragon-shard inside. It glowed softly, the lines of his mark casting a reddish glow over the inside of the leather pouch. He traced the lines with his eyes, felt them tug at his mind, inviting him to lose himself in their winding paths again, but he resisted. "No," he whispered.

The Prophecy had spoken of the Storm Dragon crossing the bridge to the sky, becoming a god and leaving the world behind. So how could it account for all that had happened since he faced the Soul Reaver? He had bent the fluid verbs of the Draconic text to chart his own path, choose his own destiny. As far as the Prophecy was concerned, shouldn't he be finished? The Storm Dragon had done what he was put in the world to do. Perhaps he hadn't bent the Prophecy at all. Perhaps it accounted for his choice at Starcrag Plain, his trip to Argon-nessen, and everything else he had done. Was he just a player in a scripted drama after all?

Damn the Prophecy, he thought. You're not part of me any more—I'm not part of you. My destiny is what I choose.

The sun warmed the back of his neck again, and he looked around the plaza. An airship drifted slowly toward the mooring tower. Soon, he thought with a smile, he would be aboard such a ship, sailing for home. With any luck, soon he would find Rienne. Then the rest would fall into place, one way or another.

Gaven saw Cart and Ashara at the door of the Ruby Chalice. It was time. He stood, patted his pouch to make sure the dragonshard was safely in place, and walked slowly, enjoying the sunshine, to meet them.

* * * * *

"Gaven, look." Cart thrust a leather folder across the table at him. Gaven took it, noting the embossed cockatrice seal of House Sivis on the cover. Inside was a single sheet of vellum adorned with a sketchy portrait of Cart and a faintly glowing arcane mark.

"It says here you're twenty-three years old," Gaven said.

"That's right. The twenty-second of Zarantyr, in the Year of the Kingdom 976—that's when the creation forge gave me life."

"That makes you pretty old for a warforged, doesn't it?"

"I suppose it does. The first of us were made in 965, but there aren't too many of that generation still around."

That meant the first warforged were made only eight years before Gaven was locked in Dreadhold. He had known of them, of course. They were big news at the time. He remembered a parade in Fairhaven where a company of warforged soldiers marched at the back of the battalion, on their way to their first battle. But he had never seen one any closer than that, until Cart lifted him out of his cell.

"And you were born—or made, here? In Fairhaven?"

"I was. It was strange, when we arrived here from the Dragon Forge, right into the Cannith enclave, it was familiar to me. Even though I hadn't been inside in twenty-three years."

Gaven looked at the paper again. The sketch was fairly crude, but it gave careful attention to the mark on Cart's forehead, the signature of the Cannith creation forge. He compared it to the original, trying not to stare too hard at Cart's face. It was very accurate.

Gaven's head swam, and for just an instant he thought he saw meaning in the simple shape of the line, just an echo of Prophecy, some hint of destiny in the stamp of the forge. Then the feeling was gone, fading like a dream. He handed the folder back to Cart.

"Congratulations," he said. "This is the first time you've had papers?"

"Yes," Cart said. "Thank you."

Gaven was struck again at the warmth of Ashara's smile as she gazed at Cart. She was nearly bursting with pride.

"It's funny," Gaven said. "I've known you all these months now, and I never knew those simple facts about you. Where and when you were born, your service record in the war. I knew you were Haldren's aide, and that's all."

"You were born in Stormhome on the seventh of Rhaan in 939. Your father was Arnoth d'Lyrandar, born on the twenty-first of Rhaan in 902. Your mother was Sheira Laran, born on the nineteenth of Lharvion in 903, died on the eighteenth of Lharvion in 944, giving birth to your brother Thordren."

"How do you know all that?" Gaven said.

"We were briefed. Before we broke you and Haldren out of—"

"Best not to mention it," Ashara interjected, glancing around at the nearby tables.

Gaven followed her gaze. No one seemed to be listening, but he cursed himself. He hadn't been paying attention. Cart had just identified him as a Lyrandar to anyone who might have cared, and had as much as said he was an escaped prisoner. If anyone came looking, here were a number of witnesses who could attest they had seen him.

"Sorry," Cart said. "I keep doing that."

"It's all right," Gaven said. "So where is Aunn with my papers, I wonder?"

"Good question," Ashara said, frowning. "He's late."

"Again." Gaven looked around the room. "I hope he didn't run into more trouble."

"Gaven, listen." Cart leaned forward over the table and lowered his voice. "It took me a long time to come around and do what was right, and by then it was too late for me to stop . . . what they did to you. I'm sorry for that."

"You have more than made up for it since."

"No, I don't think I have. I'm not sure I ever will."

"I wouldn't have made it out of there without your help. Both of you," he added, smiling at Ashara. "You got me out of Phaine's tent to safety, and then you went back to the forge with me. You helped me recover what they took from me."

"Gaven," Ashara said, looking at the table, "I carry far more blame than Cart for what happened. I know it doesn't mean anything, but I'm sorry as well. The Dragon Forge, the whole thing was largely my work. Kelas might have operated it, but I built it—I took your mark from you."

Gaven didn't know how to answer. He had been furious at the forge, when they first met—only a few days ago, but it seemed so much longer. But, as Cart had pointed out then, she had saved his life, tending his wounds after their narrow escape from Phaine and the dragon-king. She seemed committed to goals that he and Cart shared, now, perhaps trying to make restitution for the wrongs she had done.

"Can you restore it?" he said.

Ashara's eyes met his and widened in surprise. "I . . . I don't know." She frowned and looked away. "I can imagine another device, like the Dragon Forge, built to undo its work."

"Powered by dragonfire?"

"I said I could imagine it. There's no way I could build it alone. But maybe a simpler item . . ." She trailed off, eyes closed in concentration.

"What?"

"It's possible I could mount the shard in a staff or rod, to let you access its power by holding the haft."

"I can access its power by just holding the shard."

"Oh. Of course. It is still your mark, clearly."

"So you're saying that such an item would let anybody access its power, not just me? The way the Dragon Forge let Kelas call that storm and send it to Varna?"

"Yes, although the Dragon Forge was designed to amplify the effect of the mark."

"This would just let anybody wield the power of the Siberys Mark of Storm," Gaven said. "Have you ever known a Siberys heir in your own House, Ashara? Is there a Siberys Mark of Making loose in the world right now?"

"There was, a few years ago. She came from Zorlan's branch of the family, in Karrnath, but she turned rogue."

"You mean she refused to let the House keep her on a short leash in Korth."

"Right."

"And what happened to her?"

"First, Jorlanna and Merrix tried to bring her under their thumbs. When that failed, all three branches of the House worked together to eliminate her."

"If there's one thing that can make the three Cannith barons work together . . ."

Ashara finished his thought. "It's the threat of a Siberys heir loose in the world."

"So imagine House Lyrandar's reaction if they even learn that this dragonshard exists. The Siberys Mark of Storm, not just scribed on the skin of an excoriate criminal like me, but loose, so anyone could pick it up and use it. In Jorlanna's hands, or Phaine's?"

"I hope you haven't been showing it around," Cart said.

"Of course n—"

A voice behind him cut Gaven off. "Good evening, Ashara."

Gaven turned in his seat. It was a human man, with the Mark of Making on one temple, right beside a shock of white hair. The man glanced at Gaven as he turned, then looked back at Ashara.

"Hello, Harkin." Ashara's voice was cold and flat, and her eyes went to Cart.

Harkin's eyes followed hers, and he grinned. "And . . . Barrow, wasn't it? Carrying the dying from the field of battle?"

"Cart," the warforged said.

"Of course. And I don't believe I've had the pleasure." He looked at Gaven.

Gaven stood, putting his eyes at a level with Harkin's. "I'm Keven," he said, taking Harkin's extended hand.

"Harkin d'Cannith." He gripped Gaven's hand firmly and gave it a cursory shake.

"Don't you mean ir'Cannith?" Ashara said. "We're a noble house now."

"Of course," Harkin said. His eyes ranged over Gaven's face and arms, and Gaven realized he was looking for a dragon-mark. "Are you part of the family, Keven?"

"No," Gaven said. He hadn't given any thought to a family

name for "Keven," but making himself a Cannith—either with a dragonmarked d' or a noble ir'—seemed like a bad idea.

"Yet I've seen you before, haven't I?"

Gaven frowned. He had the same feeling, a nagging sense of familiarity, but he couldn't find a specific memory. It seemed like something in a dream.

"Yes, I have," Harkin said. His eyes narrowed. "In the enclave, last night. With Ashara and ir'Darren—he called you their prisoner, and the warforged led you out like a helpless child. Jorlanna seemed particularly furious when I told her about you. I wonder why."

None of what Harkin said sounded familiar, but Gaven's pulse quickened. If Harkin recognized him as a prisoner, there could be trouble.

"Listen, Harkin," Ashara said. She stood and took Harkin's arm, lowering her voice to a whisper. "This isn't the time or place to explain all this. I'm willing to help you with the family matter we discussed, so the Baron certainly doesn't need to know anything about this meeting, right?"

"Of course." Harkin's smile did little to reassure Gaven. "I had hoped to discuss that family matter with you in more detail, but it can wait for your convenience."

"Tomorrow would be better," Ashara said. "Perhaps luncheon? Here? I'm told this place offers private meeting rooms, if you know the right person to ask."

"I would enjoy a private meeting with you," Harkin said.

Ashara dropped his arm and stepped back, putting Cart between her and Harkin and resting a hand on the warforged's shoulder. "The three of us will have a great deal to discuss, I'm sure," she said.

"Oh, you'll be joining us then, Keven?"

"No. I think Ashara was referring to Cart."

Harkin's eyes fell on Ashara's hand. "I see. Well, I'm sure that will be enlightening." He turned and extended a hand to Gaven again. "It was a pleasure to meet you, Keven, and I hope to see you again. Ashara, it's always lovely to see you, and I look forward to our meeting tomorrow. Good-bye."

He turned and strode away, weaving through the tables, stumbling once as he tripped over a cloak trailing off someone's chair. He did not look back.

"I'm sorry to say this, Ashara," Cart said, "but I don't like him very much."

Ashara sighed and sat back down beside Cart. "Neither do I. But he could be very useful to us and to Aunn."

Gaven dropped back in his chair as Harkin finally stormed out the door. "But where in the Ten Seas is Aunn?"

Chapter
18

Rienne stood near the front of the lines of Eldeen defenders as the Blasphemer's horde drew near. The Reachers were mostly farmers and herders drafted into the militia, handed spears and told to defend their lands, with only a few professional soldiers, officers scattered among the lines to enact a modicum of strategy. The front lines were reinforced with great Eldeen bears, giant animals wearing spiked plates of leather armor to reinforce their thick hides. Stretching to the tips of her toes, Rienne couldn't have reached a hand to the top of a bear's back. She found a position among the farmers and bears and waited in the darkness of night for the attack the Reachers were sure would come at dawn.

The dragons were the first to attack, and they didn't wait for dawn. They were dark shapes set against the bright Ring of Siberys, outlined by the light of twelve moons—most of them about the size of the bears, with great wings blotting out the light behind them. Rienne gripped Maelstrom's hilt as three of them winged toward her position, painfully reminded of sailing into Argonnessen with Gaven. A terrible roar from the bears greeted the dragons' approach, then screams joined the chorus as the dragons unleashed great gouts of fire and lightning, flashing in the darkness.

Rienne spun into motion, launching herself at the nearest dragon. Its scales gleamed gold in the light of the fiery wisps that surrounded it, exuded from its scales to sear the flesh of the two enormous bears that tried to hold it in their claws. Rienne reached it just as it sank its teeth into one bear's throat. She felt tiny beside the dragon and the great bear, all the more so when the dragon heaved the bear's corpse over her head to crash into the quivering soldiers behind her. The remaining bear stood on its hind legs to grapple the dragon, and she barely reached the bear's waist. Bony spurs jutted from its skull, spine, and shoulders, and its teeth were swords scrabbling against the dragon's plated scales.

But they were not Maelstrom, the legendary sword of Lhazaar. Rienne came in beneath the dragon's notice and sliced a long gash across its belly. Fire erupted from its mouth like a cry of pain, casting pale golden light around the dark battlefield. Maelstrom whirled around her and deflected the full force of the blast, spinning it into a cyclone of fire that surrounded her without burning her. Without Maelstrom's protection, the second bear slumped to the ground, smoke wafting up from its scorched fur and skin.

Lunging like a snake, the dragon snapped at her before the last of its fiery breath had dissipated. She couldn't bring Maelstrom around in time to block it, and the dragon's teeth slashed her shoulder. Rienne cried out in a reflex of pain, but she felt nothing. She brought Maelstrom up in an arc beneath the dragon's throat, but it pulled its head back just in time. Her blade cut through a scaled tendril that hung beneath its jaw, and the dragon hissed in irritation, shuffling back to open the distance between them.

The dragon's hiss became words—words she could understand, spoken in the Common tongue. "I know that blade," the dragon said.

"You won't be the first dragon Maelstrom has killed," Rienne said.

"Maelstrom," the dragon repeated. Rienne thought she saw fear in its eyes. "*Barak Radaam,* the Whirlwind Sword."

"That's right." Rienne swung Maelstrom around herself, then let herself spin behind it, whirling back into motion toward the dragon. She planted a foot on the fallen bear's shoulder, then launched herself up to drive her blade into the dragon's eye. Too late, the dragon lunged at her, snapping its teeth inches from her face, but its lunge drove Maelstrom deeper into its brain. It fell onto the smoldering corpse of the bear and lay still.

Dragons fly before the Blasphemer's legions—the Prophecy whispered in her mind, stilling the chaos of battle around her—*scouring the earth of his righteous foes.* Well, she thought, that's one less dragon to do any scouring.

Her shoulder stung with a distant echo of the pain she should have felt, easy enough to ignore. She looked for another dragon and spotted an eruption of lightning piercing the darkness nearby. A dragon stood facing another Eldeen bear, lightning cascading from its mouth as the bear swiped at it. A squad of soldiers stood in a clump that bristled with spears, like a hedgehog rolled into a ball and hoping the predator wouldn't bite. As Rienne ran toward them, a few of the soldiers, caught in the blast of lightning, fell to the ground, screaming out their last breaths.

The blue-scaled dragon lowered its snout, tipped with a jagged horn, and used the horn to toss the bear toward Rienne, but she vaulted over the mangled carcass without slowing her charge. Maelstrom seemed alive in her hand, her body just an extension of its will as it propelled her forward.

Why had the gold dragon known and feared Maelstrom? *Barak Radaam*—what part did the Whirlwind Sword have to play in the Prophecy? If her destiny was bound to her blade, what part would she play as the Prophecy unfolded?

She felt as though she were watching from some other place as Maelstrom launched her body into a whirlwind of death. Each cut and block happened without any act of conscious will on her part, perfectly timed and flawlessly executed. Could she so expertly carry out her destiny, whatever it was?

Lightning burst from the dragon's mouth again as Maelstrom cut a deep gash in its shoulder. She staggered backward, every nerve in her body screaming its agony. She drew a deep breath and felt the pain and all the energy of the lightning pool together, low in her chest. Maelstrom crackled and sparked as it cleaved through the dragon's skull, cutting it neatly in half.

Three dragons had flown toward her position—where was the third? She scanned the battlefield but didn't see it. To one side of her, the Reachers were arrayed in a ragged line, clutching spears and peering anxiously into the darkness. Opposite them, she heard a low roar, slowly growing in volume. As her pounding pulse quieted in her ears, the sound became clearer: hundreds of voices shouting, howling as the barbarians rushed into battle. The darkness of the forest cloaked them, but she felt the same fear that gripped the Reachers bite at the back of her mind. An unseen foe was far more fearsome. Perhaps that was why the Blasphemer had chosen to attack at night.

She settled into a waiting stance and glanced to her sides. A sergeant had placed one of the great bears to her left and another to her right, widely spaced but clearly intended as a first line of defense against the onrushing barbarians. Soldiers clutched their spears and clustered around the bears and around her, as if they were seeking shelter from an onrushing storm. She smiled to herself—in the Reachers' minds, apparently, she was equivalent to one of their bears.

She thought of Gaven, imagined telling him about the three dragons she had slain and how the Reachers made her into a bear. For a moment she saw him as she had in her dream, the strange vulture-Gaven hopping on the airship deck. She lifted her eyes to look for Jordhan's airship, but instead she found the third dragon, just as it joined a circle of wyrms winging around the sky above the barbarian forces. She tried to count them, but they ducked and weaved around each other, and the moonlight gleaming on their scales wasn't enough for her to distinguish them from each other. She guessed at seven.

As she watched, one by one, the dragons dove from the sky. She braced herself for a renewed assault, but the dragons weren't diving at the Eldeen defenders. They disappeared into the dark forest. A moment later, flames erupted in the darkness. The barbarians' yell grew into a howl, a primal scream that made even the Eldeen bears shift backward nervously, and then Rienne saw them, silhouetted against a curtain of fire behind them.

The dragons had ignited the forest behind the Blasphemer's horde, cutting off any possibility of retreat.

* * * * *

The earth groaned in protest and pain as the dragonfire coursed over it. Kathrik Mel crouched down and placed his palm on the ground. The grass died at his touch, and the earth's outcry grew louder in his ears. He lifted his hand, looked at his fingers, and rubbed away flecks of gray ash from the tips. He drew a slow breath, and the mingled aromas of autumn and smoke turned to rot in his nostrils. He stood, stretched his arms wide, and shouted.

"Forward! Trample their bones into the ground! For Kathrik Mel!"

His warriors took up the cry: "Kathrik Mel! Kathrik Mel!"

He felt the heat of the dragonfire at his back and smiled. The warriors before him were too slow. He spoke a word, and fire leaped around him to lash at their backs, impelling them forward. For a moment he was bathed in fire, and he cackled.

As he strode behind his onrushing horde, he listened to the cries of the earth, searching for the painful harmonies of the Gatekeepers' seal and the stifled chorus behind it. Softly, he began to hum his part of that entropic chorus, a song of madness that would unmake the seal—the song that would soon unmake the world.

* * * * *

Lit by the fire behind them and roaring what she guessed was the proper name of their leader, the barbarians charged into Rienne's whirling storm. They were tall, even the women, towering head and broad shoulders above her—which made it easier for her to move them around, crashing them into each other or throwing them sprawling to the ground where Maelstrom could finish them easily. Black hair fell in matted tangles over their shoulders. The men wore old scars instead of beards, and the women too were disfigured by scars that gave them an almost demonic appearance. Their armor was leather or hide, and most of them used heavy, two-handed maces or axes that left them off-balance after a clumsy but powerful swing.

She could have closed her eyes—she was not seeing, but feeling the rhythm of their approach and their attacks. She dodged and ducked almost effortlessly, and Maelstrom was a blur of steel and blood in the air around her. The barbarian wave crashed upon her and broke against solid rock, unable to move her.

But it could flow around her. She glanced to one side as a great bear roared in pain, and she saw it go down under the press of warriors. Other barbarians were already sweeping over the lines of militia behind her, pushing them back toward the ancient druids' seal. Rienne could hold her ground, perhaps indefinitely, but she would soon be a lone island in a stormy sea, and her defiance would mean nothing. She began a slow retreat, letting the tide carry her closer to the other defenders even as she continued her deadly dance.

She began to see some variety among the onrushing barbarians. She had heard that the Blasphemer united many disparate tribes to form his horde, and she started noticing differences that might be tribal. Some wore the black feathers of carrion birds and proudly bore the sores and scars of plague on their skin. Others wore patches of scaled black hide on their shoulders and thighs, and bone needles pierced through the skin of their cheeks and bare chests. A few had taken the scarification of their faces to an extreme, actually stripping away skin and muscle to expose their teeth in a hideous grin. She even saw a small pack of shifters, presumably traitors from the Eldeen Reaches, since she had never heard of shifters among the Carrion Tribes before.

No matter how many she killed, more kept rushing at her, around her, past her. If they recognized her as a serious threat, they didn't show it—wave after wave of barbarians crashed around her, undaunted by the corpses around her and the dead she left in her wake. They never spoke, except to chant their leader's name with their last living breaths. As more and more of them came at her and died at her feet, a weight descended on her heart. These barbarians—these people were weapons in the warlord's hands, their wills utterly subsumed to his. Could they have stopped fighting if they wanted to? Could they have avoided an obviously superior foe? Were they capable of giving a thought to self-preservation, or were they just animals herded to the slaughter? Rienne was the instrument of their slaughter, and she did not relish the role.

She also, with some shock, realized that she was getting tired. How long had she been fighting? The first dragon, the gold one, had come in the darkness of night, what seemed like hours ago. A hint of morning tinged the sky—had she been fighting all night? Her shoulder burned where the gold dragon's teeth had torn her flesh, and a hundred other cuts and bruises gnawed at the distant ends of her nerves. The barbarians rarely landed a blow on her, but fatigue alone was wearing her down.

Just as that realization settled upon her, two dragons fell from the sky. Barbarians scattered away from her as the dragons—one scaled in blood red, one plated in iron—settled to the ground on either side of her.

"The Blasphemer wants to know," the red one said in a whispering hiss, "why you aren't dead yet."

"The Blasphemer wants you dead," the iron dragon added, rumbling and loud.

Rienne tried to steady herself, calm her pounding heart and relax the muscles clenched in her shoulder and legs. "Then he'll have to kill me himself," she said.

CHAPTER
19

"Why all the interest in the Lyrandar?" Thuel demanded.

"I always knew Kelas had an interest in the Prophecy of the Dragons," Aunn said. "It seems that was an interest he shared with Nala."

"And he's supposed to play some part in this prophecy?"

"It makes me dizzy." Aunn stared into the fire in Thuel's office. "Kelas sent me to help get Gaven and Haldren out of Dreadhold. As far as Haldren was concerned, Gaven was important only because he knew so much about the Prophecy. He thought Gaven would help him and Vaskar achieve their goals—get the Eye of Siberys, find the Sky Caves of Thieren Kor, and turn Vaskar into the Storm Dragon. That's not what happened, and somehow I think that's never what Kelas meant to happen. Or Nara."

"What did they intend to happen?"

"I think they always knew that Gaven would become the Storm Dragon."

"And he did."

"Yes."

Thuel folded his arms and looked intently at Aunn. "And what does that mean, exactly?"

Aunn rubbed his temples. He had been talking with Thuel for hours, and he was exhausted. "I'm not entirely sure. I know he came back from the Sky Caves much more powerful than he was before—beyond what I've read about other Siberys heirs of House Lyrandar. He defeated the Soul Reaver at Starcrag Plain, the leader of all the monsters that spilled from the earth there. Then he went to Argonnessen, and ended up at the Dragon

Forge, and Kelas stripped his mark from him. I'm afraid I don't know much more than that."

"And Nara wants him for some kind of reunion."

"That's what she said."

"And what does he want to do? What's he doing right now?"

Aunn looked to the window and saw the dark evening sky. He and Thuel had talked long past the time he was supposed to meet Gaven and the others back at the Ruby Chalice. He shot to his feet.

"What's the matter?" Thuel said.

"I was supposed to meet him for dinner, along with Ashara and Cart. I came here to get him some traveling papers."

"Sit down. We're not finished here."

Aunn looked at Thuel, keenly aware of the threat in his voice. He sank back in his chair, wondering what Gaven was doing.

"Where's he planning to travel?"

"He wants to go to Stormhome."

Thuel's eyes went wide. "An excoriate and a fugitive? To Stormhome? Why?"

"He and Rienne were separated in Argonnessen. He doesn't know where she is, and he's desperate to find her."

"Why Stormhome?"

"They had magic tokens to transport them back to Stormhome. If she made it back from Argonnessen, she probably went there."

"Interesting. I had a report that she was held briefly in a jail in Thaliost last week."

"What? Really?"

"Yes. Traveling without papers, suspicion of stowing away on a Lyrandar galleon. And of course assisting a fugitive."

"But she was only held briefly?"

Thuel snorted. "House Kundarak and House Lyrandar declined to press charges, and her fines were paid. Very heavy fines were paid."

"Who paid them?"

"A Lyrandar pilot, if I remember correctly."

"Is that all? Do you know anything more? Where they might be now?"

"I haven't received any further word. However, before you get too excited, let me remind you that what Gaven does at this point is a matter of national security. He doesn't have much choice in the matter, and I don't think that having him travel to Thaliost or Stormhome or anywhere else at this moment is in anyone's best interest."

Fear clutched at Aunn's stomach. "What do you intend to do with him?"

"Well, he needs to be off the streets, clearly. He's a danger. We can't have him falling into Nara's hands just yet, or Jorlanna's. Or anyone else's, for that matter."

"He can take care of himself."

"Clearly. Which makes him that much more of a threat." Thuel leaned forward. "Look. I can see that you think of Gaven as a friend. But you can't let friendship interfere with your duty. You know that. I know Kelas taught you."

Aunn stared into the fire again. Evidently Thuel saw more emotion on his face than he was used to showing, but he couldn't bring himself to care. Thuel was right—he did think of Gaven as a friend, perhaps his only friend. Thuel said them much more kindly, but the words were right from Kelas's mouth: *You have no friends. If you love, if you care about anything, you will suffer. You will fail!*

What about Aundair? What about the queen and the crown? He was supposed to love his country and queen, wasn't he? That was why he was here, telling Thuel everything he knew—already, perhaps, betraying his friends.

Yes, that was what Kelas was saying: love queen and country, and everything else comes after. And perhaps in this one thing he was right, Aunn thought. If Gaven had to suffer in order to prevent Jorlanna and Nara from overthrowing Aurala and seizing the crown, shouldn't he be willing to let that happen? Weren't the crown and the people of Aundair—hundreds of thousands of people—more important than Gaven or the bond of friendship they shared?

"Yes," he said at last, a heaviness settling in his chest. "I do know that."

"Good."

"Shall I bring him in?"

"I think not. Tell me where to find him, and I'll send a team. I'm not going to take any chances."

"Don't be a fool," Aunn said. He ignored Thuel's glare and pressed on. "Three dragonmarked houses haven't been able to bring him back to Dreadhold yet. You think three of your spies can capture him where Sentinel Marshals, the Ghorad'din, and House Thuranni's best assassins have failed?"

"Yes, I do," Thuel said, his voice cool. "As I understand it, House Kundarak would have returned him to Dreadhold by now if their ranks hadn't been infiltrated by a spy who helped him escape. And if what you tell me is true, Kelas had him in his grip as well. I suggest you put aside your friendship and your pride and do your damned job." Thuel stood and folded his arms. "Where can we find Gaven?"

"I don't know. I was going to meet him at the Ruby Chalice for dinner, and give him papers, which I haven't had time to make up."

"You needn't worry about that now."

"No, I didn't think so."

"Who is he expecting to see? Does he know what you are?"

"Yes, he knows I'm a changeling. I've been wearing Kelas's face, but he knows this one."

"And how was he planning to reach Stormhome?"

"He hoped to get on a Lyrandar airship in the morning."

"Very good. This interview is concluded. We will resume in the morning, early. And you will remain in this tower until that time."

Aunn got slowly to his feet. "Am I a prisoner, then?"

"Not yet. But if you attempt to leave, I will imprison you. Good night."

Thuel let Aunn make his own way out of his office, but he knew the Spy Master was already issuing orders—his every move within the Tower of Eyes would be watched, and if he tried to leave, he would be stopped. There was no denying it, he was a prisoner. He had some freedom, for now, but it was a precarious and very limited freedom.

What have I done? he thought. I'm sorry, Gaven.

* * * * *

"I don't think he's coming," Ashara said.

Cart leaned forward on the table. "Something must have happened to him."

"So what do we do?" Gaven said. "Head back to the Tower of Eyes and try to rescue him?"

"I think that would be foolish," Cart said. "If he's been discovered, we have no friends there."

"Thunder!" Gaven leaned back in his chair and stared at the ceiling. "Nothing's ever simple, is it?"

"No, it never is," Ashara said.

"I have no idea how we would go about finding him," Gaven said. "In the past, he's always found me. How do you find a Royal Eye, or someone who's been captured by the Royal Eyes? Especially when he's a changeling?"

"Shh." Ashara glanced around at the empty tables surrounding them. They had waited in the Ruby Chalice for hours, and the crowd of dinner patrons had long since departed, leaving them alone with the few serious drinkers getting an early start on their late-night revels.

"Maybe we just have to trust that he'll find us again," Cart said. "He has proven himself resourceful enough in the past."

"But what do we do in the meantime?"

Cart shrugged. "Carry on with what we were doing, I suppose."

"How can I do that? Without papers, I can't get to Storm-home. I can't even get a room to sleep in tonight."

"We can get you a room, at least," Ashara said. "Perhaps by morning Aunn will reappear."

"All right, then. Let's go." Gaven pushed his chair back from the table and stood. His body ached, and the thought of spending a full night resting in a real bed suddenly sounded very appealing, even if it meant a sleep haunted by dreams.

Ashara and Cart followed him out of the Ruby Chalice and into the plaza outside. The night air was cold, promising a bitter winter, but the sky was bright. The Ring of Siberys stretched across the southern sky like a glowing golden cloud. The light of half a dozen moons and a thousand brilliant stars washed the plaza in silver light. All around the square, lovers strolled arm in arm, groups of revelers stumbled to their next amusement, and a few travelers emerged from late-arriving Orien coaches.

Gaven's eyes kept drifting to the airship he'd seen earlier, now moored at the tower that defined one end of Chalice Center. Crew members were still moving around on the deck, loading or unloading cargo, checking her for wear. As he looked, a group of three travelers, probably the last passengers to disembark, emerged from the base of the tower. Gaven stopped, his heart suddenly racing. The one in the middle—a woman in flowing silk, a sword stuck through a sash at her waist, long black hair draped over her shoulders—it was Rienne.

* * * * *

If he was to be confined to the Tower of Eyes, Aunn decided to make the best of it. Wearing Kelas's face again, he sat in his old master's study and started reading. A small key in Kelas's pouch opened the drawers in the desk, where he found a few files—precious little, considering Kelas's position and the number of projects he'd been involved in. Either Kelas had more files elsewhere—in a secure vault in the tower, or perhaps in his home—or he'd kept most of his secrets in his mind. Unfortunately for Aunn, the latter seemed more likely.

He found almost nothing written in Kelas's hand—only letters and documents from agents and other contacts, some of them in code. The papers seemed to be organized by author, wrapped in packets of thin leather and bound with string to keep letters from the same agent grouped together. He opened each one, checking the authors of the documents inside. He made a mental list of names to watch for: Nara, of course. Jorlanna, Ashara, or Wheldren. Any of the other conspirators Cart and Ashara had mentioned—Bromas ir'Lain, Kharos Olan, Janna Tolden, or the half-orc from Droaam. Arnoth d'Lyrandar, for Gaven's sake. Or a mysterious, nameless changeling, but he didn't really expect to find anything from the spy he'd faced in Kelas's house, any more than he thought to find a letter or report he'd written himself. Kelas and his agents were smarter than that.

His vision began to blur as he stared at a coded message—a hundred blocks of five letters each, each letter representing one of five different letters depending on its position in the block—and tried to puzzle out its sender and its contents. He leaned back, rubbed his eyes, and yawned. When he looked back at his desk, the crystal orb was glowing again.

Nara. She had promised to contact him again tonight, but in the frantic activity of the day he'd utterly forgotten. He had nothing he could tell her—should he ignore the glowing orb? She would be furious. Best to stumble through another conversation with her. He reached for the crystal, and as soon as his fingers touched the surface the light diminished and Nara's face appeared in its heart.

"Good evening, Kelas," she said. "I have exciting news."

CHAPTER
20

R ienne!" Gaven ran across the square. She turned and
searched the square for the source of the call, then a
smile spread across her face. She started away from her
companions—two women he didn't recognize—and then she
was in his arms, weeping into his chest.

He lifted his face from Rienne's hair—something was
wrong—the smell of her hair, the feel of her in his arms. Her
companions moved closer, circling to either side. They were
armored, and when they realized he'd seen them they sprang at
him. He tried to push Rienne away, but she clung to him.

She had betrayed him again. The thought was cold steel in
his heart.

"No!" he cried. His voice was thunder, and it threw Rienne
away from him. Her two companions, each clutching a jagged
blade, staggered away from the blast, but they recovered
quickly and lunged at him, both blades darting at him.

He felt the dragonshard in its pouch at his side, his mark
coiled inside it like a sleeping dragon—and he felt the wyrm
awaken in fury. It was still a part of him—its rage coursed
through his veins and out through his hands, joining him
to the two assassins in a bolt of lightning that stretched
across the plaza. His enemies were on their knees, smoke
wafting from their clothes and hair as they struggled to stand,
and Rienne lay on the ground before him, tears streaking her
horrorstruck face.

"Gaven, no," she sobbed.

How could she have betrayed him again? Some part of
Gaven's mind screamed at him to stop and think, to make sense

of what was happening, but the storm churned in his chest and surged in his veins, a fury that wouldn't be contained.

Gaven raised his arms and looked up into the storm-darkened sky. Thunder rumbled, so close and loud that the ground shook. Then everything was brilliant white, and a deafening crack split the air. When his vision cleared, the two attackers lay blackened and still on the ground. Rienne was scrambling to her feet, no longer pleading but trying desperately to flee.

Gaven heard Cart's heavy footsteps running toward him, and Ashara calling his name. He didn't turn. He pulled his sword from its sheath on his back and walked toward Rienne. Lightning danced along the edges of the blade and sparked from the point.

Rienne looked over her shoulder as she found her feet, eyes and mouth wide with terror. Her face was badly burned, almost unrecognizable—and then Gaven realized it wasn't her face.

"Gaven!" Cart caught up to him and grabbed his arm, pulling him to a stop.

Gaven watched Rienne run away, her streaming dark hair becoming short and blond, her lithe body growing wider, more masculine. The changeling—she'd been a changeling, of course—stripped off some of the distinctive red silks as he ran, then he disappeared at the edge of Chalice Center.

"Aunn?" he murmured.

"Gaven, we have to get out of here." Cart's voice was loud and urgent at his ear, and his grip was painfully tight. "A dozen witnesses just watched you kill two people with a freak storm out of nowhere."

"What?" Gaven heard the words, but he couldn't quite understand them. They didn't make sense. Nothing made sense. He looked around, stared at the bodies on the ground, then gazed in the direction the changeling had run.

A changeling—she wasn't Rienne at all. Rienne hadn't betrayed him again. Relief washed through him, mingled with horror at what he might have done to Rienne if it had been her.

He sagged in Cart's grip, stunned at the destruction he had wrought so quickly, caught up in his rage.

"Soldiers or Sentinel Marshals will be here any second, Gaven," Ashara said, seizing his other arm and helping to steady him on his feet. "Run!"

Together they pulled him into a stumbling run between them, and they made their way into the nearest alley, behind the mooring tower.

"Now what?" Ashara said, looking to Cart. The warforged looked around, uncertain.

One feeling surged to clarity in Gaven's jumble of thoughts—he needed to be alone. "We should split up," he said. "You two shouldn't have let yourselves be seen with me."

Ashara glared at him. "We were helping you," she said.

"Which is a crime you committed in public view. We were going to part ways anyway. You two lie low in the city someplace. I'll get out of here—there's nothing here for me anyway."

"What about Aunn and your papers?" Cart said.

"A changeling just tried to kill me. I'm not dealing with Aunn anymore."

"You think that was him?"

"I . . . probably not. He mentioned facing a different changeling in Kelas's house. Maybe it was that one. I don't know—how many changelings are there in this city?"

"Aunn's your best hope for getting papers," Ashara said. "Shouldn't you—"

"I'll find a way. Thank you for your help. Now go."

"Gaven," Cart said, extending a hand, "I hope you find what you're looking for."

Gaven clasped his hand. "Thanks, Cart. I wish you the best—both of you." He clapped Cart's shoulder. "Now get out of here. I'll draw their attention." He turned back toward the plaza. A soldier's voice was barking orders.

"Gaven," Ashara said.

"Will you two go?" He shot a glance over his shoulder. Cart had started in the opposite direction, but Ashara hadn't moved. "What is it?"

"I'm sorry," Ashara said. "For my part in all this."

"Go!" Gaven chose a path that would take him near the plaza again but not quite into it, and he started to run. He didn't look back.

* * * * *

Running with Ashara was awkward, Cart realized. If he ran, he quickly left her behind—her short legs didn't move fast enough to keep pace with him. If he walked, even his fastest stride left him lagging behind her. So he fell into a sort of trot, half walking and half running, alternately surging ahead and falling back while she maintained a steady pace, as fast as her legs could carry her, away from Chalice Center and toward . . . he wasn't sure.

"Where are we going?" he asked.

She had trouble speaking as she ran, with her body demanding more air, drawing it in and expelling it in great gasps that interfered with her voice.

"Following you," she managed to say.

"Oh. I thought I was following you." Cart slowed, trying to get his bearings. He hadn't been paying attention to their route—

He stopped dead as the buildings fell away, and he saw again the horrible dreamscape Havrakhad had shown him. Gaven's storm overhead trailed streams of purple and red fire down to the earth, where they swirled into cyclones of terror among shadowy crowds. In contrast to the silent lightning of the night before, thunder rumbled in the storm, accompanying flashes of yellow, orange, and blue. It was unreal, and yet somehow more real than the normal world—it seemed heavy with meaning, with significance. Cart's every sense was on edge, tingling at the edge of pain.

Cart saw barbarian hordes, natural catastrophes and horrible crimes enacted in endless repetition. Then he noticed that the worst horrors seemed to ripple outward from a single point, waves of disturbance in the collective soul of the city. At the center of that nightmare, he saw again the monstrous form Havrakhad had identified as a quori.

In its general form, it was almost like a snake or an enormous, reddish-pink worm. Its long body trailed into the mists of nightmare behind it. The vaguest hint of a humanlike chest, armored in black chitin plates, loomed above the mists. Two thick arms ending in pincerlike claws darted among the screaming mob around it, selecting prey from the tortured dreams of the city's people. Numerous smaller arms jutted from its flanks, some ending in fleshy hands, others in chitinous claws. Its shoulders were crowned with a bulbous mass rather than a head, studded with a dozen eyes, each one a different color and no two looking in the same direction.

Except that as Cart stared at it in horror, one of its eyes fixed on him, and one by one the others joined it until the thing's entire fractured gaze focused on him.

You can see me. Its voice manifested in Cart's mind as the buzzing of a thousand insects in imperfect unison. *Why can you see me?*

Cart cast his eyes around in a panic, looking in vain for Ashara. The quori was advancing on him, slithering and squirming among throngs of souls—some screaming in terror, some staring in shock, some cowering on the ground and covering their heads, and a few, most frightening of all, just observing without a hint of fear.

Why can you see me? the quori repeated. Its voice became the hissing of a hundred snakes, a whispered threat of poison and death.

Cart reached for his axe, but it was not at his belt. He looked down at his body and saw not armored plates protecting fibrous cords, but skin—delicate, light brown skin stretched over muscles and organs, held up by a framework of bones. He was naked and defenseless as the quori surged forward.

A small, soft hand clutched his arm, and he wheeled to see Ashara, concern but not panic written on her face. For a moment, his skin tingled with fire at her touch, and he wanted to take her in his arms, heedless of the danger. But metal plates interposed between his skin and hers, spreading from her touch to cover his body again, to encase him in his armored shell.

"What's wrong?" Ashara said.

Close your eyes, whispered the voice in Cart's mind, a rustle of feathers. Pain stabbed through the back of his head, where it met his neck, and his vision blurred for a moment.

Cart turned, but the quori was gone. The storm—Gaven's storm—still rumbled overhead, but its lurid colors and deadly fire were gone. The buildings of Fairhaven stood where they always had, as their inhabitants slept their troubled sleep, feeding the quori with their nightmares.

"Cart, what is it?" Ashara's touch was still soft and warm.

"The turning of the age draws near," Cart said. "Come on."

* * * * *

At first Gaven felt the wind on his face, just the resistance of still air against his sudden movement. Then the wind stirred around his feet as they hit the flagstones, and then it blew at his back, carrying him along through the streets and alleys. Thunder rumbled in the sky, lightning flashed around him, and a torrent of rain began to fall.

I am still the storm, he thought. They stripped it from my skin, but it's still mine.

He heard shouts behind him, but a rumble of thunder drowned out the words. He didn't know where he was going— he'd never known Fairhaven as well as Stormhome, and it had changed far more during the years he spent in Dreadhold than his old home had. His first thought was simply to draw them away from Cart and Ashara, and it seemed he had accomplished that much. Beyond that—well, he needed a plan, and it was hard to come up with one while running at top speed in the midst of a raging storm.

It was all too easy to get lost in the storm. The wind that carried him so he barely touched the ground, the rain cascading around him, the lightning that flashed above—he felt each gust of wind and rumble of thunder in the depths of his body, like the beating of his heart and the flexing of his muscles as he ran. He felt like a thunderhead surging across a lake. . . .

He saw Varna lying in ruins beneath him, laid waste by the fury of his storm. He saw the two would-be assassins lying charred and dead in Chalice Center, and the shattered glass of Kelas's window cutting into his knees. He saw the wreckage of the Dragon Forge, torn apart by the hurricane of his wrath, in retribution for what it had done to him.

"I hope you find what you're looking for," Cart had said as they parted.

What am I looking for? he wondered.

He'd been determined to find Rienne, but perhaps he wasn't ready to find her. For a moment he'd held her close to his heart, and in the next instant he was caught in the fury of the storm. If that had been Rienne, he might have killed her. He had become a force of destruction, wild as the storm— particularly, it seemed, since the Dragon Forge had stripped his mark from his skin. He couldn't risk hurting her.

In his mind, he was racing on the wind through the streets and alleys of Stormhome, Rienne at his side, leaving Bordan and Ossa's team of dwarves behind them. Then he was running, free for the first time in decades, through the Aerenal jungle, racing to the Eye of Siberys.

In Aerenal, Senya's ancestor, long dead but enshrined in unlife in the City of the Dead, had recognized him—or, rather, the dragon whose memories were stored in his mind—from a past visit, some four or five centuries before he returned with Senya and Haldren. "Twice you have come to me now," she had said. "The third time, you will finally find what you seek."

A plan formed in his mind, as much raging storm as conscious thought, and he chose a path through the streets of the city.

CHAPTER
21

"G ood evening," Aunn said. He tried to find just enough
warmth for his voice, with a hint of excitement about
the news Nara had promised, without revealing any
hint of his fear. "What is it?"

"I'll tell you in a moment." Nara's smile, tiny and distorted
in the glass orb, struck him as odd. There was too much of the
predator in it, and Aunn couldn't be sure whether Aurala was
the prey or he was. "You first."

Behind a bemused smile, Aunn tried desperately to think.
He had to trust that the secret of his identity was safe with
Thuel—they had agreed that he would continue playing
Kelas's role in the unfolding drama. But he couldn't count
on any other secrets. Anything that anyone knew—anyone
besides himself and Thuel—Nara could find out.

"It's been an interesting day," he said, and sighed. Nara gave
the slightest nod, and Aunn knew he was right—she already
knew much of what had made it interesting.

"Gaven emerged from his stupor," he said, "and escaped
my control."

He braced himself. If this was a surprise to Nara, she would
almost certainly erupt in anger.

"So I have heard," she said.

Aunn tried not to let his relief show, even as he wondered
who her source was. "Thuel has involved himself in the matter,
and sent a team of agents to capture him this evening. I haven't
been told yet whether they were successful."

"They were not."

Who could have told her that before anyone told him?

One of the agents Thuel sent?

"That's unfortunate." Aunn measured his response, just as Kelas would have done. Nara had started the conversation on a cheerful tone—she wasn't as angry as circumstances seemed to warrant, so there must have been something important she hadn't told him yet. "What happened?"

"Gaven killed two of the three agents, right in the middle of Chalice Center. In full view of a dozen witnesses. I'm surprised you haven't heard yet."

"As I said, Thuel has involved himself. He's watching me very closely, and evidently not telling me anything. It will pass. It always does." That was fair—Kelas had been through similar periods before, when Thuel decided in a fit of pique or jealousy to involve himself more closely in his underling's affairs. It never lasted long.

"Don't you want to know how I know all this?" Nara said. She was smiling, and Aunn found it unsettling.

"I've never been naive enough to assume I was your only contact within the Royal Eyes."

"Oh, Kelas, are you jealous?"

What was she playing at?

"Of course not." Aunn let some of his irritation filter into his voice. "But I am tired of this game. Why don't you just tell me your 'exciting news' and we can get on with figuring out what to do next?"

"Well . . ." She hesitated, waiting for something.

A knock came at Kelas's door, and Aunn looked up, startled. "Damn," he said. He glanced around the office, looking for something he could drape over the orb to hide it from view.

"You should answer the door, Kelas," Nara said. "Don't worry about the orb."

Aunn looked back at Nara's face in the orb. She wore the same disturbing smile. She knew who was at his door, he realized. Had she sent an assassin to punish him for his failures?

"N-Nara," he stammered. It was more than he could take—too much in a single day, from appearing in Jorlanna's enclave before dawn to his audience with Thuel in the afternoon, and now this.

Her smile vanished. "Answer the door, Kelas."

He stood and fumbled with Kelas's sword. Gripping its hilt, standing behind the cover of the great desk, he called out, "Come in." His voice didn't quite carry the authority he tried to weight it with.

The latch rattled and the door swung open, and Aunn saw a face that registered as familiar, but he couldn't place it. A nondescript face on an average man—medium height, medium build, neutral hair. The kind of face that witnesses have trouble describing. He knew the kind, because Kelas had guided him in developing his own version of the same face. The perfect killer's face. Aunn hadn't worn his killer's face in many years, and he didn't even have a name for it.

The killer stepped into the room, cautiously, but he didn't have a weapon in his hand.

"Kelas," Nara's voice still came from the crystal orb in front of him, "you know Vec."

Vec? It sounded like a changeling name, and the newcomer confirmed the suspicion by dropping the killer's face, leaving no face to replace it, just featureless gray skin and limp white hair. Was Vec the changeling who had appeared in his office the night before, and the same one he'd faced in Kelas's house?

"Vec led Thuel's mission to capture Gaven, and failed—of course. Thuel doesn't know what he's dealing with, so Vec was not properly prepared. But Vec and I have spoken, and I'm convinced that he's the ideal person to fill your other changeling's role in our plan."

Vec pushed the door closed and leaned against it, his lipless mouth twisted in a strange sort of smile.

"Vec will kill the queen," Nara said.

Kill the queen—the other changeling's role? Kelas and Nara had planned for *Aunn* to be the assassin?

"I see," Aunn said. His eyes were fixed on Vec's blank white orbs.

"There's just one flaw in your plan, Nara," Vec said. His face began to change again—soft and round, with dark hair hanging over pale blue eyes. "This isn't Kelas ir'Darren." The face of the servant girl from Kelas's house wore a triumphant expression.

"You damned fool," Nara said.

Vec's triumphant smile dropped from his face as he tried to see into the crystal globe. Aunn glanced down at it as well. Nara looked disgusted.

"Do you actually think I was ignorant of this deception?" she said. Her gaze was turned in Vec's general direction. "As long as he thought I believed his ruse, he was still useful to me."

Aunn tightened his grip on Kelas's sword and glanced at the door. If he struck now—

Vec must have had the same thought, for he looked up at Aunn in a sudden panic, a dagger appearing in his hand.

"Now kill him," Nara said, "and prove your value to me." But the two changelings were already in motion.

Aunn jumped onto the chair and stepped up onto the desk, both to clear his path to the door and to maximize the advantage of his longer blade. He swept the blade wildly as Vec tried to stab at his legs, and drew one cut across the other changeling's forearm.

"You fool," Aunn snarled, doing his best impression of Kelas in a fury. "You've ruined everything." He shot a foot at Vec's head and managed a glancing blow. For a moment, he thought it might work—Kelas clearly had Vec cowed, and the changeling recoiled from both the blow and the rebuke. But then Vec stood straighter and began to change, taking on Kelas's face himself.

"Do you mock me, changeling?" Vec roared in Kelas's voice. "You think it's funny to wear my face?"

Cold fear gripped Aunn's chest—not fear of Vec, but the raw terror that Kelas had instilled in him over years of training. He fought it, trying to fix the image of Kelas's dead body in his memory.

"I already killed Kelas once," he said through gritted teeth.

"You dare to threaten me?" Vec yelled, and he launched a fresh assault, beating Aunn back. As Aunn shuffled back out of his reach, Vec stooped to grab the legs of the desk and heaved. The desk reared up under Aunn's feet and threatened to crush him against the wall. He managed to jump clear, toward the door.

The door burst open, and Aunn saw one of the soldiers stationed to guard the Tower, gawking in at the two Kelases in the office. Clutching a longsword in front of him, the soldier glanced between the two changelings, panic on his face.

"He's a changeling and a traitor!" Vec yelled, pointing at Aunn. "Seize him!"

"Idiot!" Aunn drew himself up to Kelas's full height and tried to wrap Kelas's imperious air around him, but Vec had a head start on that. "Don't involve yourself in something you don't have the wits to sort out." And don't get yourself killed, he added silently—I don't want to watch this bastard kill another innocent.

"You'll see the truth when he dies!" Vec shouted, and pain stabbed through Aunn's side.

Aunn cursed himself. He had let the guard distract him, let himself worry more about the guard's survival than his own. He batted at Vec with Kelas's blade, and he felt the dagger slide out through the muscles of his lower back. As he turned his full attention back to the assassin, he tried to assess the wound, probing the mutable flesh around it with his mind. He would probably survive it, assuming the blade wasn't poisoned—and assuming he didn't take any more wounds like it.

Vec lunged at him again, but Aunn deflected the blade with an awkward parry. The guard stupidly inserted himself between them, pushing Vec back with his shield.

"Drop your weapons, both of you!" he said. "I'll take you both to Thuel and let him sort it out."

"Are you blind as well as stupid?" Vec roared. "Can't you recognize a changeling when you see one?"

Aunn knew what Vec was doing. It never occurred to most people that anyone of their acquaintance could be a change-ling. People knew they existed, of course, but mostly from outrageous tales and occasional reports in the chronicles. And that ignorance made them very susceptible to suggestion—once the idea was planted, they'd start to see changelings everywhere. Even the guards in the Tower of Eyes were easily fooled.

Sure enough, the guard turned to examine Aunn's face, suspicion in his eyes, exposing his back to Vec's blade.

"Watch out!" Aunn shouted, but in the same instant the guard's eyes went wide with pain, then his knees gave out.

"And so the queen will fall," Vec whispered, a feral grin twisting his face.

Aunn spent only an instant weighing his options. He could stand and fight, but he was already badly wounded and hold-ing a weapon he didn't favor. He could try to run to Thuel for help, but Thuel was probably at home asleep, despite the guard's brash declaration. Besides, Aunn was no longer any use to Thuel, and the Spy Master was bound to figure that out soon enough. He needed to get out of the Tower of Eyes, out of Kelas's body and clothes, and out of the whole damned mess he'd put himself in.

He bolted out of the room, pulling the door behind him. The guard's body and the door would slow Vec slightly—just enough to allow Aunn to escape, he hoped. He tore down the deserted hall, Vec's footsteps pounding behind him.

"Coward!" Vec shouted, still playing Kelas's role to the hilt, trying to batter Aunn's will into submission—and perhaps to rouse more guards. "Come back and accept the punishment you've earned!"

Pain seared across Aunn's back from his wound with every step he ran. A moment with one of his wands would close it, but he didn't have a moment to spare. The pain sapped the strength from his legs and made his head swim. He felt as though he were running in a dream, making no progress through an end-less tunnel, with his pursuer closing quickly.

He burst through a door into the center of the tower, with a wide stair twisting down to the ground floor. Aunn vaulted down, stumbled on the stairs as a fresh jolt of pain stabbed across his back, and ran as fast as he could manage down the winding stairs. A knife clattered against the stone just ahead of him, then nearly sent him tumbling down the stairs as he tried not to step on it. In that off-balance moment, a second blade bit into his shoulder—a small cut, but Aunn didn't need any more wounds. He fumbled in a pouch at his belt as he continued down the stairs, searching by touch for a wand he normally kept close at hand.

Polished wood, a smooth stone at the tip, fiery lines of power twisted and coiling inside—he found the wand he sought, drew it out of the pouch, and pointed it up the stairway. He had to pause a moment, stopping his rush down the stairs, to focus on loosing the knot of magic in the wand's core. A spark flew up from the wand as if from a bonfire, and erupted in roaring flame above him. As the fireball filled the stairway, Aunn ran again, and a moment later he burst through another door onto the ground floor of the Tower of Eyes.

Two soldiers posted at the entrance turned at the sound of the door, hands reaching for their swords. They were all that stood between him and freedom, but how was he going to get past them? They had orders not to let him out—not Kelas nor anyone else who might be a changeling, which meant anyone at all. There wasn't a face he could put on that would convince the guards to let him through the doors. He fingered the wand in his hand, toying for just a moment with the idea of blasting the guards out of the way.

No, he thought, I'll leave killing soldiers to Vec.

He changed his face quickly, before the guards could get a good look at him in the hall's lantern light. "He tried to kill me!" he shouted, finding and slowly settling into Thuel's pitch and clipped accent. He was breathing hard, out of breath, bleeding—the guards wouldn't think twice about his voice not sounding quite right. He pointed at the door he'd just burst through. "The changeling!"

The guards got their swords out and hurried toward him.

One stammered, "Sir, I—I thought you left the tower...."

"I came back," Aunn barked. He wasn't dressed like Thuel, and the other guard was thinking a little too hard about the situation, from the look on her face.

"We didn't see you—" she said.

"You don't think I have ways of getting in my tower that you don't know about?" he roared. "Now get ready to stop that maniac!"

The guards positioned themselves between Aunn and the swinging door, and Aunn heard Vec's steps coming down after him. They were uneven, as if Vec were half stumbling down the stairs. Aunn edged back from the soldiers, toward the beckoning freedom of the tower's exit, but the suspicious guard shot a glance at him.

"Haunderk!" Kelas's voice roared from the doorway, sending a lance of cold fear though Aunn's heart. He knew Kelas was dead—he'd stripped the clothes and armor from the dead body himself—but he couldn't forget a lifetime of lessons so painfully learned.

When Vec appeared in the doorway, he did not look like Kelas anymore. The burst of fire had burned his clothes and seared his skin, leaving pinkish-gray welts across his face and chest. His hair was white except where it was blackened by fire, and his face was frozen somewhere in between a horribly disfigured Kelas and his true changeling visage. The soldiers recoiled in horror, and Aunn used that moment to bolt for the door.

Am I leaving them to their death? he wondered. Letting Vec kill them so I didn't have to dirty my own hands?

"Stop him, you fools!" Vec called behind him.

"Come back here!" the suspicious guard shouted.

Well, they'll get through this all right, Aunn thought. Another few steps, and he felt the cold night air on his face. He ran across the broad, well-lit street that radiated out from the palace and past the Tower of Eyes, chose the narrow mouth of an alley and ran into it, letting its darkness close around him.

He ran through dark alleys and across bright streets until his breath failed him. He stopped, tried to quiet his breathing enough to listen for the sounds of pursuit, and heard nothing. He sank down against a wall and sat in the darkness until his breath came more easily.

He unfastened one of Kelas's belt pouches, opened it, and dumped the contents out onto the ground. A glowstone clattered on the cobblestone, shedding a faint light that let him see the rest of his and Kelas's belongings he'd dumped out—a ring of keys, a small knife with its blade folded into its hilt, several sets of identification papers, his wands. He found the wand he needed and touched its tip to the wound on his back, then his shoulder. Tingling warmth spread through his body, knitting his injured flesh back together and restoring some of his flagging energy.

He removed another pouch and dumped its contents out with the rest. More papers, the shard of masonry he'd taken from Gaven's cell, the silver torc he'd removed from Dania's body and then taken from the wreckage of the Dragon Forge. He found a tinder box as well, and set it in his lap.

He had one more pouch, which he removed and dumped out, and then he unbuckled his sword belt and took off his clothes as well. Naked but not feeling the cold, he changed— he let his body relax into no form at all. It was hard at first, to resist shaping himself and instead just let his body be what it wanted to be, but once he began letting go, his flesh gladly slid from his control. Shorter than Kelas, slender and smooth, gray-skinned and white-haired. He tried to look at his face in the blade of Kelas's sword, but he didn't have enough light.

"I am Aunn," he murmured.

He crouched back down to the ground and began to sort the things he'd dumped out of his pouches. Everything that belonged to Kelas went in one pile, everything that was his in another. Using Kelas's identification papers as kindling, he started a small fire in that pile, then one by one, he added his own belongings—starting with his own sheaf of identification papers, showing half a dozen different names and faces he never wanted to wear again. He fastened Dania's torc around his neck, rubbed the masonry shard between his fingers, and watched his old life and Kelas's slowly burn away in flame.

"I am Aunn," he said again. "This is who I am."

CHAPTER
22

"The turning of the age?" Ashara said. "That's what Havrakhad said."

Cart nodded. "Yes. And now I understand it." He strode through the streets, forcing Ashara to hurry her steps, half running, to keep up.

"What are you talking about?" The pace was making Ashara breathe heavily again, and her words came out between deep gasps for air.

"He could explain it better than I."

"But he didn't, did he? Cart, what's going on?"

"I saw something," Cart said. He wasn't sure he could describe it, or in any way help Ashara understand what was suddenly clear to him. "We live in an age of darkness, but it's drawing to a close."

"You sound like Gaven now."

Cart slowed his pace just slightly. "Do I? Interesting."

Ashara caught up and took his arm. "The Time of the Dragon Below he was talking about, and the rise of the Blasphemer—is that the end of this age?"

"Perhaps it is."

"So what does the next age hold?"

Cart looked down at her and was struck again at the expressiveness of her face. Shadows and lines beneath her eyes, which he hadn't noticed before, told him how tired she was. Creases in her brow spoke of worry and anxiety. The hint of a smile at one corner of her mouth, and something in the warm brown of her eyes whispered of what he was coming to recognize as her affection for him, mixed with something else—something else that made her want to smile, or made her think of a reason to smile.

"I think that's largely up to us," Cart said. "Now come on!" He stepped up his pace again, and Ashara had to let go of his arm as she hustled to keep up.

"What's the hurry? Do we have to save the world right now?"

"We might."

Ashara gave up asking questions after that, saving her breath for running as he led the way back to Havrakhad's apartment.

As he walked, Cart imagined his footsteps—the steady beating of the metal and leather in his feet against the cobblestones—as one beat in a larger cadence, as if he were part of an army marching toward the kalashtar's home, an army of truth and light marching forth to do battle against the darkness. It comforted him to think in those terms, as if the axe at his side could help him against the nightmare monster he'd seen, as if the age of darkness were an enemy army he could stand against. As if he and Ashara were not alone in the dark streets of Fairhaven, cut off from what few allies they had.

But if his steady strides were a marching cadence, a steady drumbeat impelling him forward with determination and resolve, Ashara's steps were a fluttering descant that lent a hint of panic to the march. They reminded him of the frightened mobs he'd seen fleeing from the quori or screaming at the barbarians' approach in his visions. Part of him wanted to join his steps to hers, to run from the threat they faced, to pretend there was nothing they could do but wait for the age to turn.

Then his steps brought him into the small immigrant neighborhood where Havrakhad lived. There weren't enough kalashtar in the city—or members of any race native to their homeland of Adar—to form a district of their own, the way that dwarves had established a community around the Kundarak enclave or Karrns clustered around Drake Street on the east side. Instead, the kalashtar lived in an apartment building of Aundairian construction, which would have blended perfectly with the white plastered buildings on either side if it weren't for the colorful banners that streamed from balconies and windows on every one of its four stories. On their previous visits, Ashara had mentioned another distinguishing feature that he was blind to—the aroma of Adaran cooking, which made use of spices and seasonings unfamiliar to Aundairian nostrils.

"Cardamom," Ashara said. "Oh, Cart, I wish this were all over and I could just go home and cook a good meal, relax in front of the fire, and sleep in my own bed."

The yearning in her voice made Cart melancholy. She was longing for simple comforts and pleasures that meant nothing to him, and he couldn't imagine what it would be like to share them with her. When this was all over, would there be room in her life for him?

He pushed open the door to the apartment building and started up the stairs. Ashara trailed behind him in silence, perhaps lost in her reverie, perhaps wondering why he hadn't answered her. He took the stairs slowly, one at a time, so she could keep up. And, he told himself, so he didn't make as much noise.

At the top of the stairs, Ashara broke her silence. "What will you do? When it's all over?"

Cart shrugged. "I don't know. I've always been a soldier. Already I'm feeling my way in the dark, but at least I have a purpose. I suppose it's just a matter of finding a new purpose."

"One mission after the next."

"Something like that." Cart reached the door to Havrakhad's home. Ashara started to say something else, but he held up his hand and she stopped. The door was open.

"Havrakhad?" he called quietly.

The door didn't look like it had been forced, and peering into the dark room beyond he didn't immediately see any sign of violence. Even so, the situation felt wrong. He slid his axe from his belt and called out again, a little louder.

Hearing no answer, he glanced at Ashara, who nodded, and stepped softly through the open door. A dim glow filtered from an inner room, giving him just enough light to distinguish the general outline of the room.

"Havrakhad? It's Cart."

Ashara gasped, and before he could turn around, he felt a stab of pain in the back of his head, right where it rested on his neck, and his vision went black.

"Please don't fight me, Lady d'Cannith," Havrakhad's soft voice said.

Clutching his axe, Cart turned, trying to fix the voice in front of him so he could defend against another attack. Havrakhad was moving as well—Cart could hear the soft rustle of his flowing clothes.

"What did you do to him?" Ashara's voice came from the doorway. Cart tried to visualize the room, remembering his other visits, and place the three of them in it.

"It was regrettably necessary," Havrakhad said. "He carries an eye of the quori in his mind, and they must not see me. So for the time being, Cart must not see me either."

"An eye of the quori?" Cart said. He put his free hand to the back of his head. The nightmare creature had touched him there, right where Havrakhad had—what had the kalashtar done? In both cases, it had felt like the stab of a dagger, but a real blade there would have killed him.

"Come in, please, and close the door," Havrakhad said, as gracious a host as he had been before.

Cart heard Ashara move, and he shifted nervously.

"Easy, Cart," she whispered. "Maybe you should put your axe away."

"What's happening?" Cart said. He had fought in the dark before, straining to see his foes in the barest of moonlight filtered through a cover of clouds. But there had always been something to see, some shred of light he could use to find his foe or at least ward off attacks. This was different, and terrifying. It wasn't just blackness—it was as though his mind had forgotten that there was such a thing as sight. As though he didn't have eyes and never had. Worst of all, though, was the fact that his enemy—if Havrakhad was now his foe—could still see him.

"It's all right." Ashara's voice was closer now, and soothing. She touched his arm and he flinched. "It's all right," she repeated, and took his arm, and he started to relax. "Here, let me take your axe." Her soft hand was on his, and he started to relax his grip.

"No!"

He pulled away and stumbled toward the door again. What if it was all a trick? A quori or another mindbender could fool him so easily, could make him think he was hearing Havrakhad's voice and Ashara's, disarm him and capture him. He tightened his grip on his axe and tried to put his back to the door, uncomfortably aware that he had lost track of Havrakhad.

"Cart, please!" There was a note of desperation in Ashara's voice that made him even more suspicious. Did Havrakhad or some other enemy have a knife at her throat?

That thought put a new edge on his fear. If the voice he was hearing really was Ashara's, she could be in deadly danger. He could be endangering her with his actions. He couldn't do that. He let his axe clatter to the floor, then followed it down, dropping to his knees.

"I yield," he said. "Please don't harm her."

"I assure you," Havrakhad said, his voice right at Cart's shoulder, "Ashara is unharmed, and I mean you no harm either." Cart felt the kalashtar's warm hand on his shoulder. "Please come and sit with me. We have much to discuss."

Ashara moved to his other side, and together she and Havrakhad helped him stand and guided him farther into the apartment. They turned him sideways to go through a doorway, then wheeled him full around and backed him up against a couch.

"Sit," Ashara whispered, and he slowly sank down onto the soft cushions behind him.

Cart chuckled, embarrassed. "I've never felt quite so much like a cart, drawn by two horses."

Ashara's laugh bubbled with relief, setting Cart at ease. She sat close beside him on the couch, holding his arm. He heard Havrakhad settle into a different seat nearby.

"Now that we've finished with that unpleasantness," Havrakhad said, "why don't you tell me why you're here?"

"Finished?" Ashara said. "Cart still can't see."

"Nor can he be allowed to see, until I can no longer be seen."

"It's all right, Ashara," Cart said. He put a hand on Ashara's and shifted to face the kalashtar directly. "Havrakhad, I apologize. I should have realized that by coming here, I might be turning the quori's eyes on you. I was not thinking clearly."

"The ways of the quori are new to you. Your error is easily understood, and easily forgiven."

"And I'm sorry to disturb you in the middle of the night, again."

"I am growing accustomed to it." Cart thought he heard a smile in the kalashtar's voice. "But I'm sure something important must have precipitated your visit."

"Yes. I saw it again."

"I surmised as much. And it saw you, and noticed that your eyes were open to it."

"Yes."

"What did you see, exactly?"

"It was much like what you showed me last night. The city melted away, and a terrible storm raged in the sky."

"Yes, the dreams of the city are stormy tonight."

Despite the darkness of his eyes, or perhaps because of it, Cart's memory of the nightmare landscape was terribly vivid, even more frightening than when he'd seen it the first time. "All around I saw scenes of terror—collapsing buildings, murder and rape, the barbarians." Ashara's hands tightened on his arm, a gentle reminder of reality that kept him from sliding entirely into the nightmare. He planted his feet more firmly on the ground and continued. "I noticed that the horror seemed to be radiating outward from a single point, like ripples on a pond, and when I looked for the center, I saw the quori again. I heard it say, 'Close your eyes,' and I felt a jab of pain in the back of my head, right where you—what did you do to me?"

"I'll explain in a moment. What happened then?"

"Everything returned to normal. It—the quori closed my eyes, the ones you opened somehow. And suddenly I knew . . . I felt that I had to find you, I had to join you and take up arms against the darkness, to make sure that the new age was one of light. I . . . I can't really explain it."

"I can," Havrakhad said. "The quori is using you to get to me."

"What?"

"It planted a seed of its own mind in yours, so it could see through your eyes. It filled your mind with thoughts that would encourage you to seek me out."

"But . . ." Cart leaned forward, toward Havrakhad's voice. "But I *felt* those things. I *believed* them. I still do—I think I do. I want to fight against evil."

"War and slaughter can't bring the Light into the world," Havrakhad said. "The quori's interests are served by encouraging evil means toward apparently good ends."

Cart sat back on the couch. He had felt so ardent, on fire with passion to set the world right, to atone for his past actions—and inaction. Havrakhad had doused that fire.

"What about my eyes?" he said.

He heard Havrakhad rise and move around the room. Ashara gave his arm a gentle squeeze, but he barely felt it. He felt like an inanimate hunk of stone and wood. Havrakhad rustled to his left, then behind him.

"Well," the kalashtar said, "let me show you how the darkness can be overcome."

Cart felt Havrakhad's fingers on his head, and his vision erupted in golden light.

Chapter
23

Aunn sat on a bench in Chalice Center and stared
numbly at the cloud-filled night sky, lit from below
with the pale red light of street lanterns. He watched
as the sun set the last remnants of the night's storm on fire and
slowly brightened the sky. The last nighttime revelers staggered
their way back to homes and hostels. The first merchants and
travelers of the daylight hours appeared in the plaza, unlocking
doors, driving wagons, hauling luggage to the lightning rail
station or the airship mooring tower.

As the morning light fell on his gray skin and blank white
eyes, Aunn began attracting attention. He was sure he looked
like the worst dregs of the drunks and gamblers who stayed out
all night on the streets, but even the most destitute changelings
usually had the good sense to appear as downtrodden humans
or half-elves, rather than compound the hatred and prejudice
they faced. He questioned his decision a dozen times in the first
half-hour of dawn light, but he kept repeating to himself, "This
is who I am."

At last the merchant he'd been waiting for came downstairs
to his shop and unlocked the door, and Aunn rose stiffly from
the bench, shaking the night's chill from his limbs. Spending Kelas's money sparingly, he bought a new suit of leather
armor, perfectly fitted to the natural form of his body, and a
pair of boots. With that, he discarded the last of Kelas's clothes,
then went next door to a weaponsmith and bought a new
mace, which was a welcome change from Kelas's light sword.
The mace had a heft that made it feel like a real weapon, but
demanded little in the way of expertise or finesse. By the time

he was fighting for his life, Aunn had always figured, the time for finesse was long past.

His last stop was a clothier at the edge of Chalice Center, which catered as much to the wealthy residents of the neighboring Alderwood district as to travelers. He picked out a warm traveling cloak, which cost more than he really wanted to spend but helped to dispel the last remnants of the cold night, and tried it on in front of a full-length glass mirror. The mirror was the reason that Jazen was his favorite clothier in Fairhaven, though the portly human wouldn't recognize him. Aunn frequently visited Jazen's to put the finishing touches on a new disguise, carefully examining every detail of his face and body in the mirror as he pretended to fuss over choosing a new cloak.

His first impression, looking in the mirror, was that the black cloak he'd chosen wouldn't do. He needed color—something bright and vibrant, to make up for the pale gray of his skin, the white hair and colorless eyes, the blank face that seemed to be waiting for features and color and life.

Who are you? he thought, searching the eyes of his reflection for some answer.

"I am Aunn," he murmured. Behind him, Jazen glanced up from where he was busying himself with the hem of the cloak, then quickly looked away.

He let Jazen continue straightening and brushing the cloak so he could look at himself more closely. It was like seeing a stranger—a face he didn't recognize as his own. At first he thought of it as expressionless, blank, but then he noticed a crinkle of distaste at his brow, which quickly melted into a smile. The sight of his smile made him laugh out loud, which made his blank white eyes come alive.

"The cloak pleases you?" Jazen asked, looking up at the laughter. Even his perpetual scowl softened a little when he saw Aunn's smile.

"It's a fine cloak, but the color is wrong. I need something more vibrant." He watched his face as he spoke, the way his lipless mouth formed sounds. It was growing on him.

"Absolutely, I agree." Jazen stood and reached around Aunn's shoulders to unfasten the clasp. Aunn tensed—he always did. Then the cloak was off his shoulders, and Aunn felt suddenly cold. "What color did you have in mind?"

"What would you recommend?"

He watched as Jazen brought a selection of colors and draped them over his shoulder, noticed how his own complexion changed ever so slightly without any conscious effort, laughed at the horrible effect of a daffodil yellow, and finally settled on a purple that was far too expensive.

As he counted out the coins for Jazen, the clothier looked at him thoughtfully.

"I beg your pardon," Jazen said, "but have you been in my shop before?"

No more lies, Aunn thought. "I have. Several times."

"I thought as much." Jazen put the coins away in a pouch at his belt. "Well, you are always welcome."

"Thank you." Aunn knew he would not always be welcomed elsewhere, wearing his true face for all to see. But his visit to Jazen's was an auspicious start to his new life.

* * * * *

Aunn stood on the street and stared up at the abandoned cathedral like a dumbfounded tourist from the farmland. He had probably walked past the cathedral hundreds or thousands of times before, but it didn't seem to matter—he felt as though he were seeing it for the first time.

"Keep moving," Kelas barked.

Laurann quickened her steps to keep up with him, while trying to steal glances at the magnificent building. Questions churned in her mind, but she knew better than to ask Kelas.

"Come along," Kelas said again. This time, though, he looked at her, and noticed her wide eyes staring at the building. He stopped.

"You like that?" he said. "Then you like failure. That's the greatest monument to delusion and weakness in all of Aundair. That's why no one goes there any more—Aundair has outgrown its time of weakness."

But to Laurann's eyes, nothing about the place spoke of weakness.

And to Aunn's new eyes, it seemed the opposite—a testimony to the highest ideals anyone could aspire to, a monument to the sacrifice of Dania ir'Vran, Vor Helden, Farren Dorashka, and the noble warriors of Maruk Dar. And it was a monument that still stood proudly in a city that had turned its back on it eighty-five years ago, driving the priests and worshipers of the Silver Flame out of the city or into more secretive places of worship.

Even from the street, the building itself lifted his spirit. Though its stained-glass windows were shattered and its mosaics defaced, its buttresses carried the eye upward, to the silver dome it wore as a shining crown. Its pillars carved in the likeness of the saints of the faith moved him with the serenity of their faces, the quiet confidence of their faith—and their eyes, too, drew his eyes upward. The dome itself was engraved with a ring of dancing flames, gleaming in the morning sun.

Kalok Shash burns brighter.

The main entrance to the cathedral was boarded over and bound with chains. From the look of it, Aunn guessed that some of that work was recent—the city watch's one gesture toward keeping criminals from using the cathedral as a base. He chose the alley on the left side of the building and walked over heaps of trash, scanning for windows or doorways. Several high windows probably once helped light the vaulted sanctuary inside, before the neighboring building had been built so close to the cathedral. He suspected they were covered with boards, and he couldn't imagine Kelas climbing so high on the wall to get inside. A little farther on, though, with the noise of the street fading behind him, he found a smaller doorway. Boards were carefully placed over the door to give the appearance that it was sealed closed without actually preventing it from opening. With a glance up and down the alley, he pushed the door open and stepped through, into the darkness.

He pulled the glowstone from his pouch, letting its dim light surround him and sketch the lines of floor, walls, and ceiling. He was in a hallway, probably where the bishop and priests had lived when the cathedral was open. He could just make out a doorway on either side of the hall.

Aunn cursed under his breath. Ashara had told him that Kelas used the cathedral as a meeting place, but the cathedral was huge, and at least some of its space was also claimed by one of Fairhaven's criminal gangs—not a problem the Royal Eyes had ever been too concerned about. He didn't even know what he was looking for, precisely, let alone where he should look. Where would Kelas establish himself? In the bishop's quarters? That might suit his sense of irony. Aunn crept forward and pressed an ear to the door on his left.

Something was moving in the room beyond—probably rats scuttling among the old furniture. The presence of rats would suggest that the room had seen use more recently than the priests' departure, that someone had left behind something the rats considered edible. He lifted the latch and pushed the door open, cringing as the hinges let out a piercing squeak. He cast a glance up and down the hall, then gritted his teeth and pushed the door all the way open in one quick movement, ignoring its loud protest.

He stopped in the doorway, letting the dim light from his glowstone filter into the room as he listened for any sign that the noisy hinges had attracted attention. He didn't see any rats—not a surprise, since they had probably taken cover at the first squeak of the hinges. The room had been a sort of a parlor, he guessed, with a moldering sofa and two equally decrepit chairs where the priests could meet with guests and visitors. It was certainly not what he was looking for. Kelas would have cleaned the rooms where he worked, or rather, ordered some-one else to clean them. Leaving the door open and dispensing with caution, Aunn strode to the door he could just make out at the far end of the hall, which presumably led deeper into the cathedral's heart.

He opened the latch and pulled, but the door wouldn't budge—either stuck or sealed shut. He looked around for another likely route out of the priests' quarters but didn't see one, so he gave the door another, harder, pull. This time it flew open—it was merely stuck in its frame after all. The sound of it pulling free echoed in the great cathedral's sanctuary beyond.

Sunlight shone into the broken windows and filtered through the shards of stained glass at the top of the lofty dome, casting a fractured rainbow of color across the dusty mosaic floor. Sculpted saints and dancing flame captured in solid stone supported the dome, and through either a trick of the sunlight or some lingering magic, they all seemed to shine with the faintest of light, filling the dome with silvery radiance.

Aunn's feet carried him into the sanctuary as his eyes drank it in. Tattered tapestries hung on the walls, their colors surprisingly vivid despite the passage of years and the depredations of rats and moths. Strands of silver thread still gleamed in some of them, though in places he saw the work of knives where thieves had cut the precious metal out of the fabric. The tapestries showed more saints of the Silver Flame, he imagined, engaged in the acts that had made them objects of the church's veneration. None were familiar to him, but he saw mostly crusading warriors in gleaming armor, locked in mortal struggle with dragons, demons, undead horrors, and werewolves.

"I'm no saint," he said aloud. His throat closed as tears sprang to his eyes. One of the tapestries showed a knight locked in battle with a giant, and for a moment he thought it was Vor, roaring to Kalok Shash as he confronted the demon-giant of the Wastes, his sword blazing with silver fire. The weight of all Aunn's deeds and failures came down on his shoulders, too much to bear. He fell to his knees, then put his face to the cold stone floor.

Kelas had trained him practically since his birth to be a Royal Eye—a spy, an infiltrator, an assassin. He'd been taught to kill without pity or remorse, to lie with every breath, to betray those who considered him a friend, and he'd done it all very well. He probably could have risen to Kelas's position, perhaps even Thuel's, with time.

Instead, he was kneeling on the floor of Fairhaven's grand cathedral. He was an utter failure as a spy—twice in as many days, his disguise had failed and he'd been discovered, nearly costing him his life. But his failure had begun long before, when he allowed grief and remorse to gnaw at his heart, when he allowed the stirrings of conscience to blossom into actual morality. After he caused the deaths of Sevren Thorn and Zandar Thuul, he tried to make a new life for himself, a new identity that would live according to his new principles.

And even that had failed. Donning Kelas's face had turned him into a spy again. He had let innocents die in order to protect his disguise, and he had let his life become a web of lies again.

He lifted his head and wiped his eyes, his spine tingling faintly. He looked at the floor, where his hands had disturbed the dust and revealed the mosaic beneath—the image of a foot armored in silver plate. Looking around, he could make out some of the image, except where it was covered by a large round table—an armored figure enfolded by a leaping tongue of silver flame. He crawled toward the figure's head, sweeping the dust aside so he could see her face.

"It doesn't look anything like her," he said aloud, but hearing the words aloud made him realize the absurdity of the thought—he'd expected to see Dania's face enshrined in a mosaic on the floor of a temple that had been abandoned at least forty years before she was born. No, he realized—this was probably Tira Miron, the paladin who had joined herself with a pillar of supernatural fire to become the Voice of the Flame, the founder of the faith.

She floated in the midst of the fire, holding a sword aloft in one hand. Her face was exquisite, even from a merely artistic perspective—a look of rapture in her uplifted eyes and full lips. There was something at once erotic and unspeakably holy about her face. The tingling at the back of his neck turned into a chill washing through his whole body, a cool fire that coursed through his veins.

Why do you resist me?

He wasn't sure whether he heard the voice or remembered it from all his fevered dreams, but it seemed suddenly as though Tira's eyes gazed directly into his.

"Because I'm not worthy of you," he said aloud. He closed his eyes, trying to hold back a fresh flow of tears.

Then he felt a soft hand on his cheek, and without thinking, he pressed his lips to hers. They were warm and moist, and her breath filled his lungs like searing fire.

You are worthy, she breathed into his mouth, *and you are mine.*

Chapter
24

W ind and thunder followed Gaven through the
streets of the city. If soldiers were still chasing him,
they had only to follow the beacons of lightning
that flashed over him. It didn't matter—he couldn't have
stopped the storm if he had wanted to, and if his plan somehow
worked, he would soon have sanctuary of a sort.

He had never known Fairhaven especially well, and he
hadn't been in the city in more than a quarter century. But
the elves of Aerenal preserved traditions stretching back ten
thousand years—he doubted that their descendants in this city
had moved their little enclave since the last time he'd seen it.
The trick would be finding his way there, once he left the old,
straight streets that defined the basic pattern of the city.

Those streets, like the spokes of a wheel with the palace
at its hub, brought him quickly to the southwestern part of
town, then he lost himself in a maze of smaller streets and
alleys. The storm's fury died as he tried to navigate through
the neighborhood, as the panic of his flight faded into per-
plexity. If pursuers still followed him, they had lost their
lightning beacon.

So many new buildings filled the area that he began to
question whether he could be in the right place, unless the
Aereni had abandoned their enclave. Then he decided to turn
down an alley he had already walked past twice, and suddenly
he was there. One moment, the buildings crowding close on
either side were freshly plastered white apartment homes,
smooth, windowless walls rising high overhead, but a few
steps later the alley widened into a little courtyard paved with

ancient flagstones, and the buildings on its three sides might have been transplanted directly from Aerenal. Built of exotic woods, the buildings rose in tiers topped with sculpted spires and magical flames that washed the square below in dancing green and purple light.

Apparently unwilling or unable to trust Fairhaven's city watch to protect their little enclave, the elves had their own soldiers, gaunt warriors in ornate armor, carrying poleaxes with elaborately carved, probably impractical heads. The elves stood at attention as Gaven blundered out of the alleyway, shifting their grips on their weapons. The one on the left, Gaven noticed, bore a tattooed skull design that obscured his true face, making him look like one of the deathless. He fixed a wary gaze on Gaven and scowled. The one on the right, though, was already dead—his withered flesh clung to his bones and dim green flame flickered in his eye sockets.

They didn't immediately accost Gaven—they were probably accustomed to people stumbling into their little enclave, looking around incredulously, and hurrying back out. Gaven didn't see anyone else in the courtyard, so he steeled himself and approached the soldiers.

"Have you lost your way?" the living soldier asked coldly. He spoke Common with a thick accent.

"I know where I am," Gaven answered in the best Elven he could muster. "I—" What was the correct phrase? "I invoke the right of counsel."

The guard's face was as expressionless as his skull tattoo as his eyes searched Gaven's. Then the deathless soldier's bony hand lashed out and struck Gaven's face. A last echo of thunder rumbled overhead, but Gaven squelched his surging anger.

"The Right of Counsel?" the living soldier said in Elven. "You have no such right. You should leave this place before my friend's righteous anger increases."

"My ancestors fought under Aeren as yours did," Gaven said. He wasn't surprised, except perhaps by the violence of the deathless guard's response. But he had no alternative plan. He couldn't give up without a fight.

"Name them," the dead soldier demanded.

"I am an heir of House Lyrandar," Gaven said. It was the best answer he knew. The first Lyrandars had already been half-elves, their elven blood mixed with a noble human line from Khorvaire. But perhaps the elves knew more about his ancestry than he himself did.

"No doubt you have ancestors among the elves of Aerenal," the living soldier said, "but their names are not honored, nor were they worthy of joining the ranks of the deathless."

"Name them," the guard repeated. "Name a single ancestor you claim among the Undying. Whose counsel do you seek?"

"Alvena," Gaven blurted. "In the name of my friends Mendaros Alvena Tuorren and Senya Alvena Arrathinen, I seek the counsel of Alvena."

Both guards took half a step backward, and they exchanged a glance. Gaven wasn't even certain he'd blurted out the right name, and he had no idea whether it was Alvena or the name of one of his friends that had given the soldiers pause.

"I shall go," the living soldier said. With a quick glance at Gaven, he hurried across the courtyard.

"Wait here," the other soldier said. "On your knees, and do not speak to me again."

Gaven didn't know what was happening, but at least he'd made something happen. He decided it was best to obey the undead soldier, so he dropped to his knees and waited. Clutching his poleaxe in both withered hands, the guard stood a few steps away, his burning eyes fixed on Gaven in an unwavering stare.

Gaven watched the living soldier climb the wide stair at the far end of the courtyard and disappear into a darkened archway at the top. What was he doing? Whatever had provoked them, it had clearly suggested a course of action so obvious that the only question was which soldier would carry it out.

"You Khoravar," the deathless guard muttered, half to himself, "so full of human arrogance." He stepped closer and addressed Gaven directly. "The Undying exist only because of the veneration of their descendants. You hybrids who can't even remember the names of your ancestors—if it were up to you, the Undying would all fade into death. Memory is life. Without memory, your people are already dead. You don't know who you are—you might as well be beasts."

Gaven bit his tongue and stared at the flagstones. The soldier had ordered him not to speak, so he bit back an angry retort, but as he did, the guard's words echoed in his mind. Gaven's memories were a jumble, a shattered mosaic of his own past and the memories of the other. The time before he found the nightshard was shrouded in fog, particularly now that Rienne was gone. When he'd been with her, that time had seemed clearer in his mind.

"Gaven?"

Gaven looked up and scanned the courtyard. The living soldier had emerged from the building and started back down the stairs, followed by a woman in a plain white robe. Her head was shaved bald, and her face bore a skull tattoo like that of the soldier.

The deathless soldier stepped back and watched the others approach. Gaven started to stand, but the guard turned and glared at him, so he stayed on his knees. The woman hurried toward him, sandals slapping against the flagstones. Gaven watched curiously—there was something familiar about the woman, but he couldn't place her in the fragments of his memory.

Finally she stood before him, a little breathless, her slight smile strangely out of place on her tattooed face. "Gaven," she said Common, "I'm glad to see you again."

Gaven stared dumbly.

"Gaven, it's Senya."

"Senya?" Gaven gaped at her, trying to see Senya's face past the tattoo. Her full lips, no longer painted scarlet, had been made to look like stark white teeth, and the eyelids she had colored blue before were black, so that when she blinked, they might have been empty sockets. Her bald head was perhaps the most disconcerting, but when he tried to imagine a full head of curly black hair, he could almost see her face.

"Yes, it's really me." She bent down and kissed his cheek in greeting. She smelled of incense and spice, not the flowered fragrances she'd worn before.

"You have changed," Gaven said.

She laughed. "Yes, I have. You may stand." She offered her hand to him, and he took it as he rose to his feet. "And I have you to thank for it."

"Me? Why?"

"You helped me discover who I am. You gave me the courage to stand up to Haldren. You taught me . . ." She looked away. "Many things." Glancing at the two soldiers who frowned at them, she took Gaven's arm. "Let's discuss this indoors. It's cold out here."

"One moment, priestess," the living guard interrupted in Elven.

Gaven looked at Senya again. Priestess?

"What is the matter?" Senya said in the same language.

"This man you greet with such familiarity has spoken blasphemously of the revered ancestors and demanded a right he does not have. I would see him punished."

"I will bring your concern to the ancestors," Senya said. She tugged Gaven's arm. "Come with me," she added in Common.

"But priestess—"

"That is all. Return to your post."

Both guards bowed and stepped back from them, and Senya led Gaven toward the building she had emerged from.

"Priestess?" Gaven said, once they were out of the soldiers' earshot.

"Indeed. Much has changed since you left me outside Vathirond."

"You were at Starcrag Plain," Gaven said. "With Haldren. Darraun and Rienne captured you."

"Yes. We'll discuss it inside."

Gaven walked beside her up the wide stairs to the many-tiered tower. The warmth of her hands on his arm stood in strange contrast to the death mask inscribed on her face, and when he wasn't looking at her it was easy to imagine her at his side in Korranberg, too close for his comfort, flirting seductively. But then he looked at her again, and all he could see was a priestess of the Undying Court, her body shrouded in her shapeless robe.

"Senya?" he said as they passed through the arch at the top of the stairs.

"Yes?"

"I'm glad to see you, too." Strangely, he meant it.

Senya smiled up at him, clutched his arm a little more tightly, and led him toward a narrower stairway inside the building—which Gaven suddenly recognized as a temple. A pair of tall doors were carved with Elven invocations to the Undying Court and adorned with images of skulls and swords, honoring the warrior ancestors of Aerenal. Braziers outside the doors smoldered with coal and incense, waiting for morning when their flames would be stoked to life again for the next sacrifices. In the night, the whole building was as quiet as a tomb.

Senya released his arm and led the way up the narrow stairs. They climbed three flights in silence, then down a short hall, and she led him into a small chamber. A curved couch, made for reclining, stood against one wall, a table and a single chair opposite it. Between them was a tiny altar on the floor, with a straw mat set before it. In an icon above the altar, Gaven recognized the deathless ancestor he had met in Aerenal.

Senya closed the door behind him and sat on the couch. He was suddenly uncomfortable again, alone with her in her bedchamber. His discomfort must have shown. "Sit," she said with a laugh, gesturing at the chair across the room. "And don't worry. I'm done with all that."

Gaven felt his face flush and turned away, taking longer than he needed to pull the chair out from the table and turn it to face her. When he sat down and looked at her again, she was grinning.

"What's so funny?" he asked.

Her grin became a full-throated laugh. "You are," she said. "I'm sorry. I must have been truly awful."

He was struck, suddenly, by the brilliant blue of her eyes, which he hadn't noticed in the darkness outside. "Awful? No. You were quite persistent, though."

"I'm sorry." The smile faded from her face.

"It's all right."

"It's not—not for me, anyway. I had the opportunity to learn from you, to study the Prophecy of the dragons at your side, and I squandered it. I think I knew what I really wanted, but I translated that into the only desire I really understood at the time."

"What did you really want?"

"The same thing my mother and all my ancestors wanted for me—what all the universe wanted for me." She extended an arm, vaguely encompassing the room and the temple beyond. "This."

"Your destiny?"

"Exactly."

CHAPTER
25

The iron dragon loosed its breath first, cascading waves of lightning pouring from its mouth. Maelstrom spun to life around Rienne, gathering the lightning into a whirlwind that crackled and sparked around her but didn't harm her. Drawing a deep breath at the eye of that storm, Rienne planted a foot firmly on the ground and directed a focused blast at the red dragon, just as it was inhaling in preparation for loosing its own gout of fire. The lightning struck it in the face and filled its mouth, turning its exhalation into a roar of pain.

"*Barak Radaam,*" the iron dragon rumbled. "I didn't believe it."

"We will deliver it to the Blasphemer," the red one said, wisps of smoke trailing from its mouth. "With the body of this one."

Rienne was too tired to repeat her boast that the Blasphemer would have to take her himself. She crouched, waiting for the dragons' next attack, trying to keep them both in view as they circled her warily.

The red dragon lunged first, springing at her with surprising speed, half running and half flying. She ducked and sprang aside so the dragon's mouth snapped at empty air, but the iron dragon—smarter than it had first appeared—had anticipated the direction of her dodge, and it was ready. Its heavy claw lashed out and raked across her back as she tried to arch away from it, pushing her back, stumbling, toward the red.

Maelstrom swung around and bit into the red dragon's snout as it snapped at her again, and trailing a line of steaming blood, it cut into the other dragon's claw. Rienne followed its momentum, whirling dangerously close to the iron dragon's claws until it stumbled over her. For one terrifying moment, the dragon's feet were stamping the ground all around her. She swung Maelstrom up to cut a wide gash across the dragon's belly, showering blood around her, then it staggered past her and crashed into the red, landing on its side.

Rienne wiped the acrid blood from her face as the iron dragon scrambled to its feet and the red circled her again. The barbarian tide had parted to give her and the dragons a wide berth, and at a glance Rienne couldn't see any of the Eldeen defenders behind her—the barbarians must have pushed the line back. She was alone, then.

The prospect of dying on this battlefield had not occurred to her until that moment. Her dream in Argonnessen had convinced her that she was fated to confront the Blasphemer at the Wynarn—alone and perhaps in failure, but at least not yet, not until the barbarians had advanced that far. But now she stood alone in the midst of the horde, flanked by dragons as her every muscle screamed in exhaustion, cut off from any aid. She shook her head ruefully.

Then a shriek like an eagle's cry pierced the air overhead, and she glanced up to see three hippogriffs circling in the brightening sky. Both dragons chose that instant to lunge at her, coming in from opposite sides. The iron one was slower, perhaps because of the wound in its belly, so she leaped toward it to avoid the red's bite. As the iron dragon opened its jaws to snap at her, she threw herself at its mouth. She planted one foot just behind its front teeth, and before it could close its jaws on her leg she flipped up and over its head, landing solidly between its shoulders. The dragon reared up to throw her off, but she grabbed a wing to steady herself, and drove Maelstrom down behind its shoulder. With a roar that made lightning crackle in its mouth, the iron dragon collapsed.

Now the red was distracted, looking up at the sky. Rienne followed its gaze. Two of the hippogriffs were still high above her, but the third was swooping low, and she saw Sky Warden Kyaphar on its back. Did he hope to extract her from a losing battle? As she and the dragon both watched, Kyaphar stood up in his stirrups and lifted one leg over the hippogriff's back, then jumped off. Rienne gasped—he was still a long way from the ground. But Kyaphar spread his arms wide and they became wings, and the rest of his body transformed until he was a great eagle, diving rather than falling down to her side as his hippogriff flapped upward.

The red dragon roared a tremendous blast of fire. Rienne pulled the dead dragon's wing up as a shield to block the brunt of it, and she saw Kyaphar pull up from his dive in time to avoid most of the flames. Emboldened by the Sky Warden's unexpected appearance, Rienne charged.

The dragon reared up to meet her charge, exposing its belly to Maelstrom's arc. But in order to reach it, she would have to put herself in easy reach of the dragon's claws. She didn't look up, but she could hear the beat of Kyaphar's wings, so she took the bait, leaping the last few yards with Maelstrom drawn back over her shoulder, ready for a mighty swing. As she reached the dragon, she saw its head and claws start down, but when Maelstrom cut through the scales of its belly, Kyaphar swooped past the dragon's head and slashed his talons across the dragon's eyes. It pulled back away from the eagle and fell wildly off balance. Rienne drove Maelstrom into its heart.

She heard a rustle, then Kyaphar stood beside her, clutching a short wooden rod adorned with eagle feathers. "Perhaps you didn't need my help after all," he said with a smile. "I've never seen anyone wield a sword quite like that."

"I appreciate it nonetheless," Rienne said. She looked around at a wide circle of barbarians watching her. They had kept their distance while she fought the dragons, and they seemed reluctant to approach now that she'd killed both wyrms, but she suspected their leader would soon drive them forward again. "Can you get us up and out of here?"

In answer, Kyaphar gave a piercing whistle, and his hippogriff swooped downward. But the encircling barbarians also seemed to take the whistle as a signal to charge. With a ragged shout, "Kathrik Mel!" they surged in from all sides.

Kyaphar held out his feathered totem, and a blast of icy wind threw barbarians back into their fellows, collapsing one side of the closing circle. Rienne crouched and waited for the nearest ones to reach her, but the hippogriff was faster. Kyaphar leaped onto its back before its feet touched down, and he held a hand out to Rienne. She swung Maelstrom in a wide sweep that killed three plague-marked men, then took Kyaphar's hand and vaulted into the saddle behind him. A pair of shifters, their bodies and faces warped in their bestial rage, pounced on the hippogriff as its wings beat the air. Kyaphar kicked at one as Rienne slashed at the other, then the hippogriff bounded up and out of reach.

"Thank you again," Rienne said. All her pain and exhaustion suddenly crashed down on her, making her vision swim for a moment—or perhaps it was the vertigo of their hasty takeoff. "How goes the battle?"

"Poorly," Kyaphar said over his shoulder. "The Blasphemer's horde keeps pushing our defenders back. Even our bears can't stand against the dragons, let alone the farmers who call themselves soldiers. There are only a handful of us who are making any difference in the battle, and most of us are as tired and bloodied as you are."

"What about the seal?"

"The Blasphemer marches at the back of his forces— there." Kyaphar pointed down and behind them, turning the hippogriff slightly to give Rienne a better view. "He has almost reached the outer lines."

From their altitude, the figure Kyaphar identified as the Blasphemer was a tiny shadow against a wall of flame. The forest blazed at his back, and he seemed to wield tongues of fire like whips to drive his horde forward. Even at such a distance, the sight of him brought her dream vividly to life in her memory—his demonic visage, his sword alight with blood red fire. Darkness closed around her vision.

Kyaphar caught her before she slipped off his mount, jolting her back to her senses. Only then did she see what Kyaphar had been trying to point out—the dimly glowing purple line that she had seen from the sky before the attack had already been crossed by the front lines of Kathrik Mel's horde, and the Blasphemer himself would reach it soon.

"Are you hurt?" Kyaphar asked, his arm awkwardly holding her in place, pressed against his back.

"I'm fine. We should head back down. We have to stop him."

"The Mosswood Warden is planning to lead a counterattack to drive the Blasphemer back from the seal. We will join her shortly, but you'll see a healer first."

"No, really, I'm fine."

"You're covered with blood."

"Dragon blood! I've killed four dragons—"

"And no one alive can take down four dragons without suffering a single wound. Look at your shoulder. You'll see a healer."

Rienne looked down at her shoulder, where she had a vague memory of being injured. It did look terrible—the gold dragon's fangs had pierced and torn the flesh, and it must have had fire in its mouth as well, for both skin and clothing were scorched black around the wound. She felt dizzy again, and looked away. "Very well," she said. "I'll see a healer."

"Don't worry. We'll have you back on the front lines in no time."

Rienne closed her eyes and rested her head against Kyaphar's shoulder.

* * * * *

When she opened her eyes again, Rienne saw trees stretching up to a smoke-filled sky, and Kyaphar's face looking down at her. The Sky Warden was carrying her, and his face betrayed his concern even as he smiled with relief. "Good morning," he said. "We're almost to the healer now. Stay with me, all right?"

She could manage only a nod. She watched his face as he carried her a dozen more paces, then she heard someone say, "Put her there." Kyaphar looked around, took a couple of steps, and gently laid her on a bed of moss at the roots of one of the towering trees.

Startled, Rienne tried to lift her head and see where she was. A healer, to her mind, meant an heir of House Jorasco, a skilled halfling who combined the magic of the Mark of Healing with careful study and perhaps prayers for divine intercession. The Jorasco Houses of Healing were immaculately clean and almost as comfortable as the hostels run by the other dragonmarked halflings, House Ghallanda. Her mind had not been prepared for a bed of moss.

Nor could she have anticipated the healer, a shifter woman clad in leather and fur. Her wild mane of hair was woven with beads and bones, making her look every bit as savage as the shifters in the Blasphemer's horde who had tried to pull the hippogriff back down to earth with their claws. Even so, she smiled as she crouched at Rienne's side, and Rienne instantly warmed to the compassion in the woman's eyes.

"So you are the dragonslayer," the shifter said. "I am honored to have you in my care, Lady Alastra."

"Thank you."

"I am Kauna."

As the healer spoke, Rienne saw an enormous bear lumber up behind her, then realized that she could still see the trees and sky through the bear's smoky form. Kauna smiled and looked over her shoulder at the bear, then back down at Rienne.

"The bear is my link to the spirit world." The smile faded from her face. "The spirits are troubled this morning. We must get you back to the battle."

Kauna produced a basin and washed Rienne's shoulder. Pain stabbed through her at first, but then the bear started a low grumble and she felt better. She could barely hear the low pitch of its voice, but it seemed almost like a song, and its vibrations soothed away the pain and weariness from her body. Kauna began to hum softly as well, and Rienne felt warmth spread gently up from the moss beneath her, as if she were drawing strength through roots like the tree that towered above her.

She closed her eyes again, lost in the peaceful song. She felt as though a warm river washed over her body, carrying away all her aches and wounds, cleansing her and refreshing her spirit. She started drifting to sleep, reached for it with longing—

The bear spirit roared—a terrible, pained sound that jolted Rienne awake. Kauna spilled her basin in surprise, and Rienne saw her panicked face as she looked at the bear.

"There is no more time," Kauna said. "On your feet, Lady Alastra. Kyaphar will take you where you must go."

As Rienne got to her feet, her eyes fixed on the bloodstained water from Kauna's basin as it slowly seeped into the earth.

CHAPTER
26

A door slammed somewhere in the cathedral, jolting Aunn to his feet. He shook his head to clear it and looked down at the mosaic. Tira's face in colored tile seemed to smile back at him, urging him on his way.

"I am yours," he whispered, "and if by my life or death I can make your flame burn brighter, I will."

The noise had come from an open doorway across the sanctuary from where he'd entered, so he crept to that entrance and listened. A stairway led down, presumably to offices or storerooms, perhaps catacombs. He heard footsteps echoing in the stairwell, but they receded as he listened. He followed them, cupping his glowstone in his hand to light the stairs as he descended. At the first landing, he found a door, which he suspected led to another alley outside the cathedral—probably the door he had heard.

He felt as if he were walking in a dream, moving for the sake of moving without knowing why, with no idea who or what he was following. Was it some angel of the Silver Flame sent to lead him to what he sought? A criminal using the cathedral as a hiding place, drawing him down into an ambush? A haunting spirit? He had no idea, but he felt drawn to follow it, and the part of his mind that questioned why was not strong enough, or perhaps awake enough, to stop him.

Light washed over the bottom of the stairs, and Aunn pocketed his glowstone as he moved to the shadows at the outer edge of the stairway. A narrow passage stretched back under the cathedral from the bottom of the stairs, with doors every few yards on both sides, and at least one intersection where passages branched out in each direction. Everbright lanterns hung at intervals from the low ceiling, bathing the entire hall in bright light. And the figure turning a corner at the far end of the hall gave more credence to the haunting spirit idea—it looked like Kelas.

He felt a brief tingle of fear, but stifled it. After all, he had seen Kelas just the night before—for that matter, he had *been* Kelas. The figure in the hall was more likely to be the changeling, Vec, than some kind of ghost. And that suggested that he'd been right to come to the cathedral. Or at least, Vec shared his suspicion that Kelas might have kept useful information there.

Aunn started to pursue the shade or changeling or whatever it was, but he stopped just short of the doorway. The cathedral cellar looked like a labyrinth, a perfect place for an ambush. There could be Royal Eyes lurking behind every door in the hall, waiting for him to walk into their midst.

He hesitated for just a moment, then decided he had to take the risk. If Kelas had used the cathedral as a base of operations, then some clue to help Aunn unravel Nara's plans might be in this cellar, and that was worth risking his life for. He slid his mace from his belt and stepped through the doorway.

The walls became the rocky sides of a blasted canyon surrounding him, the floor was strewn with rubble, and the low ceiling turned into a smoky red sky far overhead. He was in that other Labyrinth, with the demons of the Wastes a very real and present threat. He could feel the presence of the shapechanging fiend that had attacked him there, wearing first his own, new face, then so many other faces in quick succession—Vor's, Dania's, Kelas's, and the shape of a demon bear. But he also felt the presence of the Silver Flame, the presence that had driven the fiend from him in the Wastes. He felt a surge of magic, like a knot in his chest suddenly loosed, and the illusion vanished in a flash of white light. The cellar was just plastered walls and tiled ceiling again.

"What is going on here?" he muttered.

Clutching his mace, he hurried as quietly as he could to the point where the second passage crossed the one he was in.

No unseen assailants leaped from doorways, and as he peered down the crossing passage he saw no sign of danger. He stepped through the intersection and down to where he'd seen Kelas turn the corner. The only footsteps he could hear were his own, as much as he tried to soften them.

A door stood open halfway down the corridor, and Aunn could see a shadow cast into the hall from a light in the room beyond. He cursed his new armor and boots, which creaked as he crept down the hall. As he drew near the open door, he heard the rustling of papers, drawers sliding open and banging closed. Perhaps the other visitor was making too much noise of his own to hear the sounds of Aunn's approach.

He was only three steps from the door when the noises from inside the room stopped.

"Who's there?" a voice called from the room. It was not Kelas's voice, but a woman's. Familiar, but he couldn't place it.

Aunn's mind raced. His first instinct was to put Kelas's face back on, to swagger into the office full of bluster and rage, and he actually felt his face begin to change before he reminded himself to stop. "My name is Aunn," he said, addressing himself as much as the woman in the room. He slid his mace back into his belt and inched toward the open doorway.

The woman laughed, high and musical, and Aunn finally recognized the voice. "Colonel Tolden?"

The laugh cut off abruptly. "Do I know you?"

Aunn took the last step into the doorway, hands in front of him, palms out. Janna Tolden sat behind a large wooden desk, with a crossbow cocked and pointed at his chest.

How did I mistake her for Kelas? he wondered.

Her hair was the same light shade of brown as Kelas's, and that might have been enough to explain his mistake. She wore it only slightly longer than Kelas had, framing her face and brushing the lines of her jaw. She wore a bulky traveling cloak, so he hadn't really seen her body, which was nothing at all like Kelas's.

"We have met," he said, "though you wouldn't know this face." No one would.

"Or the name," Janna said. She scowled. "So you've lied to me before. Who were you pretending to be?"

"Ah, that's a complicated question." Answering it would be tricky. How much did Janna already know?

"No, it's not. It's a very simple question. Who did you claim to be?"

I'm through with lies, Aunn thought. "General Jad Yeven." Her eyebrows rose. "The real general died at the battle of Starcrag Plain. From then until he was reported dead, I wore his face."

Aunn watched as her eyebrows drifted back down her forehead, her eyes lost their focus and strayed to the side, and her brow furrowed. He imagined her thoughts, as she tried to recall every interaction she'd had with him, believing he was Yeven. There hadn't been much, but she had always adopted a much more flirtatious manner in private with him than he would ever have suspected her capable of, judging from her more public persona.

"That explains a lot," she said, bringing her gaze back to him. "So who are you really? A Royal Eye?"

"Yes. Or at least, I was until recently."

"You worked for Kelas, then."

"Yes."

"Where is Kelas?"

"Dead."

"At the Dragon Forge?"

"Yes."

Janna sighed and pushed a drawer in the desk closed. Had she been looking for something Kelas might have brought back from the Dragon Forge? Gaven's shard, perhaps?

"So what are you doing here?" she asked.

"I might ask you the same question."

She laughed again, and her grip on the crossbow finally relaxed. "I wondered when you were going to turn the tables on me."

"I hope I've demonstrated that I want to deal honestly with you now. I'd hope for the same in return."

Janna smiled. "I don't know. I think I still owe you some lies."

"I can't argue with that. I'm sorry that my mission required deceiving you."

"You are a very curious Royal Eye. I've never known such an honest spy."

"I'm no longer a Royal Eye."

"And what? Leaving the Eyes made you suddenly honest?"

"Something like that."

"So what are you doing here?" Janna repeated. Her eyes narrowed and one corner of her mouth twisted in a smirk. She was playing with him, dodging his questions while barraging him with her own. He already suspected that they were here at cross purposes—he to foil Kelas's plans and she to further them. If that was the case, he didn't want to answer her question, at least not while she still had a crossbow pointed at him.

At least, he didn't want to answer her completely. He could say much of the truth without revealing all of it. "I came here hoping to find any notes that Kelas had left behind. Just as you did."

Janna's face brightened. "Kelas's death doesn't have to mean the end of his vision for Aundair," she said.

So Aunn had been right. Janna had come to the cathedral to see if she could pick up where Kelas had left off. She seemed completely unaware that Nara was still working to carry out the plan, which had been hers all along. And now she thought that Aunn was a fellow conspirator. Of course, he'd encouraged that misapprehension—he'd fallen so easily back into his life of lies.

Aunn stepped into the room, closing the distance between the door and the desk in two quick steps before she realized what he was doing. He knocked the crossbow from Janna's hand, sending its bolt clattering harmlessly to the floor. Janna pushed the chair back from the desk and sprang to her feet, drawing her sword as she rose.

"What are you doing?" she said. Fear and confusion twisted her face.

Aunn spread his arms wide again, showing her that he wasn't reaching for his mace. He took a few steps back, so he wasn't in easy reach of her short, heavy blade. "I didn't want your crossbow pointing at me when I told you that my purpose here is actually the opposite of yours. I'm here to ensure that Kelas's plan does not get carried out and his vision for Aundair never becomes reality."

Janna laughed again and lowered her blade. Aunn found himself warming to her ready laugh, despite himself.

"I must say," she said, "your honesty is refreshing. What was your name again?"

"Aunn."

"Aunn. So did you know I was here, or did you suspect someone else of planning to carry on Kelas's work? Or did you just come to destroy all his notes and make sure no one ever could?"

Aunn scowled. She was flirting again, quirking her lips and looking sidelong through her eyelashes, as if he were back in Yeven's face. Toying with him, trying to extract as much information as she could. "I wanted to be honest with you, Janna. But I have to draw the line at giving you information that might help you in pursuing goals that I'm opposed to."

She laughed again, feigning delight at his words, but he saw it in her eyes. She realized exactly what he'd just told her: someone else was already carrying on Kelas's plans. Frustrated, he walked out the door before turning back to Janna.

"Listen," he said. "As a Royal Eye, I promised to give my life in service of the queen. Her Majesty is hardly blameless in all that's happened, but I will not stand by and watch a thousand years of Wynarn rule get tossed aside so she can be replaced with the likes of Jorlanna d'Cannith, Arcanist Wheldren, and you. If you continue to pursue Kelas's schemes, you will make me your enemy."

Janna's smile became a wolfish grin. "Oh no," she sneered. "Perhaps you'll bore me to death with your speeches."

Anger boiled in his chest, and he suddenly couldn't believe he'd ever harbored a pleasant thought about this woman. "Don't underestimate me," he said. "Kelas didn't die in the storm at the Dragon Forge—he died at my hand."

"Was that a threat? Why not fight me now, Aunn?" She stepped around the desk, sword at the ready. "I'm not going to turn back. I'll find the others, and together we'll finish what Kelas started. Are you going to stop me?"

Aunn pulled his mace from his belt. "I am."

Her demeanor changed so quickly that he thought for a moment he was facing the changeling after all, but it was still Janna before him—the laughing, flirtatious Janna of a moment before. She toyed with the hilt of her sword as she took a step toward him, looking coyly up at him.

"But why?" she said. "Why do you care so much for the queen? Why cling to your old loyalties when Aundair could be so much more?"

Aunn knew she was trying to distract him as she advanced within reach of him, but whether she meant to or not, she had struck a nerve. He had admitted it himself—the queen was not blameless in this whole affair. She hadn't ordered the construction of the Dragon Forge, but she had willingly accepted its use in destroying Varna. She had been goaded into attacking the Eldeen Reaches—largely through his own actions—but she had only done what she had always wanted to do. The barbarian invasion just gave her a pretext. In short, the queen was already a pawn of the forces that wanted control of the nation, which begged the question of why Nara wanted to overthrow her at all. Why replace a government she already controlled with an illegitimate government that would draw the ire of the rest of Khorvaire?

Only two possible answers made sense. One possibility was that Nara wanted to reignite the Last War, probably believing that Aundair could win it this time—that a new ruler could govern not just Aundair but all of Khorvaire. That had been Haldren's goal, after all, and when Janna spoke of Kelas's vision for a glorious Aundair, he suspected that's what she had in mind.

But if that was what everybody seemed to believe, then in all likelihood the other possibility was the real truth: it was all about the Prophecy—which, as always, made his head spin.

But he was finally beginning to glimpse the still center of that whirlwind.

Janna watched his face with evident interest, as if she was trying to guess the thoughts running through his mind. She was close enough to strike with her blade, but she hadn't yet, perhaps waiting for some kind of answer to her question.

It was Aunn's turn to laugh. "You won't sway me, Janna. Kelas's vision wasn't what you think it was. Pore though his papers—see if you find anything about the Prophecy, or any clue who he was working for. I'll bet you won't. Go ahead and chase the dream he sold you, and play right into their hands."

Janna's brow furrowed. "Whose hands?"

"When you figure that out, you find me." Aunn turned his back on her and strode back around the corner, down the main passage, up the stairs, and out of the cathedral.

CHAPTER
27

Slowly, Cart began to understand.

Havrakhad spoke in his mind, words that soothed and guided him. He saw visions amid the explosions of golden light that replaced his sight—visions of memory and history, portent and nightmare. His mind was a stormy sea of emotion—raw terror, exultation, steely determination, love— but Havrakhad's voice coaxed him up above the storm, to float above the waves and ride them through the tumult. It was no different, really, from the discipline of a soldier, fighting on despite the fear and pain, careful not to be carried away by the surge of joy that came with each small victory.

He couldn't express or explain what he came to understand, but he knew that it left him changed.

"Listen carefully, Cart," Havrakhad said to him at last. It had been hours—he had no idea how many hours. "In a moment, I will remove the quori's eye from your mind. But before I do that, I have to restore your own sight. When I do, you must not turn and look at me. You *must not*. It will try to make you turn, but you must resist. Use what you have learned, and resist it."

"I understand."

"Not yet, but you begin to. Are you ready?"

"Wait. Where's Ashara?"

"I'm here." Her murmur came from across the room. She sounded sleepy. What had she been doing while Havrakhad was in his mind? Cart realized he had no idea.

"Will you sit beside me?" he asked.

He heard rustling and her soft footsteps, then she sank onto the couch beside him and put a hand on his arm.

"Are you ready?" Havrakhad repeated.

Cart nodded slowly.

"Then open your eyes."

He felt Havrakhad's hand at the back of his neck, and then his vision returned like a slow dawning. He saw Havrakhad's apartment, spare and clean, washed in morning light filtered through gauzy curtains over the windows. Ashara leaned into his view and smiled at him.

He had to turn and see Havrakhad. He knew—with all his being he knew—that if he turned, he would see not the beautiful man he knew as Havrakhad, but a monster veiled in flesh. Everything about Havrakhad was a lie. He fumbled for his axe, ready to turn around and strike the monster down.

"Cart?" Ashara was still holding his arm, looking up at him with worry on her face. Her hair was a tousled mess, and her eyes were swollen from sleep.

She's in league with him, he thought. Panic seized his mind, and he crouched, ready to whirl and confront the monster.

"Use what you have learned, and resist it."

Cart stopped and straightened his legs. He felt the panic in his mind, but he rose above it—he observed it and then discarded it. He felt Havrakhad's fingers on his head, probing gently into his mind, and the panic slowly subsided.

Then another jolt of pain stabbed through his head, and the fear and doubt were gone. "It's gone," he said.

"Yes." Havrakhad came around the couch and into his field of vision. He looked more exhausted than Ashara did, but he smiled. "You did well."

"Thank you," Cart said, then he looked back at Ashara. "And thank you as well."

Wrapping her arms around his waist, she rested her head against his chest. He encircled her in his arms and held her.

"I'm sorry," Cart told Havrakhad. "We'll go, and let you rest."

Cart stood and lifted Ashara to her feet.

"Il-Yannah shines in you, Cart," Havrakhad said, walking them to the door. "Not in your axe or the strength of your arms."

Cart nodded and clasped the kalashtar's hand, Ashara gave a slight bow, and they stepped out into the stairwell of the apartment building. Ashara sighed and took his arm, and they walked together down the stairs.

"Where to now?" Ashara said.

"Do you need more sleep?"

"No. I slept just about the whole time we were there."

"How long was that?"

"All night. What did he do to you?"

"He taught . . . or showed me—" Cart shrugged. "He opened my eyes."

"After he blinded you."

"Hm." That was literally true, but at a different level, Cart felt like he had never learned to see before he met Havrakhad.

"So what now?"

"How about some breakfast?"

"What an excellent idea. I know just the place."

"Then lead the way."

Ashara held his arm as they walked away from the apartment building with its streaming banners and back in the general direction of Chalice Center. When they left the narrow residential streets and walked along more crowded roadways, though, Cart noticed hostile stares directed at them. Ashara didn't seem to mind, but Cart was uneasy. He patted her hands on his arm, then gently extricated himself from her grasp.

"Who cares what they think?" Ashara said.

Cart didn't want to look at her, so he let his gaze range over the wide street, with its row of trees down the center, bare as winter drew near. "In my experience, I find it better to avoid giving offense than to deal with angry people. Especially when they get violent."

"Violent? Because I'm holding your arm?"

"People get violent when I walk into their favorite tavern. Or because I'm on the wrong side of the street. Or because someone's brother died in the war and somehow I'm responsible. People don't need good reasons to be unreasonable."

Ashara laughed at his choice of words, and Cart hung his head. She could take the matter lightly, because she had never known the reality of life as a warforged. Quite the contrary— as an heir of House Cannith, she had enjoyed the servitude of the House's warforged creations for most of her life. She could still rightly command Cart's loyalty, as much as she wanted him to think of her as a friend.

She tried to take his arm again, but he pulled away. They walked in silence the rest of the way to Ashara's choice of break-fast locations—a bakery in Chalice Center. Cart didn't notice its name.

* * * * *

Cart sat with his arms folded across his chest and watched Ashara eat. The sting of her laughter was fading, and he was trying to remind himself to rise above it, to observe the storm of his emotions without being carried away by it. He liked watching people eat, except when they ate things that didn't seem to fit in the category of food—clams, mushrooms, pota-toes. He particularly liked the way the muscles of Ashara's jaw flexed as she chewed, and the obvious pleasure on her face as she licked the dusting of cinnamon and sugar from her fingertips.

Her smile vanished as her eyes fell on something behind him, by the door. The smile returned a moment later, but dif-ferent, perhaps forced. Cart heard footsteps behind him.

"Hello, Harkin," Ashara said.

Cart turned in his seat to see the blond Cannith heir stand-ing behind him. He didn't return Ashara's smile.

"I thought I might find you here." Harkin seized a chair from another table and sat between them.

"What do you mean?" Ashara asked. "We were going to meet for luncheon."

"You were quite the scandal in Fairhaven this morning, walking arm in arm with your warforged like lovers."

Ashara's face turned crimson. "Why is it anyone's business what we do?"

Harkin laughed. "It's not, but that won't stop them from talking. Particularly when they can see the dragonmark on your arm. I understand the baron is in a fury."

"Jorlanna has already excoriated me. What else can she do?"

"You really don't know what you're in the middle of, do you?"

"Why don't you spell it out for me, Harkin?"

"Very well, Ashara. Jorlanna has decided to cast aside the Korth Edicts and swear allegiance to the queen, turning her part of House Cannith into an Aundairian noble family and its enclave into a Ministry of Artifice, responsible for producing armaments for the crown."

"I'm well aware of what Jorlanna has done," Ashara said.

Cart nodded. When the first King Galifar united the Five Nations under his rule, he signed accords with the leaders of the dragonmarked houses that prevented such close ties between the houses and the crown, but in the chaos of the Last War those agreements had grown increasingly tenuous.

"Of course you are." Harkin sneered. "But fourteen other dragonmarked barons are watching very carefully. Some of them have been stretching or outright breaking the Korth Edicts for years. There's no way Lyrandar's operations in Valenar are legal—they have a standing army there, and a fleet of flying warships. Aurala even married an heir of House Vadalis—and now she's gone and destroyed the city Vadalis calls home. No wonder some of the Houses are very nervous about what could happen if Aurala or some other sovereign starts getting ideas. House Orien's headquarters are down in Passage, and I know they're worried that Aurala's going to annex them next. More than any other House, Orien needs to be able to operate across national borders—that's the whole point of the Mark of Passage, right?"

"What are you getting at, Harkin?"

Harkin leaned over the table. "There's a war brewing, Ashara, and we're right in the middle of it."

"The barbarians? What—"

"Not the barbarians. The Houses. Look around you. House Cannith is about to split like Phiarlan and Thuranni did, if it hasn't already. The rest of the Houses are lining up on one side or the other, some trying to preserve the Korth Edicts, the rest trying to continue tearing them down until the dragonmarked rule Khorvaire."

Cart shifted in his seat. Harkin's words rang true, and Cart suspected that this dragonmarked war ranged farther than Harkin was aware. Did he know about the Dragon Forge and Phaine's involvement in it?

"Where does House Thuranni stand in all this?" Cart asked.

Ashara looked at him thoughtfully, but Harkin seemed annoyed at his intrusion. "They haven't made their position known," he said.

"You're thinking of Phaine," Ashara said. Cart nodded. "He was part of Jorlanna's plan, but that doesn't mean his whole house was involved."

"Phaine?" Harkin said. "A Thuranni?"

"Yes," Ashara said, still looking at Cart.

Harkin snorted. "If one Thuranni is involved, you can be sure their baron knows about it."

"But why was he involved?" Cart asked. He was trying to piece it together in his mind, but he felt as much adrift as he had when he was working with Haldren—caught up in political games far beyond his expertise. The night before, in the Ruby Chalice, Gaven and Ashara had been talking about what might happen if the dragonshard ended up in Phaine's hands. Perhaps, he thought, House Thuranni sought to undermine House Lyrandar, or maybe they hoped to build more Dragon Forges and steal marks from all the Houses. He wasn't sure if that had anything to do with the Korth Edicts, though. And he didn't want to talk about it in front of Harkin.

Ashara seemed to share his reluctance, which made him strangely glad. She reached across the table and took Cart's hand. "I still don't see what this has to do with me and Cart."

Harkin looked down at their hands as if he were regarding a dead thing on his plate. "Don't you? Aurala and Jorlanna have just thrown the Korth Edicts out the window. The vigilant protectors of the Korth Edicts are the Sentinel Marshals of House Deneith. Or, as some people like to say, House Deneith uses the Marshals to make sure that nobody *else* violates the Edicts by creating an army that could challenge Deneith. So the Sentinel Marshals are looking for a way to interfere with Jorlanna, to get Cannith West back where it belongs—in a private enclave, and out of the government."

Cart shifted uncomfortably at the mention of the Sentinel Marshals. At Haldren's command, he had attacked the Sentinel Marshal who captured Senya. That was not one of his proudest moments.

"There's a marshal in town right now," Harkin continued, "quietly asking questions about this whole affair, and by now I expect she's heard quite an earful about the Cannith heir seen walking through the streets this morning, hanging on the arm of a warforged. The key question, I think, is whether she knows that the baron declared you excoriate. If she doesn't, she might try to use you to trap Jorlanna. If she does, she might be asking for your help."

"I don't want to talk to a Sentinel Marshal." Ashara groaned.

Harkin smirked. "That, my dear, is why you should have kept a lower profile this morning. Now, it's too late. The Sentinel Marshal I spoke of has just walked into this bakery."

Ashara looked at the door, over Cart's shoulder, and her eyes widened. Cart turned in his seat and saw them as well. A tall human woman wearing gleaming chainmail beneath a leather overcoat, resting a hand on the basket hilt of a rapier, cast her eyes around the room until they fell on Cart. She gestured to her companion, a female dwarf whose scarlet silk shirt provided stark contrast to her deep brown skin, and the two of them made their way to the table where Cart and Ashara sat.

CHAPTER
28

Senya tucked her feet under her and smiled. "So why did you come here?" she asked.

Gaven leaned back in his chair and sighed. Why had he come? "I'm not sure, actually."

"Really?" Senya shifted forward slightly. She wasn't mocking him—she seemed genuinely intrigued.

"Well, I got to thinking about what your ancestor said to me in Shae Mordai. 'The third time, you will finally find what you seek.'"

Senya nodded. "'Twice you have come to me now,' she said. You never did explain that."

"The first time, it wasn't me. A dragon disguised in human form went with Mendaros to see your ancestor."

"What? If it wasn't you . . ."

"That dragon's memories took root in my mind. That's why—well, basically that's why I went to Dreadhold. So when you took me before your ancestor, she recognized the dragon in my mind. That was the second time."

"The dragon's second time."

Gaven frowned. "Sort of." It didn't make sense, as he thought about it. The dragon had visited Senya's ancestor once, four or five hundred years ago. If Gaven's visit was the second time, then the ancestor had been talking about the dragon, not Gaven. Perhaps he'd been fooling himself to think that Senya's ancestor could give him anything he sought.

"So that's why you asked about Mendaros," Senya said.

"Yes. When we were in Shae Mordai, I was overwhelmed with the memory of being there before, walking up those stairs with Mendaros beside me. I remembered him as a good friend."

"A good friend to a dragon. Hence his disgrace in our family."

"Yes. You said that he opened the door for an invasion of dragons."

"He did. I have learned more about him in the last few months, if you're interested."

Gaven leaned forward. "Quite interested. Please."

Senya smiled. "Well, Mendaros Alvena Tuorren was born in 398, in Galifar's reckoning, just over six hundred years ago. He was born in Shae Cairdal, but by the mid-four hundreds he was wandering around Khorvaire, already sort of an outcast from the family. He was evidently very interested in the Prophecy of the dragons, and in 512 he was involved in the construction of an observatory in the Starpeaks."

"King Daroon's observatory?" Gaven said. As ruler of Galifar, Daroon had grown obsessed with predicting the future by studying the moons and stars.

"I suppose so, yes. It's not clear to me what his involvement with it was, and I don't know what his connection to the king was."

"I might have known once." Gaven wasn't sure how he knew about King Daroon. Was that something he had learned in his studies, or the echo of the dragon's memories in his mind? He shook his head.

"Mendaros only exercised his Right of Counsel once," Senya said, "and he brought a friend from Khorvaire—a human, or he seemed to be—with him. I assume that human was actually the dragon you described. Mendaros asked questions about the Storm Dragon, and received answers similar to what you and I heard on our visit. They went on to ask about the Time of the Dragon Between, and the Time of the Dragon Below. Mendaros, apparently, was particularly interested in the Blasphemer."

"The Blasphemer?"

"My ancestor, in her wisdom, perceived that, while Mendaros's human companion fancied himself the Storm Dragon, Mendaros imagined himself to be the Blasphemer."

"Dragons fly before the Blasphemer's legions," Gaven said, and visions of bone-white banners danced in his memory.

"And apparently, as dragons winged across the sea to attack Aerenal, Mendaros commanded a fleet of warships full of his mercenary legions."

Gaven sat back and ran his fingers through his hair. "And when was that?"

"That was in 537."

"So more than four hundred years ago. What happened? You said it was a devastating invasion."

"It was. Taer Senadal was burned to the ground, and both Var-Shalas and Shae Thoridor were in flames before the dragons were routed."

Gaven had studied maps of Aerenal before, but the names meant little to him. Taer Senadal was a fortress—he could figure that much from the name. He nodded for her to continue anyway.

"Mendaros made land near Var-Shalas," Senya continued, "and tried to bring his legions upriver to the town, but they didn't get very far. He was killed in the battle."

Gaven rested his forehead in his palm and tried to make sense of this information. The dragon had sought to become the Storm Dragon more than four hundred years ago, and then, when its memories found their way into Gaven's mind, he had followed along a similar path. Mendaros had set himself up as the Blasphemer four centuries ago, and now a new Blasphemer had arisen out of the Demon Wastes. Was the Prophecy fulfilled in cycles, so that every age had its Storm Dragon and its Blasphemer? Or were Mendaros and the dragon deluded, pursuing the Prophecy when the time of its fulfillment was still far off? Or perhaps they were all deluded—neither Gaven nor the dragon actually fulfilled the Prophecy of the Storm Dragon, and the warlord from the Wastes was no more the Blasphemer than Mendaros had been.

Senya got up and stood before Gaven, filling his nostrils with the smells of incense and spice. She held out a hand, and Gaven took it.

"Why did you come here?" she asked again.

Gaven's eyes stung. "I was hoping someone could tell me what it is I'm supposed to be looking for."

Senya nodded. "Come with me." She squeezed his hand, and he stood beside her.

Senya led him out of her room and back down the stairs, her hand soft and warm in his—so alive, in contrast to the death mask on her face. She led him to the tall doors across from the entrance, and there she released his hand.

"Just a moment," she whispered.

Gaven watched in silence as she busied herself around one of the braziers outside the doors. Scented smoke billowed up from the coals, and she moved to the other and sent another offering of smoke into the air. Then she stood before the doors and sang softly in Elven. Gaven caught only a few words speaking of honor, reverence, death, and wisdom. She touched a few of the carved images as she sang, and when she was finished with the song the doors swung open like arms reaching to enfold her.

She was smiling when she turned back and extended a hand to him. He stepped forward and took her hand, and she drew him into the interior of the temple. The doors swung shut behind him, and he was in darkness.

His eyes, growing accustomed to the dark, found the dim glow of coals just before they flared to life at Senya's touch. The tiny fires did little to illuminate the cavernous room, though. Gaven wasn't sure what he had been expecting—something more like the small tomb where Senya's ancestor had granted them an audience in Shae Mordai, he supposed. Instead, the room was the size of a grand temple of the Sovereign Host.

Senya took his hand again and led him to the center of the room. "Kneel," she whispered, and he obeyed. A woven mat of dried reeds offered a meager cushion between his knees and the stone floor.

As Senya drifted away again, Gaven found himself wondering how old the temple was. Shae Mordai was ancient—the elves had started its construction more than twenty thousand years ago, although surely not every building could be that old. But when had the population of Aereni in Fairhaven grown sufficiently large to support a construction project on this scale? It felt old, but he suspected that had as much to do with the burning incense and the presence of the deathless than with the actual age of the building.

Two more braziers flared to feeble light in front of him, where Senya stood in front of a carved altar. The altar looked as old as anything he'd seen in Shae Mordai, and Gaven wondered if it had been brought from Aerenal, perhaps as sort of a foundation stone for the whole community of Aereni here.

Senya turned and smiled at him, then sat cross-legged on the floor in front of the altar and closed her eyes. In the half-light of the flickering braziers, her face was an ornately decorated skull floating above her shoulders. When her eyes were closed, they could easily have been gaping sockets. He watched her chest rise and fall three times with slow, even breaths, and then her eyes shot open.

Her eyes, though, were no longer sparkling orbs of sapphire blue, but pale yellow flames that seemed to dance in empty sockets. And when she spoke, her voice had become the cold, clear voice of her long-dead ancestor.

"Gaven, Storm Dragon, dishonored child of Lyrandar, what do you seek?"

Gaven pressed his forehead to the ground as he had seen Senya do in Shae Mordai, surprised to find tears already welling in his eyes.

"I—" His voice caught in his throat, and he cleared it as he rose to look at Senya again. "I don't know."

"How can you hope to find it, then?"

"I thought . . ." Gaven peered at her. "Senya?"

"My daughter cannot hear you right now. Speak to me."

"I'm sorry. Senya's . . . you told me, in Shae Mordai . . ."

"The third time, you will finally find what you seek."

"Yes."

"And you hoped I could tell you what your desire is? Only you can name that, Gaven."

Gaven sighed. "There's so much."

"And you don't want to appear greedy? Is that it?"

Gaven frowned. "I suppose it is."

"I have not promised to grant you any wish you might voice, Gaven, and I cannot magically solve all the difficulties facing you. I offer you counsel, even though you have no right to claim it—it is my gift to you."

"Why do you offer this gift?"

"Three times you have come to me now," Senya said. "The first time, you were a dragon seeking the power of the Storm Dragon. The second, you were a man dreading that mantle, as the dragon's thoughts within you encouraged you to seek it. Now you are a man, and you have been the Storm Dragon, but you did not choose the path that the dragon before you sought. You have shown insight and restraint. I am pleased to offer my wisdom to aid you."

"I am grateful." Gaven bowed to the floor again, trying to collect his thoughts. "The first time, though—that wasn't me. It was the dragon." The name surfaced in his memory. "Shakravar."

"And who are you?"

"I'm Gaven. Just the man, not the dragon anymore."

"Here, then, is my gift of wisdom for you. You cannot cut time with a knife, as if the present were utterly separate from the past and the future. Who you are now is who you have been and who you are yet to be. You are Gaven. You are the Storm Dragon. You are a dishonored child of Lyrandar, cut off from your line but still a product of it. You are Shakravar, and you are the murderer of the Paelion line."

Senya's words hit him like a blow to the stomach, and he bent forward to the floor again. "I wish that were not true."

"But you know that it is. However, you are also, in this moment, who you will choose to be, and that is a far better thing."

"How do you know? Is it written in the Prophecy what I will become?"

"You know the answer to that. You have read it in your own dragonmark."

"There are many paths traced in the lines of my dragonmark."

"Yes, there are many paths you could choose, many paths you might have chosen but did not, paths you have turned away from but could yet return to. The Prophecy, like the lines of your mark, offers many possibilities."

"Then how can you say what choices I will make? How can I already be what I have not yet decided to be?"

"Because who you will be in that moment includes who you are now."

"That moment? One particular moment?"

"There are many moments, past and future, that define who you are. There is one decision coming upon you soon that defines the shape of your destiny."

"What is that?"

"In the darkest night of the Dragon Below, storm and dragon . . ."

Gaven joined his voice to the thin voice of Senya's ancestor. ". . . are reunited, and they break together upon the legions of the Blasphemer."

"But what—"

"The maelstrom swirls around him," the ancestor continued. "He is the storm and the eye of the storm. His is the new dawn, and in him the storm cannot die."

Gaven leaned forward, trying to imprint the words in his memory. His eyes fixed on Senya's face, he fumbled at his pouch and withdrew the shard that held the glowing lines of his dragonmark. Light spilled from it and spread to fill the enormous temple.

"His are the words the Blasphemer unspeaks, his the song the Blasphemer unsings."

Senya closed her eyes, and the lambent flames were extinguished. Gaven glanced down at the dragonshard, but it was glowing so brightly he had to look away. He looked up instead, and saw the lines of his mark etched over the ceiling and every wall, as they had been in the Dragon Forge.

All the lines of his mark, the paths that delimited the possibilities of his life—they were all laid out before his eyes. Layer upon layer of meaning was contained in the twisting patterns, and he lost himself in them as if he were walking the Sky Caves of Thieren Kor again.

"His are the words the Blasphemer unspeaks." He saw that path—that network of paths, that expanse of possibility. "His the song the Blasphemer unsings." He saw creation undone, reality unwoven, his power of creation and the Blasphemer's sword of annihilation rending the fabric of time and space.

He knew at last what he would do, and who he would become.

CHAPTER
29

Gaven stared at the lines of his dragonmark until the light faded from the shard and draped the room in shadow again, and then he stared at the ceiling until Senya, standing beside him, nudged him back to his senses.

"Did you find what you seek?" she said, holding a hand out for him.

"I believe I did." He took her hand and got to his feet. The braziers' fire had already died down, so the only light in the temple came in through the open doors.

"Where will you go now?"

Gaven looked back up at the ceiling as though the lines of his destiny were still visible there. He knew his destination, but he still had a choice of paths to get there.

"West," he said. She started to pull her hand away, but he gripped it with both hands. "Senya, thank you. Thank you so much."

Senya beamed at him, her blue eyes sparkling in the firelight. "The fact that I was able to help you is atonement for a great many past sins. You might not recognize it, but you have helped me as well."

Gaven released her hand and drew her instead into a tight embrace, which she returned. He closed his eyes as he held her, and for that moment he thought he saw the twisting lines of her destiny as well, all the mad rush of her past, but only serenity ahead, the peace of communion with her ancestors and service to her people.

"Now," she said, pulling out of his embrace. "I meant where will you go *now?* When's the last time you slept?"

Gaven laughed. "It has been a while since I had a good night's sleep."

"You'll sleep in my room tonight, then."

Gaven started to stammer a protest, but she cut him off.

"Don't worry, I'll leave you alone. You need sleep tonight."

He hadn't realized until that moment how tired he was. Without another word, he let Senya lead him back upstairs to her room.

"Sleep well, Gaven." She kissed his forehead and left him alone in the warm darkness as sleep reached to claim him.

* * * * *

The morning sun dazzled Aunn's eyes, accustomed as they were to the dim light of the cathedral. He scanned the sky for a storm cloud that might point him to Gaven, but the Storm Dragon was not making it that easy to find him. Aunn bit his lip and tried to think. Where would Gaven go?

As far as Aunn knew, Gaven had no papers. Aunn had promised to get him some and deliver them to the Ruby Chalice the night before. Without them, he would find it difficult, if not impossible, to board a Lyrandar airship, the lightning rail, or even an Orien coach.

He had done it before, Aunn reminded himself. Gaven and Senya had taken the lightning rail from Korranberg well into Breland. But that was before the skirmish at Starcrag Plain and the all-out war now being waged in the Eldeen Reaches. Security would be much tighter . . . unless . . .

Unless Gaven managed to talk his way onto an airship. It was unlikely, but if he found someone he knew, an old friend who'd be willing to take a big risk for his sake. Jordhan had done it, first ferrying Gaven and Rienne from Sharavacion to Stormhome, then taking them all the way to Argonnessen.

Drawing a deep breath of the wintry air, Aunn got his bearings, then set out toward Chalice Center. He had to find Gaven. The fate of much more than the queen might depend on it.

* * * * *

Harkin sighed. "Well, this should be interesting," he muttered as the pair approached the table.

"Ashara d'Cannith?" the tall human woman asked. The dwarf stood behind her, arms crossed over her chest, glaring at Cart.

"I suppose that depends," Ashara said. "My baron and the queen would have us say ir'Cannith."

"By the terms of the Korth Edicts, they would be wrong to give land and noble rank to heirs of a dragonmarked house."

Ashara smiled. "And your name?"

"Sentinel Marshal Mauren d'Deneith." She gave a slight, stiff bow. "And this is Ossa d'Kundarak."

The dwarf turned her gaze from Cart and smiled briefly at Ashara, then recrossed her arms and resumed her staring.

"This is Harkin," Ashara said, "also of my House, and this is Cart."

"Cart?" The Kundarak's gaze sharpened. "Haldren's Cart?"

That explained the harsh stare, Cart supposed. How did this dwarf know him?

"I beg your pardon?" Ashara said.

Ossa stood with her hands on her hips and brought her face unpleasantly close to Cart's. "Are you the Cart that belonged to the late Haldren ir'Brassek?"

"The last time I belonged to anyone, it was to the army," Cart said. "By the terms of the Treaty of Thronehold, it would be wrong to call me anyone's property."

Ashara beamed at him, but Ossa's face darkened and Mauren scowled as well.

"What's wrong, Ossa?" the Sentinel Marshal asked.

"A warforged named Cart helped ir'Brassek escape from Dreadhold," Ossa explained. "I chased them from Cape Far to Stormhome."

"It's hardly an uncommon name for warforged," Ashara said. "This one has been with my House since the war."

"He has a very independent mind for a Cannith warforged," Ossa observed. It was true—the warforged at the Cannith enclave had been docile servants.

"But clearly you've grown very attached to him in that time," Mauren said, "which is part of the reason we're here."

Cart shot a glance at Harkin, who was leaning back in his chair, legs crossed, hands folded on one knee. He didn't seem inclined to betray Ashara's lie, but he wasn't leaping to Cart's defense either. His face had a bemused expression, as if he were interested to see how Ashara would worm her way out of the situation.

"You're here because I've become friends with a warforged?" Ashara said. "Surely the Sentinel Marshals have more important things to do with their time than chase down every soldier, artificer, and dockworker who's struck up a friendship with a warforged."

"We're not interested in every soldier, artificer, and dockworker, Lady Cannith," Mauren said. "We're interested in you."

* * * * *

Gaven awoke to sunlight streaming through a high window he hadn't noticed in the dark of night. He felt rested, for the first time he could remember. He wondered whether Senya had used magic to knock him out, and how long he'd slept, but he decided it didn't matter. He stood and stretched, and even then the complaints of his cuts and bruises were diminished, if not entirely absent. He felt good, and ready for what fate had in store for him.

He pulled his chainmail shirt back on and slung his scabbard over his back, wondering where Senya might be and whether his emergence from her room might arouse scandalized speculation among the other residents of the temple. As he stepped forward and reached for the door, though, glowing red lines flashed across his vision, part of his dragonmark as it appeared in the shard. He paused, trying to sort out a vague sense of imminent danger and make sense of the pattern he'd seen.

He felt a presence behind him an instant before he heard the soft rustle of silk, and he spun and ducked away. A blot of shadow in the streaming sunlight slashed past him, and a black blade cut across his arm, drawing a thin line of blood that burned even as icy cold spread from the wound. The shadowy figure spun to follow him, relentless in its attack. He yanked his sword from its sheath on his back as he dodged again and his eyes struggled to pierce the shadow that cloaked his assailant.

The figure lunged again, and Gaven tried to bring his sword around to block the blow. His left hand, though, was numbed by whatever toxin coated the assassin's dagger, making his grip on his own sword unsteady. He banged his elbow against the wall as he maneuvered his sword in the tiny room, and the black dagger slipped past his guard and toward his neck.

His attacker's face was close enough that Gaven could see through the veil of shadow. "Phaine," he breathed.

Time seemed to slow to a crawl as the point of the elf's dagger touched the skin of his neck and pressed inward. Then a burst of blinding white light drove away Phaine's cloak of shadows and threw the elf back as a crack of thunder exploded between the two men. Gaven and Phaine slammed against opposite walls of the room.

Phaine struggled to his feet, his breath rasping. "The power of the storm is still with you after all," he said, scowling. His eyes ranged over Gaven's body, lingering at the pouches at Gaven's belt. "So you must have the bloodshard."

The cut on Gaven's arm was on fire, even as his hand grew increasingly numb and cold, and the toxin spread up into his shoulder as well. His heart pounded in his chest, which he knew would just send the poison coursing more quickly through his veins.

"Isn't that why you're here? Malathar never did give you a chance to study it, did he?"

"He didn't," Phaine said. "You have disrupted a great many plans."

"Considering that those plans involved torturing me and stealing my dragonmark, I can't say that I'm sorry."

"You will be." Phaine's shadow-filled eyes were fixed on Gaven as if he were watching the poison spread through his body, waiting for him to keel over. As if in response, a sharp jolt of pain stabbed through Gaven's chest.

Gaven fumbled with his numb left hand at the pouch that held the dragonshard, then shifted his sword to that hand and reached for the shard with his right. Phaine chose that awkward instant to leap at him again, his dagger poised to swing in a broad arc across Gaven's neck.

Gaven's fingers touched the smooth crystal and lightning gave shape to his fury and hatred, leaping out from him to engulf Phaine. The elf's black eyes shot wide as twisting tendrils of lightning suspended him in the air between floor and ceiling, with a stream of blinding light connecting him to Gaven.

Gaven withdrew the shard from his pouch and shook it in Phaine's direction. "Is this what you came for?" Sparks danced in his mouth as he spoke. A second bolt of lightning shot from the shard to spear through Phaine's middle for a moment, and smoke started to billow from his scorched clothes and hair. "Here it is, you bastard. Want to take it from me?"

Gaven was a pillar of crackling lightning. It coiled in arcs around his body and cascaded down his outstretched arm, and tendrils of it danced over the walls of the room. He was more than the storm—he was destructive energy barely contained in mortal flesh, annihilation he couldn't restrain.

"Gaven?" The door swung open, and a tendril of lightning leaped to course over Senya.

"No!" He let go of the dragonshard, but it clung to his flesh as lightning continued to flow through him and dance across the walls, up to the high window and the ceiling, across the floor, and over the still forms of Phaine and Senya where they hung suspended in the air.

* * * * *

A sharp crack that sounded like thunder, muffled but not distant, caught Aunn's attention as he hurried toward Chalice Center. He slowed his steps, trying to determine what he had heard and decide whether to investigate. He scanned the sky, but it was clear and cold with winter's approach, with no sign of a brewing storm, either natural or sprung from the twisting lines of Gaven's mark.

He heard some commotion, distant shouts and running feet. Clearly, he hadn't imagined the sound. He was in a part of the city he didn't know particularly well—he remembered a tiny enclave of Aereni immigrants nearby, elves who clung to the ways of their ancestors, unlike most of the urbanized elves of Khorvaire, who worshiped the Sovereign Host and fit in smoothly with their human, dwarf, and gnome neighbors. What would Gaven be doing in that neighborhood?

A chill ran up Aunn's spine as he remembered the undead thing Senya had addressed as a revered ancestor, and he shuddered. "All right," he muttered, "I'm coming." He listened for the nearest sounds of commotion and followed them.

* * * * *

"Who you are now is who you have been and who you are yet to be."

The cold, clear voice of Senya's ancestor echoed in Gaven's mind as he hung suspended in time, lightning like the twisting lines of his dragonmark binding him together with Phaine and with Senya. Pain seared along his every nerve, power too great for his body to contain.

"You are Gaven. You are the Storm Dragon. You are a dishonored child of Lyrandar, cut off from your line but still a product of it. You are Shakravar, and you are the murderer of the Paelion line."

I've killed her, he thought. He tried to shake the dragonshard from his hand, but it was a part of him. He struggled to lower his hand, to bring it in to his chest so his other hand might pry the dragonshard free, but the lightning was like a swift-flowing river that would not release his arm.

"However, you are also, in this moment, who you will choose to be, and that is a far better thing."

And so, Gaven thought, I now choose this.

He closed his eyes and drew a deep breath. The air, heated by lightning, seared his throat and lungs, but he focused his thoughts on the dragonshard in his hand. He saw the lines of the Prophecy winding within its rosy heart, and words formed in his mind—words he might have known once, in this life or another, but which were now part of his destiny and part of himself:

Under the unlight of the darkened sun, the Storm Dragon lays down his mantle; he stops his song before it can be unsung, and so his storm is extinguished.

The dragonshard clattered to the floor in a shower of sparks, and the writhing tendrils of lightning withdrew into its gleaming surface. Phaine and Senya, released by the storm, fell to the ground, shrouded in reeking smoke.

"Senya!" Gaven gasped. He stepped toward her, but his leg faltered under his weight and he toppled onto the floor beside her. He was vaguely aware of voices outside the door, chattering in confusion and alarm, but he couldn't lift his head to look. His face pressed against the cold stone, he could see only the death mask of Senya's tattooed face.

"Senya, I'm sorry," he gasped.

Blackness swallowed his vision, but he thought he saw two smoldering green flames looking into his eyes before the darkness claimed him.

* * * * *

It would have been easy for Aunn to put on an elven face and blend in among the dozens of elves rushing into their temple to find out what was going on, but he did not. He saw some bluntly hostile glances, but no one accosted him as he moved through an open courtyard outside the temple. Flickering light—white like lightning, not the red of a fire—lit a high window near the top of the temple, and Aunn could feel the ground beneath his feet rumbling with the thunder of Gaven's storm. He could feel the fear of the elves around him, and it was no wonder. Aunn was terrified, and he had a pretty good idea what was going on. To the elves, this must have seemed like an angry divine manifestation.

As he climbed the stairs to the temple, he drew more angry glares. A few elves shouted at him in Elven, which he couldn't really make out. "No go in," one managed in Common, but Aunn ignored her and pushed his way into the building.

A pair of tall stone doors stood open inside the temple, and a few of the elves gathered inside, seeking solace in the spiritual presence of their ancestors in the absence of any priests. A dozen or so more huddled around the bottom of a staircase leading up in the direction of the storm-filled window, as if waiting for news to be delivered from on high. The flickering light cast eerie dancing shadows down the stairs, and the building trembled with the rumble of thunder. Aunn hesitated, unsure if he'd be allowed to climb the stairs or if he could even make it through the press of elves.

The building stopped shaking abruptly, and the flickering light went out. A hush fell over the crowd, but in a moment there were shouts from the top of the stairs. A murmur spread through the elves around him, and they turned toward the temple sanctuary.

Aunn bit his lip and started walking against the crowd. There weren't that many elves, but they were crammed into a narrow antechamber and moving with some urgency in the direction opposite the one he wanted to go in. Every time he collided with an elf, he provoked shouts and glares, and he understood just enough Elven to know quite clearly that he wasn't welcome.

Finally he reached the bottom of the stairs, and stopped in his tracks. A deathless soldier blocked his way, clutching the haft of a poleaxe with both bony hands and staring at him with eyes of green fire.

"You are not welcome here," the soldier said. "This is where we pay honor to our ancestors."

Aunn swallowed hard. His fear of the undead was utterly irrational, but that didn't make it any less paralyzing. It took root in him years ago, on one of his first missions during the war, in Atur—the Karrn city rightly called the City of Night. He tried to answer the soldier, but his voice froze in his throat.

You are mine. He felt Tira's breath on his lips again. *I did not call you to live in fear.*

"Please," he said, the memory of the presence in the cathedral giving him strength. "My friend is upstairs."

"Your friend? The Khoravar?"

It took Aunn a moment to recognize the word, a term for half-elves. "Yes! Gaven."

The undead guard made an eerie sound that was half growl and half wail, and Aunn's fear returned in force. "Your blaspheming Khoravar friend killed our priestess."

CHAPTER
30

S omeone shouted her name. Rienne looked up from the blood-soaked ground and saw Kyaphar at the edge of the clearing, beckoning to her.

"The Mosswood Warden calls us to battle!" he cried. "Come!"

It's too late, Rienne thought. The battle is over.

The healer's spirit bear shifted nervously on its feet, punctuating its whimpers with an occasional quiet roar. The healer herself seemed lost in a trance, one hand planted on the ground, grave concern written on her face. The Blasphemer had already started to break the seal, and the battle was lost.

"We can still drive him back!" Kyaphar shouted. "We can limit the damage he does! Come!"

Rienne forced herself into a run. Kyaphar was probably wrong—this final charge had little chance of success, and was most likely just a headlong rush into destruction. But she had to try. She had committed her sword to the defense of this site, and she would not back down.

"This way," Kyaphar said.

Rienne shot past him, unhindered by armor and empowered by the energy coiled in her soul. She heard him laugh behind her—grimly cheerful on this day of doom—and then his laugh turned into a growl. He loped beside her in the shape of a shaggy black wolf, easily keeping pace with her light steps.

They charged together through the woods, bounding over fallen trees and scrambling beneath low branches. It was exhilarating. The leaves and twigs that brushed her as she passed seemed to gift her with some of their life, as if the forest was fortifying its defender. Kyaphar must have felt it as well, for his bestial form raced with increasing vigor, keeping pace with her as she sped up.

He barked and jerked his head to the side, and they altered course. A moment later, they emerged from the grove onto the slope of a hill overlooking the battlefield, and Rienne slowed her pace, then stopped. The sky was a black dome of smoke, neither day nor night but a ruddy twilight of fire and shadow. From her higher ground, she saw the barbarians arrayed in a wide arc, with a wall of flames at their back, driving them forward at their fiendish leader's urging. The Eldeen defenders were a ragged ring, unable to hold the barbarians back. Dragons flew here and there above the fray, occasionally loosing blasts of fire or frost, bolts of lightning or sprays of acid down onto the soldiers below.

Rienne couldn't see any sign of the seal breaking, but she could feel it—a sense of wrongness radiating up from the violated land. It reminded her of Starcrag Plain, the feeling she'd had as wave after wave of monstrosities, the hordes of the Soul Reaver, spilled out of the earth and washed over her.

Elestrissa stood a few paces away, surrounded by a clump of warriors, mystics, and rangers. The men and women gathered around the Mosswood Warden wore superior armor and carried weapons that shone with magic, clearly setting them apart from the rank and file soldiery. A few of them, like her, bore the signs of their own struggles against the Blasphemer's dragons. These, she guessed, were the greatest heroes of the Eldeen Reaches, gathered from across the lands that the Blasphemer had already devastated—a half-dozen humans, about as many shifters, a few elves and half-elves. Two dwarves covered in thick hide armor stood beside a goliath who towered over them; its leather armor left much of the patterned markings and rocklike protrusions on his stone-gray skin exposed.

"Ah! Kyaphar," Elestrissa said, gesturing toward them. Rienne turned to look at the Sky Warden, and saw the tall, proud man once more where the wolf had been a moment before. "And Lady Alastra Dragonslayer. Good! We have precious little time."

Elestrissa turned back to face the battlefield, and Rienne stepped forward to join the others at her side.

"There he is," the Mosswood Warden said, pointing toward the center of the arc of flame. "The Blasphemer, the opener of the seal. He has spread his forces thin, because he knows that our defense is thinner still. That means there aren't many soldiers between us and him. Our plan is as simple as it is desperate: We charge straight for the Blasphemer. The greater our speed, the less chance he will have to put more of his forces in our way. If we're fast enough, we'll cut right through his lines and get to him. One man cannot stand for long against twenty of us. And when he is dead, our hope—our only, desperate hope—is that his sundering will cease. Perhaps none of us will survive this day, but if we succeed, the world can rest tonight free from fear."

Elestrissa turned and let her eyes range over the men and women gathered around her. Rienne watched emotions flit across her face as she met the gaze of each individual—it was clear that Elestrissa knew all of these people personally and held them in the highest respect. Rienne felt sadly out of place.

"Sky Warden Kyaphar," Elestrissa said as her eyes fell on him, "your place is not at my side this day. I want you with the Lyrandar airship."

Jordhan! Rienne couldn't believe that she had all but forgotten him in the press of the battle. She searched the sky, and saw the airship drifting over the glade behind her, as if it had followed her from the healer's clearing. Elestrissa must have held it in reserve for this moment, knowing that revealing it too soon would make it a target for the dragons.

Elestrissa was still addressing Kyaphar. "You may choose a few others to join you, and your task will be to rain the fury of wind and storm down upon our foes. If we succeed in destroying the Blasphemer, the survivors will need help getting back through his forces. Clear them a path."

Kyaphar bowed. "As you command," he said. He sounded pained, as though he wanted to be part of the ground assault— or else he was already grieving those who would surely fall.

Then Elestrissa stood before Rienne and looked solemnly down at her. "And you, Lady Dragonslayer. Do you still wish to stand with us in our foolhardy defense of this place?"

But the Blasphemer's end lies in the void, in the maelstrom that pulls him down to darkness. Rienne's dream flashed through her mind, and briefly she wondered whether she should flee—fall back to the river, join the Aundairian defenders there, and seek to bring about the Blasphemer's end the way her dream suggested.

"What is the Prophecy?" she asked.

Elestrissa looked confused.

"Is the vision in my dream an immutable image of what will be, regardless of what I choose? If it is, then what I do now doesn't matter—one way or another. I'm fated to end up facing the Blasphemer at the river. I can join your charge knowing that somehow I'll survive, even if no one else does, because my destiny is to face the Blasphemer in two weeks, when he reaches the Wyr."

"But we and the Eldeen Reaches are doomed," Elestrissa said, scowling.

"Or perhaps my vision was just a glimpse of what could be, a foretaste of what might come to pass if I make the choices that lead me to that point. In that case, I'm free to choose a different path and perhaps arrive at a different destination. That would mean I could die in this foolhardy defense, or I could defeat the Blasphemer two weeks early."

I wish Gaven were here, she added silently.

Elestrissa frowned. "Such questions are best discussed in the groves of the druids in times of peace," she said. "Now is a time for action." She took a deep breath, and seemed to swell with it, growing taller and broader. "Perhaps we all die here today, but perhaps our charge is necessary to weaken the Blasphemer so he can fall at the river." Her skin, where her hide armor left it exposed, was transforming into thick bark, and leafy twigs appeared in her hair. "Perhaps you will live to see the Blasphemer fall, Lady Alastra." Her voice rumbled and resounded like thunder over the noise of the battle, and her limbs became the mighty trunks and branches of an oak. "Then you can tell the tale of this day, and ensure that the story of the defenders of the Mosswood is told until the end of days!"

A cheer went up from the battle-worn heroes, and Rienne smiled. She would fight beside Elestrissa, and if fate allowed, she would destroy the Blasphemer before his fated day. Perhaps she would die without having seen Gaven again, but after all the times she had told Gaven that he was the author of his own destiny, she couldn't do otherwise.

Elestrissa raised her war club over her head and roared, drawing another cheer from the heroes around her. She turned and began a lumbering stride in the direction of the barbarians.

Thoughts of Gaven filling her mind, Rienne drew Maelstrom from its sheath and looked down at the blade.

Gaven faced her in Jordhan's cabin, Maelstrom's gleaming blade between them. "The day you first touched that sword," he said, "you set a course for a much greater destiny. It's a sword of legend, Ree. Great things have been done with it, and more greatness will yet be accomplished. Can't you feel that?"

She still felt it, and she had come to believe—to hope, at least, or maybe to fear—that the rest of Gaven's words might be true, that she was the one fated to accomplish so much with it.

"You and Maelstrom are linked in destiny," Gaven said, "as surely as you and I are."

Tears streaming down her face, she lifted the blade above her head, gave a wordless shout, and joined the last charge of the defenders of the Mosswood.

* * * * *

The song of unmaking boomed from his throat, each note throbbing in dissonance with the protesting chords of the Gatekeepers' seal. Slowly his song bent the druids' harmonies, twisted their chords into terribly cacophony, and snapped the lines of the binding. The chorus of madness rose from deep below and echoed in his ears, giving strength to his voice. This was why the Blasphemer had come—the beginning of the unmaking of the world.

He crouched and cocked his head, listening. The mad chorus had been clear to his ears for hours now as the battle raged, but he was beginning to hear the high keening notes of a single voice raised above the others. Its song was at once a chant of war and a summons, drawing its kindred from across the depth and breadth of Khyber to come to the opening of the doorway.

I am here, Kathrik Mel sang in his wordless, tuneless song, *and the door will soon be open.*

The distant voice answered with a banshee's wail, portending the death of the world.

* * * * *

The defenders of the Mosswood advanced in grim silence. Elestrissa strode forward like a walking oak imbued with the primal power of her woodland home. The goliath kept pace beside her, resting a greataxe on one broad shoulder. Rienne had never seen a goliath in person before, but she knew of them—the wild mountain-folk of the western Reaches, more at home on snow-capped peaks than in city streets.

Both dwarves had shaggy boars by their sides, but one was a hazy spirit like the healer's bear while the other was real flesh and bone. Some of the shifters walked upright, but others switched between a crouching run and scampering leaps, pausing frequently to sniff the air or just let the group catch up. Rienne saw humans and elves armed with bows and clad in leather, and others covered from head to toe in plates of metal armor, holding finely crafted swords and heavy metal shields. It was as motley a collection of warriors as she'd ever seen, all united under the Mosswood Warden's banner to make a final stand against the Blasphemer.

Much like the Blasphemer's forces themselves, she reminded herself. According to Kyaphar, the Blasphemer had united members of many different Carrion Tribes under his bone-white banners, leading them in a common cause to conquer the lands east of the Shadowcrag and Icehorn Mountains.

Elestrissa's charge reached the bottom of the slope, and the sounds of the battle engulfed them—the clash of steel against steel or swords splintering wooden shields, the shouts of enraged warriors as they hacked into their foes, the roars of dragons and the great Eldeen bears, and the pitiful screams of the dying.

"For the Reaches!" someone near Rienne called out, and the rest of the charging warriors took up the call.

"For the Reaches!"

"For the Wood!"

Barbarians streamed toward them from both sides, having beaten past or broken away from the Eldeen soldiers that tried to hold the line. Several of the charging warriors slowed, readying to meet them, but Elestrissa urged them forward. "On to the Blasphemer!"

Lightning flashed in the sky, and Rienne looked up—half expecting to see a dragon breathing lightning down on them, half hoping to see Gaven's dreadful storm. Instead she saw Jordhan's airship skimming low over the battlefield, the fiery ring of its bound elemental bright against the smoke-blackened sky. As she looked, another bolt of lightning streaked down from a figure on the deck—Kyaphar or one of his druids, she supposed—and struck in the midst of a thick clump of barbarians, knocking them to the ground.

The barbarians closed around the heroes of Elestrissa's charge like the jaws of a dragon, roaring and howling as they swung their mauls and axes. Rienne was sheltered from the initial assault, surrounded by allies who prevented Maelstrom from meeting her enemies. Inevitably, though, the warriors on the edge of their ragged formation slowed, and as Rienne continued to advance she found room to maneuver, and Maelstrom began its whirling dance of death.

A plague-scarred barbarian thrust his leering visage in her face as she dodged his hammer's swing. His eyes went blank as

Maelstrom bit through his flesh and found his heart. A shifter, his skin splotched with horrible burns, stumbled back, trying to dodge the flashing blade, but Maelstrom sliced through his throat and he fell on his back. A Carrion Tribe woman clanged two rough blades together in challenge, blocked Maelstrom's first slash, whirled forward in answer, then stopped dead as Maelstrom severed a tendon in one arm, took off the other hand, and finally sank into the barbarian's chest.

Elestrissa strode in front of Rienne, swinging her club back and forth in devastating arcs that sent barbarians flying away from her and crashing into each other, clearing a path to the Blasphemer. Rienne kept pace, but what had been a tight formation charging ahead started to thin as the warriors slowed to engage their enemies and some fell under the overwhelming tide of the barbarians. Maelstrom kept her moving forward even as it whirled and cut, jabbed and killed.

The elf just behind her, his two curved blades flashing in the firelight, stumbled as a barbarian's club swung low at his legs, and Rienne hesitated.

"Keep going!" he screamed at her, then the barbarian's club smashed his skull.

Maelstrom darted out and slit the Plaguebearer's throat, and Rienne left him sprawled across the body of the hero he had slain, the elf whose name Rienne had never learned.

* * * * *

Dragonfire leaped and roared at Kathrik Mel's back, adding its dissonant voice to the distant chorus down in Khyber. The howls of rage-filled warriors and the agonized screams of the dying sang his song of dissolution. The Gatekeepers' seal itself, groaning as its bindings weakened and broke, added voices to the song, a crescendo of chaos building to the inevitable climax.

He stepped forward, and the tread of his armored foot turned a new circle of grass to ash, adding the tiny dying breaths of the leaves to the grand cacophony. He looked down and saw a line of the seal, flaring with purple light in protest as the song tore at it.

The Blasphemer spoke a word that was no word, and fire erupted beneath his feet. Like lightning, the flames coursed along the ground, tracing the lines of the seal and igniting them. Fire licked the sky, burning through all the colors of the spectrum until it burned black and terrible.

The flames died, their fuel extinguished. The seal was undone, and the chorus of madness swelled in triumph. The keening voice surged louder as its owner rose to pass through the open doorway.

PART

III

In the Time of the Dragon Below,
the moon of the Endless Night turns day
into night,
and so begins the darkest night.

* * * * *

In the city by the lake of kings,
the city scourged with his storm,
the Storm Dragon becomes as the Devourer,
and he opens his maw to consume the world.

* * * * *

Under the unlight of the darkened sun,
the Storm Dragon lays down his mantle;
he stops his song before it can be unsung,
and so his storm is extinguished.

CHAPTER
31

Aunn gaped, trying to see past the deathless guard and up the stairs. Silence had fallen over the temple, and he was desperate to know what was happening on the upper floor. Why had Gaven killed an Aereni priestess? What was he doing here at all?

"You had better come with me," the soldier said, clutching Aunn's arm in his shriveled hand. His touch was ice cold and seemed to sap the strength from Aunn's muscles.

Without thinking, Aunn wrenched his arm from the deathless soldier's grip and bolted past him up the stairs.

The soldier shouted, "Stop!" and then something in Elven.

Revulsion and terror impelled Aunn up the stairs. He leaped out of the path of the guard's poleaxe as it swung at his feet, vaulting up a few more steps to the first landing. The guard was still shouting in Elven as he scrambled up the stairs behind him, jabbing his spear at Aunn's feet.

A few more guards stood at the top of the stairs. Mostly their attention was focused upward, looking at something on the next flight, though one woman was drawing a curved sword and shifting to block Aunn's way. Aunn hesitated, but a clatter on the stairs at his feet warned him just in time—he hopped up as the other soldier's poleaxe swept under him, and kicked down, trapping the weapon against the stairs. The haft broke with a loud crack, drawing a string of Elven curses from the guard.

The guard at the top of the stairs barked something to her companions, but whatever was happening on the stairs above them must have been riveting—they barely gave Aunn a glance before looking back up. The soldier below him shook the axe head free of the splintered haft and repeated the eerie growl he'd made before. Aunn still hadn't drawn his weapon—he didn't want to kill any of the guards, but he was starting to wonder, as rational thought reasserted itself, how he could get out of this mess without the use of his mace. Not giving those thoughts a chance to settle in, he charged up the rest of the stairs, keeping a wary eye on the curved blade of the guard above him.

Instead of blocking his path, the guard fell back from his charge, and Aunn saw the other soldiers around her fall to their knees, heedless of any danger. He cleared the stairs, put his back to the wall, and looked past them.

An elf woman draped in a simple gown descended the last few stairs, carrying Gaven's unconscious form in her slender arms without apparent effort. Her face was a mask of death, tattooed to resemble a stylized skull, but her eyes were green flames. The other elves had their faces to the ground, ignoring him, and he decided to follow their example rather than draw the ire of this being. She reminded him of Senya's ancestor in the City of the Dead.

Senya!

Aunn looked up, and the elf's fiery eyes burned into his. Her head was shaven clean, the skull tattoo obscured her features, and her eyes were not the sapphire blue they had been, but this was unmistakably Senya.

"I know you," she said. Her voice was not Senya's husky purr, but a cool, clear song.

How could she know him? Senya had never known what he was, as far as he knew.

"You were with this one and my daughter Senya in Shae Mordai."

The terror that had gripped him through their entire stay in the City of the Dead returned, a cold hand on his heart. As frightening as the haunted City of Night had been, years ago, to a young spy on his first mission, Shae Mordai had been far worse, a place where the undead walked openly among the living. Senya's ancestor had been the most terrifying part of a truly horrible day, for in the brief moment when the burning eyes in her empty sockets had met his gaze, he had felt himself utterly exposed to her. It appeared that, somehow, he was facing Senya's ancestor again—enshrined in Senya's body.

"Senya?" he said quietly.

"My daughter is dying." She looked down at Gaven's limp form in her arms, as if suddenly remembering what she was doing. "You will help me. Come."

"Revered One," the deathless soldier behind Aunn said, "these men are intruders into the sanctity of your temple."

"Do you presume to bind what I have chosen to loose? You may assist us if you wish, but you will not stand in the way any longer."

Senya strode forward and started down the stairs. Aunn followed close behind her, giving the deathless soldier a wide berth. The soldier glared at him, clutching the haft of his broken poleaxe, but he obeyed Senya and stayed out of Aunn's way. Senya seemed to float down the stairs, still showing no sign that carrying Gaven's heavy body was the least bit difficult. Indeed, each step she descended—each step that brought her closer to the sanctuary at the heart of the temple building—seemed to increase the sense of power or presence that emanated from her.

The entry area at the bottom of the stairs was deserted and deathly still. Aunn wondered where the dozens of elves who had been there a moment before had gone, but then he saw them all gathered in the sanctuary, kneeling on the floor in silent prayer or contemplation. Senya walked directly to the sanctuary, but Aunn hesitated.

"Stay with me," Senya said, not looking back at him. "I need your help."

What is going on? Aunn wondered, hurrying to catch up.

In Shae Mordai, Senya's ancestor had been imperious, angry with her wayward descendant, and uncooperative. Now she was imploring him for help. Was Senya engaged in some elaborate hoax, pretending to be a representative of her ancestor in order to swindle her distant relatives? It didn't seem likely—Senya was a mercenary, not a thief. She could be manipulative, but she usually preyed on men's desire rather than their piety. And if all this was an act, it was a very convincing one.

The elves gathered in the sanctuary had left a path open from the door to a raised area at the far end of the room, flanked by smoldering braziers that breathed billowing clouds of perfumed smoke. Senya drifted between the kneeling crowds, an almost palpable aura of holy power surrounding her now that she was in her sacred place. The elves pressed their faces to the floor, and Aunn stumbled along behind her, not sure what to do but unwilling to be separated from the one person who accepted his presence in the temple.

Senya dropped to one knee and laid Gaven on the floor between the braziers. Aunn hurried to his friend's side. He hadn't noticed upstairs how ashen Gaven's face was, or the cut across his upper arm. Gaven was still breathing, but slowly. Aunn pulled Gaven's broken armor out of the way and examined the wound. Its blackened edges suggested the work of a poisoned blade.

"What happened?" he asked Senya. "Who did this?"

"I do not know," Senya said. "There was another body on the floor."

Aunn glanced at the door, and saw two elf soldiers carrying a body between them. Wisps of smoke still rose from the figure they carried. Elves kneeling near the door turned to look and wrinkled their noses.

An assassin? he wondered. Here? Why did Gaven come here at all, and how had an assassin found him here?

"You asked for my help, lady," he said softly. "What would you have me do?"

"Save Gaven."

Aunn pressed his fingers to Gaven's neck to feel his pulse. It was an excruciating moment before he felt a single beat. "Have you no power to aid him?"

"First I must heal this body. That will require time that Gaven does not have."

Aunn slid his healing wands from his pouch and chose the most potent of the three—the one he had once told Dania could bring her back from death's door. Remembering Dania's face and Tira's holy kiss, he breathed a silent prayer that its magic could help Gaven. He felt the wand tingle in his hand, and power coursed through his other hand where it rested on Gaven's chest. A blush of color spread at once across Gaven's face, and he drew a deep, shuddering breath.

Aunn sighed with relief and slid the wand back into his pouch. The wound on Gaven's arm had closed, and the blackened flesh was slowly regaining its normal color as the healing magic continued its work.

* * * * *

Gaven heard the sound of a great kettle drum, a single beat that echoed once, like distant thunder. He was walking on a stone floor between two rows of round columns. Shadows flitted behind the columns, hazy memories and indistinct visions that refused to resolve into defined shapes, sliding away from his gaze. He had a vague sense that his father was nearby, but his voice and his footsteps echoed in the great stone hall and drew no answer.

Another beat of the drum, louder, startled him. There wasn't supposed to be another beat, he felt, though he couldn't quite understand why he believed that. He stopped walking and looked around, behind him, and up past the towering columns to a star-filled sky, and another beat came.

The next beat was softer, as though Gaven was soaring up and away from the great drum, but now it was a steady pulse, and he could feel it in his chest even after he could no longer hear it. He opened his eyes.

He lay on his back on a cold, hard stone floor. Someone or something was kneeling beside him, leaning over to peer at his face with blank white eyes. The creature had no face, just an expanse of gray skin with the merest hint of a nose and a lipless gash for a mouth, all surrounded by wild shocks of white hair. His first thought was that this was some sort of wraith whose task was to receive him into the land of the dead, for the room he was in seemed fitting for the marble halls of Dolurrh, the shadowy realm where souls were said to pass when their mortal life had ended.

But no, he felt quite alive, his heart beating strong and steady in his chest. And the faceless thing had broken into a smile with surprising warmth, which made its white eyes sparkle. "Gaven!" it said. "Welcome back to the land of the living. How do you feel?"

The voice was familiar, but . . .

"Who are you?" Gaven asked.

"Oh!" The face pulled back, and it seemed to take on more definition, fleeting through vague hints of a few other familiar faces. "I'm Aunn."

"Aunn?" The assertion made no sense at first. He knew at least three different faces that Aunn had worn—Darraun's, the one he had called Aunn, and Kelas's. Was this what a changeling looked like when he wasn't . . . changed?

"This is my real face," Aunn said. "I don't want to hide it any more."

Gaven's mind was beginning to clear, and memories washed over him. "What happened? Where's Senya?"

"Senya's right here." Aunn jerked his head behind him.

Gaven lifted his head and saw her, kneeling on the floor behind Aunn, her back turned toward him. Then he saw what she was facing—a temple full of elves!

"Thunder!" he breathed. "What are all these people doing here?"

"I think they came for the same reason I did," Aunn said. "They heard thunder in their temple."

"Phaine attacked me in Senya's room."

"Phaine?" A look of alarm transformed Aunn's face, and he turned to look toward the temple doors. "I think you killed him, Gaven."

"Finally." The memory of Phaine torturing him at the Dragon Forge was still fresh.

"I wouldn't be so dismissive if I were you," Aunn whispered. "The death of a dragonmarked heir is going to be investigated, even if he was an assassin. That's attention you can't afford, and there are a lot of witnesses here."

Gaven sat up. He still wasn't sure why he'd been lying on the floor of the Aereni temple, but he felt healthy and strong—almost as good as he'd felt just before Phaine attacked him. "You're right," he said. "Time to run again. And I'm guessing you don't have traveling papers for me."

"I'm sorry. But even if I did, they wouldn't do you much good after this."

Senya still knelt with her back to him. Was she angry with him? And why were they here in front of this silent assembly of somber-looking elves?

"Senya?" he called.

Aunn shifted between them. "Uh, Gaven—"

Senya stood slowly and spread her arms to the assembled elves. Her skin had an unhealthy pallor he didn't like, and he started to his feet behind her, but Aunn pulled him back down.

"She's not well," Gaven whispered.

Aunn shook his head.

"Sons and daughters of Aerenal," Senya said—but it wasn't Senya speaking, it was her ancestor's voice, speaking in clear Elven. She was channeling the spirit of her ancestor again, as she had the night before. "I thank you for your concern for this temple of your ancestors and for your priestess, my daughter Senya. I am sorry to inform you that Senya Alvena Arrathinen is dead."

Gaven bolted to his feet. "Dead?"

Aunn took his arm and pulled him back to his knees. "It appears you killed her as well."

CHAPTER
32

Flames erupted from the Gatekeeper seal, just ahead of Elestrissa's charge. The Mosswood Warden stumbled as though an arrow had hit her, and Rienne's first impulse was to scan for the archer. Then the flames raced along the lines of the seal, forming a wall of terrible fire encircling the battlefield, burning in every color and no color at all, and Rienne understood. The seal was broken, the battle lost, just as victory came within their grasp.

"We are undone," Elestrissa said, her pace faltering.

"Keep going," Rienne said. "We might still defeat the Blasphemer, keep him from breaking the next seal."

"It is not to be. Your dream—"

"Damn my dream! I'm writing my own destiny today."

Elestrissa seemed to take heart, but she couldn't match her earlier pace, and Rienne surged ahead. Maelstrom was a whirlwind of steel surrounding her, cutting a path through a fresh wall of barbarian resistance.

Then she heard the voice.

It was a high keening, like a woman mourning or the call of a falcon, and it seemed to sing in her mind as much as in her ears. Beneath it was the merest hint, beyond hearing, of a thousand unearthly voices babbling, which reminded her of the inhuman sounds of the Soul Reaver's hordes at Starcrag Plain. The voices were drawing nearer, like a dragon eel slowly surfacing in dark water.

One challenge at a time, she told herself. First the Blasphemer, and after that—if there is an after—I can deal with whatever is coming through the seal.

Barbarians fell away from her like water before the prow of a ship. Elestrissa, at least, was still behind her. If others survived, they were straggling farther behind, caught in the mire of the barbarian hordes.

She saw the Blasphemer, silhouetted against a wall of dragonfire, and her dream sprang to life around her. He was a towering figure in blood-spattered plate armor, twisting horns rising above his fiendish visage. A long tail snaked out behind him as he strode toward her, behind the last remnants of his personal defenders.

He spoke, and his voice rang in her ears above the din of battle. "So here is the one they are calling Dragonslayer, the bearer of *Barak Radaam*." He pointed his own curved sword at her, and she felt a twinge of fear. "Destroy her!" he shouted, and the barbarians around him roared in fury as they surged ahead.

Maelstrom sprang back into motion, parrying every blow that came at her, killing in a ruthless rhythm. Maelstrom whirled and Rienne danced, her body and the steel blade in perfect coordination—a step, a parry, a jab, a jump. Then the Blasphemer began a strange chant, words she didn't recognize, words that couldn't possibly be words in any mortal tongue, and pain stabbed through her ears. Her feet faltered, nearly sending her onto the point of a barbarian's sword, but Maelstrom accommodated, dashing the other sword aside and whirling around to take off its wielder's head.

Maelstrom wanted to get to the Blasphemer.

It was a strange realization. Rienne had never been inclined to personify her blade, as strongly attached to it as she was. It was precious to her, but it was steel, a weapon—not a person. It was an extension of her body and her will—she had never imagined it had a will of its own.

Perhaps it was merely that she had never before been this close to what Maelstrom apparently wanted. Or perhaps it had concealed its desire from her, all the while impelling her to follow the course that had brought her here. Had Maelstrom planted the idea in her head, when Jordhan rescued her from the Thaliost jail, to fly westward into the Reaches? Had it convinced her not to pursue Gaven when she saw his storms in the south? Was she the tool in Maelstrom's hand, the extension of its will, rather than the other way around?

Whether its influence had been absent or merely subtle in the past, there was no denying it now. When one barbarian fell, the blade led her into the open space left behind, drawing her closer to the Blasphemer. Every step away from him felt heavy, every step toward him easy and light. He was a force of gravity, drawing her in through her sword.

Why? she wondered.

As Maelstrom brought her closer to the Blasphemer, his maddening chant grew louder and her pain intensified with it. The words assaulted her, and blood began to trickle from her ringing ears. Suddenly, she understood the title he bore in the Prophecy—his words were a blasphemy, an utter denial of existence and meaning.

But the Blasphemer's end lies in the void, in the maelstrom that pulls him down to darkness.

The words of her dream renewed her courage. They also seemed to give her respite from the pain, so she tried speaking them aloud. "Dragons fly before the Blasphemer's legions, scouring the earth of his righteous foes." She could barely hear her own voice, but the pain in her ears faded—and she realized she couldn't hear the Blasphemer while she spoke, as though the words of the Prophecy negated his blasphemous chant. "Carnage rises in the wake of his passing, purging all life from those who oppose him."

He grinned as if he'd heard her, sharp white teeth gleaming in his red devil's face. She was almost to him now, close enough to see the sweat on his brow and feel the searing heat of the wall of flames behind him.

"Vultures wheel where dragons flew, picking the bones—"

The earth beneath her interrupted, rumbling, then shaking so violently that the barbarians surrounding her staggered into each other or fell on the ground. She rode the bucking earth, hopping lightly as she felled more of her enemies, drawing ever closer to the Blasphemer. But she expected to see the ground split open at any moment and release its brood of chaos, as it had at Starcrag Plain.

Instead, it erupted. Huge boulders streamed up from the ground and hurtled into the sky. Rienne watched in horror as a jagged shard flew skyward and crashed into Jordhan's airship. Wood splinters flew out from the ship in every direction, then the fiery elemental ring burst loose, turning the ship into a tiny sun, a blinding flash of light. Then the light and the ship were gone.

Rienne went numb. Maelstrom was a dead weight in her hand, and she couldn't feel the ground beneath her feet. If her heart still beat, she couldn't feel it—just the vise grip of dread clutching her chest. Jordhan was gone.

The rock had erupted near the center of the seal, and the largest boulders were falling back down in that area. Rienne thought of the healer who had tended her, the faithful elders and children who, unable to fight, had sought to sustain the seal with their devoted prayers. They were certainly lost, caught in either the erupting stone or its return.

A hail of smaller stones, shattered from the great boulders, fell around her even as the ground kept roiling under her feet. She lost her balance, crashing into a barbarian. The collision sent the man's club flying, but he clutched at her, pinning her sword arm against her side.

"I have her!" the barbarian shouted. "Hit her!"

An axe swept toward her face, but she planted her feet on the ground, shifted her weight low, and swung the man holding her into the weapon's path. He lost his grip on her as the axe cut his spine, and Rienne shrugged him off before whirling to kill the axe wielder.

She found her balance and looked for the Blasphemer. With the eruption of the ground, chaos had seized the battlefield— any hint of formation or lines of engagement had vanished. She couldn't see the Blasphemer, and Elestrissa's towering form was nowhere in sight. Barbarians and Eldeen defenders alike scattered, running with their arms thrown over their heads to shield themselves from the falling stones. She heard no horns sounding a retreat, saw no banners marking a rallying point for either side. The only sounds were the rumble of the earth and the clatter of stones falling against shields and helmets and bodies. Soldiers and farmers, the barbarians of the Carrion Tribes and the wild folk of the western Reaches all ran headlong in every direction, barely bothering to swing their weapons at each other.

"Reachers!" she shouted over the tumult. "To me! For the Wood!"

Too much noise, too much confusion—

She held Maelstrom high and repeated her call. More boulders, smaller fragments of the shattering earth, flew into the air and crashed to the ground, more gravel pounded from the sky.

She searched the ground—someone in Elestrissa's charge had carried a standard, the emerald oak symbol of the Reaches. She couldn't see it. She started running back the way they had come, against the tide of people fleeing from the erupting stone.

She spotted a flash of green, all but trampled into the dirt, and made for it. A shifter swung a clumsy blow toward her head, but she ducked it and gutted her foe, and then pulled the standard from the sod and gore. She hoisted it over her head and cried out once more, "For the Reaches! For the Wood!"

Holding the standard high, she started back away from the center of the seal—not in the direction of Elestrissa's charge, but off to the side, away from where she'd seen the Blasphemer, away from the wall of dragonfire. "For the Wood!" she cried again, and a few of the fleeing Eldeen defenders veered toward her.

Jordhan is dead, she thought. Elestrissa is fallen and her charge failed. The Gatekeepers' seal is broken and Sovereigns know what's emerging through it. But I can't let these people scatter like sheep before wolves.

A ragged band formed around her, mostly farmers drafted to the militia who had managed to survive the onslaught of barbarians and dragons—most likely by running away. A few battle-worn soldiers fell in alongside her, and some rangers and hunters. Some shifters joined the band who might have been part of the Blasphemer's forces for all she knew, but they took up the cry—"For the Reaches! For the Wood!"—and walked as comrades with the other Reachers, so she let them come.

One of the first to join the group was a human girl—Rienne couldn't help but think of her as a girl, since she couldn't have been older than twenty—armored in a suit of worked leather far too large for her slight frame. Her spear and armor both looked fresh from the artisan's hands. She didn't say a word, just drifted closer and closer to Rienne as more and more of the remnants of the Eldeen forces gathered around the standard.

"For the Reaches!" Rienne shouted for the hundredth time, lifting the banner as high as her arms could manage. The weight was too much for her fatigued body, and she stumbled off balance. The farmer girl caught her by the arm and took the standard from her hands.

"For the Wood!" the girl screamed.

Rienne smiled, and the girl smiled bashfully back.

"Thank you," she said. "I'm Rienne."

"Oh, I know who you are!" the girl said, beaming. "Everyone's been talking about the Dragonslayer."

"Have they?" The thought saddened her.

"I'm Cressa," the girl offered.

"Where are you from, Cressa?"

"I grew up near Riverweep. It's a little village on the river."

Rienne smiled at the suggestion that Cressa—this girl one-third her age—was done growing up. "But now?"

Cressa's smile faded and her eyes grew weary, and she suddenly looked older than Rienne had first thought. "I had just moved to Varna when the storm came."

The storm. Rienne remembered watching it from the deck of Jordhan's ship, as it formed in the Blackcaps and then swept across Lake Galifar to wash over Varna. She wondered again what part Gaven had played in that devastating tempest, but she no longer questioned whether she had made a mistake by not turning south to look for him.

"Lady?" Cressa said.

Rienne put a hand on the girl's shoulder. "I'm glad you escaped the city," she said. "Did you fight the Aundairians there?"

Cressa snorted. "I fled the storm. I didn't join the militia until after, thinking I'd get back at them."

"But instead you faced the Blasphemer's horde."

"And fled again." Cressa's shoulders slumped. "I'm no warrior."

"There are other parts to be played."

Cressa brightened. "Do you think so?"

"Of course." She thought of Jordhan, bravely but ineffectually clutching an axe and running to her side as she fought the black dragon. He'd been a pilot, never a warrior, and he met his end as a pilot.

The ground bucked beneath them again, sending farmers and rangers tumbling into each other all around her. Rienne kept her feet, and she noticed with approval that Cressa did as well—keeping her feet planted wide, her weight low, and her arms out for balance.

More shards of stone flew into the air, followed by columns of strange yellow fire roaring into the sky. Several people in Rienne's little band cried out in fear. Cressa's knuckles were white as she clutched the standard, but she shouted, "For the Reaches!" with such conviction that even Rienne felt stirred by her passion.

"For the Wood!" Rienne yelled with the rest of the survivors. "And for the world," she added under her breath.

CHAPTER
33

I t was an accident," Gaven said. An icy dagger of pain
stabbed through his chest as Senya's body turned to face
him and her eyes burned into him. "She opened the door
while I was fighting Phaine, and the lightning leaped to her. I
tried to stop it!"

"But you could not," the cold, clear voice of the ancestor
said. Senya's chest didn't move with breath, though her lips
moved to form the words. She extended a stiff hand to point a
finger at Gaven. "And that failure is at the heart of the choice
you must make."

Gaven dropped his chin to his chest. "Yes." He saw again
the lines of his dragonmark twisting around him, like pathways traced in blood. He put a hand to his pouch, just to feel
the weight of the dragonshard—

"Where is the shard?" he said, looking up at Senya again.
"It was in your—in Senya's room, in my hand. Where is it?"

"It is still there," the ancestor said.

He leaped to his feet and started for the door, Aunn right
behind him, but the kneeling elves stood to block their path.
One drew a scimitar from his belt. Gaven looked back at Senya.

"Let the changeling go," the ancestor said.

The elf with the scimitar made a show of letting Aunn past,
with a slight bow, but he resumed his position, frowning at
Gaven, as soon as Aunn had gone by. Gaven watched the rest
of the assembled elves make way for the changeling and then
close ranks behind him. Panic surged in his chest—he was
trapped, held captive by these elves, and without the power of
his dragonmark to call upon.

He took a deep breath, trying to steady his nerves. The ancestor had said the shard was right where he left it, and Aunn had told him that Phaine was dead. In a moment, Aunn would return with the dragonshard, and Gaven would have his mark back. He might still be captive, but at least he would be whole.

* * * * *

As he passed through the ranks of elves, Aunn tried not to watch their stony faces or meet the eyes that followed his passage. He fought the urge to blend in, to mimic their high cheekbones and pointed ears, their bright, colorful eyes, and their long, straight hair. He hated their attention and wanted to hide, to lose himself in their midst, but he could not.

As he drew near the door, he saw where the elves had laid Phaine's body. The elf was severely burned, far worse than Senya or Gaven had been, but Aunn could still see the tracings of the Mark of Shadow on his cheek and the side of his neck. He still clutched a dagger with a strange black blade, as if it were made of solidified shadow. His eyes were open wide, but they were gleaming black pools, like a dark reflection of the opalescent eyes of the eladrins he'd met in the Towering Wood. Pupilless as they were, Aunn couldn't help the feeling that they were watching him as he walked by. He hurried his pace and left the temple sanctuary.

The entryway and staircase were deserted. Aunn ran up the stairs, Phaine's dead gaze haunting his thoughts. He reached the top floor and looked around. A hallway stretched away to either side, lined with small doors. One door stood open, a half-dozen yards to his left, and he had to assume that was his destination. Suddenly cautious, he moved slowly and as quietly as he could manage, sliding his mace from his belt as he crept toward the doorway.

He reached the door and peered around the corner. His trepidation had been for nothing, it appeared—no enemy crouched in the room waiting to attack him, and he spotted the blood-red dragonshard on the floor by the bed. He let out his breath and stepped into the room.

A cloud of shadows began to billow and pool in one corner of the room, fighting back the sunlight that streamed from a high window over the door. Aunn stopped and stared into the shadows, which deepened as he looked. A long steel blade caught the light as it emerged from the shadows, then the darkness melted away from a black-clad woman. The black eyes staring out from the cowl of her cloak suggested that this was another Thuranni, come to finish what Phaine had started, perhaps, or to find out why he hadn't returned.

She turned her head with quick, small movements that made Aunn think of an insect looking for prey. Although it was hard to tell exactly where she was looking, Aunn was fairly sure her gaze lingered longest at the dragonshard on the floor across the room from her before she turned her full attention to him.

"Phaine is dead," she said flatly. There was no doubt in her voice or on her face, as if Phaine's death were the only possible explanation for his failure to return. Perhaps it was—Aunn had certainly been on more than one mission where he had been expected to take his own life if threatened with capture.

"Yes." Aunn's eyes darted to the shard and back to the elf woman. He saw her tense, ready to spring if he made a move for it. He decided not to make a move for it just yet.

"And Gaven?" This time it was a question.

Aunn chose his words carefully. "Phaine's poison did its work." Let them think he's dead, he thought.

Her smile sickened him. His answer apparently gave her all the information she needed about the situation, because she stepped forward and swung her blade in a shining arc at his neck. He ducked the gleaming steel and dived for the dragonshard on the floor. He watched her feet as she reacted, spun, and lunged at him again, and he twisted away from where he thought her blade must be. One hand brushed against the dragonshard, then it skittered out of his grip, spitting a trail of sparks across the floor. He heard the woman's blade scrape against the bed as she swung at him again.

Reaching for the shard again, he swung his mace in a back-handed arc with his left hand, trying only to give himself a bit of distance from her relentless attacks. She rewarded his desperate swing by taking a couple of quick steps back, even as the tip of her blade cut across the back of his hand. The mace slipped out of his grip and crashed into the wall, but he got his hand around the dragonshard.

The explosion threw him against the wall, stole his sight, and set his ears ringing so loudly he couldn't hear any other sound. He fell onto the bed, tried to lift himself and found he couldn't move at all. With the taste of Senya's bedclothes in his mouth, he lay there and waited for the Thuranni's blade to fall.

As his vision began to clear, he saw the elf's shadowy shape heaving herself up off the floor. The thunder and lightning must have knocked her back as well, which explained why he was still alive. She staggered next to the bed, and Aunn still couldn't move. Instead of swinging her scimitar at him, she yanked a pouch off her belt, then bent down and used the blade to nudge the dragonshard into it. She cast a glance over her shoulder, took a slow breath that seemed to draw shadows in to gather around her, and vanished in the gloom.

The shadows dissolved into wisps of dark mist as Aunn's nerves prickled with the return of sensation and the echoes of pain. With a mighty effort, he worked his splayed arms beneath his body and heaved himself up off the bed, sending jolts of agony through his limbs and his head. The pain made his head swim again, and darkness close in around the edges of his vision, but he forced himself to stand. He had to find her, follow her somehow—or at least tell Gaven that the dragonshard was gone, stolen by House Thuranni.

House Lyrandar's most prized possession, the one thing they owned that no one else could obtain, was now in the hands of a rival House.

* * * * *

"Gaven, Storm Dragon, hear my words." Senya took his hand in her cold grip and drew him back before the altar. "I must soon depart from this place and let my daughter sleep. My people gathered here demand some satisfaction from you, for two children of Aeren are dead by your hand. Nor is their blood the only stain on your soul."

Gaven fell to his knees as strange memories washed over him.

His magic let him scale the wall of the Paelion tower as easily as a spider, unseen beneath the dark clouds of the brewing storm. He—he who was both Shakravar and Gaven, dragon and meat—slipped like a shadow through a high window. It should not have been so easy, but it didn't matter. Of course the elf had set him up. It didn't matter. The Prophecy mattered.

All he needed to do was find something to steal, something to prove he had been in the tower. With that and the letter he had already carefully crafted, the Thuranni line would have the evidence they needed to strike.

The Paelions would die, House Phiarlan would split, and thirteen dragons would rule the land. As the Prophecy required.

"I admit my guilt," Gaven said. He heard a murmur spread through the gathered elves, the first sound he had heard from the crowd. "But what satisfaction can I give?"

"Would you give your life?" the ancestor asked.

A few voices raised above the softer murmur of the onlookers, expressing approval of that idea.

Gaven looked down at the floor. On some basic level of arithmetic, it seemed like a fair request. He had killed Phaine quite intentionally, and killed Senya by accident. That alone was two lives weighed against his, and as Senya's ancestor had said, theirs was not the only blood on his hands. Add in the Paelions, and his life seemed like far too small a price to pay for what he had done.

But he couldn't accept it as a simple matter of arithmetic. Phaine had been trying to kill him, and had nearly succeeded. The Thurannis had used him, manipulated him when he was not in his right mind—and all he did in the end was help provide them with a pretext to do what they wanted to do anyway. That left Senya, whose death had been a terrible accident. Of them all—of all the lives he had taken—she was the one who grieved him the most, the one who could almost make him consider giving his own life as restitution. Was that simply because he had known her, because he cared about her? Perhaps it was.

It didn't matter. "No," he said at least, looking up to meet Senya's fiery eyes again. "I will not give up my life to pay for the death of an assassin, and not even the accidental death of your daughter. I regret her death, but my destiny lies beyond this place."

"What makes you think you're so damned important, Gaven?" Bordan thrust his face into Gaven's. *"You think you're more important than the people you've killed? Is your life worth more than theirs?"*

Senya's ancestor watched him as if she expected an answer to Bordan's question, and Gaven wondered if she had dredged up these memories. Was this some kind of trial?

He had answered Bordan with belligerence, and while he argued, the dwarves with Bordan had captured Rienne. He closed his eyes, briefly entertaining the notion of fighting his way out of this temple, even if it meant more elven blood on his hands. . . .

A crack of thunder shook the building. For a moment Gaven thought it was an echo of his violent thoughts, then he remembered—Aunn had gone to retrieve the dragonshard that held his Mark of Storm. Where was he?

"The time has come for you to make your choice," Senya's ancestor said.

Gaven stood up and turned to look at the open doorway. He heard no sound of a struggle, no shouts of alarm. He wondered if Aunn were dead, and the thought filled him with sadness.

Is that all? he thought. How can I be so calm?

He felt the ancestor's presence behind him, and she seemed no longer contained within Senya's slender form. Her presence was larger, somehow—larger than the frightening deathless form he'd seen in Shae Mordai. It was as though she were just one of a host of elders assembled at his back, like a great tribunal seated for his judgment, or perhaps a council gathered to advise him.

He closed his eyes. From far away, it seemed, he heard Aunn shouting his name, and he knew the dragonshard was gone, and with it the dragonmark Kelas had stolen from him at the Dragon Forge. The choice that lay before him now was simple and yet utterly profound: To pursue whoever had taken the shard, or to relinquish the shard, the Mark of Storm, and the power contained in them.

"Gaven, Storm Dragon, dishonored child of Lyrandar." It was a chorus of voices behind him now. "What do you choose?"

Storm Dragon, Gaven thought. Can I be the Storm Dragon without the Mark of Storm?

He turned back to face Senya. Her head lolled back slightly, as though the ancestor's hold on her body were slipping.

This is what that power has brought me, he thought. It's beyond my control. It's no longer a tool in my hands, but the other way around.

"Let it go," he said softly.

Senya's dead face smiled. "She is pleased, Gaven," the ancestor whispered, "and she wants you to know she forgives you."

Tears sprang to Gaven's eyes. "I'm so sorry."

"Let him go," Senya's ancestor proclaimed, and the flames in her eyes faded as she slumped into Gaven's arms.

CHAPTER
34

"hy don't you tell me what this is all about?" Ashara
said.

The Sentinel Marshal grabbed a chair from a nearby table and swung it around, sitting across from Harkin but focusing her attention on Ashara. Cart glanced at the dwarf, who was still glaring at him.

"I've heard reports that House Cannith recently undertook a significant construction project in the south of Aundair, between Arcanix and the Blackcaps. The Arcane Congress might have been involved, in fact."

Cart turned his gaze to Harkin, wondering again whether he knew anything about the Dragon Forge. Cart couldn't read his face, but it was clear from the way he leaned forward slightly that he was interested in what Mauren was saying.

"I might have heard something about that project," Ashara said. "What of it? House Cannith has a hundred construction projects going on at any given moment. That's what we do."

"Indeed," Mauren said wryly. "Give a House the Mark of Making, and watch them make. Well, my House has the Mark of Sentinel, so you should not be surprised that we keep watch. And our observation suggests that you know more of this project than you admit."

"Again, what of it?"

"What were you building there?"

"Forgive me, Sentinel Marshal, but you must also understand that our House must often keep its operations confidential. Perhaps if you discuss this matter with our baron, she can decide whether your need for this information outweighs our need to protect our secrets."

Ossa snorted. "Not likely, I'd bet."

"To put it a bit more delicately," Mauren said with a smile, "if your baron is engaging in activities that defy the Treaty of Thronehold, she's not likely to tell me."

So that's it, Cart thought. She thinks the Dragon Forge was creating more warforged.

The Treaty of Thronehold had brought an official end to the Last War, but it also included a number of provisions relating to the legal status of the warforged in Khorvaire. By the terms of the treaty, warforged already in existence were free—some nations had held them as slaves during the war—but House Cannith was prohibited from creating any new warforged. Given enough time, the warforged race would die out.

Except, Cart thought, that rumors suggested Merrix d'Cannith might be making new warforged somewhere in Breland.

"In case you hadn't noticed," Ashara said, "the Treaty of Thronehold isn't holding up so well these days. I hear Breland has sent troops into the Reaches to make sure Aundair doesn't overstep its bounds."

"Indeed," Mauren said. "And Queen Aurala and King Boranel of Breland will have to answer for their actions. But my concern is with Jorlanna."

"She's broken the Korth Edicts," Cart said, "but you can't do anything about that. Too many of the Houses are stretching the provisions of the Edicts already."

"To say the least," Mauren said. "I wouldn't say there's nothing we can do, though. It's the goal of my House to bring all the other Houses back into full compliance with the Edicts."

Cart nodded. "So now you're looking for a different crime you can blame her for, something that will turn popular opinion against her."

"And the opinion of the other Houses," Ashara added.

"What we're looking for," Ossa growled, "is an answer to the question. What's Jorlanna up to in the Blackcaps?"

"You know Jorlanna won't incriminate herself," Ashara said. "So what makes you think I would tell you anything—if we were in violation of the treaty?"

Mauren smiled. "Didn't I hear that you weren't exactly in the baron's good graces?"

"True enough."

"Well, it's simple, really. If you—either of you"—Mauren acknowledged Harkin for the first time—"can provide me with useful information about the baron's activities, I can ensure that you're rewarded for your cooperation."

"I'm sorry to disappoint you, Sentinel Marshal," Ashara said, "but our project in the Blackcaps had nothing to do with the creation of warforged, nor did it violate any other provision of the Treaty of Thronehold."

Cart wasn't sure that was entirely true, since the Dragon Forge had been used to launch an attack on a sovereign nation recognized by the treaty. But he wasn't about to contradict her.

"You speak of it in the past tense," Ossa observed.

"Yes," Ashara said. "The project was not successful, and it now lies in ruin. Jorlanna holds me responsible for the failure, and thus she has cast me out of the family."

"In ruin?" the dwarf asked. "A catastrophic failure, then."

"Thank you for rubbing it in."

What's the dwarf getting at? Cart wondered. Why is she even here?

Mauren rubbed her chin. "So there's no evidence left."

"There was never any evidence you could use against Jorlanna," Ashara said. "I told you, it was nothing more than a failed experiment."

Cart clenched his jaw. Ashara was not exactly lying outright, but if she told the truth about the Dragon Forge, she would give the Sentinel Marshal what she needed: the dragonmarked houses would rise as one to condemn Jorlanna for daring to steal Gaven's Mark of Storm. Why not just tell them?

"I see," Mauren said. "So you do not wish to assist us in bringing Jorlanna to justice for her crimes?"

"I would if I could, but I have no information to give."

"And you, Harkin? Can you offer us any further insight?"

Harkin merely smiled and shrugged.

"I see. Then I will be forced to treat you both as willing accomplices when I do bring charges."

"As I said, I would help if I could," Ashara said.

"Well, if you think of anything you might have forgotten to mention, do let me know. I'm staying at the Scarlet Bastion, in Chalice Center."

"I hope you enjoy your stay in Fairhaven, Sentinel Marshal."

Mauren stood up and frowned down at the three of them. "I had hoped we could be allies in this just cause. I am a dangerous adversary."

Ossa brought her face close to Cart's again and whispered so only he could hear her. "Don't think I fell for your innocent act. I'm watching you, Cart. I'm watching all of you."

With a lingering last glance, Mauren made her way out of the bakery, Ossa trailing along behind her.

Ashara let out a long sigh and put her head on the table. "That was unpleasant," she said into her arm.

"I'm confused," Cart said. "Why didn't—?"

Harkin interrupted. "What was that project in the Blackcaps, anyway?"

"A weapon," Ashara said, looking up. "It brought the siege of Varna to a quick close."

Harkin whistled. "Doesn't sound like a failed experiment to me."

"Well, it did what it was supposed to do at Varna. But there were flaws in the design."

"So why not tell—?" Cart began.

"Flaws?" Harkin interrupted again, and Cart thought he caught a sidelong glance that suggested he did it on purpose, trying to irritate Cart. Ashara didn't seem to notice. "What kind of flaws?"

"Central to the design. It drew on unstable sources of power—sources we shouldn't have been dealing with at all."

Harkin smiled. "Now you have me intrigued."

"I don't want to talk about it."

"You know you can talk to me—you always could." He shot another glance at Cart. "Remember how we used to talk through projects together?"

Ashara's face flushed bright red and she avoided Harkin's gaze. "Stop," she said.

Harkin turned to Cart, a broad smile on his face. "It's remarkable, really," he said. "You can find flaws in a weaving so much more easily if it's traced on your skin."

"Harkin, stop," Ashara said again.

"What's wrong? Are you afraid the warforged will get jealous? Can it even do that?"

Cart stood. He could almost hear Havrakhad's voice in his mind, reminding him to float above the tumult of emotions he was feeling, but he didn't want to. He wanted to be caught up in his rage, to give Harkin the pummeling he so richly deserved, to show Ashara that he wouldn't let an oaf like Harkin upset her.

"Oh, are you leaving?" Harkin said.

"No," Cart said, "you are."

"Not yet. Ashara and I have matters to discuss. Why don't you get some fresh air—stand outside and make sure the Sentinel Marshal doesn't come back?"

That sealed it. Cart seized a handful of Harkin's coat and shirt in one metal-bound fist and heaved him to his feet.

"Unhand me!" Harkin yelped.

Cart's eyes fell on Harkin's dragonmark, a small pattern on his left temple, and he almost obeyed the Cannith heir's command out of pure reflex. "No," he said. He lifted Harkin off the ground, carried him to the door of the bakery, and tossed him out.

Harkin landed on his feet, stumbled a few steps, and drew himself up, his face livid with fury. "You should not have done that, warforged. My House gave you life, and my hands have the power to take your life away."

"I was birthed in a Cannith forge, it's true," Cart said, folding his arms across his chest. "But that doesn't make you my father. Aundair's army gave me my training, my discipline. Haldren gave me my post and taught me much about the world. Ashara restored me to health when an assassin's blade might have killed me. Havrakhad gave me my first glimpse of real understanding. I owe much to many people, but to you . . . your family name alone does not command my respect."

"So you *are* Haldren's Cart." Harkin sneered. "You'll pay for this, warforged, and so will Ashara." He spun and stormed down the street as Cart observed the cresting wave of rage that had surged in his chest subsiding, replaced by a growing feeling of dread.

* * * * *

Aunn appeared in the doorway, breathless and disheveled. "I'm so sorry," he panted. "It's gone."

"I know." Gaven lowered Senya's body to the ground and tried to arrange her in a position of dignity, painfully aware of the eyes of the assembled elves boring into his back.

"Another Thuranni," Aunn said. "She can't be far. If we hurry—"

"It doesn't matter." Senya's hands were so cold that they seemed to sap the warmth and life from his own as he folded them over her chest.

"What happened?" Aunn was right behind him now, looking over his shoulder.

"Her ancestor's presence was the only thing keeping her upright. And she could only linger here so long, I guess." Gaven stood up and looked down at the body.

Senya sat on the ground by the river outside Paluur Draal. She stretched her long legs in front of her, and leaned back on her hands. He'd never seen her so beautiful, so alluring. Her hair was wet, clinging to her face and neck, and drops of water glistened on her bare shoulders. "It's still early," she said with a flirtatious smile.

Gaven turned away and started pulling his boots on. "You never give up, do you?"

"Not when I know what I want."

Goodbye, Senya, he thought. I'm glad you managed to find what you truly wanted. Thank you for helping me do the same.

Aunn stepped to put Gaven partly between the elves and himself, glancing nervously at the assembly. "So what happens now?"

Gaven turned to face the elves. "What would you have me do?" he said. He had no idea whether they would respect the ancestor's last command and let him leave in peace, not after the murmurs he'd heard calling for his death.

A man at the front of the gathered elves stood and stepped forward. He wore a shapeless robe similar to Senya's, which suggested that he was a priest like she was, though he didn't wear the same skull tattoo disfiguring his face, and his reddish hair cascaded over his shoulders.

"We have funeral rites to perform," the priest said, "which outsiders may not attend."

A few voices in the crowd seemed to suggest that some of the elves, at least, weren't happy with the ancestor's command, but the priest silenced them with a commanding glare. He stepped closer to Gaven and lowered his voice.

"I would very much like to understand what happened here, if you can come outside with me and explain it before you leave."

"I'd be happy to," Gaven said. He smiled at the priest. "Especially since you seem to have the authority to get me out of here alive."

The priest did not return his smile. "Which I do only because our ancestor commanded it. That is part of what I wish to understand."

"Fair enough," Gaven said. "Shall we step outside?"

"Sons and daughters of Aerenal," the priest said, "make ready the rites for the departed."

A few elves stood again, some who might have been temple acolytes, others who looked more like warriors—including the one who had barred Gaven's path before, who again drew a scimitar and stood in the way of the door.

"Stand down, Vieran," the priest said. "You heard the command."

The warrior's face was a grim mask, and Gaven felt his body tense in preparation for a fight. The priest stood face to face with Vieran and put his hands on the warrior's shoulders.

"Let her go, Vieran."

Gaven saw tears form in Vieran's eyes, but finally the elf's shoulders slumped and he stepped to one side. The priest clapped Vieran's shoulder and walked past him toward the door. Gaven wanted to ask the man if he had been a relative of Senya's, what she meant to him, but Vieran wouldn't look at him as he walked by, and his knuckles were white from clutching the hilt of his scimitar.

With Aunn close on his heels, Gaven followed the priest past Vieran and out the door. Gaven felt every eye on him, but he kept his own gaze fixed on the priest's back until they were out in the entryway and the priest closed the sanctuary doors behind them.

"I can't believe she's gone," Gaven said to Aunn.

"I can't believe you found her in the first place," the changeling replied. "What brought you here?"

"That was the first question on my mind as well," the priest said, turning away from the door. "Why were you in Senya's room this morning?"

"I came here last night," Gaven said, "hoping to consult with the priests."

"The Khoravar do not often turn to the Undying Court for counsel," the priest said.

"I visited the City of the Dead with Senya a few months ago, and her ancestor—I suppose you'd say she foretold that I would return and find what I sought. So I came in hope of finding that."

"So you didn't know that Senya was here?" the priest asked.

"I had no idea. But she took me in, brought me into the sanctuary there, and . . . I don't know, she let the ancestor take over her body, just like this morning."

"There he is!" a voice cried from the temple entrance.

Gaven whirled and saw a young elf in the entry, breathless from running, his hand extended to point at Gaven. Behind him appeared first one and then a second soldier in the green tabards of the city watch.

"Well, I think you've answered all my questions," the priest said. "You're free to go."

CHAPTER
35

The tumult of the battlefield faded into the distance, as the ragtag band of survivors around Rienne grew steadily larger. Cressa's periodic shouts seemed to give the stragglers courage and perhaps even a shred of hope, though Rienne couldn't imagine what they thought they could hope for. She didn't know what was emerging through the sundered seal of the Gatekeepers, but between it and the barbarians, she felt sure the Eldeen Reaches was beyond all hope.

She saw no sign, yet, that the Blasphemer's forces had managed to regroup after the sundering of the seal threw the battlefield into chaos. Rienne and her band saw one small gang of barbarians crouching on a ridge, looking like they were waiting to prey on stragglers fleeing the battle, but they were daunted by the size of Rienne's group and fled into the woods. Was it possible that the sundering of the seal had wreaked as much havoc on the Blasphemer's horde as it had on the Reachers? Rienne didn't dare to hope as much.

When the noise had faded and the earth no longer shook beneath their feet, Cressa fell into step beside Rienne once more.

"What's your plan, Lady?" Cressa asked.

"Plan?" Rienne shook her head. She had been thinking only about getting the survivors out of immediate danger.

Cressa's face fell, and Rienne hurried to create the impression that she knew what she was doing. "Here's what I want you to do," she told the girl. "I need to know how many of us there are in this group, and whether there are any officers or elders, or any priests, druids, or shamans among us. Find someone to help. Can you do that for me?"

"I can," Cressa said, beaming.

"Let me take the standard."

Cressa carefully transferred the ragged battle standard back to Rienne's hands, and bounded off to the nearest clump of people to begin her survey. Rienne watched her with a smile, amused by the girl's boundless energy and enthusiasm.

"Now to come up with a plan," she muttered to herself.

She had started walking vaguely eastward, ahead of the general direction of the barbarians' movement and toward the river that marked the Aundairian border. She tried to picture in her mind the maps that she and Jordhan had studied on their airship journeys, squelching the grief that surged in her chest at the thought of Jordhan. The barbarians had cut a swath through the Towering Wood, running more or less directly east from the Shadowcrags. They had reached the edge of the Towering Wood, and would soon emerge into the fields of the agricultural east. If they continued due east across a few hundred miles of farmland, a stretch of forest called the Riverwood stood between them and the Wyr River. If they turned to either side, they'd enter smaller woods—the Mosswood to the northeast, the Wolfwood to the southeast. Or they could follow the fields and farms, turn south around the Riverwood, and reach the river near Varna.

How much did the barbarians know? She doubted they had maps to plan their assault, but Kyaphar—also likely dead on Jordhan's ship, she realized with a fresh pang—had said that their path had taken them from one Gatekeeper seal to another, breaking each one in turn. What magic guided them to the seals, and where would they go next? She couldn't possibly guess, but if there were druids or elders in the group, she reasoned, they might know more.

Of course, it was pointless to think about the path of the Blasphemer's hordes unless it meant that her little band of farmers and foresters could join a larger force of real soldiers. Aundair had ostensibly sent troops into the Reaches to stop the barbarian advance, but they started by sacking Varna, and Sovereigns knew where they had gone from there. They could have followed the road westward toward Cree, perhaps, on a path of conquest to the druidic capital of Greenheart. Was it too much to hope, she wondered, that they struck out to the northwest, along the same path of cleared ground that might lead the barbarians around the Riverwood?

The more she thought about it, the more Rienne desperately wanted to reach the river. It was a far more defensible position than anything she could think of in the Reaches, and it would mean that she could take another stand against the Blasphemer with Aundair's armies at her back and the prophetic weight of her dream behind her. But even by the most direct route, the river was some two hundred miles away, easily two weeks' journey on foot. Probably more, with such a large group.

"I'm back!" Cressa announced, still beaming with evident pleasure at being chosen for such an important task.

"And what news do you bring?"

"I've brought a count of the troops at your command." Cressa gave a clumsy salute.

"My command?" Rienne scoffed. "I'm not an officer."

"No one here is, and they all agree that they'd rather follow Lady Dragonslayer than anyone else."

"No officers at all? What about druids or elders?"

"Well, I'm not sure, but that eagle seems to be following us." She pointed into the sky, and Rienne squinted against the afternoon sun.

A large bird of prey circled high overhead. It wasn't big enough to be an Aundairian dragonhawk, unless it was much farther away than it appeared. It might have been a druid—she didn't dare to hope that it was Kyaphar—but she supposed it didn't matter until the druid decided to reveal himself.

"That's all?" Rienne asked.

"Twelve soldiers from the Reaches' standing army march with us. The rest are militia—a few veterans, mostly new recruits."

"And how many are we?"

"All told, we number seventy-six."

Cressa said it with pride, as though it were a huge number, but Rienne almost gasped at how few had escaped the battle. She closed her eyes in a silent prayer that other survivors had made it to safety, but it didn't give her much comfort. Twelve regular soldiers, fifty-three militia, a druid or perhaps a hungry eagle, and Rienne herself—arrayed against the Blasphemer's tens of thousands.

The eagle started a dive, but its path took it to the ground a few miles north of Rienne and her tiny army. So it's just an eagle after all, she thought, swooping down on a rabbit that spent too long in the open.

The thought made her scan the sky nervously, thinking of the Blasphemer's dragons. Some dragons remained with the horde, she knew, despite her best efforts. From the air, they could lead the barbarians right to the survivors as they moved across the plains and fields.

"Lady?" Cressa said, concern creasing her brow.

"Thank you for the report." Rienne sighed. "I wish you had brought better news."

"There's one more thing." Cressa seemed reluctant to say it. "Most of us are tired. I'm not, of course, but I saw a lot of people who could barely stay on their feet. Many of them are wounded. I think they're wondering if we might stop and rest soon."

Rienne rubbed her temples. "Rest where?" she wondered aloud. "How far away from the Blasphemer's horde is far enough? What if they're right behind us?"

Once again Cressa's face fell, as though Rienne's lack of a clear plan was a personal attack on her idealism. And again Rienne wanted to say something to comfort and reassure her, but this time nothing came to mind. Even keeping up the appearance of hope was beyond her.

"All right," Rienne said. "We clearly need to make camp. I'm glad you're not tired, but I can barely lift my feet off the ground anymore."

Cressa laughed. "I'm almost too tired to breathe!"

"Well, I have one more task for you. Find a couple of scouts and ask them to find a relatively safe place for us to make camp. Can you manage that?"

"Of course!" Cressa gave another awkward salute and hurried off, clearly less exhausted than she claimed.

The eagle was circling overhead again, and somehow that gave Rienne comfort, as if it were keeping watch over her little army. "Thank you," she whispered to it, and she imagined she heard its answering cry.

* * * * *

Three scouts went out at Cressa's suggestion and found a defensible position for a camp, at the top of a low hill with a good view of the surrounding fields and the forest behind them. They also brought word that what looked like another group of Reachers was making its way toward their position. They estimated that group at about fifty, which almost doubled the count of the battle's survivors. They were still at least an hour away, so Rienne set people to work on establishing a camp large enough for a hundred and twenty-odd. The professional soldiers set up watches and basic fortifications, while foresters and farmers gathered food and set up simple shelters.

As the sun disappeared behind the smoke that blanketed the western sky, Rienne watched the eagle plummet to the ground again, back in the direction of the forest. She watched the spot where it went down, waiting for it to rise up again. It took far longer than she thought it should, but at last it took to the air again, wings beating furiously. A moment later, she saw another group of people near where the eagle went down. They were walking over a rise, and heading more or less directly toward the camp. She looked up at the eagle again, positive now that it was more than it appeared. Perhaps it was a druid, not just following her band of survivors, but searching the land for others and pointing them in the right direction to join Rienne's army.

When the first group the scouts had spotted reached the camp, Rienne's impression was confirmed. She met them at the edge of the camp, and a young man stepped forward to talk to her. A bandage wrapped around his shoulder showed blood soaking through.

"Lady Dragonslayer," he said, dropping to one knee and bowing his head.

"There's no need for that," Rienne said. "On your feet. What's your name?"

"Sergeant Kallo, lady. Is there any more room in your camp? These people are exhausted."

"We saw you coming, and made sure to leave room for you all. You're most welcome."

"I am grateful, and at your service."

"How did you find us, Sergeant?"

"A Sky Warden in the form of a bird flew down and told us to follow him. He said that survivors of the battle were regrouping nearby."

Rienne's heart leaped in her chest. "What was his name?"

"I'm afraid I didn't catch it."

"A dark man, darker than me? With long black hair and a neat beard?"

"Yes, that sounds like him."

Kyaphar! It seemed he had survived the crash of Jordhan's airship after all. Might he have saved Jordhan as well?

"Please make yourselves comfortable in our camp. Sergeant. You're the ranking officer here, so I'm happy to relinquish command to you."

"Oh, no, lady. I'm just a sergeant. I wouldn't presume to give you orders."

Rienne sighed. She didn't particularly want the responsibility of commanding this tiny army, but there didn't seem to be any hope of escaping it. "Very well. Cressa here will show you the camp. Rest well, and tend to your wounds, but I'd like to consult with you at sunrise."

"I would be honored. Thank you, lady."

Kallo bowed, and Rienne returned it, feeling foolish and awkward. Despite her noble birth, she'd never been comfortable with the formal manners of the nobility, the elaborate etiquette of their social affairs, and particularly the subservience of others. She'd always been happiest delving into the caverns of Khyber with Gaven, far removed from family intrigue, social obligations, and manners. She smiled as Kallo walked away, thinking of Gaven and their utter disregard for polite manners while exploring the deeps.

The eagle wheeled in the sky, and Rienne imagined that it was beckoning the other group of survivors, urging them onward to something like safety. Somehow, she reflected, she had become a rallying point for the remnants of the Eldeen forces. As a girl, she'd been socially awkward, impatient with conversation because she always knew what people were going to say, and she had immersed herself in her training with the sword to insulate herself from interactions with other children. She had ended up with Gaven because both families wanted an alliance, and both families had problem children they couldn't otherwise marry off. Together, they had utterly disregarded their families' expectations and flitted off together on their adventures, prospecting dragonshards for House Lyrandar, circumventing the normal trade with House Tharashk. They had been young, impetuous, rebellious, and very much in love. Through years spent with Gaven, she managed to dodge the responsibilities of life in a noble family of Aundair. Then when Gaven went to Dreadhold, she'd been swallowed up in those responsibilities again—twenty-six miserable years filled with formal occasions and business negotiations. At least after a few years her parents had stopped trying to arrange engagements with other men.

Gaven had escaped, and it was like old times again—traveling across the countryside at Gaven's side, from the edge of the Mournland to Sharavacion and Stormhome and the Starcrag Plain, then all the way to the interior of Argonnessen, the grandest adventure of her life. And then Gaven disappeared, and suddenly her life was different than it had ever been before. She was alone in the Land of Dragons, neither doing family business on her own nor adventuring at Gaven's side. She had discovered new reserves of strength and independence in herself, and for the first time in her life she'd felt like she was pursuing a destiny that was uniquely hers, something the world needed her to do, which only she could do.

Now she began to wonder whether that destiny really had anything to do with slaying the Blasphemer at all. Perhaps it was more about providing leadership and hope to these people in the aftermath of the utter desolation of their homeland. She could see it on the faces of the people she saw in the camp—the sacredness of the land was part of who they were, their identity as a people. These weren't Aundairians, she realized, though their political independence from Aundair was only forty years old. They were part of the Eldeen Reaches, part of its land, and it was clear from the way they carried themselves and the expressions in their eyes that the devastation of the Blasphemer was a wound from which they might never recover.

To them, she was Lady Dragonslayer—a symbol, she suspected, of resistance to the Blasphemer. His dragons scoured the earth, but she was the slayer of dragons. Perhaps she could be more than that.

Darkness settled over the camp, and Rienne moved among the cookfires and makeshift shelters, offering what expressions of comfort she could muster. The mere fact of her presence seemed to be a help to many of the people she saw, whose faces brightened when she drew near, who stood and pressed food into her hands, or who leaped to their feet and embraced her, shaking with sobs as they clutched her to their hearts. It was humbling, strangely—it seemed that there was something greater than her at work in her, using her body and her voice as a tool to reach and comfort these people. It made her think of the shaman who had tended her in the grove, with the spirit bear beside her, a conduit between the world and the realm of the spirits of the land. Had those primal spirits chosen her as a vessel?

A cry of alarm arose at the western edge of the camp, and Rienne tore herself from a cookfire to investigate. She expected to find the other group of survivors she had spotted, and at first that's all she saw. Then her eyes distinguished a cloud like roiling smoke behind them—a swarm of flying insects pursuing the Reachers as they ran in a panic toward the fires on the hill. Even at such a distance, she could hear the angry droning of the swarm beneath the screams of its victims.

CHAPTER
36

Cart stood in the bakery's doorway and watched Harkin slink off. Harkin shot one bitter glare over his shoulder, then defiantly kept his back to Cart until he rounded a corner and disappeared. Cart stepped aside to let a mother and small child enter the bakery around him, glancing fearfully at him as they passed, but he kept his eyes fixed on the last place he'd seen Harkin until he was satisfied the human wasn't coming back.

He turned to go back into the bakery and found Ashara standing behind him, her cloak wrapped tightly around her.

"Are you finished?" he asked.

"Isn't it obvious? Cart, that really wasn't wise."

Cart turned back in the direction Harkin had gone. "I don't care," he said. "He deserved it."

Ashara started walking, quickly, in the opposite direction. "What does that have to do with it?"

Cart caught up quickly. "Everything. He was being awful. He interrupted me every time I spoke. He was trying to provoke me."

"He does that. But it doesn't mean you have to rise to it."

"And you just let him do it. You were ignoring me, too."

"I wasn't ignoring you."

"You were. Every time I tried to speak, he cut me off and you listened to him. You could have stopped him. You could have asked me what I was going to say. But you let him cut me off, pretend I wasn't there."

"So you threw a tantrum and threw him out the door."

"Yes I did. Why are you defending him?"

"Don't you see? He's going to find that Sentinel Marshal and tell her everything."

"How much does he know?" Cart said. "He sounded like he had no idea what the Dragon Forge was about."

"He probably knows more than he let on, and we told him enough to get us all in trouble."

"So why didn't you tell the Sentinel Marshal the truth in the first place?"

Ashara stopped in her tracks. "Are you crazy?"

Cart stopped as well and faced her. They were drawing stares, though, so he grabbed her arm and walked her farther down the street, whispering as they walked. "She was looking for something she could arrest Jorlanna for. Why not give it to her?"

"I'm not about to tell a Sentinel Marshal and a marked heir of House Kundarak that I helped build an eldritch machine that stripped the dragonmark off Gaven. They wanted an excuse to arrest Jorlanna, not an excuse to launch a crusade against all of Cannith West."

"A crusade?"

"Punishing Jorlanna wouldn't have been nearly enough. They'd want to lock up everyone involved in that disaster. Including you and me." She shook her head. "Especially me. I'd end up taking the fall and being executed or thrown in Dreadhold, while Jorlanna got a slap on the wrist."

"Executed?" The possibility hadn't occurred to Cart. He slowed his pace.

"Yes!" Ashara stopped and spun to face him again. "Cart, Gaven might say he forgives me, but if he really does, I don't know how he managed it. And all the Houses aren't going to be so quick to forgive a crime like the Dragon Forge. What we did there . . . can't you grasp the magnitude of it?"

Cart looked into her eyes and saw her fear—the same wild panic that sometimes gripped soldiers on the battlefield when they knew they were trapped. He saw echoes of the nightmares he'd glimpsed, the terror that swept over the sleeping city as the troubled age drew to a close. His eyes fell to trace the lines of the dragonmark on her shoulder. Was her terror at the thought of losing her mark?

"No," he said. "I suppose I can't." He put his hand to her chin and cradled her cheek. "What is it that frightens you so?"

She closed her eyes and nuzzled against his hand, clasping it in both of hers. "Do you love me, Cart?"

The change of topic surprised him, and he wasn't sure how to answer. Her eyes opened, and they were wet with tears.

"Never mind," she said, her face flushed red. She let go of his hand, but he didn't pull it away.

"Ashara," he said. "If I had ever before in my life admitted to loving something or someone, I would have been laughed from the army, mocked by anyone around me. You're the first person who has ever accepted the possibility. If that were all, that would be enough. But there are so many more reasons why I do love you."

She seized his hand again and pressed her lips to his palm. Tears ran down her cheeks, but she smiled between each kiss. "Hold me," she whispered, and he gathered her into his arms.

Her voice came out muffled against his chest. "That canyon was a place of evil, Cart. We should never have gone there, we shouldn't have tried to tap into the power in the crystal there. The forge was evil in its making, evil in its purpose, evil in its use." She sobbed. "We let it out, Cart—I let it out. I'm filthy with the taint of it."

Cart heard again the voice of the Secret Keeper in his mind, a harsh whisper that sapped his will as he walked through the narrow passage to the Dragon Forge.

"You walk boldly to your doom," the presence in shadows whispered. *"You think to stand before a power that was already great when Karrn the Conqueror took his first infant steps. Malathar the Damned will consume your body and annihilate your soul."*

"It lies," Gaven protested. *"Truth would burn its tongue. It's the Keeper of Secrets."*

"You think she cares for you? You think she could ever dream of loving you?"

"It's trying to sow despair," Cart said, feeling the despair clutch his chest and squeeze the energy from his body.

"We stopped it," he whispered, stroking her hair with his clumsy metal-bound hand. For a moment he dreamed that he was flesh, like the vision the quori had planted in his mind, and her body was soft and warm against his. In that moment he saw the taint in her, smelled and tasted it on her skin and her soul, and he started to recoil—until he realized that it was in him as well. The revulsion faded, replaced by a new understanding, and he held her closer.

Havrakhad had spoken of the spirit of the age—the unfathomable being at the heart of Dal Quor, the Region of Dreams. The present age had a spirit of malice and darkness, and so many things he saw now as expressions of that spirit: the influence of the Secret Keeper escaping through the Dragon Forge, the barbarians attacking the Eldeen Reaches, the nightmares of the city, Haldren and Kelas's plot against the queen. The turning of the age, Havrakhad said, draws near—and the hope of the kalashtar was that the spirit of that new age would be one of light, *il-Yannah*, "the Great Light." The darkness could be fought, yes, but even more important were the ways they sought to express the Great Light.

Though his body was wood and metal, fiber and stone, he held Ashara as tenderly as he could manage, clinging to the hope that the love he felt was a bastion against the darkness that threatened to overwhelm her.

* * * * *

Gaven glared at the priest, who wore an expression of smug self-satisfaction. "She told you to let us go," he snarled.

"The sons and daughters of Aerenal will do nothing to impede your departure," the priest said.

"Except keep me busy with questions while someone fetches the watch. I hope you enjoy your next conversation with your ancestor."

The soldiers, though, seemed reluctant to approach. Aunn had his mace in his hand and faced them warily, so Gaven slid the sword off his back.

"Give yourselves up!" one of the soldiers ventured, clutching his own sword in a trembling hand. He was a human man of maybe twenty with a long scar down his face, perhaps a mark of the Last War—or of some back-alley scuffle. The other soldier, an older human woman, shot him an incredulous glance.

"You seem to have some inkling what you're up against," Aunn said calmly. "I suggest you leave us in peace. You can tell your officers that we were gone when you arrived."

The older soldier looked as though she were considering the offer, but her eyes went to the two elves who would certainly complain to the watch and contradict that lie. The young man shouted back, "I suggest you surrender. Give yourselves up to justice!"

Gaven scratched his cheek, listening to the patter of rain in the courtyard outside. "We don't want to fight you," he said, "and it's clear you don't want to fight us, either."

"You were warned about us," Aunn said, advancing slowly. "Who told you? What did they say?"

The soldiers exchanged a glance, then the woman spoke up. "The Royal Eyes issued warnings about both of you. They said you killed some people in the Tower of Eyes, and he killed some spies in Chalice Center. Right in the open."

"I didn't kill anyone in the Tower of Eyes," Aunn muttered. "But I should have."

They were close enough now that Gaven could see past the soldiers and out into the courtyard, where rain was splattering against the cobblestones.

"No, I'm the killer here," Gaven said. "Once the storm gets started, it's hard to stop it. Look outside, it's already raining."

The soldiers stepped back at that. Clearly they had heard how the spies in Chalice Center met their end.

Even as the soldiers retreated, though, Gaven saw two other figures enter the courtyard at a run, then slow as they splashed into the puddles already forming among the cobblestones. The one in front was a tall woman in a leather coat, wearing chainmail beneath it, a rapier at her belt. Lagging a few paces behind was a dwarf in a scarlet shirt.

"It's the Kundarak," he said to Aunn.

"And it looks like she has a new friend," Aunn noted.

"Too bad. I rather liked Bordan."

Aunn shrugged. "So much for getting out of here without a fight."

The two women hurried across the courtyard. At the bottom of the stairs, the human looked up and took in the scene.

"Fairhaven watch!" she cried out. "Stand down, by order of the Sentinel Marshals!"

The soldiers looked relieved, and immediately backed away from Gaven and Aunn, afraid to turn their backs but not too proud to retreat. Gaven followed them outside to the top of the stairs. The rain was cold, but it soothed his skin.

"Thank you, Sentinel Marshal," he said, resting his great-sword on his shoulder. Thunder boomed overhead, and Gaven felt a thrill pass through his body. His dragonmark was gone—stolen, now—but the storm was willing to answer his call again. He was still the Storm Dragon, he realized.

"Don't thank me, vermin," the Sentinel Marshal said. "I was only trying to protect them."

"I'm grateful you got them out of the way before the storm grew too violent." Lightning flashed across the sky, casting strange shadows across the plaza.

"Gaven," the dwarf rumbled. "I suspected I'd find you here."

"You're quite persistent, Kundarak, I have to grant you that. But my position hasn't altered since we last met in Storm-home: You're wasting your time chasing me. And you don't have Rienne to take hostage this time."

"Don't I?"

A bolt of lightning struck the roof of the temple as fury surged in Gaven's heart. "You have her? Where is she?"

"I don't have her," Ossa said, "but I know where she is."

"Oh!" Aunn exclaimed from behind him. "I'm sorry, Gaven, I forgot to tell you—Rienne was briefly imprisoned in Thaliost last week."

"Imprisoned in Thaliost?"

"She left with a Lyrandar pilot who paid her fines."

Ossa scowled, and Gaven suspected that Aunn had just told him all the information that Ossa had hoped to use as a bargaining chip. So Rienne was with Jordhan. The sky rumbled with his pang of jealousy, but he felt relief as well, knowing that she had safely returned from Argonnessen and escaped whatever prison she'd been in.

The Sentinel Marshal was a few steps up the stairs, with Ossa right behind. "Gaven, excoriate of House Lyrandar," the Marshal said, "by authority of House Deneith, I place you under arrest for murder. I suggest you come without a fight, rather than adding to your crimes."

"Oh, so you make that suggestion out of concern for me?" Gaven said. "Not out of fear for your life?"

"My concern is that justice is done."

"Whose justice?"

The Sentinel Marshal looked perplexed, like the question made no sense to her.

"Enough of this bluster and boasting!" Ossa bellowed, tromping up a few more steps.

"I told you before, Kundarak—you can't handle me." Lightning slashed across the sky to emphasize his point, and thrilled in Gaven's veins.

The dwarf stopped in her tracks, staring at Gaven's face and neck, bewilderment on her face. "Your dragonmark," she said. "It's . . . not just covered up."

A dragonmark was a difficult thing to hide, partly because the pattern was typically raised above the level of the surrounding skin, and partly because using its power made it stand out even more, and typically melted away makeup used to cover it. Gaven had never tried to cover his, but as large as it had been, he doubted he would have had any success. Now, of course, his mark was gone, though the storm clearly still flowed in his blood—and the skin of his neck and chest burned furiously as the lightning flashed overhead.

"No, it's gone," Gaven snapped. "But that won't stop me from blasting you to the Outer Darkness if you take another step closer."

To Gaven's surprise, Ossa held up her hands, and even the Sentinel Marshal dropped one step back.

"What do you mean, your dragonmark is gone?" the Sentinel Marshal said quietly.

"I mean that House Cannith, House Thuranni, Arcanix, and the Royal Eyes of Aundair built a device that stripped the dragonmark off my skin." Thunder rumbled as he descended one more step. "They put it into a bloodshard and channeled its power into a storm that brought the siege of Varna to a speedy end. But I understand I'm a threat to society, so you'd better get me back to Dreadhold."

Lightning struck the steps right next to him, sending the Sentinel Marshal staggering backward, stumbling on the stairs.

"If you can take me!"

Another bolt crashed to the ground between the two women, tossing them aside. Ossa rolled quickly back on her feet, but the Marshal was slower to stand.

"Gaven!" Aunn's voice was right at his shoulder, and he felt the changeling's hand on his arm. Power surged in Gaven's blood, thunder rumbled in the sky and shook the ground, but he bit back a thunderclap that would have thrown Aunn back away from him.

"Give them a chance to talk," Aunn said.

The Sentinel Marshal was in a crouch, her empty palms turned out to Gaven, her rapier on the ground a few feet away. Ossa, too, had her hands well away from the weapon at her belt, as her eyes continued to search Gaven's skin for any sign of his mark.

"So talk!" Gaven shouted.

"Where was this device?" Ossa said, glancing at the Sentinel Marshal.

"Near the Blackcaps."

"I knew it!" the dwarf exclaimed.

"And House Cannith built it—Cannith West?" the Sentinel Marshal asked. "With help from all the others you mentioned? Arcanix and the Royal Eyes—and House Thuranni?"

"Yes," Gaven said.

"Not exactly," Aunn interjected. "One officer of the Royal Eyes was involved, but he's dead now. And I don't know how involved House Thuranni was."

"And that officer died in the . . . catastrophic failure of the device?" Ossa said. Gaven couldn't read her expression, but there was more she wasn't saying.

"We destroyed the Dragon Forge," Gaven said, "but Kelas met his end earlier."

"Who from House Cannith was involved?" the Sentinel Marshal asked.

"A whole platoon of magewrights," Aunn said quickly. He was trying to hide Ashara's involvement, Gaven realized.

"But what about the baron? Was Jorlanna aware of it?"

"I saw her there once," Aunn said. "She demonstrated the device to the queen."

Ossa and the Sentinel Marshal shared an excited glance. "We have her!" the Marshal exclaimed.

Ossa grinned. "We've got them all."

CHAPTER
37

A unn stepped in front of Gaven, hoping the storm might calm if Aunn took the reins of the conversation and let Gaven cool his head.

"You're looking for information you can use against Jorlanna?" he asked.

The Sentinel Marshal nodded.

"Then you need to know that she's part of something larger."

"Larger?"

"At minimum, it's a plot against the queen, but I fear it's more than that."

"I'm listening," the Sentinel Marshal said.

"Should we go someplace more private to discuss this?" Gaven said.

Ossa scoffed. "So you have a chance to lose us in the city streets?" she said. "I don't think so."

"Here is fine for now," the Sentinel Marshal said. "Let's hear what you have to say, changeling."

"My name is Aunn." It still felt strange to say it aloud. "I was with the Royal Eyes."

"That much I knew," the Sentinel Marshal said. "The Royal Eyes issued a warning to the city watch about you. I'm Mauren d'Deneith."

"Mauren," Aunn repeated. It was a name he might have used for one of his faces. He had been a Vauren, a Maura, and a Laurann in the past. He felt a sudden strange pang—he missed them, somehow, or grieved the life they represented. It was followed by a sudden stab of suspicion: What if Mauren was the changeling, Vec? Vec had used one of Aunn's faces, appearing as Haunderk. Might he also use a name similar to one he would use?

"Mauren, forgive my impertinence," he said, "but could I please see your dragonmark?"

Mauren's mouth quirked in a funny smile. "You don't want to see my papers or my badge? Just my mark?"

"I'm a Royal Eye, Sentinel Marshal. I know how easy it is to acquire papers and badges."

"You're also a changeling," she said. She fumbled at a buckle near her shoulder as she climbed the steps. "And you know how hard it is to imitate a dragonmark."

"Exactly."

"It is not easy to show," Mauren said, still smiling, her fingers working at a different buckle. Ossa climbed the stairs behind her.

Aunn tensed. That could be a convenient excuse, though Mauren didn't look like she was preparing an attack.

Mauren slipped her leather coat down off her shoulders and turned partly away from Aunn. "Come here," she said.

Aunn stepped beside her, feeling awkward.

"There's a flap at the shoulder you should be able to open," Mauren said.

Aunn reached out and pulled at the chainmail that covered her shoulder. As Mauren had said, a flap of mail attached to leather and backed with cotton pulled away, revealing bare skin beneath—and the tracings of the Mark of Sentinel, a bit like a rampant dragon, with its head, tail, and wings forming a sort of cross shape. If she was a changeling, she had mastered a talent he found impossible.

"I'm sorry I doubted you," he said quietly. It was a strange moment of intimacy.

"I'm glad you're satisfied. Maybe now we can work together from a position of trust." She pulled the armor flap back over her mark and her coat back over her shoulders as Aunn stepped back. "You were going to tell me about Jorlanna's involvement in a plot against the queen."

"Yes. We believe that Nara ir'Galanatyr is behind the whole

scheme, though almost everyone else involved thought that the mastermind was Kelas ir'Darren."

"I know the Galanatyr name," Mauren said. "She was head of the Royal Eyes during the war, right?"

Aunn nodded.

"But I don't know ir'Darren."

"He was my superior in the Royal Eyes. He brought together Jorlanna, Arcanist Wheldren of the Arcane Congress, former Colonel Janna Tolden, and a few financial backers to overthrow the queen."

"You said you feared it was more than just a plot against the queen. What more did you mean?"

"I'm not sure yet." He turned to Gaven. "Listen. You know how the Prophecy confuses me. But I realized something this morning."

"Is this the time to talk about it?" Gaven said, glancing sidelong at Ossa and the Sentinel Marshal.

"We don't have much time left, Gaven. Listen. Nara's been masterminding this whole affair, from breaking you out of Dreadhold"—he saw Ossa stiffen—"to the Dragon Forge. When I talked to her she was excited about the 'storm and dragon reunited' line. But that's crazy. That means that she knew you were the Storm Dragon, even when Haldren thought it was Vaskar. She knew you would face the Soul Reaver but you wouldn't become a god, because you had to be around for the Time of the Dragon Below. Each time you've thought you were taking control of your own destiny, you were doing what she expected you to do. You were fulfilling the Prophecy in the way she planned for it to be fulfilled."

Gaven scowled. Aunn could understand why he might not want to think along these lines, but he had to convince him.

"So she's planning to overthrow the queen, but now Kelas is dead and her plan is in a shambles. Or is it? Maybe she's counting on someone else carrying it out—she already has another changeling lined up to stab the queen, and Janna Tolden is snooping around Kelas's office in the old cathedral. But maybe she's planning for them to fail as well, because she knows that we're aware of her plot. Maybe the Prophecy says she's going to fail—but that means it's not a failure! It's what she wants to happen, because it's not her true goal."

"So what is her real goal?" Mauren said.

"I have no idea!" Aunn put his hands on Gaven's shoulders. "You're the only other person who could possibly know. There has to be something in the Prophecy that's her real goal, something that's supposed to happen in the Time of the Dragon Below. Or maybe something that's supposed to happen years from now."

Gaven frowned. His eyes were focused somewhere behind Aunn's head, and his lips moved without forming words. For a moment Aunn was afraid that Gaven was sinking back into the catatonic state he'd entered at the Dragon Forge.

Then Gaven gave voice to the words on his lips. "His are the words the Blasphemer unspeaks, his the song the Blasphemer unsings."

"What is he saying?" Ossa demanded.

Gaven whirled on her. "You, Kundarak, have been chasing me for months, since I first set foot outside of your family's impenetrable prison. And all this time, here is what you have failed to understand: My destiny does not lie in Dreadhold."

"Any common thief might make that claim."

"That's what Bordan said. But I am not a common thief. My fate is woven into the verses of the Prophecy."

"And what is that fate?" Mauren asked.

"I must face the Blasphemer."

Mauren cocked a quizzical eyebrow at Aunn, since Gaven's gaze was still fixed on the dwarf.

"The leader of the barbarian horde," Aunn explained.

"And what?" Ossa said. "You're the one who kills him? You save Aundair from the rampaging barbarian menace? Is that what the Prophecy says?"

"No." Gaven's voice was quiet, distant. "The maelstrom swirls around me. I am the storm and the eye of the storm." Thunder rumbled again, but it too seemed far off.

"What does that mean?"

"In the city by the lake of kings, the city scourged with his storm . . ." Gaven's voice trailed off.

"I don't understand," Mauren said. "You say your fate is to face the Blasphemer, that it's part of the Prophecy that ir'Galanatyr has been trying to fulfill. But you're not saying that you're going to defeat the Blasphemer—in fact, as far as I can make out you might be saying the opposite. So you're saying we should let you go so that you can go get yourself killed by the Blasphemer, which might be exactly what Nara wants to happen."

Aunn frowned. Mauren was right—Gaven's words didn't exactly fill him with confidence about a potential confrontation between the Storm Dragon and the Blasphemer. "What happens in the city, Gaven? Is that Varna?"

"Who is Nara?" Gaven whispered, his eyes wide.

"Gaven!" Mauren grabbed Gaven's shoulders and shouted into his face. Thunder rumbled and Aunn winced, but the explosion of wrath he feared didn't come. "We need you to talk to us, explain what's going on!"

"It is simple," Gaven said. "In the Time of the Dragon Above, the Storm Dragon arose after twice thirteen years, he walked the paths of the First of Sixteen in the Sky Caves of Thieren Kor, and he faced the Soul Reaver and blocked the bridge to the sky. In the Time Between, the pivotal moment of history, the touch of Siberys's hand passed from my flesh to Eberron's blood at the Dragon Forge. Now the Time of the Dragon Below is upon us, and both history and prophecy flow toward the city by the lake of kings, the city scourged with my storm, where storm and dragon will be reunited, where the Words of Creation will be sung and unsung, where the Blasphemer will meet his end. I will be there—you will not stop me. You might as well try to stop the world from spinning."

"Simple?" Mauren said. She looked utterly bewildered.

Ossa crossed her arms and glared up at Gaven. "Four of us came before the Lord Warden when you escaped, you know. Four representatives of four dragonmarked lines. Sentinel Marshal Evlan d'Deneith. Bordan d'Velderan of House Tharashk.

Phaine d'Thuranni. And me. You killed the other three. Now I'm the only one left. I'm the—"

Gaven interrupted her. "Killed Bordan?" he said. "I didn't kill Bordan."

"Then who did?" Ossa demanded. "He chased you when you fled Stormhome. I followed with my team, but he outdistanced us. By the time we caught up to him, his lifeblood was soaking into the sand."

"I never saw him again after I left the city," Gaven said. "I wouldn't have wished him dead."

"The Sentinel Marshals you killed, though? And now Phaine?"

Gaven turned away.

"Anyway," Ossa said, "the point is that I am now the only one who can restore my family's pride and honor as the keepers of Dreadhold. And I can do that only by returning you there, because even Haldren ir'Brassek is dead now, I'm told. I can't tell you how much it would please me to lead you back to Dreadhold in chains, slung across the back of a manticore and wracked with its poison."

"You can't take me." The threat was gone from Gaven's voice, and no thunder underlined his words—it was a simple statement of fact.

Ossa dropped her hands to her sides and her shoulders slumped. "No, I can't. But maybe I have to live with that. Perhaps there is more at stake than the honor of my family. If what you say is true, this is about more than bringing a fugitive to justice." Her hand rubbed absently at a spot beneath her left collarbone—Aunn guessed that was the location of her dragonmark. She looked as though she were torn between her duty to her House, symbolized by her Mark of Warding, and the thoughts she was straining to put into words.

Aunn glanced at the Sentinel Marshal, who looked similarly uncomfortable. Both of them seemed to be contemplating what could be seen as a serious dereliction of their duty, in service to a higher purpose. Aunn could understand why they found it so difficult.

"Your duty is to capture Gaven," Aunn said. "But your duty isn't always the right thing to do." He thought of Sevren Thorn and Zandar Thuul, screaming out their last breaths in the Demon Wastes, because Aunn had done his duty. He thought of Vor Helden, cut down by the giant's blade in the Labyrinth, because Aunn had done his duty.

Kalok Shash—the Silver Flame—burns brighter.

"You could not understand, changeling," Ossa said. "Even Gaven might not understand, because his mark was the touch of Siberys. For those of us who bear the more common dragonmarks, the mark is our destiny, not just our duty. It is how we fit into the symphony of the world, the part we play. I carry the Mark of Warding." She put her hand on the spot she had rubbed earlier, confirming Aunn's hunch. "It is not a decoration—it's who I am. I'm sure it is no different for Mauren with the Mark of Sentinel. I am a warder, a *Ghorad'din*. It is written in my very being. And yet . . ."

"And yet Jorlanna could strip that mark from your skin and your soul," Gaven said. "And yet the Blasphemer comes— the Blasphemer, whose words are the antithesis of what is written in your dragonmark, the negation of all being. My destiny, too, is written in my dragonmark. Not service to House Lyrandar, but . . ." He seemed at a loss for words. "I must face the Blasphemer."

Ossa nodded slowly. "Gaven, excoriate of House Lyrandar," she said, "House Kundarak renounces its claim on you. You are free."

"Free?" Gaven looked as surprised as Aunn felt.

"Not entirely," Mauren said. "Other Houses have claims on you as well, and not just for the crimes that sent you to Dreadhold in the first place. But if Ossa chooses not to pursue you now, I will not either. I suggest you find yourself a fast horse and make for Varna."

Gaven turned to Aunn. "But I still have no papers."

Mauren pulled a sheet of parchment and a small writing set from inside her coat, glanced at the sky with a look of relief that the rain had passed, and quickly scrawled something on the page. Aunn noticed that the paper already carried an arcane mark placed by House Sivis, along with the three-headed chimera seal of House Deneith. "This will get you to Varna," she said as she handed it to Gaven.

"You're coming with me, aren't you?" Gaven asked Aunn.

Aunn shook his head, unable to speak.

"Your destiny lies elsewhere," Gaven said.

"Here, at least for now," Aunn said. "I intend to stop Jorlanna and protect the queen, even if that is exactly what Nara wants and expects me to do."

"Ossa and I would welcome your help," Mauren said.

Gaven clasped his hand. "Aunn, Darraun, dwarf with the manacles." He smiled. "I owe you my life and my freedom, such as they are. Thank you, friend."

Tears sprang to Aunn's eyes and words failed him again, so he pulled Gaven close and embraced him.

"Farewell," Gaven said.

"I hope you find what you seek," Aunn said.

"I already have."

"Give Rienne my best when you see her."

"She's very fond of you, you know. I will."

"Then I'll see you when this is all over," Aunn said, releasing him.

Gaven gave him a weak smile and turned away.

CHAPTER
38

Rienne started down the hill at a run, focusing all her energy toward greater speed. She heard confused shouts behind her—her troops expected orders, she realized, not their leader tearing off alone.

Well, she thought, they chose to follow me. They had better get used to me.

The droning of the insects grew louder as she approached, as did the cries of their victims. The creatures formed a black cloud that surrounded the fleeing Reachers, swirling in giant eddies and clinging to exposed skin and hair. People in the front of the group ran with their arms over their faces, heads down, blindly seeking an escape from the horror as winged monsters the size of their hands bit into skin or sawed through leather with enormous mandibles.

Rienne drew Maelstrom as she ran, though it was hard for her to imagine even her legendary blade causing much harm to the swarm. She could kill hundreds of the insects and leave the swarm undiminished. Nevertheless, she drew the blade, and she felt the energy flowing through her body focus and extend through her blade, as if it were part of her.

Then she was in the midst of it. The droning of the insects' wings surrounded her, and the creatures—as if smelling her unprotected skin—swarmed close around her. She didn't give them a chance to approach. Maelstrom sprang to life in her hand, whirling around her, slicing through chitin and diaphanous wing and forming a barrier of swirling wind.

Inspired by her presence, a few of the nearby farmers pulled out battered swords—most of them probably handed down

from a parent or grandparent who fought in the Last War—
and tried to imitate her example. She saw one fall to his knees,
screaming in pain, his sword clattering to the ground.

"No!" Rienne screamed. "Keep running!"

The breath and energy she spent shouting lowered her
defenses for a moment, and one of the insects sank its mandibles
into the back of her neck. The pain was excruciating, far worse
than the bite alone as venom spread up and down her neck and
back. She snatched the creature and wrenched it free, causing a
fresh jolt of pain as it tore flesh away in its jaws, then crushed it
in her hand. Violet blood oozed between her fingers, distinctly
unnatural, and revulsion welled in her gut. She fought it down
and continued Maelstrom's whirling dance.

She drew a slow, deep breath as Maelstrom whirled, and the
cloud of insects around her darkened, drawn into the vortex of
wind she created. She held the breath, and flames burst from
Maelstrom's blade, trailing along behind the steel like a banner.
She let her breath out slowly and the flames formed a curtain
around her, then widened inch by inch to encompass more and
more of the swarming horrors.

When her breath was expended, the flames faded, but
the ground around her was littered with the charred bodies
of the swarm. The air was still dark with them, though, as
Maelstrom's whirlwind drew them in toward its flashing blade.
Rienne glanced toward the camp and saw perhaps a dozen
people running clear of the swarm, almost to safety. More were
still trapped within the cloud, though. For a moment she wondered whether rushing headlong into the midst of the swarm
had been wise.

A burst of fire erupted in the air above her. She threw
herself to the ground and rolled beneath the flames, springing
to her feet as the flames died and a shower of blackened insect
corpses fell to the earth. She looked around for the source of the
flame and saw a dark figure standing outside the cloud, dressed
in hide armor and a tattered green tabard. Kyaphar!

Another insect found its way to her arm and bit through
her clothes, sending a lance of pain down to her hand. Her

muscles convulsed as poison coursed through them, and Maelstrom fell to the ground. She faltered in her whirling dance, and more insects attached themselves to her flesh, wracking her body with their painful venom. She stooped to retrieve Maelstrom, but as she did an insect bit and her leg buckled beneath her, sending her sprawling. Before she could draw a breath her body was covered with writhing and biting insects, their wings still droning as they cut into her skin.

Another burst of fire erupted around her, washing over her with a strangely pleasant warmth. The insects around her shriveled and burned in the flame, but the fires only soothed her skin and eased the pain of the poison. Rienne grabbed Maelstrom's hilt and sprang back to her feet, waving her thanks in Kyaphar's direction. Maelstrom flew back into motion as Kyaphar hurled smaller bursts of fire into the diminishing remnants of the swarm.

Once again Maelstrom whirled around her until it formed a great funnel of wind—

But the Blasphemer's end lies in the void, in the maelstrom that pulls him down to darkness.

For a moment she seemed to see the Blasphemer's leering face form in the black cloud of insects before her, and the words from her dream echoed in her mind.

She was the center of a mighty storm, her own Storm Dragon even without Gaven at her side. She drew another slow breath, feeling the energy of it build inside her like an elation she could barely contain. Holding that energy in her belly, she tumbled out of the center of the storm, turned to put the mass of the cloud in front of her, and let her breath out as a tremendous blast of flame.

Blackened husks swirled in the wind like cinders over a mighty fire, their droning silenced. Rienne surveyed the plain as Maelstrom whirled around her. Insects still flew here and there, but they had lost any coherence as a swarm, and they seemed to have lost their aggressive instincts as well. Rienne let Maelstrom slow its dance, cutting through a few last insects before coming to rest at her side.

Two dozen or more survivors walked or ran in the direction of the camp, some limping, some carrying a fallen comrade, one she noticed crawling on hands and knees. Kyaphar walked among the fallen, looking for any who might still be within life's reach. The fallen, Rienne was pleased to see, were few—at a quick count, only seven, and as she looked Kyaphar stooped over one of the seven and began tending the man's wounds.

She slid Maelstrom into its sheath and fell to her knees. Blackened chitin crunched on the ground beneath her, and even the sound it made was somehow wrong—like the words of the Blasphemer that could not have been words. She gingerly lifted one of the charred husks and examined it. It looked like no insect she'd ever seen, its six thick legs more like a spider's than the wasp it superficially resembled. It bore huge mandibles that pulsed with the poison inside, and the chitin plating its body had an unnatural purplish sheen.

"The Depravation," Kyaphar said.

Rienne looked over her shoulder and saw him standing behind her, concern etched on his face. "What's that?" she asked.

"We see it sometimes in areas where the influence of the daelkyr seeps into the earth from the Realm of Madness they call home. It happens when the seals of the Gatekeepers weaken, and madness leaks through, and in places where daelkyr or their brood that dwell in the depths of Khyber make their way closer to the surface. Usually its influence is slight, subtle, and slow."

"But with the breaking of the seal it's much worse," Rienne said. "Bad enough to generate swarms like this in a few hours' time."

"Exactly."

Rienne stood up and smiled at Kyaphar, even as tears welled in her eyes. "I'm glad you survived the battle, Sky Warden. I saw the airship go down."

"I tried to save Jordhan, but there was nothing I could do. I'm sorry."

"I understand. Thank you, Kyaphar."

The Sky Warden put his arms around her and her resolve broke. Tears streamed down her face and she shook with sobs as she thought of Jordhan—the dear friend who had aided and abetted her and Gaven on so many of their adventures, the greatest of which was their grand expedition to Argonnessen—lying dead amid the wreckage of his airship. Kyaphar held her as she wept, and only released her as the tide of grief subsided.

Drying her eyes, she thanked Kyaphar again and hoped that no one at the camp had seen Lady Dragonslayer break down so completely.

* * * * *

Free.

Gaven turned the word over in his mind as he made his way back to Chalice Center, trying not to look like he was in any more of a hurry than would be normal for people in the busy capital city. Ossa had renounced her House's claim on him, declared him free of Dreadhold. Free.

Don't get too comfortable with that idea, he reminded himself.

Mauren had stressed the point that he was still a fugitive from justice, still subject to arrest for any number of crimes. He still didn't have identification papers, let alone formal traveling papers, so he would have a hard time living anything like a normal life.

On the other hand, he was about to travel to Varna to face the Blasphemer. What kind of normal life was that? He had money in his pouch that would buy him a fast horse, he had Mauren's letter that would get him across the river despite Aundair's military presence there, and he had a sword on his back and the storm in his blood, even if his dragonmark was gone, off in the hands of House Thuranni somewhere. There was nothing normal about his life, and really never had been.

Still, somehow, it made a difference to know that he was

free—in whatever limited, narrow sense of the word actually applied to him.

In Chalice Center, he haggled with a horse trader as he had done in the years before Dreadhold, no longer caring if he made a strong impression in the man's memory that might help the authorities follow his trail—and he still spent entirely too much of Kelas's money on a magebred horse. Haggling had always been Rienne's specialty.

He thought of Rienne as he bought a saddle and bridle and other gear for his journey, and ended up paying far more than he should have because of his distraction. She'd been held in a jail in Thaliost—he didn't even know why. Jordhan had paid her fines and taken her away, and he didn't know where. Was she looking for him?

Or was she, as he was, drawn to the west by the call of her destiny? Aunn seemed to think he would find her, and the strange waking dream he'd had in Kelas's house suggested it as well—

A demon in man's shape stood before Rienne, lifting a curved sword as the sounds of the world's unmaking spilled from his mouth . . .

"Are you ill, master?" The shop clerk peered at his face curiously.

"No, I'm fine. Sorry." Gaven scratched at his neck—his skin was on fire.

"Strangest weather we've been having," the clerk remarked, turning to look out the window. "Clear and cold one minute, then clouds and rain, the rumble of thunder like the drums of war. Can't say I like it."

"Sorry."

"Well, that's autumn in Fairhaven for you. You know what they say, 'If you don't like the weather, wait a bell and it'll change.'" The clerk laughed.

Gaven paid for his supplies and hurried out to his horse. He bid Fairhaven and its mercurial weather farewell and rode out of the city, delighting in the wind on his face.

* * * * *

Kyaphar spent the night searching for more survivors of the battle and leading them, in groups of three to perhaps three dozen, to Rienne's camp. Rienne tried to rest, but each time a new group approached the camp she rose to greet them, speak to their leaders, make sure the wounded found care, and offer what comfort and encouragement she could. Two other sergeants found their way to the camp, and even a lieutenant, but no one was interested in relieving Lady Dragonslayer of her command. Besides Kyaphar, Rienne discovered one more druid among the survivors, a white-bearded man named Fieran. By dawn, she was in command of an army of just over two hundred and fifty, according to Cressa's enthusiastic report, and a council of two druids, four officers, and Rienne herself—with Cressa at her side as her aide—gathered in a large tent that someone had erected for Rienne's use.

Rienne decided to dispense with any pleasantries or introduction. She waited until the elders and officers were gathered in the tent, entered with no introduction or fanfare, and asked, "Who can explain to me what happened yesterday?"

Kyaphar frowned. "The Gatekeepers' seal was broken."

Fieran snorted into his beard. "Obliterated would be more accurate."

"What do you mean?" Rienne asked.

Fieran leaned back in his flimsy chair, steepled his fingers beneath his chin, and looked up at the roof of the tent. "Ordinarily, when we see one of the Gatekeepers' seals break, we observe a gradual process by which the energies of the Realm of Madness slowly begin to eat away at the seal, break it down slowly, until it is weak enough that they can push it aside, as it were. This was different."

"It was sudden, immediate," Rienne said. "What else?"

"It was completely undone. There is nothing left, no residue or remnant we could hope to use to begin repairing it. It is as though the seal simply never existed."

"And what happened when it broke, or vanished?"

"You saw it," Sergeant Kallo said. "You were there. The land erupted."

"Yes, that's what I saw. But I want to know why it happened. Did something emerge from the ground, pushing the rock out before it? What came out?"

"From what I could see," Kyaphar said, "what came out was madness and chaos. I didn't see a daelkyr come forth, or any of their brood. But I have never seen the Depravation spread so quickly or so far."

"So there is no horrible spawn of madness rampaging across the Reaches?"

Kyaphar shook his head. "Not as far as I could see from the air. But remember, I was dodging boulders spewed up from the earth. I could have missed much."

Rienne nodded, her fingers idly toying with Maelstrom's hilt. "Kyaphar, you told me before that the Blasphemer's path took him across the Reaches from Gatekeeper seal to Gatekeeper seal. The seal he broke yesterday was not the first, just the largest seal he has undone. But was it the last? Was this great seal his goal, or is there a greater prize?"

"I don't think—" Kyaphar began.

"There is a greater prize," Fieran interrupted. "At the city by the lake of kings."

"Varna?" Rienne asked. A sick feeling took root in her stomach, a gnawing dread. She seemed to hear the splash and rush of the river beneath the screams and shouts of battle.

"Indeed."

"What is that prize? Was the city built over a seal?" That seemed like an unwise strategy, and it ran counter to her impression of the other seals, which she had thought were all far from cities or even villages of the Reaches.

"No," Fieran said. "It's far worse than that. At the city by the lake of kings, it is said, the Blasphemer will unmake the world."

CHAPTER
39

Aunn sat in the back corner of the Ruby Chalice, the hood of his purple cloak pulled down to shroud his face in shadow. It would have been so much easier to just put on an innocuous human face, round and flushed with drink, and blend right in with the rest of the evening crowd. The temptation was strong, but he fought it, clinging to his new sense of identity. Instead, he wore his true face but hid it in shadow and distance, staying on the fringes of the crowds.

Five days had passed since Gaven left Fairhaven—Aunn figured he was probably almost half way to Varna. Aunn had spent the time working with Mauren and Ossa to unravel the strands of Nara's plot, but he took every chance he could to stop in the Ruby Chalice in hopes of seeing Cart and Ashara. It was the only place he could think of they might return to, if they were looking for him. He had tried a more active search for them, but after they created a significant buzz by walking arm in arm through the city, on the day Gaven had left, they seemed to have disappeared from public view. As far as he knew, Mauren was still ignorant of Ashara's involvement in the Dragon Forge, but he wasn't sure how long that could possibly last.

Aunn had led the Sentinel Marshal to the basement of the old cathedral, where they found Kelas's office ransacked, stripped bare of any clue to what he was involved in. Aunn suspected that either Janna Tolden had taken everything with her, or Nara had sent Vec to do the job. Since then, Mauren had arrested Kharos Olan and Bromas ir'Lain, two of Kelas's co-conspirators. Their involvement in the scheme had been almost exclusively financial, though, and they didn't have much additional information to offer. Janna Tolden and the half-orc from Droaam remained at large, to Aunn's and Mauren's increasing frustration.

Vec proved to be a tricky quarry. An individual changeling was almost impossible to track down, of course. The fact that he was an agent of the Royal Eyes made the situation much more complicated. In theory, the Royal Eyes should have cooperated with a Sentinel Marshal trying to prevent the assassination of the queen. In practice, Mauren had met nothing but resistance. She and Ossa were at the Tower of Eyes now, still trying to arrange an interview with Thuel, but Aunn didn't expect a breakthrough after five days of stalling and posturing.

He sighed and swirled the wine in his glass, watching the light from the candle on his table filter through the golden liquid. It reminded him of the Eye of Siberys, which sent his thoughts back over all the events and plots of the past year. For just a moment, the whole room seemed bathed in the golden light, and he felt an inexpressible sense that there was a purpose at work in it all—not just Nara's sinister plot, whatever it was, but some contrary intention. He felt as though he were seeing his own path laid out in the swirls of golden light, his own part in the Prophecy. He smiled as peace washed over him.

A woman draped in blue appeared in the doorway, and Aunn watched as she scanned the crowded room. When her face turned toward him, his heart leapt—it was Ashara. He adjusted his hood just enough that she could see his gray face, and she hesitated. He waved and let his face suggest Kelas's features for an instant. Ashara smiled and made her way to his table.

"Aunn, thank the Fire and Forge," she said, collapsing into a chair across from him. "We've been looking for you for days."

"Where's Cart?"

"He's waiting in the square. If I don't come out in a moment, he'll come in. We've found it's best not to be seen together."

Aunn nodded. Separately, neither of them was distinctive—most people had a hard time telling one warforged from another. It was their obvious affection for each other that drew attention.

"What happened to you?" Ashara asked. "We agreed to meet back here for dinner, and you never came."

"My trip to the Tower of Eyes didn't go as I'd planned."

"And so you're not trying to be Kelas any more."

"Right. Oh, there's Cart."

The warforged stood in the doorway, scanning the room. He spotted the blue of Ashara's cloak and strode over to join them.

"Aunn?" he asked, staring at the unfamiliar blank face.

Aunn stood, smiling, and extended a hand to Cart. The warforged pulled him into a clumsy embrace that threatened to squeeze the breath from his lungs.

"We were concerned," Cart said. "Have you seen Gaven?"

It still came as a surprise to Aunn that anyone would be concerned for him. "Yes," he said, blinking. "He's on his way to Varna."

"Varna? Why?"

Aunn shrugged. "The Prophecy draws him on, as always. Listen, there's a Sentinel Marshal in town—"

"Yes, we've spoken with her," Ashara said.

"And the Kundarak with her," Cart added.

"You have? When?"

"A few days ago," Ashara said, looking to Cart for confirmation.

"The morning after we saw you last," Cart said.

Aunn thought back over the last several days. He had first met Mauren and Ossa the same morning, and he'd been with them for most of that day. They must have met Cart and Ashara just before that. Aunn thought it strange that the Sentinel Marshal had never mentioned Ashara.

"You told them nothing about the Dragon Forge?" Aunn asked.

"I told them enough to get them off our backs," Ashara said. "I told them it was a catastrophic failure that led to my disgrace and excoriation."

A sick feeling clutched Aunn's gut. "You admitted that you were responsible for it."

"I suppose so. What of it?"

Suddenly Aunn understood much of what had been confusing him for days. He had wondered why the Sentinel Marshal seemed to be moving so slowly, unwilling to make any direct move on Jorlanna or House Cannith. He suspected now that she wanted to avoid causing too much alarm until she had Ashara in custody.

"Mauren knows what the Dragon Forge did," Aunn said.

"Mauren? The Sentinel Marshal is a friend of yours?"

"I've been working with her to stop Jorlanna. It would have been better if you had cooperated with her as well."

Ashara's eyes were wide with fear, and Cart rested his hand on top of hers.

"It's not too late," Aunn said. "I'll tell her you're willing to help—tell her all the ways you've already helped. I couldn't have undone the magic of the Dragon Forge without you."

Ashara shuddered and looked down at the table, seeming more vulnerable than Aunn had ever seen her before.

Cart squeezed her hand. "He's right," he said. "It's better this way."

"I should have listened to you," Ashara said, smiling at Cart. "But I was too afraid."

"Fear is a gateway for the Dark to enter the world," Cart said.

Aunn cocked his head at that—it didn't sound like anything he'd heard Cart say before. He glanced at the runic mark on Cart's forehead, reassuring himself that this was the right warforged. Imprinted at the creation forge, those marks were unique to each individual warforged. Satisfied, Aunn smiled to himself. Cart was proving himself more complex—more "many-layered"—with each passing week.

"So what about you?" Cart said. "You've been working with the Sentinel Marshal? What have you learned?"

"It's starting to come together—at least, I think it is." Aunn sipped his wine and gathered his thoughts. "Kelas sent me to the Demon Wastes to stir up the barbarians, to get them to strike eastward. I know that Nara was behind that mission, and I'm pretty sure the goal—or one goal—was to get Aundairian troops as far away from the capital as possible. Most of our army is either in the Reaches already or guarding our borders with Thrane and Breland. But rather than leave the capital entirely unguarded, the queen hired mercenaries, quite a lot of them. Now, normally, if you want to hire mercenaries you go to House Deneith or House Tharashk. But the queen's not in a position to deal with the dragonmarked houses right now, especially not Deneith."

"So she's hired mercenaries from Droaam," Cart said. "Led by the half-orc who was at Kelas's council."

"Exactly. A whole company of minotaurs, disciplined and ferocious, marched into the city today. As far as I know, Janna Tolden is still involved in the plot as well, and even though she's been discharged in disgrace, she still commands devout loyalty from some number of soldiers. So our working assumption is that the entire military forces of the city, with the possible exception of the palace guard, are more or less directly under Nara's control."

"So you think they're going to seize the palace?" Cart asked.

"I expect they'll try. And in the confusion of the skirmish the assassin will strike at the queen. The key question is when—and here's where I wish Gaven were still around. I figure there has to be a significant moment, something related to the Prophecy, that will signal the attack."

"Then, when the queen is dead," Ashara said, "the mercenary army installs Jorlanna on the throne?"

"I suppose. Jorlanna's involvement is still not clear to me."

"Jorlanna doesn't dare take part in the battle openly," Ashara said, "in case it doesn't go according to plan."

"But she can help covertly," Cart said. "We found out that the mercenaries are armed with weapons made and enchanted in Cannith forges."

"Which means Jorlanna spent a small fortune already,"

Ashara added. "And those weapons might be enough to tip the scales of the battle."

"I can see that," Aunn said. "But they're also physical proof of her involvement, aren't they?"

"Probably not," Ashara said. "Ordinarily, the magewrights would stamp the House seal in the tang of the blade, but Jorlanna probably ordered them not to for these weapons."

"But what about the enchantments they carry? Where else would a band of mercenaries from Droaam get magical weapons?"

"I'm not sure that constitutes physical proof," Cart said.

"And my House has devised some temporary enchantments," Ashara said. "I'd bet that within a day or two of the battle they'll be ordinary, if well-crafted, blades."

Aunn stared into his glass, empty except for a few drops of the golden wine. "So how do we prove Jorlanna's connection to this whole scheme?"

A voice from behind Ashara startled him—he hadn't seen the man approach. "Exactly what I've been trying to figure out," Harkin said.

* * * * *

Rienne's ragtag army marched toward the ruins of Varna as fast as her would-be soldiers could manage. It wasn't a march, really—the farmers and foresters walked in casual clumps of two to five, sharing stories or singing songs as they went. The handful of real soldiers began the trip marching, lined up in formation, but their rigid lines soon dissolved as the soldiers drifted off in ones and twos to join the clusters. Rienne smiled, watching it. She understood the need for discipline in an army, but it heartened her to see hope take root among those she had come to think of as her people.

The march brought them through miles of farmland and past the occasional tiny village where they could stock up on food—freely donated, more often than not, by the farmers who pegged their sole hope for the Reaches' survival on this straggling army. Rienne had been concerned that some of her followers would drift away in each village, but in fact their numbers swelled—a few survivors of the battle who had made their way separately to these communities rejoined the army when it passed through, and a handful of hardy men and women who had never joined the militia took up weapons that had lain unused since the Last War and joined Rienne's march to Varna.

Cressa was her nearly constant companion on the march, a fountain of energy and a source of unending chatter whether or not Rienne had anything to add to the conversation. Slowly, Rienne let her guard down—she stopped worrying quite so much about conveying the impression that she had everything under control, and began confiding in the girl as she would to an old friend. By the end of the first week, she had told Cressa about Jordhan—starting with his death at the Mosswood, then slowly working backward through their long history together. That forced her to tell the girl all about Gaven, which occupied the beginning of the second week.

Cressa seemed shocked, at first, to learn that Rienne's betrothed had gone to Dreadhold, and even more surprised when she learned that Rienne helped Gaven after he escaped from that supposedly inescapable prison. As Rienne told more of her long tale, though, Cressa looked on Rienne with even more adoration in her eyes, as though she were a true hero because of the devotion she showed to her true love. Rienne almost laughed, but the girl was so earnest—and in fact, Rienne's heart ached with the truth of it. She had sacrificed everything to help Gaven, to be reunited with him . . . only to have him stolen from her side in the depths of Argonnessen. Now, as her story came to what seemed like the end, she was going to face the Blasphemer alone, still wondering where Gaven was.

Night fell early as winter spread its icy claws down from the Frostfell, and the lights of the night sky did little to illuminate the ground. Even so, Rienne ordered torches lit so the army could keep moving—they had to reach Varna before the forces of the Blasphemer caught up with them. When they finally did make camp each night, Rienne walked among her people, talking with them and hearing their tales, watching as the more experienced soldiers offered some basic training to the freshest recruits, as conversations struck up on the march continued and expanded and blossomed into friendships. Before allowing herself the luxury of sleep, she consulted with Kyaphar and Fieran, and sometimes with the officers as well.

Kyaphar spent most of every day on the wing, flying in wide circles around the army to watch for threats from the Blasphemer or the spreading Depravation. He reported that the Blasphemer's horde was close on their heels, fully regrouped after the chaos of the breaking seal and now no more than a day's journey behind them—and Rienne was deeply grateful for that day of distance. Then in the middle of the second week, he reported that Varna was in sight—as was a battalion of Aundairian soldiers, heading along the edge of the lake from the west toward the ruins of the city.

"Thank the Sovereigns," Rienne said. "We won't have to defend it alone."

Kyaphar shook his head. "It sickens me," he said. "They sacked Varna on the pretext of holding the barbarians back, protecting their borders. Then they struck farther and farther into the Reaches, utterly ignoring the barbarians. Only when the Blasphemer threatens to actually cross the Wyr into Aundair do they return to do the job they supposedly came here to do in the first place."

"I only hope they're not too late," Fieran added.

"How far did they get?" Rienne asked. "They marched west from Varna—did they take Cree? Or sack it?"

"I don't think they made it as far as Cree," Kyaphar said. "It's only been two weeks since they left Varna—that's barely enough time to get to Cree, turn around, and come back. Of course, they could have sacked the town quickly, so it's not outside the realm of possibility. Especially if half the city's defenders were facing the Blasphemer at the Mosswood."

Rienne sighed. "How long until we reach Varna?"

"Two or three days."

"Let's make it two." She stood and touched each of the men on the shoulder. "Rest well, friends. I want an early start in the morning."

CHAPTER
40

Cart sprang to his feet at the sight of Harkin, and Ashara paled, making Aunn wonder what had transpired between the two of them and Harkin since they left the Cannith enclave.

"What are you doing here, Harkin?" Ashara asked, turning in her seat.

"I thought we had agreed to help each other stop Jorlanna's madness," Harkin said, putting a hand on her shoulder.

Cart clenched his fists at his side. "I thought I made it clear that we don't want you around anymore."

"You certainly made your opinion clear, warforged." Harkin's voice was ice. "But you don't speak for Ashara."

"He does in this case," Ashara said. "Leave us alone."

"Ashara, listen," Harkin protested, stepping back away from Cart. "As much as I hate to admit it, I need your help. So does your House."

"It's not my House anymore, remember?"

"For my sake then, for the sake of the love we had . . ."

"Is that what you call it?" Ashara's face had gone from white to red, and she stood to face Harkin. "If you ever loved me, which I doubt, you could show a shred of respect for Cart."

Aunn watched Harkin stammer, trying to come to terms with an idea that was obviously foreign to him and counter to everything he felt about Cart. At the same time, he realized that the argument was drawing the attention of the other patrons.

"All of you, stop," Aunn said quietly. "Sit down and stop making a scene."

Ashara turned her back on Harkin and returned to her seat, but Cart and Harkin stayed on their feet. The question of whether Harkin was staying or leaving wasn't resolved, and there was only one more chair at the table.

"Pull up a chair, Harkin," Aunn said.

Cart looked at Aunn as he settled into his own chair, and Harkin borrowed a chair from another table nearby.

"We should probably leave," Cart said. "We drew too much attention."

"I expect the Sentinel Marshal to arrive within a few moments," Aunn said. "But I'm not sure that's a bad thing."

"What?" Ashara said.

"You're the best chance we have to prove Jorlanna's involvement in all this," Aunn said. "You and Harkin."

"Have we met?" Harkin asked, looking at Aunn for the first time.

"Yes, in your forgehold. I told you I was Kelas ir'Darren. My real name is Aunn."

Harkin arched an eyebrow. "Interesting," he said. "So what's your connection to all this intrigue?"

Aunn glanced at Cart and Ashara. Much like them, he realized, his connection to this mess was that he had played an unwitting part in Nara's plans and was trying now to undo the harm he'd wrought. And, he supposed, trying to imagine and live out a life that was less tangled and shady, more honest, more pure. Cart and Ashara might not express it like that, but Cart's comment about the Dark using fear as a gateway to enter the world resonated with Aunn's own thinking.

For Harkin, though, he decided on a simpler answer. "I've been working with the Sentinel Marshal to investigate Jorlanna's plots."

"Harkin, listen," Ashara said, staring at the table and carefully keeping her voice low. "I think you should leave. We might have common purpose, but I don't think we can work together."

"Particularly after you threatened us," Cart said.

"I can appreciate that," Harkin said. "I'll admit that when Cart threw me out of that bakery, I was furious, and I spoke in anger. But once I calmed down, I realized that I'd be a damned fool to throw away our chances of saving House Cannith because of my injured pride. I'm willing to put that unfortunate incident behind us for the sake of our common cause."

Harkin had addressed Ashara, but her eyes went to Cart, waiting for him to respond to Harkin's overture.

"I also let my anger get the better of me," Cart said. "I apologize." He extended a hand to Harkin, who at first seemed not to notice.

Then he half-turned to Cart, clasped his hand as he flashed a forced smile, and turned back to Ashara. Cart bristled, and Aunn began to understand how Harkin had stirred up Cart's anger.

"Well, Ashara?" Harkin said. "Can I still count on your assistance?"

"Not until you find it in yourself to treat Cart like a person. He's not a tool, Harkin. He's the best and bravest man I've ever known. You owe him an apology."

Harkin scoffed, and Cart drew himself up further. "Man?" Harkin said. "A man is born from a womb, not made in a creation forge. A man breathes and eats. A man has a soul, Ashara. And a man can sire children of his own. Your warforged might be a loyal companion, and I can understand that you have some affection for him. But he's not a man you can love and wed."

Aunn gave Cart a great deal of credit. Cart must have been furious, but he showed no hint of it, sitting perfectly still, proud and tall in his chair. But Ashara's fists were clenched on the table before her, white-knuckled, her face was bright red, and tears lined her eyes.

"You had better leave, Harkin," she said, her voice strangled.

"Grow up, Ashara," Harkin said. "I haven't said anything you don't know is true. You'll be happier in the long run if you face reality now."

"Please go."

"Ashara . . ."

"She asked you to leave," Cart said. "Don't make me carry you out again."

Harkin slammed his hands down on the table and stood. "When this is over, I'm going to be in charge of the forgehold as Baron Merrix's lieutenant. I could have asked him to reverse Jorlanna's ban of excoriation, to welcome you back into the family. Instead, I'm going to make sure your life is miserable. You should have listened to me, Ashara."

Aunn watched him stomp to the door and abruptly stop. He backed away as the Sentinel Marshal and Ossa entered, and his shoulders slumped as they led him back to the table. With Mauren at his back, he sat back in his chair, avoiding everyone's gaze.

"Well, here's an interesting assembly," Mauren said, sweeping her gaze around the table.

"We've been discussing matters of interest to you," Aunn said. "I understand you're acquainted with Ashara and Cart, and clearly you know Harkin."

"Yes, we've all met before. Perhaps you'd like to explain why you're having a friendly chat with the mastermind responsible for the device that stripped the dragonmark from your friend Gaven."

Ashara's knuckles were white again, but Cart put a hand on her arm to reassure her.

"Cart and Ashara have been helping me make more sense out of the plot on the queen. Those mercenaries from Droaam—did you know that Jorlanna armed them?"

"Kol Korran's beard, changeling!" Ossa grumbled, pulling another chair over to the table. She sat down and crossed her arms, scowling. "You're not going to convince us to let another criminal go!"

Aunn's brow went cold. "She can help us get Jorlanna and put a stop to all this."

"So you've decided to cooperate now," Mauren said, "is that it?"

Ashara glanced up at the Sentinel Marshal, then at Cart. "I suppose I have."

"You heard that I've made a few arrests already, and you got scared."

"No, that's not—"

"Why didn't you come clean before?"

"I was afraid—"

"What about you, Harkin? Have you also decided to help in a desperate attempt to save your skin?"

Harkin ignored her, staring at the wall.

Aunn recognized what Mauren was doing—firing off questions more quickly than they could be answered, trying to put Ashara and now Harkin off balance. This meeting was not going as he had imagined.

"Mauren, why don't you sit down?" he said.

"I don't want to sit down. I want to take our friends here to the city jail where they can start getting used to spending the rest of their sorry lives in Dreadhold. I've been looking for you for five days, Ashara. Now that I've got you, you and your baron are going to see just how much trouble you're in."

"No," Aunn said. "We need her help."

"What in sea or sky do we need her help for? We know the Dragon Forge stripped the Mark of Storm off your friend Gaven. We know his dragonmark powered the storm that destroyed Varna. Ashara told me herself that she was responsible for the project—that's why Jorlanna excoriated her." She wheeled on Ashara. "If you'd told me five days ago what I needed to know, I could have protected you from prosecution and even from the reprisals of your House. But now? I have no more need of you. I just want to see you locked up to make sure you can't strip the dragonmark off anyone else."

"Mauren, listen," Aunn said. "She's already realized her mistake . . ."

"Mistake? Stripping off a Mark of Siberys was a *mistake*?"

"Yes!" Ashara said, drawing stares. "We never should have drawn on the power we did."

"And she helped me disable the Dragon Forge," Aunn said.

"Then perhaps she'll receive a lighter sentence," Mauren said. "But I'm not letting this one run free."

"Will you sit down and talk this through?" Aunn barked. "Is a moment of civil conversation too much to ask?"

"With the likes of her?" Mauren said.

"Pull up a chair, Mauren," Ossa said. "Let's hear the changeling out."

Finally the Sentinel Marshal complied, settling in a chair and pushing a stray lock of blond hair behind her ear. "Very well, Ashara. Five days ago you told me you had no information to give that would help me bring your baron to justice. What has changed?"

Aunn bit his tongue, unsure what Ashara would or could say to blunt the force of Mauren's anger toward her. He wished they all had left the Ruby Chalice before the Sentinel Marshal had arrived.

Ashara took a slow breath and reached into a large pouch at her belt. Aunn tensed, and he saw Mauren and Ossa stiffen as well. She produced a battered roll of paper and smoothed it open on the table.

"What is this?" Mauren asked, the anger draining from her voice.

Aunn saw at once what it was—and from the man's low whistle, Aunn figured Harkin did as well. The paper was covered with intricate diagrams, and Aunn recognized the column of blue stone that featured prominently in every view. Part physical plan and part instructions for the magical artifice, the papers detailed Ashara's plans for the Dragon Forge.

Ashara pointed to the corner of the paper. "No member of House Cannith can undertake a project of this magnitude without the approval of the baron," she said.

Aunn peered at the page where she was pointing. The signature was illegible, but the arcane mark beneath it clearly identified it as the seal of Baron Jorlanna d'Cannith.

* * * * *

To Cart's tremendous relief, Mauren had proven more reasonable than she had first seemed in the Ruby Chalice. Once she realized the significance of what Ashara had shown her, she arranged for

Cart and Ashara to stay in the Ghallanda hostel near the city's northeastern gate, where they could be assured of privacy and security until Jorlanna was safely in custody and Ashara could appear at her trial.

They spent a week there, waiting for any word from Mauren or Aunn, enjoying the luxury provided by House Ghallanda's Mark of Hospitality. Ashara reveled in it—soaking in a hot bath every evening, then wrapping herself in a warm blanket and sitting in front of a roaring fireplace to enjoy the fabulous meals the halflings provided.

Remembering the yearning in her voice when she had described the comforts of her own home, Cart was pleased to see her finding such enjoyment in those simple pleasures. He was even more pleased to find that he could enjoy them with her, or at least vicariously through her. The aromas of the halfling cooking meant nothing to him, but the pleasure on her face as she smelled and then ate their meals brought him new experiences of delight. He began to feel that perhaps, when her life returned to normal, there might still be room in it for him.

At night, he watched her sleep in the soft bed, but he kept his axe and shield in hand, standing guard—unnecessarily, he thought, given the importance that House Ghallanda placed on the security of its guests. But on the sixth morning of their stay, when three warforged barged into the room, he was glad he was there to block their entry.

"Cannith excoriate," one of the intruders said, "surrender and appear before your baron."

The other two, meanwhile, forced Cart back into the room at swordpoint. He gripped his axe and shield, but they circled around him, forcing him to retreat if he wanted to keep them both in his field of vision.

"Jorlanna has grown desperate indeed," Ashara said, "if she's willing to draw the ire of House Ghallanda as well as the Sentinel Marshals." She stood on the bed, her hair tousled from sleep, clutching a blanket around her out of a sense of modesty that Cart found oddly endearing in the circumstances.

"The baron will not long have anything to fear from the Houses," the warforged said. He edged toward Ashara, keeping clear of Cart and the other two warforged. Cart considered breaking away from the two that engaged him and charging the leader, but he decided to wait. He didn't want to start fighting until it was clearly necessary.

"Except perhaps her Kundarak guards in Dreadhold," Ashara said. She was doing something with her hands—Cart realized suddenly that the blanket might not have anything to do with modesty after all. He started calculating his rush at the leader, though he wasn't sure what Ashara would do and how it might alter the battlefield.

"This is foolish," Cart said. "You three can't take us alone."

To make his point, he lunged at the warforged on his right, swinging his axe where his opponent could easily block the blow. As he expected, the other warforged brought his sword into a basic parry but at an awkward angle, and Cart's blow knocked the sword from his grip. Without looking behind him, Cart heaved his shield back, where it collided with the other soldier's weapon and sent it flying. He planted his foot on the first one's sword and brought his axe around to rest on the shoulder of the other.

It was over in seconds, giving the leader no time to react. He stared at Cart, his face unreadable, but his paralysis a sure sign of fear.

Ashara pulled a short rod from beneath the blanket and touched it to the leader's back. "And now that you know who's in command here," she said, "you will take us to see the baron after all."

* * * * *

"Well, we finally saw Thuel Racannoch," Mauren said, sliding down the bench of the private booth to make room for Ossa.

"And?" Aunn asked.

"Like much of the last week, it was frustrating and not at all productive."

"What did he say?"

"He said nothing at all," Ossa said, scowling, "in a great many words. Full of bluster and bile."

Mauren shrugged. "He said that our investigation overstepped the authority of the Sentinel Marshals, that a plot against the queen—if one existed—would be an internal Aundairian matter and none of our damned business."

"That . . . doesn't sound like Thuel," Aunn said. "Bluster and bile? I've seen Thuel angry, but those aren't words I'd use to describe it."

"I'd say they're accurate enough," Mauren said. "He insulted me enough that I might have arrested him, but I didn't want to create any more trouble than we're already in. Oh, and then there was the leering."

"Leering?"

Mauren rolled her eyes.

Ossa gave a harsh laugh. "He couldn't take his eyes off her. I thought at one point he might drool on her."

"Now I'm sure that wasn't Thuel," Aunn said. Thuel was refined and polite, a gentleman in every way—even when he was angry. "It was probably Vec."

Mauren raised her eyebrows. "You think Thuel is dead?"

"Almost certainly. Vec would have to be a fool to impersonate the Spy Master of the Royal Eyes in his own office if the Spy Master were still alive to get wind of it. Well, in case there was any doubt before, I guess that makes it quite clear that I can't go back to the Tower of Eyes."

"And it means we can't rely on any help from them, either," Mauren said.

"Neither can the queen," Ossa added. "If the assassin's posing as the head of the Royal Eyes, he doesn't even need the distraction of a battle to get into the palace."

"I wouldn't bet on that," Aunn said. "There are enough magical wards protecting the palace that he'd probably be revealed before he got close enough to hurt her."

"So the plan probably remains in place," Mauren said. "The mercenaries attack, and that's when Vec strikes."

"And so the question remains—when?"

Mauren leaned over the table. "In your conversations with Nara, she said nothing?"

The details of his conversations with Nara were a blur in his mind, all but erased by the stress of the encounters, pretending to be Kelas and acting as though he had some idea what Nara was talking about. "She did say something," he said, grasping for the memory. "About how I should lock Gaven away, because he needed to be in place when the time was right."

"That's all she said? 'When the time is right?' "

"For the reunion, she said."

"What reunion?" Ossa said. "Is she planning a gathering of those who are loyal to her?"

"No, wait," Aunn said. "Gaven said something about the reunion—there was something in the Prophecy." He closed his eyes and let the memory rise to the surface. " 'In the darkest night of the Dragon Below, storm and dragon are reunited.' And he said the Time of the Dragon Below was beginning now, or a couple of weeks ago."

"So what's the darkest night?" Mauren asked.

"It doesn't matter," Aunn said. As much as he hated trying to wrap his mind around the intricacies of the Prophecy, it seemed to be drawing him along its twisted pathways. "The reunion had something to do with Gaven arriving in Varna. Remember? Gaven said as much before he left."

Mauren scowled. "So?"

"Gaven will probably arrive in Varna in the next day or two—he's been traveling almost two weeks. Whatever the darkest night of the Dragon Below might be, that's when it's going to happen. And I'm certain that Nara is planning some kind of grand conjunction of historical events, sending the assassin to strike at Aurala at the same moment the Storm Dragon confronts the Blasphemer. That's the moment we're looking for."

Ossa clapped her hands together. "I'll contact House Sivis and see if there's any news of a battle near Varna. Last I heard, Aundair's troops were pulling back toward the remains of the city."

Aunn nodded. Besides scribing arcane marks and official documents, House Sivis also operated a network of magical communication, so they would be the first to know of an impending battle anywhere in Khorvaire. He got to his feet.

"The time is close, I'm sure of it," he said.

CHAPTER
41

Cart and Ashara walked behind the three warforged, leaving no question who was in command of the little procession. All three of the Cannith warforged were unarmed, their weapons on the floor back in the Ghallanda hostel. Cart's axe was at his belt to avoid drawing too much of the wrong kind of attention as they walked through the city, but his hand was never far from its haft, in case one of the warforged tried anything. But they were back to their docile, obedient manner, in the presence of a Cannith heir who had the power—if not the legitimate authority—to command them, and they walked to the Cannith forgehold without ever looking back at him or Ashara.

Ashara seemed confident, but beyond a hastily whispered assurance that it would be all right, she hadn't had a chance to explain why they were marching willingly into the stronghold of their worst enemy. They had been in the forgehold once already, and it had been all Aunn could do to get them out without turning Ashara over into the baron's custody. Cart was not eager to return, but he trusted that Ashara knew what she was doing.

They reached the forgehold, spewing its black smoke into the sky. The leader of the warforged pounded a metal fist on the door, and Cart heard the whir of locks and sliding bolts before the door creaked open. Fear surged in his chest, but Ashara quelled it with a smile. The warforged leader looked back at them for the first time, Ashara nodded, and they all strode into the forgehold together.

A murmur traveled through the forgehold as they entered, and even the din of machinery and working hammers seemed to fade as magewrights and warforged ceased their work to stare down at the excoriate who so boldly entered the enclave of her angry baron. Cart stared around at the angry faces of the Cannith heirs throughout the large room—and the blank expressions of the warforged.

"*What god watches over my people, Gaven?*" Cart asked as he stared down into the gaping maw of the stone dragon, the bridge to Siberys. "*Which Sovereign has our interests at heart?*"

"*Are there gods for each race and people?*" Gaven said. "*Doesn't the whole Host keep watch over us all?*"

"*Perhaps. But the gods made all the other races. We were made by artificers and magewrights. Does Onatar then care for us, the god of the forge? Or perhaps the warlord Dol Dorn, since we were made for war? Or do they see us as many mortals do—simply as tools for war? There is no god of swords or siege engines. Perhaps there is no god for us.*"

"*You want to be one, then?*" Gaven asked. "*What would you do as god of the warforged? Would you urge them into war?*"

No, Cart thought as he looked around at the blank faces of the Cannith warforged, I would urge them to love.

"Ashara!" Jorlanna emerged from a workshop somewhere above and leaned over the rail of a balcony that encircled the great room.

Cart found the sight amusing. The only other time he'd seen Jorlanna, she had sat at Kelas's table like a dignitary, clothed in finery, her hair carefully sculpted to rise from her head in an elegant design. Now she wore comfortable, practical clothes beneath a thick leather apron and boots. She pulled heavy gloves from her hand as she looked down, and pushed wayward strands of hair from her soot-blackened face. The Mark of Making on her cheek said it all—for all her aspirations to nobility, even royalty, she was born to the forge, destined to *make*.

"Good morning, Jorlanna," Ashara said, pointedly ignoring the proper way to address the head of a dragonmarked House. "Cart and I were delighted to receive your invitation. It's nice to be here again. I do hope you're serving breakfast."

"Oh, Ashara." The baron seemed genuinely distraught, making Cart wonder what the real purpose of this audience was. "Let me come down and see you."

Jorlanna disappeared from the balcony. Ashara glanced at Cart, looking as perplexed as Cart felt. He shrugged, then the baron reappeared at an archway to their left.

"What a terrible mess this has become," Jorlanna said as she strode toward them. "I would so much rather be working with you than against you in all this."

"Perhaps you should have considered that before declaring her excoriate," Cart said.

Jorlanna shot Cart an irritated glance, then looked back at Ashara. "So this is the warforged I hear so much about. It should know its place, Ashara."

Cart drew himself up and stepped closer to the baron, interposing himself between her and Ashara. "I do know my place, Baron. According to the Treaty of Thronehold I am a free citizen of Aundair, an honored veteran of the Last War, and worthy of the same rights and privileges afforded to every other sentient and civilized race."

"Perhaps it escaped your notice, warforged, but the Treaty of Thronehold is no longer upheld in Aundair, and the provisions you mention will be among the first things to change in the new Aundair."

"The new Aundair is a pitiful delusion, Baron."

"Ashara." Jorlanna stepped around Cart and took Ashara's hands, a strangely intimate gesture. "That Sentinel Marshal has arrested Harkin."

Cart watched Ashara's reaction carefully, and he was pleased to see not a hint of concern for her former lover. "What of it?" she said. "I expect you'll be next."

"Me? Ashara, I'm concerned for you."

"You're concerned." Ashara's disbelief dripped from her voice.

"Yes." Jorlanna's voice revealed just a hint of steel. "Harkin knows just enough about the Dragon Forge to get you in serious trouble."

"Is that a threat?" Cart said, putting a heavy hand on the baron's shoulder.

Jorlanna turned and fixed him with an icy glare. "Unhand me."

"Funny, that's just what Harkin said to me. And here's what I told him." Cart raised his voice, enough to ensure that every warforged in the room could hear him. "I have this House to thank for my existence, it's true. I was birthed in the womb of your forges. Are you then my mother? If so, you sold your offspring into servitude, to Aundair's army, where I learned to be a soldier, to do my duty. I owe you nothing—you have already been paid for the work you did to bring me into the world. The debts I owe are debts of true gratitude—to the people who have gradually driven the idea through my very hard head that I am a person worthy of respect, of friendship, and even of love."

Ashara took his hand, and Cart heard gasps of outrage from some of the onlookers.

"I am not an automaton," he continued, ignoring Jorlanna's furious glare. "I was made for war, just as you were made for making. But that is not all I am. Like you, I am capable of courage, of hope and dreaming, of loyalty, of fear and hatred, and of love. And until you realize that you are lording it over a forge full of people like me, you rule a very precarious domain."

He let go of Jorlanna's shoulder, and the baron whirled around in a fury, fixing every magewright and warforged in the room with her glare. "Listen and heed me," she said. "I will not tolerate insubordination, not from marked heirs of House Cannith, not from anyone associated with the House, and not from the warforged we made."

Ashara squeezed Cart's hand. "Let's go," she said, smiling up at him.

"Goodbye, Baron," Cart said with a hint of a bow.

"Ashara," Jorlanna said, anger seething in her voice, "I have not finished with you yet."

Ashara half-turned as they walked toward the door. "You are finished, Jorlanna. All your building has come to ruin."

Nearing the door, Cart kept an eye on the three warforged who'd been sent to bring them here. They were still unarmed, but for a moment he thought they might try to block their exit.

Instead, they parted—the leader to one side, the other two to the other. Beyond them, Cart saw Mauren and Ossa striding toward the forgehold, coming at last to make their arrest. Cart nodded his thanks to the warforged, and as he and Ashara passed between them, the leader put a hand on Cart's shoulder.

It was enough.

* * * * *

Four soldiers formed a ragged line blocking access to the bridge across the Wyr that linked Varna to the trade roads of Aundair. Gaven considered storming past them, not wanting to slow his horse to deal with them, but they gripped their halberds as he galloped toward them, and he decided to stop.

"The bridge is closed," one of the soldiers shouted. Her insignia, a set of linked gold rings at her shoulder, marked her as a sergeant.

Another soldier snickered. "So's the city."

The sergeant shot him a rebuking glance.

Gaven walked his horse forward and stopped in front of the sergeant. "Who's in command here?"

"I am in command of this bridge, and I'm telling you to find another route. The west bank will be a battlefield in an hour."

Gaven scratched at his shoulder, growing impatient, and glanced at the sun. "Who's in command of the forces here?"

"Who's asking?"

Gaven pulled the Sentinel Marshal's letter from the pouch at his belt and handed it to the sergeant. Her eyes scanned the page, widening as she read, and she handed it back to Gaven.

"My apologies, master. You'll find Lord Major Parak ir'Velen in a pavilion just inside the remnants of the city wall." She gestured vaguely behind her, across the bridge. "Just follow the road, you can't miss it."

She moved aside for Gaven to pass, bowing as he walked his horse through the gap she left. "Thank you, sergeant."

His horse's hooves clattered on the cobblestones of the bridge and scattered broken pieces of rubble left behind by the fury of his storm. The city came into clearer view as he neared the end of the bridge, its once-proud walls now a shattered ruin. North of the ruins, he saw line upon line of soldiers arrayed on the riverbank, Aundair's blue banners whipping in the wind above them.

A strange pall of shadow fell over him, and he glanced up at the sun again.

It has begun, he thought.

In the Time of the Dragon Below, the moon of the Endless Night turns day into night, and so begins the darkest night.

He wasn't sure where he learned those words, whether he had read them in his explorations of Khyber or the other, Shakravar, had learned them and shared that knowledge with him through the nightshard. Certainly he had forgotten them for a long time, but now they were as clear in his mind as if someone had just spoken them.

A single figure stood at the other end of the bridge, waiting for him. Draped in what looked like ceremonial robes, with ornate crests at the shoulders, the figure wore a featureless white mask.

In the darkest night of the Dragon Below, storm and dragon are reunited, and they break together upon the legions of the Blasphemer.

His horse's hooves impelled him forward, toward the shrouded figure. The skin of Gaven's chest and neck burned, and the darkening sun hid behind churning clouds that formed from nowhere. Gaven reined in his horse, bringing it it to a stop some ten paces from the end of the bridge, and dismounted.

"The darkest night of the Dragon Below is upon us," the figure said. The voice, a rich alto, was familiar, but she was too far away for him to place it. He started walking toward her, sliding his sword from its sheath on his back.

"Storm and dragon are reunited at last!" the masked woman cried.

"Who are you?" Gaven called.

"You don't know me?" She withdrew her hands from her sleeves, and Gaven saw a gleaming red stone in one hand—the dragonshard that held his mark. "I certainly know you, Storm Dragon."

He recognized the voice, finally—the same voice he'd heard from the crystal globe in Kelas's study.

"Nara," he said. "You have my dragonmark."

She chuckled. "Yes, I am Nara ir'Galanatyr." She removed the mask, revealing a severe face with dark eyes. She tossed the mask aside, then opened her robe and shrugged it off. Standing naked before him, she changed.

Blue scales covered her skin as her body grew to enormous proportions. Her hands fell to the ground as they grew into claws, and wings spread from her back. Her face lengthened into a snout with a jagged horn at the end, above a mouth filled with teeth like swords.

"And I am also Shakravar," the dragon said.

* * * * *

Aunn leaned against the trunk of a bare maple tree and looked up at the Tower of Eyes across the street. Ossa's first report from House Sivis had confirmed his gut feeling—a battle near the ruins of Varna was imminent, and this morning word had come that the remnants of the Reacher army had joined up with the Aundairian forces outside the city and were awaiting the barbarians' attack. He'd taken up his position outside the tower shortly after dawn.

The alabaster tower, with its decoration of blankly staring eyes subtly blending in among leaves and branches, had been his home for his entire life. Kelas had raised him there, taught him the life of a spy, instilled in him a loyalty to Aundair and the queen that still guided his actions when everything else was gone. Until just a few years ago, the tower had been Nara's domain, and from time to time she had taken a passing interest in his tutelage. If Kelas had been his surrogate father, Nara was something like a distant grandmother, stern and unloving.

Aunn frowned, pulled his cloak closer for warmth, and for the hundredth time checked his gear—a pouch of wands on one side of his belt, mace on the other, and a light crossbow with a quiver of bolts slung on his back. He had killed his father, as it were, and was trying to unravel Nara's plot. He felt a bit like a disobedient, ungrateful child, but then he remembered Tira Miron, remembered why he had done what he did. *Kalok Shash burns brighter.*

A strange shadow fell over the street, as if echoing the darkness of Aunn's thoughts. He glanced up, and saw a dark shadow biting into the edge of the sun, one of the larger moons moving to block the sun's light. As he looked, he heard cries of alarm from behind him, where soldiers of the palace guard poured out of the garrison building on the other side of the street, presumably rushing to meet the threat of soldiers moving toward the palace. He turned his gaze back to the Tower of Eyes, just in time to see a man stride out the front doors, dressed in black and gray and wearing a perfect killer's face.

The killer paused in the doorway, looking up the street after the rushing palace guard. Aunn stepped behind the trunk of the old maple, hoping to avoid his gaze. The killer's eyes swept across him as he turned to look toward the palace, and then came back to linger on the line of bare trees that divided the wide street. Aunn couldn't tell if he'd been seen or not, but the killer stepped onto the street and walked briskly in the direction of the palace.

Aunn waited a moment and stepped out after him. Between the Tower of Eyes and the great Crown's Hall at the heart of the palace grounds was only a wide courtyard cobbled in faded blue stone. The courtyard was not thickly crowded, but the eclipse and the shouts of soldiers added significant elements of chaos to the crowd as people stopped dead and pointed to the sky or looked frantically about them. Aunn couldn't find the killer at first, and he quickened his pace as he scanned the crowd for the man he'd seen.

Then he saw a woman with long, fair hair, trailing an overlong black cloak. Now certain that he was following Vec, Aunn slowed his pace and tried to melt back into the crowd, keeping his eyes fixed on the changeling's blond hair.

Vec led him on a path circling Crown's Hall, staying close to the outer edge of the courtyard. She slowed her pace and lingered at a shop window just past the garrison building, pretending to check the wares while she actually watched the reflections of people passing. Aunn continued past her, rounding the corner of the courtyard, turning his face away from her view. He started to regret buying the expensive purple cloak that made him stand out in the crowd.

He made his way to the royal museum and ducked inside. Smiling at the obsequious attendants, he pulled the cloak from his shoulders and handed it to one of them, along with a gold galifar. The attendant bowed and smiled, then pressed a ticket into his hand that would allow him to reclaim the cloak when his visit to the museum was concluded. Aunn changed then, ignoring the gasps of the attendants, taking the first face and name that sprang to his mind.

Who are you?

As he tightened his belt and adjusted his clothes, he caught a glimpse of himself in glass—long brown hair, soft and curved. I am Caura Fannam, he thought. *You were very kind.*

As the attendants protested, he strode back out of the museum, scanning the people on the street, looking for Vec. His thoughts were a jumble, thinking of Jenns Solven and the green dragon in the forest.

Vec had changed as well—Aunn saw a burly man, dressed in the same gray and black, looking closely at his face as he walked past. When their eyes met, Vec flashed him a grin like a hungry wolf, then hurried ahead of him.

Crown's Hall loomed across the courtyard. Aunn loosed his belt and changed again, ignoring the gawks and gasps of the people who witnessed the transformation.

Who are you?

He felt solid and strong in his dwarf body. I am Auftane Khunnam, he thought, and Dania ir'Vran called me friend. He touched the silver torc he wore, which was not tight despite the thickness of his dwarf neck, and felt its fire course through him.

The burly Vec glanced over his shoulder and scanned the crowd, and he seemed not to see Aunn. Then Aunn lost sight of him in a knot of people gawking at the darkened sky.

Someone screamed, and many of the people around Aunn pointed down the wide avenue leading south from Crown's Hall. Aunn glanced down that street and saw a few squads of minotaur warriors marching toward him. He looked back at the hall, where lines of the palace guard were forming up to meet the attackers. The crowd was in full panic, racing in every direction to get out from between the two forces of soldiers before they clashed.

A slender elf in gray darted around the palace guard toward Crown's Hall, and Aunn ran toward him, changing his face again as he ran.

Who are you?

He was tall and strong, his shirt tight across his chest, with a thick neck and crooked nose. I am Kauth Dannar, he thought, a hard man for hard work. His long strides helped him gain on Vec.

Vor's face, lying dead on the Labyrinth's floor, haunted him. Why didn't you come back? Aunn asked the dead paladin. Was it my lack of faith? Or was it because you had found peace and were content to stay dead?

Crown's Hall was an enormous structure the size of an arena, consisting of the central audience chamber surrounded by four wings jutting out in the cardinal directions, symbolizing Aurala's willingness to hear petitions from every quarter of her nation. Four towers rose up at the corners of the structure, containing the rich historical archives of the Royal Collection in one tower, the Courts of Justice and its prison in another, and the residences of the queen and her brothers with their families in the remaining two towers.

Vec darted into a short and narrow alley between one of the wings and towers. At the end of the alley, he threw open a door and disappeared inside. Aunn hesitated—the door was one way into the heart of the palace, but it would ordinarily be heavily guarded with both soldiers and magical wards, easily defensible. Was Vec counting on the distraction of the soldiers in the courtyard, or were there agents on the inside—unwitting Royal Eyes, or soldiers loyal to Janna Tolden—who were responsible for removing both guards and wards?

Aunn reached the door and leaped over the body of a palace guard slumped on the floor. Vec was fast.

I have to catch him before he gets to the queen, Aunn thought.

Who are you? Tira Miron asked him.

Aunn let Kauth's face fade and didn't replace it, reverting to the blank gray and white of his true face. "I am Aunn," he said aloud, "and I'm yours."

CHAPTER
42

Aunn heard footsteps racing up a staircase through an archway ahead of him, and ran after them.

"Stop!" someone cried.

Aunn reached the stairs and saw Vec, now back in his unremarkable killer's face, raced up toward a soldier of the palace guard who pointed a spear down the stairs at the approaching assassin. Vec dodged around the soldier's thrust and knocked the spear out of his hand, but Aunn noted with satisfaction that the soldier already had a sword in his free hand, and he swung a strong, accurate blow at Vec. The palace guard was a cut above the rank-and-file soldiery of Fairhaven.

Vec parried the guard's blow, slowing enough for Aunn to gain a few steps on him. If the guard could just hold him another moment—

Vec's blade sliced across the soldier's neck, and his other hand pulled the man forward so he tumbled down the stairs toward Aunn. Aunn couldn't get out of the way fast enough, and the soldier's foot caught him in the face, pulling him back down to the foot of the stairs, with a few hard collisions on the way.

Aunn pulled himself back to his feet and looked up the stairs. Vec was out of sight. Ordinarily, three or four guards would have blocked the stairway, with the two in the back thrusting spears around their comrades in front. Someone— perhaps a traitor in the palace guard, perhaps just someone who viewed the attacking mercenaries in the courtyard as a greater threat than someone sneaking through less obvious passages—had diverted the bulk of the palace guard to deal with the minotaurs.

Aunn raced up the stairs and found himself in a guard post, now deserted. The room stretched ahead a few paces and then bent around the wall of the adjacent tower. He crept to a point where he could see around the corner, expecting Vec to leap out at him as he drew near. He saw another soldier bleeding out her life at the top of another staircase, but no sign of the assassin. A door of heavy darkwood engraved with arcane sigils stood closed beside each stairway. It didn't seem that either seal had been broken.

Where did he go? Aunn wondered.

Following the trail of blood, Aunn went to stand beside the fallen soldier. He bent to check the woman's pulse while he listened for footsteps. The woman was quite dead, and all he heard was the sounds of fighting from the courtyard. Vec might have gone down the other stairs and back out into the fray, but Aunn couldn't imagine that he would get this far into Crown Hall and then retreat.

Frowning, he stood at the door near the dead guard. He closed his eyes and let his fingertips graze across the surface of the door, not quite touching the wood but feeling the lines of the magic that coursed within it. The ward was strong, but Aunn felt a weakness in it as well, the echo of Vec's passage through the door.

"Damn," Aunn muttered, opening his eyes and letting them wander over the sigils on the door. The ward was designed to prevent the door from opening. Vec hadn't opened it—he'd gone right through it.

Aunn weighed his options. With enough time, he could either bypass the door's wards or he could weave an infusion into his armor that would let him pass through the door as Vec had done. But time was exactly what he didn't have. If Vec was on the other side of the door, he could be a blade's length away from the queen already.

He took a closer look at the sigils on the door, a slightly crazy idea taking form in his mind. His hunch proved correct—the ward wasn't so much designed to prevent the door from opening, but to kill anyone who opened it without disabling the ward, while raising an alarm throughout the palace. One of those results was actually desirable under the circumstances, and the other . . .

"I think I can handle it," he said aloud. "Please, let me survive this."

He traced a quick ward of his own across the front of his belt, giving himself some protection from fire. It wasn't enough to shield him completely, but it might keep him alive. With that ward in place, he threw himself against the door.

An inferno erupted around him as the door gave way, and every nerve in his body screamed its agony as he fell to the floor. His ears rang with the noise of it, which at least gave him comfort that an alarm would be raised.

He heaved himself up from the floor and looked around. He was on a narrow balcony, with the magnificent ceiling of Crown's Hall arching high above him. Every inch of the ceiling was covered with gold leaf that seemed to glow with an inner fire of its own, bathing the hall in warm light. The balcony extended all around one wing of the great hall, offering a vantage point where the palace guard could keep their watchful eyes on the queen's visitors below.

Sliding a healing wand from his pouch, he got his feet beneath him and pulled himself up on the balcony railing, searching the hall below for Vec. Chaos reigned in the hall, with every face upturned to the source of the explosive sound, and many fingers raised to point at him. Shouts of alarm were raised as soldiers ran for stairways and clustered beneath him in case he jumped off the balcony. Aunn swore to himself—with his noisy entrance, he had probably created the distraction that would allow Vec to get close to the queen.

Queen Aurala stood in front of the gilded throne where she granted audiences. Aunn cursed her as he felt the healing power of his wand course through him—she should have retreated to safety when the first alarms were raised. Her pride had almost certainly prevented it.

He spotted Vec, a dark figure lurking at the edge of the hall, perhaps ten yards from the queen. Aunn shouted and pointed down at Vec. "He's the assassin! Guard the queen!" A few soldiers paused and stared around the hall, trying to follow Aunn's pointing finger, while Vec darted toward the queen.

More soldiers started to pour onto the balcony from stairways to either side. Aunn had no choice but to jump down and hope he could reach Vec before Vec reached the queen.

"I think I can handle the fall," he muttered, smiling to himself. "Please, let me survive this!"

He ran along the balcony to get as close as he could to the throne before going over the edge. Soldiers ran toward him—one tossed a javelin that flew right by his ear. No time to lose—he looked over the railing, and saw Vec withdraw a bloody dagger from the queen's ribs as she sank to the ground.

* * * * *

"Storm and dragon are reunited," Gaven breathed, turning the Draconic words over in his mind as he stared up into one of the dragon's enormous yellow eyes. His chest was tight and his mind reeled at the sight of the magnificent beast. Shakravar had left his memories in a nightshard at least four hundred years ago, and Gaven had always had the sense that the dragon was already centuries old at that time. How incredibly ancient was the creature revealed before him?

"Listen to me, Storm Dragon," Shakravar said. "We stand at the culmination of six centuries of planning. You have a part to play. So far, you've done everything I desired, unwitting though you were. You need only continue on the course you've already chosen for a few more hours, and this will all be over."

"And if I refuse?"

"Why would you do that? Just to spite me? You can't refuse. The Prophecy is unfolding exactly as I planned."

Gaven shrugged. Senya's tattooed face smiled in his memory. *Who you are now is who you have been and who you are yet to be.*

"Give me the dragonshard," he said.

Shakravar chuckled—a low rumbling that Gaven felt in his gut and through his feet. The dragon reached out, and

Gaven saw the bloodstone pinched between the scythe blades of Shakravar's claws. He took it and felt its power coursing through him.

"So what happens next?" he asked.

"Look at the sun, Storm Dragon. 'The moon of the Endless Night turns day into night.' We face the Blasphemer's forces together!"

"Where are they?" Gaven asked.

"They approach from the northwest."

"Then we'd better get moving. This darkness can't last long."

The dragon lowered his head almost to the ground. "Climb on my back, Storm Dragon. We will fly as one."

"And break as one," Gaven said, stepping up to the dragon's shoulder. He reached a tentative hand up, found a hold, and pulled himself onto Shakravar's back.

"As a storm breaks, Storm Dragon—a storm such as this world has never seen."

Gaven found an awkward seat at the dragon's shoulders, behind the spiny crest that ran down his neck and in front of the larger spines running down its back. As he was still settling, Shakravar spread his wings and leaped up, beating his wings fiercely to catch the air and lift them skyward.

Gaven scratched fiercely at his neck and chest, and started in surprise as he felt a raised pattern emerging on his skin.

Storm and dragon are reunited indeed, he thought.

Clouds formed above and around them as they flew, thunder echoing through every part of Gaven's body and shaking the dragon's wings. Shakravar flew over the Aundairian legions, sending waves of fear rippling through the soldiers' orderly lines but not breaking them. They soared across acres of swamped and trampled farmland and swept down upon the massed hordes of the Blasphemer.

Three smaller dragons rose into the air as they approached, circling warily around the ancient Shakravar, who roared a challenge to them. As one, they swooped in to attack from all sides, but Shakravar snapped his wings and thunder boomed around them. Gaven spread his arms and drew lightning out of the surrounding clouds, spearing all three dragons as they reeled in the thunder of Shakravar's wings. Lightning flowed through him and the dragon beneath him, binding them together in the heart of the storm.

I am the storm, Gaven thought. The lightning sang as it coursed through his veins, thrilling every nerve. He stood on the dragon's back, rooted to Shakravar's scales by the lightning still coursing through them. We are the storm!

Shakravar swooped lower as the three small dragons plummeted to the ground. A great wind howled past Gaven and swept over the barbarians massed below, and bolts of lightning crashed to earth from his fingers and Shakravar's gaping maw. Chaos and devastation rained down on the Blasphemer's forces, and the barbarians scattered.

Shakravar rose higher and wheeled around for another pass over the horde, and Gaven saw the Aundairians charging in their wake, rushing in to take advantage of the destruction they had wrought. Shakravar swept back over the barbarians, flying low to batter them with the thunder of his wings as Gaven streamed lightning down on them from the stormclouds.

At the front of the Aundairian charge, a tattered green banner rode amid a ragtag group of what looked like Eldeen militia—like a herd of cattle driven to slaughter ahead of the regular troops. A figure draped in red near the banner caught Gaven's eye and made his heart leap in his chest. It was Rienne.

* * * * *

"For the Reaches!" Cressa screamed.

"For the Wood!" came the cry in answer, three hundred voices managing a ragged unison. That was Rienne's army—making up in fervent enthusiasm what they lacked in training and discipline. Rienne's heart swelled.

The blue dragon wheeled in the air and began another pass over the Blasphemer's forces, flying low and battering the barbarians with thunder and lightning. She didn't dare to hope—

But then she saw him, standing tall on the dragon's back, streaming bolts of lightning linking him to the sky and to the ground. Gaven was here after all, wreathed in storm like a vengeful god of thunder, smiting the Blasphemer with his wrath. She watched him fly overhead, tears filling her eyes.

The momentum of the charge carried her forward, and Maelstrom sprang to life as she reached the first ranks of the barbarian horde. The Blasphemer's forces were in disarray, still reeling from the assault of Gaven and his dragon. Maelstrom cut a swath through them, and the Reachers behind her fought with surprising ferocity, inspired by her example.

Cressa still held the tattered banner in one hand, and she clutched a light sword in the other. She seemed to fight as much with her voice as with her weapon. She shouted encouragement to Rienne and the rest of the forces in earshot—her high, clear voice carried far over the din of battle—and occasionally she struck a telling blow with her little blade. But everyone around her, even Rienne, seemed to fight harder because of her.

Rienne let Maelstrom do its work, and the barbarians fell away before her. She scanned the battlefield for the Blasphemer, conserving her strength for that final confrontation. She saw Gaven's dragon alight on the ground, the storm still swirling around it, and took comfort in knowing that she would not be alone.

* * * * *

Aunn hurdled the balcony railing and tried to brace himself for the impact of hitting the ground. He landed clear of the guards below and let his forward momentum carry him into a roll. After turning several times on the hard stone floor, he got up running to where Vec still stood over the queen's body, fencing with two of the queen's failed protectors.

Blood pooled on the floor beneath the queen, spreading quickly across the smooth marble as her heart pumped its last beats. Aunn breathed a desperate prayer as he ran, imploring the Silver Flame to close her wound and preserve her life.

Vec grinned at him as he drew closer—which meant that the assassin didn't see the faint silver glow hovering over the queen, or the slight stirring of her head and hand that told Aunn she would survive the attack.

Still grinning, Vec dropped his unremarkable killer's face and took on the blank gray and white of his natural form—which was practically indistinguishable from Aunn's face, at least to the human eyes of the palace guards. He laughed, a high-pitched cackle, as his dagger slashed across the throat of one of the guards. Before the dead man could fall to the ground, Vec yanked his body into the path of the other soldier, who stumbled back. Vec's dagger flashed, blood spattered on the floor, and both guards fell lifeless to the ground.

The nearest guards dead, Vec just waited for Aunn to draw closer—close enough that the pursuing guards would have trouble distinguishing them. Of course, Aunn doubted that the guards would even care which changeling they killed.

Rather than get close enough to use his mace to wipe Vec's grin from his face, Aunn pulled the crossbow from his back, cocked a bolt, and traced a few quick sigils on the shaft with his finger. The steps of the guards pursuing him grew louder—they were almost upon him, despite the weight of their armor. He loosed the bolt with a whispered prayer that it would strike true.

Vec was ready for it, and nearly dodged out of the way. The bolt just grazed his shoulder, though, and it erupted with writhing tentacles of gleaming silver light that coiled around Vec and rooted him to the ground. Aunn sprang back into a run, and in a few seconds he was beside Vec, standing over the body of Queen Aurala.

"Aunn, my friend," Vec said, his mocking grin replaced with an exaggerated simper, "free me, and we can still escape these buffoons."

"Friend?" Aunn said. "I doubt you know the meaning of the word." He bent down to check on the queen, opened a knot of magic to send healing power into her wounds—and then remembered that he didn't have a wand in hand. He looked down at his hands, perplexed.

The pouch where he kept his wands was empty—they must have spilled out in his fall. He'd had one in his hand on the balcony, but that was gone as well. So how had he healed the queen?

"Brother!" Vec cried, his eyes suddenly wide with fear. "Don't do this!"

"I am not your brother." Yes, there was magic in his hands, magic unlike the knots of power in his wands. Perhaps it came from the torc around his neck, or maybe it came from the Silver Flame or Tira Miron, from Vor or Dania as their spirits added their brightness to the Flame. *Kalok Shash burns brighter.*

"But you are! Kelas told me we were born of the same mother. And he always demanded to know why I couldn't be as good a spy as you, my brother."

Aunn looked at Vec with loathing. Was he lying? Had Kelas lied to him? Or was it true, that the same blood flowed in Aunn's veins as in Vec's?

The queen's eyes fluttered open just as the palace guard finally reached him. Two soldiers grabbed Vec's arms while a third held a sword to his throat, and two more seized Aunn and dragged him away from the queen.

"Stop!" Aurala commanded, and the soldiers froze. "Help me to my feet."

Aunn watched as two soldiers took the queen's arms—far more gently than those still holding him—and lifted her up from the ground. She had a reputation for beauty, and Aunn could see why. Her skin was as smooth and white as alabaster, and her hair was like gold spun into gossamer thread. She wore a velvet gown of rich green, and jewelry of thin gold wire wrapped in exquisite patterns around emeralds. Once she was back on her feet, she was a commanding presence—her authority came from more than the crown on her high brow. Aunn could think of a dozen reasons to hate her, but he was glad he saved her, and he fell to his knees before her, surprising the soldiers who held his arms.

"Two changelings came uninvited this day into my audience hall," Aurala said. "One to kill, and one to save. All beneath a darkened sun, even as the barbarian forces reach my western border. What am I to make of these portentous events?"

"Your highness, you are not yet safe," Aunn said. "Mercenaries loyal to the conspirators are battling your palace guards in the courtyard outside. You should find a more secure refuge."

"Who are you?" the queen asked him.

He dared to look up and meet her questioning gaze. "I am Aunn."

CHAPTER
43

Gaven slid off the dragon's back, gripping his sword in one hand and the dragonshard in the other as thunder crashed and lightning struck the ground at his feet. With a syllable of power, his sword erupted with crackling lightning that drew a bolt down from the sky to course through him. Each step he took brought a rumble of thunder, and when he swung his sword at the nearest barbarian, steel and lightning and thunder combined to smite the man, hurling him back and killing him before he hit the ground.

"Rienne!" he shouted, but thunder drowned out his voice.

With a growl that shook the sky, he swung his sword in an arc that cut through three men and sent their bodies flying away from him. He whirled the sword over his head, and a funnel of wind swirled around him, expanding until it caught the nearest barbarians and tossed them off their feet. Lightning shot through the walls of swirling wind, coursing through the barbarians caught in the maelstrom.

"The maelstrom swirls around me," Gaven said in a voice of thunder. He spun in a circle, holding his sword at arm's length, and killed five more barbarians. "I am the storm and the eye of the storm." Forking branches of lightning shot out from the dragonshard to engulf another half-dozen. "A storm such as the world has never seen," he added, echoing Shakra-var's words.

A blast of fire erupted around Gaven, pouring down from the mouth of a red dragon hovering above him. Gaven's whirl-wind caught the flames and drew them away from him, but the infernal heat seared his skin and burned his eyes. He blindly pointed the dragonshard at where he'd seen the dragon and sent more lightning hurtling in that direction. When his vision cleared, he saw the dragon on the ground, striding toward him through a mass of barbarians that parted like water before it. It was almost as large as Shakravar, and the scales on its belly were like polished rubies.

"I know you," the dragon rumbled in Draconic. "Storm Dragon. You destroyed the Dragon Forge."

Gaven remembered the three dragons flying up from the wreckage of the Dragon Forge. The first and smallest breathed its fire at him, but his lightning impaled it and his wind would not let it fly, and it crashed into the wreckage of the forge and lay still. The other two escaped, and the third was the largest, its belly gleaming brilliant red in the light of the storm as it flew off to the west.

He answered the dragon with a blast of lightning that danced over its scales and teeth but didn't slow its advance.

"Now the Blasphemer has come," the dragon continued, "to scour the earth."

"The Blasphemer has come to meet his doom," Gaven said in the Common tongue. "Just as you have met yours."

"My fate is immaterial. But the Blasphemer's time has not yet come. Yours are the words he unspeaks, yours the song he unsings."

"Enough of this. Have you come to fight me or taunt me with the Prophecy?"

"Both," the dragon said.

"Don't you want to let the Blasphemer unspeak my words before you kill me?"

"I am under no illusion that I will be the one to kill you, Storm Dragon." The dragon leaped at him, spewing fire from its mouth as it came—fire that bathed Gaven in searing agony. "But I do intend to hurt you," it added.

* * * * *

The tide of the battle seemed to conspire against Rienne. She tried to make her way to where she had seen Gaven's dragon alight on the ground, but Maelstrom's dance of death seemed to lead her in any direction but that one. She grew convinced that the blade was seeking the Blasphemer again and would tolerate no distraction.

Dragons flew overhead, raining fire and lightning down on the Aundairians as the full force of the army crashed against the barbarian horde. She saw one of the dragons—the largest she'd ever seen, except the one Gaven had ridden—loose a mighty blast of flame in the general area where she thought Gaven was, and her suspicion was confirmed by a tremendous blast of lightning erupting up from the ground. The red dragon landed, and Cressa shouted encouragement to Lady Dragonslayer as she started in that direction.

Rienne smiled to herself, glad that Cressa was beside her— against all likelihood. Somehow the girl had survived the battle at her side, enduring one barbarian attack after another, shouting encouragement until Rienne grew convinced that real magic flowed in Cressa's voice, healing and strengthening her for the battle. Rienne held little hope for the outcome of the battle, even after seeing Gaven, but she breathed a prayer to the nine Sovereigns, asking them to keep Cressa safe from harm.

Fire and thunder, lightning and howling wind testified to the battle raging out of Rienne's sight, behind apparently impenetrable walls of her barbarian foes. Maelstrom cut and killed in Gaven's direction, pulled her sideways to parry an attack and cut again, and the dance drew her in a new direction.

She saw a bone-white banner, whipped by the wind of Gaven's storm, marked by a twisted rune painted in blood. Maelstrom was drawing her toward that point, so at last she succumbed. Her blade wanted her to fight the Blasphemer, and her dream suggested that she was destined to slay him. So slay him she would.

* * * * *

Gaven spoke a hasty spell that bathed his body in cool flames, offering him some protection from the heat of the dragon's fire. Then the dragon was upon him, its claws slashing through the air toward him. He jabbed his sword between two claws, drawing a spurt of sizzling, steaming blood, but the blow still connected, cutting across Gaven's chest and sending him flying backward.

Gaven's pain erupted in a blast of thunder that threw the dragon back as well. His eyes flashed and lightning speared down through the roaring dragon. The winds around him picked up speed, howling as they tore at the dragon's wings.

Shakravar rode the whirlwind down and slammed into the other dragon, teeth and all four claws digging into its red-scaled hide. Gaven engulfed both dragons in a mighty burst of lightning streaming out from his hands and his mouth, and taking shape from the blood that welled in the wounds across his chest. Even Shakravar, whose breath was lightning and whose wings were thunder and wind, staggered back under the force of the assault, and the red dragon wailed in agony as wave after wave of lightning coursed over its body.

"Find the Blasphemer, Gaven!" Shakravar growled.

The red dragon folded its wings and rolled onto its back, bringing its claws around to scrabble against Shakravar's armored belly. Shakravar caught the red's mouth with one claw and wrenched its head back, then bit into its exposed neck and tore out its throat. Gaven stepped back, deciding to take the dragon's advice and continue looking for the Blasphemer—and Rienne.

The bulk of the Aundairian forces had closed the gap while Gaven faced the dragon, and bodies in Aundairian blue lay alongside those in the leather and fur of the Carrion Tribes, their blood flowing together on the gore-slick ground. As the wind whipped around him, he was a still point in the center of a raging tempest, the noise of battle swept away in the whirlwind. He was seized with the sudden sense that he'd been there before—witnessed this exact scene before. A crash of thunder shook the earth, and the wind fell.

An alien, incomprehensible sound replaced all the noise of battle and the howl of the wind—a string of syllables with no meaning, sounds that signified the unmaking of the world. They tore at his ears and ripped at his mind, defying him to form sense or reason.

All around him, soldiers and barbarians fell to the earth, hands pressed to their ears, mouths wide in silent howls of agony. They parted like a subsiding flood, leaving only two figures standing in their wake.

One was Rienne—so close, no more than ten yards away— her face wrenched in pain, both hands clutching Maelstrom's hilt. Her mouth moved, forming words Gaven couldn't understand, as though their structure and meaning were her only defense against the sound of the Blasphemy.

The other figure was a tall man in bloodstained plate armor, twisting ivory horns rising from the brick-red skin of his brow. Blasphemy streamed from his mouth as he raised a flaming sword to the sky. His burning eyes fell on Rienne and anger twisted his face, and he strode toward her to cut her down.

* * * * *

Rienne fought her way toward the banner as Gaven's blue dragon swept out of the sky to attack the gargantuan red dragon. Maelstrom spun around her like a steel whirlwind, cutting through armor and flesh, weapons and bones. Barbarians parted before her.

An eerie quiet fell over the battlefield and time seemed to slow. The only sound that reached her ears was the inhuman babbling of the Blasphemer she'd heard at the Mosswood—his unearthly chant, words defying language.

Aundairians, Reachers, and Carrion Tribe barbarians fell to the ground as one, agony written on their faces as the Blasphemer's chant tore through their minds.

Rienne clutched Maelstrom tightly and screamed words of the Prophecy again, the only remedy she had found for the pain. "The Blasphemer's end lies in the void, in the maelstrom that pulls him down to darkness!"

He stood before her, and her presence and her words

seemed to infuriate him. Fury burned in his eyes as he took a step toward her.

* * * * *

"No!" Gaven screamed. Lightning crackled across his dragonmark, now fully formed on his skin again, and crackling bolts shot to the Blasphemer, stopping him in midstride.

But the lightning didn't strike him. It coiled in blazing rings of light encircling him, and a dazzling arc bound him to Gaven's dragonmark. The fabric of creation began to unravel in the path of the lightning. The Blasphemer turned to look at Gaven, and a twisted smile formed on his face. The sounds issuing from his mouth changed, and Gaven felt a jolt of pain in his chest, not in his dragonmark but beneath it.

His are the words the Blasphemer unspeaks, his the song the Blasphemer unsings.

Words sprang to Gaven's lips unbidden—the words inscribed in his dragonmark, words in no mortal language, words of his being and his destiny—and the Blasphemer's voice devoured his speech. Utter silence swallowed them, the complete absence of sound at the edge of the absence of being.

A rift formed in the world, a tear in the dimensions of time and space where a tempest of raw elemental forces stormed, like an echo of the chaos before creation, the world unshaped. Devastation swirled out from that breach and washed across the battlefield, fire and lightning like no storm Gaven had ever made, boulders of ice crashing into the ground, slabs of stone wrenched from the earth and set free to crash among the gathered armies.

Gaven and the Blasphemer hung together in a space that was outside of all space, no part of the created world, a space of pure annihilation that slowly spread out around them.

* * * * *

A crash of thunder drowned out the sound of his Blasphemy for a blissful moment, and lightning circled the demon's towering form. A coruscating arc of lightning linked him to Gaven, to her left. Rienne almost wept with relief, seeing him so close at the moment she least wanted to be alone.

The Blasphemer turned to face Gaven. Gaven's lips moved, and a total silence fell over the world. Rienne watched in mounting horror as the air before her seemed to part, the ground split open, and chaos raged in the void. A storm of fire and ice, lightning and stone swept silently out and across the battlefield, and Rienne spun around to find Cressa huddled on the ground behind her. She crouched down beside the girl, put an arm around her shoulders, and lifted her to her feet. Tears left streaks in the dirt that caked Cressa's face, and blood trickled from both her ears.

"Sing," Rienne urged her, but her voice made no sound.

Cressa looked puzzled, but when Rienne repeated her command, puzzlement turned to a blush of embarrassment. She shook her head.

"Sing!" Rienne said a third time, just as Gaven's voice pierced the silence.

"No," Gaven said, and the storming chaos and the Blasphemer's words of madness and Cressa's choked sobs sprang to life in Rienne's ears.

* * * * *

"No," Gaven said, though it took a supreme effort of will to bring that single word to voice. The arc of lightning that bound him to the Blasphemer died, though rings of it still flew around the Blasphemer's demonic form. Gaven stood on solid ground again, and he was suddenly aware of Shakravar standing behind him, his mouth close by Gaven's shoulder.

"What are you doing?" the dragon said. "Don't stop!"

"We would destroy the world," Gaven said.

"Yes! For six hundred years I have worked to bring this about! I will not let you undo it!"

Gaven spoke in the Common tongue, but other words danced in his mind as he spoke. "Under the unlight of the darkened sun, the Storm Dragon lays down his mantle; he stops his song before it can be unsung, and so his storm is extinguished."

Rage twisted the Blasphemer's visage, and he strode closer to Gaven, his Blasphemy fallen silent.

"What is that?" Shakravar roared. "That is not the Prophecy!"

"It is now," Gaven said. "I am player and playwright." He repeated the verse, but this time his words were not Common, but the very words of creation, the tongue in which the world was spoken into being.

"No!" Shakravar howled, and the sky shook with thunder again.

The Blasphemer extended the long, clawed fingers of one hand toward Gaven and spoke again. Pain stabbed through Gaven's ears and he felt blood trickle down both sides of his neck. He let his sword fall to the ground, and the Blasphemer snarled as he drove his curved blade through Gaven's chest.

* * * * *

Cressa looked around, her eyes wide with terror, and she began to sing. Her voice was clear and pure, achingly sweet. Rienne didn't know the song—it sounded rustic and childish, but it didn't matter. She felt as though her heart might burst with the beauty of it. The Blasphemer fell silent, Gaven's dragon roared in fury, and thunder shook the sky. The Blasphemer spoke another word and Cressa's voice faltered. In that moment, Gaven died.

CHAPTER
44

Grief and rage jolted Rienne into motion. She sprang at the Blasphemer, Maelstrom exulting in her grip, and swung at him with all her strength. The Blasphemer raised his fiery sword to parry, and when the two blades met the sound was a piercing scream of metal that obliterated all other sound.

The Blasphemer's face twisted in confusion—he was evidently feeling the same sort of life in his own weapon, and it surprised him. The expression was oddly human in such a diabolic face.

"Barak Radaam," he said. "What is this?"

Maelstrom led her in its exquisite dance, flashing in circular patterns around her, drawing her arm in cuts and parries, leading her feet in lunges and dodges. Every blow struck the steel of the Blasphemer's sword, bringing the unearthly scream of the two blades.

The Blasphemer was a clumsy partner for his own blade, stumbling through the motions of its dance, which was no less intricate than Maelstrom's, if less elegantly executed. He struck when he was supposed to, fumbled into lunges as she stepped back, staggered back when she lunged. Fury twisted his face, and every blow Maelstrom blocked or dodged drew a snarl of frustration.

Rienne saw countless opportunities that Maelstrom didn't take, but when she tried to alter the course of the dance, it resisted. Slowly it dawned on her that Maelstrom wasn't interested in fighting the Blasphemer—it wanted to fight the Blasphemer's sword. The dance of the blades was not a duel intended to establish a victor in the battle, so what was it?

Another blast of lightning crashed around her and the Blasphemer, and Rienne glanced over to where Gaven had fallen. The great blue dragon had one huge claw planted over Gaven's body, and its other front claw held a shining red dragonshard. Lightning poured from its mouth and the dragonshard to whirl around them, adding to the storm of chaos that Gaven had started.

Rienne saw the rift where the Blasphemer's words and Gaven's dragonmark had torn through the world, some bizarre interaction of Blasphemy and Prophecy that threatened to unmake the creation, and she realized that the steps of the swords' dance were leading them steadily closer to that hole in reality. She saw Cressa watching the battle in stunned silence, and the rest of the armies—Aundairians, Reachers, and barbarians alike—slowly finding their feet, breaking into scattered fights again or fleeing the field in terror.

"Yes!" the dragon hissed, exulting in the devastation. "In the city by the lake of kings, the city scourged with his storm, the Storm Dragon becomes as the Devourer, and he opens his maw to consume the world."

With a dawning sense of horror, Rienne realized that the dance of Maelstrom and the Blasphemer's blade was doing more than leading them toward the rift. Each wide sweep of her blade, she noticed, tugged at the raging forces around them, shaping the storm, giving form to the chaos. The Blasphemer's sword had the same effect. She thought at first that the swords might be repairing the rift, re-creating the sundered world. But no—each cut of the blades tore at the edges, unraveling the fabric of reality still more.

"Now the world is consumed!" the dragon shouted, plunging itself into the lightless void that split the ground and air. Its body buckled and shuddered, and the rift contracted around it. The dragon became the void, spreading inky wings of nothing that annihilated everything they touched.

But if the dragon had sought to control the void by merging with it, it appeared to have failed. It hung suspended in the center of the raging storm, and the blood-red dragonshard floated at its heart, lightning streaming out from it even as it seemed to draw Rienne and the Blasphemer toward it. But the void seemed to be slowly consuming the dragonshard, drawing trickles of red like blood away from the stone to vanish in the inky depths.

The Blasphemer's fiery yellow eyes met her gaze. In her dream, she had seen him as a demon, an incarnation of evil given substance solely for the purpose of destruction. But she saw now that he was flesh and bone, that he or a distant ancestor might once have been human. He was not so different from Gaven in some ways, drawn by the Prophecy into the role it demanded of him—not so different from her, really. Could he have chosen differently? Could he have arrived at a different destiny by taking different paths along the way?

But they had both arrived at this moment, along their different paths, bound to the same Prophecy and its fulfillment. They faced each other across their whirling blades, both drawn into the dance of steel and apparently powerless to stop whatever consequence might arise from the dance. They seemed to be unwitting partners in the destruction of the world, pawns of the weapons they wielded.

Her rage subsided, and she sought the stillness in the center of her soul. She first found the depths of grief, but she plunged her mind through it to a point beyond grief, beyond concern for her life. She turned Maelstrom over in her hand, and her mind slipped from history into eternity. She stepped back from the unending dance of the dueling blades, and the Blasphemer faltered.

Somewhere—far off, it seemed—Cressa began to sing again, her voice quavering. The dragon-void writhed in pain and contracted, growing visibly smaller as its dragonshard diminished. The Blasphemer roared in fury, stumbling forward as his sword sought Maelstrom again. Rienne stepped away from his clumsy charge, keeping Maelstrom low at her side. As he fought to regain his balance, she slid Maelstrom into its sheath.

The Blasphemer grinned, running the tip of his tongue across the points of his teeth as if savoring the anticipation of her blood. "Now you die, Dragonslayer."

Rienne shook her head. She had spent her life mastering her sword, mastering her thoughts and emotions, learning discipline and technique, drawing on the deepest reserves of power in her soul. She would not be mastered by her blade or by the Prophecy—she would be a playwright as well, as she had said to Gaven so long ago. The Blasphemer, though, was willing to be a slave, enslaved to his rage, his hatred, his sword, and his role in the Prophecy. In all the ways that mattered, she and he were utterly unlike each other.

He lunged and she stepped around him, he swung his sword like a cleaver and she dodged and rolled. She found a position behind him and stayed there as he whirled in rage, trying to get her in front of him again. As the Blasphemer's rage grew, the fury of the chaotic storm diminished, no longer fed by the clash of their blades. The dragon-void grew still smaller, thrashing in impotent fury as reality repaired itself around it, woven together by the strains of Cressa's song. Finally the Blasphemer threw himself backward, thinking to knock her over, but she dodged that as well, and he landed hard on his back, right at the feet of the dragon, the very edge of the void.

The dragon's lightless maw opened as the chaos sought to engulf the Blasphemer. His upper body slipped into the void and his eyes widened in fear. Another surge of lightning crackled around him like tendrils reaching to draw him in.

Rienne almost felt pity for him, but she shook her head. "You were the author of your own doom," she said.

The Blasphemer snarled and swung his blade in a sweep at her feet. She stepped back to avoid the blow, and he tumbled into the nothingness beyond creation.

Cressa's song was the only sound. The battle was over, it seemed. Both armies had scattered from the storming chaos, and hundreds lay dead. Cressa had begun a different tune, a mournful song with Elven words that spoke of the world's first dawn. The song stilled the chaos and repaired the weave of creation, but it drew Rienne back into the depths of her grief. She searched around the field until she found Gaven's body, then she fell to her knees beside him.

Clutching his dead hand to her chest, she wept until Cressa's song was done.

EPILOGUE

T ira Miron seemed to cradle Gaven's body in her arms. A black shroud embroidered with gold, enchanted to stave off the corruption of death on the journey back from Varna, covered everything but his face, like a lifeless mask. The tracings of his dragonmark, darker than they had been before the Dragon Forge stripped them from his skin, were just visible beneath his chin and disappearing under the shroud.

Aunn unrolled the vellum scroll, a gift from the queen, and let his eyes roam over it without reading. It was utterly unlike the one he'd used in the Labyrinth, though the ritual it contained was the same in essentials. That one had been scribed by a cleric of Dol Dorn, the war god, and ornamented with images of warfare. This had been seized from the Cathedral of the Silver Flame when King Wrogar closed it, and each black letter was outlined in silver, while intricately swirling decorations of silver filigree ran along the edges of the page.

He looked around the cathedral—at the saints arrayed around the dome, at his friends arrayed around him, at the mosaic icon on the floor. He felt privileged to be in their company, honored to call these people friends. Rienne had embraced him so tightly when she saw him that he thought she might squeeze the breath from his chest. Cart and Ashara, their arms linked in obvious affection, had reported Jorlanna's arrest and joined in celebrating the unraveling of all her schemes. Rienne's young companion Cressa, a fountain of energy, seemed fascinated with Aunn and had barely given him a moment's peace since her arrival in Fairhaven.

He liked to imagine that his other friends had joined the ring of saints around the dome—Dania and Vor, Farren and the other warriors of Maruk Dar, Zandar and Sevren. The Silver Flame burned brightly in the cathedral, it seemed, despite eighty-five years of disuse. Aunn had refused to attempt the ritual anywhere else.

He let the ritual take shape in his mind complete and entire, each letter, each word contributing to a whole that was more than a string of sounds. He closed his eyes and drew a deep breath, setting fire tingling down his spine, the touch of the Silver Flame upon him. He opened his eyes again and began to read.

Once again magic streamed from the words, dissolving the ink and burning around him like a raging flame. He was the merest flicker in that great flame, and yet he felt himself cradled in divine arms, embraced, accepted, acknowledged, and loved. He did not command the power of the Silver Flame—he requested it, implored it to condescend to work through him. Flames danced from his hand to wash over Gaven's body, cleansing the stain of death from his flesh.

There was a moment of perfect silence. No one breathed, no waft of wind stirred the dusty cathedral floor, nothing moved. They hung suspended in time.

And then Gaven drew a shuddering, gasping breath, and the sky rolled with a distant rumble of thunder.

EBERRON

KEITH BAKER'S
THORN OF BRELAND

As a child, Nyrielle Tam dreamed of being a soldier. Instead, she became a spy, a saboteur, and when necessary, an assassin.

She became Thorn, Dark Lantern of Breland.

THE QUEEN OF STONE
Available Now

THE SON OF KHYBER
Available Now

THE FADING DREAM
October 2010

DON BASSINGTHWAITE'S

LEGACY OF DHAKAAN

From the ashes of a fallen empire,
a new kingdom rises.

The Doom of Kings

The Word of Traitors

The Tyranny of Ghosts
June 2010

EBERRON

PAUL CRILLEY'S

The Chronicles of Abraxis Wren

All great criminals have a complex mind.
Few are as sharp as a Master Inquisitive's.

Night of the Long Shadows
Winner of the 2008 SCRIBE Award!

Taint of the Black Brigade
August 2010

And a third Abraxis Wren adventure arrives June 2011!

RETURN TO A WORLD OF PERIL, DECEIT, AND INTRIGUE, A WORLD REBORN IN THE WAKE OF A GLOBAL WAR.

TIM WAGGONER'S
LADY RUIN

She dedicated her life to the nation of Karrnath.
With the war ended, and the army asleep—
waiting—in their crypts, Karrnath assigned her
to a new project: find a way to harness
the dark powers of the Plane of Madness.

REVEL IN THE RUIN
DECEMBER 2010

ALSO AVAILABLE AS AN E-BOOK!

DUNGEONS & DRAGONS®

FROM THE RUINS OF FALLEN EMPIRES, A NEW AGE OF HEROES ARISES

It is a time of magic and monsters, a time when the world struggles against a rising tide of shadow. Only a few scattered points of light glow with stubborn determination in the deepening darkness.

It is a time where everything is new in an ancient and mysterious world.

BE THERE AS THE FIRST ADVENTURES UNFOLD.

THE MARK OF NERATH
Bill Slavicsek
August 2010

THE SEAL OF KARGA KUL
Alex Irvine
December 2010

The first two novels in a new line set in the evolving world of the DUNGEONS & DRAGONS® game setting. If you haven't played . . . or read D&D® in a while, your reintroduction starts in August!

ALSO AVAILABLE AS E-BOOKS!

WELCOME TO THE DESERT WORLD
OF ATHAS, A LAND RULED BY A HARSH
AND UNFORGIVING CLIMATE, A LAND
GOVERNED BY THE ANCIENT AND
TYRANNICAL SORCERER KINGS.
THIS IS THE LAND OF

CITY UNDER THE SAND
Jeff Mariotte
OCTOBER 2010

*Sometimes lost knowledge is
knowledge best left unknown.*

FIND OUT WHAT YOU'RE MISSING IN THIS
BRAND NEW DARK SUN® ADVENTURE BY
THE AUTHOR OF *COLD BLACK HEARTS*.

ALSO AVAILABLE AS AN E-BOOK!

THE PRISM PENTAD
Troy Denning's classic DARK SUN
series revisited! Check out the great new editions of
The Verdant Passage, *The Crimson Legion*,
The Amber Enchantress, *The Obsidian Oracle*,
and *The Cerulean Storm*.